The Lion
Son of the Forest

More tales about the Dark Angels from Black Library

CYPHER: LORD OF THE FALLEN
John French

LUTHER: FIRST OF THE FALLEN
Gav Thorpe

LEGACY OF CALIBAN
Gav Thorpe
An omnibus containing the novels *Ravenwing, Master of Sanctity* and *The Unforgiven* along with a number of associated short stories.

LEGENDS OF THE DARK ANGELS: A SPACE MARINE OMNIBUS
Gav Thorpe and C Z Dunn
Contains the novels *Angels of Darkness, The Purging of Kadillus, Azrael* and *The Eye of Ezekiel* plus the novella *Dark Vengeance* and several short stories

More Warhammer 40,000 from Black Library

LEVIATHAN
Darius Hinks

• DAWN OF FIRE •

BOOK 1: Avenging Son
Guy Haley

BOOK 2: The Gate of Bones
Andy Clark

BOOK 3: The Wolftime
Gav Thorpe

BOOK 4: Throne of Light
Guy Haley

BOOK 5: The Iron Kingdom
Nick Kyme

BOOK 6: The Martyr's Tomb
Marc Collins

• DARK IMPERIUM •
Guy Haley

BOOK 1: Dark Imperium
BOOK 2: Plague War
BOOK 3: Godblight

BELISARIUS CAWL: THE GREAT WORK
Guy Haley

THE INFINITE AND THE DIVINE
Robert Rath

RENEGADES: HARROWMASTER
Mike Brooks

The Lion
Son of the Forest

Mike Brooks

A BLACK LIBRARY PUBLICATION

First published in 2023.
This edition published in Great Britain in 2023 by
Black Library, Games Workshop Ltd., Willow Road,
Nottingham, NG7 2WS, UK.

Represented by: Games Workshop Limited – Irish branch,
Unit 3, Lower Liffey Street, Dublin 1,
D01 K199, Ireland.

10 9 8 7 6 5 4

Produced by Games Workshop in Nottingham.
Cover illustration by Paul Dainton.

The Lion: Son of the Forest © Copyright Games Workshop Limited 2023. The Lion: Son of the Forest, GW, Games Workshop, Black Library, The Horus Heresy, The Horus Heresy Eye logo, Space Marine, 40K, Warhammer, Warhammer 40,000, the 'Aquila' Double-headed Eagle logo, and all associated logos, illustrations, images, names, creatures, races, vehicles, locations, weapons, characters, and the distinctive likenesses thereof, are either ® or TM, and/or © Games Workshop Limited, variably registered around the world.
All Rights Reserved.

A CIP record for this book is available from the British Library.

ISBN 13: 978-1-80407-356-8

No part of this publication may be reproduced, stored in a retrieval system, or transmitted in any form or by any means, electronic, mechanical, photocopying, recording or otherwise, without the prior permission of the publishers.

This is a work of fiction. All the characters and events portrayed in this book are fictional, and any resemblance to real people or incidents is purely coincidental.

See Black Library on the internet at

blacklibrary.com

Find out more about Games Workshop
and the worlds of Warhammer at

games-workshop.com

Printed and bound in the UK.

For Gav, for all the help when I was only a baby Black Library freelancer.

For more than a hundred centuries the Emperor has sat immobile on the Golden Throne of Earth. He is the Master of Mankind. By the might of His inexhaustible armies a million worlds stand against the dark.

Yet, He is a rotting carcass, the Carrion Lord of the Imperium held in life by marvels from the Dark Age of Technology and the thousand souls sacrificed each day so that His may continue to burn.

To be a man in such times is to be one amongst untold billions. It is to live in the cruellest and most bloody regime imaginable. It is to suffer an eternity of carnage and slaughter. It is to have cries of anguish and sorrow drowned by the thirsting laughter of dark gods.

This is a dark and terrible era where you will find little comfort or hope. Forget the power of technology and science. Forget the promise of progress and advancement. Forget any notion of common humanity or compassion.

There is no peace amongst the stars, for in the grim darkness of the far future, there is only war.

DRAMATIS PERSONAE

Primarchs

LION EL'JONSON	'The Lion', primarch of the Dark Angels

Dark Angels

ZABRIEL	Former Destroyer, protector of Camarth, Fallen
KAI	Fallen
APHKAR	Fallen
LOHOC	'The Red Whisper', Fallen
BORZ	'One-Eye', captain of *Honour's Edge*, Fallen
LAUNCIEL	Joint commander of Trevenum Gamma, Fallen
GALAD	Joint commander of Trevenum Gamma, Fallen
BEVEDAN	Former Librarian, Fallen
GUAIN	Captain of Echo Station, Fallen
ECTORAEL	Techmarine, crew of Echo Station, Fallen
KUZIEL	Crew of Echo Station, Fallen
LAMOR	Crew of Echo Station, Fallen
ASBIEL	Apothecary, crew of Echo Station, Fallen
BREUNAN	Fallen
MERIANT	Crew of Echo Station, Fallen
CADARAN	Fallen
PERZIEL	Fallen
RUFAREL	Fallen

The Ten Thousand Eyes

SERAPHAX	Lord Sorcerer, Fallen
BAELOR	'The Imposter', Fallen

MARKOG	Commander of the Dolorous Guard
DIMORA	Canticallax of the New Mechanicum, *Eye of Malevolence*
URIENZ	Arch-Raptor
VARKAN	'The Red', former World Eater
JAI'TANA	'The Unshriven', Apostle
KRR'SATZ	Overseer of astropaths on the *Blade of Truth*, beastman

Humans

SUTIK	Man of Camarth
HALIN	Man of Camarth
BIBA	Child of Camarth
VALDAX	Tech-priest of Camarth
M'KIA	Woman of Camarth, head of the Lion Guard
JOVAN	Man of Camarth
YINDA	Corporal of the Avalus defence force
SEENA AP NA HARAJ	Marshal of the Avalus defence force, acting planetary governor
SHAVAR	Seer of Avalus
TORRAL DERRIGAN	Admiral of the Avalus defence fleet and the *Lunar Knight*
RAULEN	Captain of the Trevenum Gamma defence fleet
MONTARAT	Captain of the *Pax Fortitudinis*, Avalus defence fleet

Blood Angels

LUIS DANTE	Commander of the Blood Angels

Part One

AWAKENING

I

The river sings silver notes: a perpetual, chaotic babble in which a fantastically complex melody seems to hang, tantalising, just out of reach of the listener. He could spend eternity here trying to find the heart of it, without ever succeeding, yet still not consider the time wasted. The sound of water over stone, the interplay of energy and matter, creates a quiet symphony that is both unremarkable and unique. He does not know how long he has been here, just listening.

Nor, he realises, does he know where *here* is.

The listener becomes aware of himself in stages, like a sleeper passing from the deepest, darkest depths of slumber, through the shallows of semi-consciousness where thought swirls in confusing eddies, and then into the light. First comes the realisation that he is not the song of the river; that he is in fact separate from it, and listening to it. Then sensation dawns, and he realises he is sitting on the river's bank. If there is a sun, or suns, then he cannot see them through the branches of the trees overhead and the mist that hangs heavily in the air, but there is still light enough for him to make out his surroundings.

The trees are massive, and mighty, with great trunks that could not be fully encircled by one, two, perhaps even half a dozen people's outstretched arms. Their rough, cracked bark pockmarks them with shadows, as though the trees themselves are camouflaged. The ground beneath their branches is fought over by tough shrubs: sturdy, twisted, thorny things strangling each other in the contest for space and light, like children unheeded at the feet of adults. The earth in which they grow is dark and rich, and when the listener digs his fingers into it, it smells of life, and death, and other things besides. It is a familiar smell, although he cannot say from where, or why.

His fingers, he realises as they penetrate the ground, are armoured. His whole body is armoured, in fact, encased in a great suit of black plates with the faintest hint of dark green. This is a familiar sensation, too. The armour feels like a part of him – an extension, as natural as the shell of any crustacean that might lurk in the nooks and crannies of the river in front of him. He leans forward and peers down into the still water next to the bank, sheltered from the main flow by an outcropping just upstream. It becomes an almost perfect mirror surface, as smooth as a dream.

The listener does not recognise the face that looks back at him. It is deeply lined, as though a world of cares and worries has washed over it like the river water, scoring the marks of their passage into the skin. His hair is pale, streaked with blond here and there, but otherwise fading into grey and white. The lower part of his face is obscured by a thick, full beard and moustache, leaving only the lips bare; it is a distrustful mouth, one more likely to turn downwards in disapproval than quirk upwards in a smile.

He raises one hand, the fingers still smeared with dirt, before his face. The reflection does the same. This is surely his face, but the sight sparks no memory. He does not know who he is, and he does not know where he is, for all that it feels familiar.

That being the case, there seems little point in remaining here.

The listener gets to his feet, then hesitates. He cannot explain to himself why he should move, given the song of the river is so beautiful. However, the realisation of his lack of knowledge has opened something inside him, a hunger which was not there before. He will not be satisfied until he has answers.

Still, the river's song calls to him. He decides to walk along the bank, following the flow of the water and listening to it as he goes, and since he does not know where he is, one direction is as good as the other. There is a helmet on the bank, next to where he was sitting. It is the same colour as his armour, with vertical slits across the mouth, like firing slits in a wall. He picks it up, and clamps it to his waist with a movement that feels instinctual.

He does not know for how long he walks. Time is surely passing, in that one moment slips into another, and he can remember ones that came before and consider the concept of ones yet to come, but there is nothing to mark it. The light neither increases nor decreases, instead remaining an almost spectral presence which illuminates without revealing its source. Shadows lurk, but there is no indication as to what casts them. The walker is unperturbed. His eyes can pierce those shadows, just as he can smell foliage, and he can hear the river. There is no soughing of wind in the branches, for the air is still, but the moist air carries the faint hooting, hollering calls of animals of some kind, somewhere in the distance.

The river's course begins to flatten and widen. The walker follows it around a bend, then comes to a halt in shock.

On the far bank stands a building.

It is built of cut and dressed stone, a dark blue-grey rock in which brighter specks glitter. It is not immense – the surrounding trees tower over it – but it is solid. It is a castle of some kind, a fortress, intended to keep the unwanted out and whatever people and treasures lie within safe from harm. It is neither new and pristine, nor ancient and weathered. It looks as though it has always stood here, and always shall. And on the wide, calm water in front of it sits a boat.

It is small, wooden, and unpainted. It is large enough for one person, and indeed one person is sitting in it. The walker's eyes can make him out, even at distance. He is old, and not old in the same way as the walker's face is. Time has not lined his features, it has ravaged them. His cheeks are sunken, his limbs are wasted; skin that was once clearly a rich chestnut now has an ashen patina, and his long hair is lifeless, dull grey, and matted. However, that grey head supports a crown: little more than a circlet of gold, but a crown nonetheless.

In his hands, swollen of knuckle and weak of grip, he holds a rod. The line is already cast into the water. Now he sits, hunched over as though in pain, a small, ancient figure in a small, simple boat.

The walker does not stop to wonder why a king would be fishing in such a manner. He is aware of the context of such things, but he does not know from where, and they do not matter to him. Here is someone who might have some answers for him.

'Greetings!' he calls. His voice is strong, rich and deep, although rough around the edges from age or disuse, or both. It carries across the water. The old king in the boat blinks, and when his eyes open again, they are looking at the walker.

'What is this place?' the walker demands.

The old king blinks again. When his eyes open this time, they are focused on the water once more. It is as though the walker is not there at all, a dismissal of minimal effort.

The walker discovers that he is not used to being ignored, and nor does he appreciate it. He steps into the water, intending to wade across the river so the king cannot so easily dismiss him. He is unconcerned about the current: he is strong of limb, and knows without knowing that his armour is waterproof, and that should he don his helmet he will be able to breathe even if he is submerged.

He has only gone a few steps, in up to his knees, when he realises there are shadows in the water: large shadows that circle the small boat, around and around. They do not bite on the line, and nor do they capsize the craft in which the fisher sits, but either could be disastrous.

Moreover, the walker realises, the king is wounded. The walker cannot see the wound, but he can smell the blood. A rich, copper-ish tang tickles his nose. It is not a smell that delights him, but neither does he find it repulsive. It is simply a scent, one that he is able to parse and understand. The king is bleeding into the water, drip by drip. Perhaps that is what has drawn the shadows to this place. Perhaps they would have been here anyway.

Some of the shadows start to peel away, and head towards the walker.

The walker is not a being to whom fear comes naturally, but nor is he unfamiliar with the concept of danger. The shadows in the water are unknown to him, and move like predators.

+Come back to the bank.+

The walker whirls. A small figure stands on the land, swathed in robes of dark green, so that it nearly blends into the background against which it stands. It is the size of a child, perhaps, but the walker knows it to be something else.

It is a Watcher in the Dark.

+Come back to the bank,+ the Watcher repeats. Although its communication can hardly be called a voice – there is no sound, merely a sensation inside the walker's head that imparts meaning – it feels increasingly urgent nonetheless. The walker realises that he is not normally one to turn away from a challenge, but nor is he willing to ignore a Watcher in the Dark. It feels like a link, a connection to what came before, to what he should be able to remember.

He wades back, and steps up onto the bank. The approaching shadows hesitate for a moment, then circle away towards the king in his boat.

+They would destroy you,+ the Watcher says. The walker understands that it is talking about the shadows. There are layers to the feelings in his head now, feelings that are the mental aftertaste of the Watcher's communication. Disgust lurks there, but also fear.

'Where is this place?' the walker asks.

+Home.+

The walker waits, but nothing else is forthcoming. Moreover, he understands that there will not be. So far as the Watcher is concerned, that is not simply all the information that is required, but all that is available to give.

He looks out over the water, towards the king. The old man still sits hunched over, rod in his hands, blood leaking from his wounds one drip at a time.

'Why does he ignore me?'

+You did not ask the correct question.+

The walker looks around. The shadows in the water are still there, so it seems foolish to try to cross. However, he has seen no bridge over the river, nor another boat. He has no tools with which to build such a craft from the trees around him, and the knowledge of how to do so does not come easily to his mind. He is not like some of his brothers, for whom creation is natural…

His brothers. Who are his brothers?

Shapes flit through his mind, as ephemeral as smoke in a storm. He cannot get a grip, cannot wrestle them into anything that makes sense, or anything onto which his reaching mind can latch. The peace brought about by the song of the river is gone, and in its place is uncertainty and frustration. Nonetheless, the walker would not return to his former state. To knowingly welcome ignorance is not his way.

He catches a glimpse of something pale, a long way off through the trees, but on his side of the river. He begins to walk towards it, leaving the river behind him – he can always find it again, he knows its song – and making his way through the undergrowth. The plants are thick and verdant, but he is strong and sure. He ducks under spines, slaps aside strangling tendrils reaching out for anything that passes, and avoids breaking the twigs, which would leak sap so corrosive it might damage even his armour.

He does not wonder how he knows these things. The Watcher said that this was home.

The Watcher itself has been left behind, but it keeps reappearing, stepping out of the edge of shadows. It says nothing; not until the walker passes through a thicket of thorns and finally gets a clearer view of what he had seen.

It is a building, or at least the roof of one; that is all he can see from here. It is a dome of beautiful pale stone, supported by pillars. Whereas before he had been finding his own route through the forest, now there is a clear path ahead, a route of short grass hemmed in on either side by bushes and tree trunks. It curves away, rather than arrowing straight towards the pale building, but the walker knows that is where it leads.

+Do not take that path,+ the Watcher cautions him. +You are not yet strong enough.+

The walker looks down at this tiny creature, barely knee-high to him, then breathes deeply and rolls his shoulders within his armour. He presumes he had a youth, given he now looks old. Perhaps he was stronger then. Nonetheless, his body does not feel feeble.

+That is not the strength you will need.+

The walker narrows his eyes. 'You caution me against anything that might help me make sense of my situation. What would you have me do instead?'

+Follow your nature.+

The walker breathes in again, ready to snap an answer, for he finds he is just as ill-disposed towards being denied as he is to being ignored. However, he pauses, then sniffs.

He sniffs again.

Something is amiss.

He is surrounded by the deep, rich scent of the forest, which smells of both life and death. However, now his nose detects something else: a rancid undercurrent, something that is not merely rot or decay – for these are natural odours – but far worse, far more jarring.

Corruption.

This is something wrong, something twisted. It is something that should not be here: something that should not, in fact, exist at all.

The walker knows what he must do. He must follow his nature.

The hunter steps forward, and starts to run in pursuit of his quarry.

II

He flows over the ground, each step sure and certain and placed to perfection. Walking is second nature and not something about which he has to think, but running awakens something within him. This sense of urgency, this sense of a goal towards which he is striving; it provides focus and clarity, and makes him not only more aware, but also more aware of his own awareness. He realises that he perceives the forest in a new way: not as a homogenous landscape, but as terrain. The ground on which tracks will be left, the plants that will show the signs of a body passing, the thickets where a predator might wait in ambush and those in which lurking would lead only to becoming a meal for the plant itself: these things are as clear to him as words upon a page.

This *is* his home, and nothing can hide from him here.

The scent leads him onwards, as distinct as a wrong note in a symphony, and strengthening as he closes on it. The Watcher is forgotten, as are the king in the boat and the shadows in the water. He is hunting beasts through the trees, just as he used to long ago, back before...

Back before what?

The hunter slows, his focus disrupted for a moment by another flash of something that is not even memory, but perhaps the shadow of one. He does not remember what came before, but he remembers that there was something to remember, which is both welcome and infuriating. All he knows is that he hunted like this in the past.

He shakes himself. Memory will return when it returns, *if* it returns. For now, he still has a quarry to chase down. He presses on, still following the scent of corruption.

The hunter is not certain when the forest begins to change character, for there was never before any way with which to mark the time except by counting his own breaths or heart-beats. However, at some point he becomes aware that the mist is thinning. The light around him has a source now, high up and to his left, and he can feel the heat of this sun upon his scalp; it is a thick heat, a wet heat, the type that reaches into the throat and threatens to clog the airways. The trees are different, as well: they are still tall, still towering, but this is no longer a world of massive, low-hanging branches. Now their crowns splay out far above him, and their trunks are bare apart from the climbing plants that seek to scale their neighbours to snatch a glimpse of light for themselves. The air is alive with the chit-tering of insects, and the hunter can no longer hear the song of the river. He pauses and reaches down into the ground once more, this time coming up with a fistful of mouldering leaves. They carpet the ground, thick and brown, and do not easily give up the prints of those who have passed over them before; not like soft earth does, the tracker's friend.

The hunter does not know where he is now, any more than

he truly knew where he was before, but he knows that this is somewhere else. He is no longer home.

The scent of corruption is still strong, though. Stronger, even. The hunter is drawn forwards, pressing on through this new undergrowth: purplish ferns, pale roots trailing down from above, hanging vines, and plants he does not know with broad, glossy leaves edged with spikes. He does not feel the same connection to this forest, but he is closing on his quarry and he will not lose it once he is this near, no matter his surroundings.

There is movement up ahead. The hunter can hear the faint creaking of stems, as his quarry passes through the brush. He begins to build a picture of what he is following. It is large, certainly, for it cannot avoid making some noise as it moves. It feels like a predator, too; its movements sound like his own, designed not to alert prey to its approach, rather than something going about its own business. He can smell the faint tang of offal and rotting meat, such as might be caught between a hunter's jaws, or smeared across its snout where it has fed on a carcass.

A large, dangerous predator. The hunter removes his helmet from where it is clamped to his belt and, with a strange familiarity of movement despite being unable to remember having ever done it before, lowers it over his head.

The helmet clicks into place, making an airtight seal. Displays power up instantly, and the hunter finds himself looking at read-outs detailing his armour's power reserves, the external temperature, humidity levels and atmospheric composition, and even the day length of the world he is on – eighteen point five-four hours – as estimated from the infinitesimal movement of the local star in the sky above him. Without knowing how he knows what to do, he blinks through the vision options available to him: standard, polarised, infra-red, thermal-imaging, and on and on.

He settles on the standard vision. Everything has its place, but he will have no need of enhancements for this. He sets the air intakes to open, allowing himself to still experience the scents of this world, and moves back into the hunt. Even clad in his armour, thick though it is, he has no problem moving stealthily. The suit responds intuitively to him, as though it is a second skin. He does not pause to ponder this. It feels as natural as breathing.

He inhales, and detects the odour of his prey. There is no wind in this dense understorey, so he has little concern about his own scent giving him away.

He inhales again, double-checking. His armour, feverishly analysing his surroundings, offers up a breakdown of molecular concentrations and pheromone trails which overlays his vision like ghostly fluorescent trails. He is not mistaken.

There is more than one predator, and they have split up, to the left and right as he looks at it.

The hunter scans the ground, but the leaf litter is as obstinate as before and refuses to divulge its secrets. Is he following two predators, or more? Even his senses, sharp though they are, have limits. Still, hesitation is not his way. He follows the trail that leads to his left, balancing speed with stealth. If he slays this corrupted beast, whatever it may turn out to be, he will need to do it quickly enough to then retrace his steps and pick up the scent of its pack mates. He blinks a command and the audio receptors on his helmet increase in sensitivity, ready to warn him if anything chooses to hunt him while he is on the trail of his quarry.

He does not hear clawed feet or muscled bodies converging on him through the undergrowth, but he does detect something else from up ahead: voices. Human voices. Not the eerie sensation of the Watcher in the Dark's communication, where meaning suddenly arrived in his head, but true voices like his own – not quiet, not stealthy, but broadcasting their position to all with ears to hear them. If the hunter is certain of anything, it is that his quarry has both the ears to hear them, and the intention of doing harm.

He breaks into a sprint, all his own stealth forgotten as he smashes through tangling underbrush. He hurdles the giant trunk of a fallen tree just in time to hear a scream, and see a monstrous shape sheathed in scales of iridescent green spring towards a huddle of humans.

The hunter launches himself into a leap, a black-armoured arrow powered by superhuman muscle and sinew. He strikes the beast in the flank with his knee, and feels rib bones the width of his wrist crack from the force of the impact. The beast sprawls onto its side with a roaring scream, its pounce cut short, but the hunter has no time to finish the job before the undergrowth rustles and two more creatures emerge on the far side of the humans.

There are three humans: two adults, and a child. All three are unkempt, dressed in ragged clothes, and the two adults sport growths of facial hair which appear to owe more to lack of grooming opportunity than to cultural significance or personal choice. The child is prepubescent, of an as-yet indeterminable gender, with long straggly hair, and eyes wide and white in a dirty face. The hunter sees this within the space of a moment as he glances past them. The humans are weak, tired, and scared, of little value as allies in this struggle, and as likely to freeze in fear as they are to respond to instruction. He dismisses them, and springs over their heads.

The predators are a different matter altogether. They each stand taller than a human at the shoulder, but the similarities between them taper off at that point. The one the hunter struck down to begin with had a scaled hide, but one of these others has purplish-green fur interspersed with patches of scales, and the third's skin appears to have hardened into chitinous carapace in many places. They all have long jaws lined with sharp teeth, but one has additional tusks that protrude below its chin, and another has large, ridged horns that curl back from above its eyes.

The hunter comes down from his leap with his hands clasped together to form one giant fist, and lands them in a titanic blow directly between those horns.

The predator's head is driven down into the forest floor so fast that the rest of its body does not have time to keep up, and its rump is still standing as the hunter rolls away and turns towards the third creature. This one faces him and opens its mouth, but no roar of rage or aggression emerges. Instead a long, thickly muscled tongue lashes out to cover the space between them, some thirty feet or more, and the tip of it engulfs the hunter's right hand with a hideous sucking noise.

Strength means little without leverage. The hunter does not have time to set his feet before he is hauled off them by the tongue, and wrenched through the air towards the creature who has snared him. He draws back his free fist, determined to turn his headlong flight into an attack, but he is smashed out of the air by a massive, clawed paw a moment before he can strike his blow.

He is pinned face down on the ground, and he automatically shuts his helmet's air intakes to prevent himself from inhaling dust or dirt. Then his concerns become more immediate, as the creature draws his hand into its mouth with its ensnaring tongue and bites down on his arm at the elbow.

The force is tremendous, and could have easily snapped a regular human in two at the waist. The hunter's armour withstands it, although red warning icons flash up into his vision to let him know how close it is to giving way. The beast shakes its head to and fro, trying to achieve through wrenching and tearing what it could not manage through direct force alone, and nearly tears the hunter's shoulder out of its socket in the process. He grits his teeth, waits for half a second to get his timing right, and hauls his arm back out of the beast's jaws in the moment that it starts to shake its head back the other way, and its grip on his limb slackens ever so slightly.

The hunter's arm scrapes free. The predator's teeth leave grooves in the smooth surface of his vambrace, then snap shut as the resistance disappears. In doing so, they sever the creature's own tongue, which still envelops the hunter's fist.

The beast screams in self-inflicted pain, and lifts its paw from the hunter's back to claw at its own mouth, from which dark blood is leaking between its teeth. The hunter springs up, shaking the tongue tip loose. Without the muscle contractions to hold it in place, it is no more than a fleshy cylinder which flops wetly onto the forest floor.

The beast lunges for him, at least two tons of flesh driving behind a fanged maw, which opens to engulf the hunter. This time, however, he has the chance to set himself. He spreads his arms wide and his fingers close for a moment on the tips of its jaws, just as he shifts his weight and twists his torso. His muscles tense, and the servos in his armour spring into action to support them.

The hunter pivots, and uses the beast's own momentum to send it spinning through the air into its horned companion, which is only now rising to its feet after being stunned by the hunter's blow. The two predators collide and collapse into a thrashing, howling pile of limbs and tails.

All of this has taken perhaps ten seconds since the hunter

first leaped over the terrified humans. He has been aware of their shrieks and gasps as he struggled with the predators, but only now does he turn back to them. They are still where he left them, their arms full of sticks: not weapons, but firewood they have collected. They are small, and weak, and unable to defend themselves against threats such as this. The hunter supposes that he might easily consider them pathetic. Perhaps he did, once, in whatever existence he had before, if he had dwelled too long on the differences between him and them.

Now, he sees only lives that need his protection. He is strong and they are weak, and therefore he will lend them his strength until they no longer need it.

The animal whose ribs he cracked is struggling back to its feet with the resilience of the wild. The hunter sees the hunger in its eyes. Its desire for flesh to eat is no more malicious than the mutations that have turned its tail into a scorpion's stinger, or the vines that constrict the trees around which they grow so tightly that the tree dies, or the fungi that grow into their victims' brains and kill them by bursting out through their skulls. It is the nature of humanity to see the fate the wild has in store for them, and cheat it. Here and now, the hunter is that cheat.

'Stay out of my way!' he shouts, the first words he has directed at the humans. He does not intend them as hostile – they are supposed to be a warning for the humans to keep their distance from the struggle – but they shrink away from him anyway with a new, sharper fear. He dismisses their reaction. There will be time enough to clarify things when he has dealt with the predators, and his primary purpose is to make them stay clear. He does not, at this point, particularly care what their rationale is for obeying him.

He sprints at the wounded beast, which snarls and lashes out at him with its stinger. The hunter catches it behind the venom bulb with one hand, and rips the weapon off with his other. The predator howls again and wrenches backwards, and blood spurts from the severed trunk to spray across the hunter's face-plate, clogging and obscuring his eye-lenses. He wipes at them, but hard, shiny armour can only smear fluids ineffectually. He can still hear the beasts around him, but hearing alone will not be sufficient to win him this fight.

He drops the stinger and reaches up, pops the neck seal expertly, and removes his helmet. He throws it towards the humans and shouts, 'Clean that!' He does not have time to see whether they scramble to obey his order or shrink from the helmet as though it is a grenade, because the now stingless beast is coming at him again.

He steps slightly to the side, and punches upwards. The uppercut crashes into its lower jaw, and is powerful enough to knock the beast off its feet and flip it over, causing its onrushing mass to miss him and come to a slumped halt in the leaf litter. The hunter pounces on it, seizes its head, and wrenches, pitting his strength against the resistance of its neck muscles and spine. It is a brief struggle: the predator's neck snaps, and when the hunter releases its head it drops limply to the ground.

That leaves two.

He picks up the severed stinger and moves to attack. The other beasts have disentangled themselves, not without a couple of snaps at each other, and spread out to flank him. The one with the severed tongue roars at him, which is its last mistake. The hunter hurls the stinger into its mouth, and the barb pierces the roof of it. The venom bulb discharges automatically, pumping toxins into its bloodstream. The creature stiffens, falls to the ground and begins to thrash, no more immune to its pack mate's venom than their prey would be.

That leaves one.

The final predator charges the hunter, faster than even he is prepared for. It ducks its horned head low and swipes upwards at the last moment, hammering its weapons into his chest. He is lifted off his feet and sent flying gracelessly through the air, the ground and the sky rapidly swapping places as he tumbles. Perhaps he would have recovered his equilibrium sufficiently to land on his feet, or perhaps not, but the sudden intervention of a tree trunk renders it a moot point. He strikes hard enough to splinter the wood, and falls to the ground.

His armour has held, but it will not stand up to many more impacts of such force. He clambers back to his feet, a little short of breath, a little shaken, and with his hearts pounding. This too is a familiar sensation, but familiarity with mortal peril does not bring any guarantee of survival. Lessons can be learned, and adjustments made, but each struggle is contested on its own merits.

The predator has forgotten about the humans. Now it only has eyes for the hunter, this thing that has stepped into its territory and challenged it. Whether it considers him to be a rival seeking to claim its food for himself, or some sort of alpha prey animal which can attack and hurt it, is of little consequence. The outcome will be the same.

Only one of them can live.

The beast comes for him again, head lowered and bellowing in rage. The hunter is better able to judge its speed this time, but he does not stand to meet it. He vaults into the air instead, inverted like an acrobat, just high enough to clear the monster's head. He reaches out and grabs the horns as they pass beneath him, then comes down astride the beast's shoulders.

It takes the predator a few more strides to realise what has happened, and it bucks in an attempt to throw him off. This was all the time the hunter needed; he now has each horn firmly in his grip, and is forcing his hands apart. The beast's thrashing works against it, as it provides just enough additional force against the hunter's pressure to break one of the horns off, halfway down.

The hunter does not hesitate. He reverses his grip on the piece of wickedly sharp keratin, as long as his forearm, and rams it into the monster's throat.

Now the beast manages to shake him loose onto the leaf litter, but he tugs the piece of horn out with him, and dark blood follows it in a flood. The predator staggers, crashing into bushes as it tries to fight against the sensation of rapidly weakening limbs, all while its powerful heart pumps its life away. It lumbers back towards him, no longer as swift or strong as it was, but still determined to kill this intruder.

The hunter is not cruel. Twisted and mutated though this creature is, it is not malicious; it is merely an animal that had the misfortune to hunt humans in front of him. It does not deserve a lingering death. When it lunges clumsily for him, he sidesteps and brings the horn down as hard as he can on the front of its skull. His great strength and the horn's own sharpness pierces the bone and drives into the brain, and the beast drops dead.

The hunter takes a moment to examine himself. The rush of battle can inure a combatant to the wounds they have suffered, but it appears that he is largely unhurt. He turns away from the corpse of his final kill, and towards the humans.

They have not moved. The child is sobbing quietly, evidently overcome by the horror and fear of what has happened. The two adults watch him with wide eyes. One of them holds out the hunter's helmet with trembling hands. The blood has been cleaned from it with leaves and, judging by the smears on the man's shirt, his own clothing.

'Thank you,' the hunter says, taking it. He does not place it back on his head. He feels that the humans will be more likely to respond better to a face they can see, a face that looks a little like their own, even if it belongs to a being so large that the adults are like children in comparison to him. 'Where is this place?'

The adults gape, uncomprehending. The hunter wonders for a moment if they do not speak the same language as he does – not that he knows what language he is speaking, nor how he came to learn it – but they clearly understood his instruction to clean his helmet. Perhaps his query was not specific enough.

'What world is this?' he tries. 'I do not know where I am.'

'C-Camarth, lord,' one of the adults manages.

Lord.

That sparks something, a flicker of memory in the back of the hunter's mind: not the name of the world, but the honorific. He has been addressed like this before, but he cannot pin down anything more. He schools down the expression of irritation that had begun to cross his face at his memory's failure, for even that hint of displeasure is enough to make the adults take a step back from him, shielding the child as best they can. They cannot think that they could protect either the child or themselves from him should he wish them harm, but it is a human instinct, and one the hunter decides not to take as an insult.

They know more about his surroundings than he does; therefore, it might benefit the hunter to remain with them for now. He clamps his helmet to his belt again.

'What are your names?'

'I am Sutik,' says the taller of the two adults, nervously but clearly. 'This is Halin, and Biba.' He gestures at the other adult first, then at the child. The hunter nods to show he has heard and understood.

'What is your name, lord?' Halin asks timidly.

The hunter shakes his head. 'I do not know. Perhaps it will come to me. Perhaps I will find a new one.' He looks at the three of them again. 'You were collecting wood. For a fire? Do you have a camp nearby? Are there others?'

'Yes, and yes, and yes,' Sutik says, nodding and eager to please. 'We would be honoured if you would come and share our fire, lord. I am sure our protector would wish to meet you as well.'

The hunter frowns. 'Your protector? They do not appear to be fulfilling their role, else I would not have had to intervene.'

'Oh, please don't say that!' Halin says hurriedly. 'He is alone, and he cannot watch over all of us at all times, but he has saved all of us at one point or another since the world ended.'

'The world cannot have ended,' the hunter says. 'We stand here. Do you believe this to be an afterlife?' He stops short, suddenly afflicted by doubt. Where *was* he, before? 'Home', according to the Watcher, but that told him nothing. Faulty memory or not, it was not a landscape that quite matched with how he thought things should be. If anything, *that* had felt more like the sort of superstitious tales of worlds a soul might go to after death. This place, on the other hand, felt vivid and real.

'A figure of speech, lord,' Halin says, with an embarrassed glance at Sutik. 'This is... This is not how our world was, until the sky opened and the Bastards came.'

'It was beautiful,' Sutik puts in. 'That was before they twisted everything. The animals, the plants, even the stars. You'll see it for yourself when the sun goes down.'

'Which will not be long,' the hunter says, looking at the sky. He can tell that Camarth's sun has moved relative to the horizon, even without his armour's sensors. 'Most forests are more dangerous at night, and I doubt this one is different. How far is the camp?'

'Not far,' Halin assures him. 'Follow us, lord, and we'll take you there.'

The hunter pauses for a moment as a new thought occurs to him. These humans are no threat, but what about their allies? Could Halin, Sutik, and Biba be bait, sent to lure him into a trap?

He dismisses the idea. How could anyone be intending to trap him? How could they know where he was to set a trap, when he does not know for sure himself? *Why* would anyone wish to hurt him? He has no context for this.

And yet, his distrust runs deep. He can feel it, like a hidden current surging beneath the surface of his consciousness. He has surely been hurt before, in the past, betrayed by those whom he considered close, and it has marked him severely enough that he carries the echoes of those wounds even though he cannot remember the cause.

Also, he is wearing armour.

He can sense no deceit from the humans in front of him. It is hard to be sure, since they still stink of the fear that came over them when they realised they were being hunted, and his own presence is as alarming to them as his deeds have been reassuring. However, the hunter is as certain as he can be that they are not intentionally misleading him.

'Wait one moment,' he says. He walks back to the body of the final predator-beast, the horned and furred one. 'Does someone have a knife at your camp?' he asks, pitching his voice to carry over his shoulder.

'Yes, lord,' Sutik replies, although it is clear from the tone of his voice that he is uncertain why this question has been asked.

'Good,' the hunter says. He reaches down, grabs the body, and heaves upwards.

The weight is immense, but so is his strength. He strains and puffs, and he can hear warning chimes from the helmet at his waist as it registers the stresses placed upon his armour, but he manages to haul the predator's body off the ground. Then, with a titanic effort, he jerks it higher still and settles it across his shoulders. Now he can carry it with the full strength of his back and his legs, and the weight is far more bearable. He returns to the three humans, and the faces of the adults leave him in no doubt as to how incomprehensible they find this feat.

'Lead on,' says the hunter.

The journey is not far, just as Halin promised. As they progress, the hunter notices signs of habitation: not buildings, power lines, roads, or fields of crops, but other, more subtle indications.

The noise of wildlife lessens, and what tracks and spoor he sees and smells grow fainter, and older. It is obvious to him that this part of the forest has been hunted out; not only that, but there is a marked absence of dead wood, which would partially explain why the humans with him were foraging so far afield for fuel.

'Why do you not cut down these trees for firewood?' the hunter asks. 'Do you lack the tools?'

'No, we can cut if we have to,' Sutik replies. 'But we're still being hunted, and fresh gaps in the canopy lead the Bastards right to us. It's safer to find dead wood, even if it means going far afield.'

'It does not seem to be that safe,' the hunter observes.

'It's still safer,' Sutik says quietly.

The hunter smells the camp before he hears it – the tang of woodsmoke and the savoury scents of cooking food, both hanging heavy in the still air – and he hears it before he sees it, but neither by much. Halin and Sutik lead him around the bole of a particularly massive tree, and through a pathway between two dense shrubs which, the hunter judges, was forced and worn over many years by the passage of larger and heavier animals than humans, and then the camp is in front of him.

Such as it is.

Sure enough, there is no clearing, save for underbrush which has been hacked away. The camp is spread out between tree trunks, apparently chosen for the thickest canopy of leaves overhead. This makes sense, since they will do the best job of dispersing the smoke from the few small, covered fires, rather than letting it rise in an obvious plume that might attract attention. There are low, makeshift roofs of salvaged material or branches, in the shadows beneath which the hunter's keen eyes detect meagre piles of cloth on which people might sleep with something to protect them from the dampness of the ground, tree roots in the ribs, or the scuttling denizens of the leaf litter, even if such protection is more theoretical than practical.

There are perhaps a hundred or so people here. There is no singing, no laughing, no joking, no speech louder than absolutely necessary. Even the children are quiet, trudging around with lowered heads and dull eyes. This is not a community, the hunter realises at once: most people here are shut off inside their own heads, unwilling to indulge in the activities that would make them human for fear of bringing ruin down upon them all. The hunter has little desire for singing, laughing, or joking for himself, but he recognises that for humans to shun such things is to doom themselves to a slow death, one of the soul if not the body.

These people have fled from death, but they are subconsciously waiting to die, simply because they have no other vision for their future.

The hunter stops at the edge of the camp, and shrugs the beast carcass off his shoulders. It lands on the ground with a dull thump, loud enough to snap up the heads of everyone nearby.

'Someone bring me a knife,' the hunter declares. 'I have a kill to skin.'

Some shrink back from him. Others press forward with open mouths, trying to simultaneously take in the concept of a dead predator this size, and the hunter himself, who is so much larger and stronger than they are. The hunter hears a whisper passing through the crowd, repeated often enough that he can make it out with certainty. It is one word.

Protector.

As if summoned by the incantation, a new figure appears out of the shadows. It towers above the humans, near to the hunter's own height, and is clad in an armoured suit of deep but battered black adorned with silver trim. On the chest, and on the left shoulder, a device stands proud: a winged sword.

The hunter blinks as his mind creaks and cracks, like glass walls finally giving in to the pressure of water from all around. Images flash through his head, too fast for even him to properly latch onto: a planet coming apart around him; a sword, or more than one, the shape and nature changing even as he tries to focus on it, or them; a monstrous, bat-winged form, all sharp edges and leering teeth, battering at him with its mind; a glowing, golden presence; a different planet, this one viewed from far above, as death ordered by his hand descends upon it as a rain of silver specks that look no larger than snowflakes, but which he knows are each the size of a hab-block; and on and on and on…

The black-armoured shape – Space Marine – hisses through his teeth, draws two weapons – *bolt pistols* – and opens fire.

IV

My name is Zabriel. Terran-born, of Stackhome Hive. Diacon of the Order of the Three Keys. Initiate of the Dreadwing, formerly the Host of Bone. Knight of the second Destroyer squad in the Third Company, Fifteenth Chapter, of the First Legion. We who were once the Uncrowned Princes, we who were the Emperor's original Angels of Death.

We who became the Dark Angels.

I scoured the Oort Cloud while the younger Legions were still being formed, cleansing dwarf planets and orphaned moons of xenos creatures which will remain forever unnamed and uncategorised, under the weak light of a sun so faint it was merely another star. I fought the rangda at Advex-Mors, and hunted their squalling remnants through the corridors of their ravaged war-moon with my brothers. We ended them with bolt pistol and chainblade, rad missile and phosphex. I was part of the host who came to the aid of the XIII on Karkasarn and repaid our debt of honour to them on the bodies of the flesh-ghola, following at the heels of the Lion.

The Lion. He who would unify us, and would sunder us once again.

To be First Legion was to be the original, the greatest, the purest. We were the mould from which the other Legiones Astartes came, the base template from which they were adapted. Some of them might, in time, come to embody certain aspects of warfare more wholly than we did, but even their specialism was rooted in our ability. The White Scars did not invent swift warfare, any more than the Iron Warriors invented siegecraft, or the World Eaters invented shock assaults, or the Luna Wolves invented striking down the enemy's leadership. All these tactics for which they became famed were born in our hidden wars, as we brought the light of the Imperium into the darkest corners of the galaxy and burned away the infestations too horrific for humanity to even know had ever existed.

Perhaps our expectations for the rest of the Great Crusade were too high. Perhaps we assumed that although our brother Legions and their innumerable human allies were not told the specifics of our deeds, of the myriad of implacable enemies we had exterminated, they would still recognise what we must have done. Perhaps we thought they would understand why we roved so far afield; perhaps we credited them with the wit to comprehend that our tally of recognised compliances was so modest because we were exterminators, the Emperor's ultimate sanction, and our talents were not to be wasted on foes who might yield. Instead, those who followed in our footsteps began to forget why we had been so feared, and who had created the road down which they now travelled with such pomp and self-aggrandisement.

The coming of the primarchs changed things, too, as was inevitable. They were the Emperor's true sons, the demigods of war. The Legiones Astartes were mighty, but we had been intended to complement our gene-fathers, not replace them. As other Legions were reunited with their primarchs, those primarchs enhanced their gene-sons; not through additional technology or gene-smithing – or at least not primarily, although the Iron Hands made no secret of their affinity for bionics, and there were always grim rumours about the World Eaters – but through their genius. Horus was the first and most fêted, of course, for he was a commander and diplomat almost without peer, but as each primarch was discovered, their Legion was newly invigorated in turn.

We were left behind. War had given us scars that ran deep, and saw us divided against ourselves as we sought the best way to reclaim our pre-eminence amongst those who had either forgotten, or never known, how we had shaped the galaxy for humanity. How could we compare, splintered as we were by the campaigning that saw us meet the galaxy's deadliest threats, and which had cost us leader after leader? Meanwhile, the Ultramarines under Roboute Guilliman rolled over human world after human world, welcomed as often as they were attacked, and carved out their own Imperium-in-miniature to their own glory.

All that changed once the Lion was found.

Just as we were the first and purest of the Legions, the Lion was the first and purest of the primarchs, late-found though he was. His mind was not diluted by any desire to seek the approval of others, his actions not weakened by instincts of diplomacy, his tactics untempered by pride. He was the embodiment of what we had always been, and what we had lost. In following and accepting him we became ourselves once again. Not only did the galaxy quake once more at the First Legion, now known as the Dark Angels, but our allies within the Imperium found a respect for us that they had lost in the intervening years.

Not everything went smoothly, of course. Those of the knightly orders of Caliban who ascended to our ranks had to be integrated, which was not a simple process, and not all of us veterans from Terra, Gramarye, and so on adapted easily to the changes the Lion made to the Legion's structures. Nonetheless, as his changes took hold we once again became a smooth blade, clean in form and function, but possessed of an inner structure and strength beyond the understanding of the casual observer.

Then Sarosh happened.

Even to those of us within the Legion, the events that unfolded were unclear. I knew that the traitorous Sarosi had been deceiving us, claiming that they had become loyal citizens of the Imperium when in fact the opposite was true. I knew that they attempted to assassinate the Lion using an atomic warhead, and I knew that they failed.

I do not know why the Lion split the Legion after Sarosh. Some of us, myself included, were sent back to Caliban under the command of Luther, the Lion's former knightly brother and the Legion's second-in-command. We were told that this was to manage recruitment from the world which had become the Legion's spiritual home in the eyes of many, but this explanation did not wash with many of us.

It was the Lion's right to deploy us as he saw fit, of course, for he was our gene-father and the Legion's master, and none could know better than he how best we could serve the Imperium. Nonetheless, it was plain that if any of us truly understood the logic, they were not happy with it. The First Legion had always been a place of secrets, of specialisms and guarded knowledge, but that was simply our way. My own Order of the Three Keys never counted many more than a hundred legionaries amongst its number, but if the Legion required us then we would step forward with what we knew. I focused on my own ways of war, and trusted my battle-brothers to have focus on theirs, each to be called upon as needed. However, knowing that others around you have knowledge that you do not, but which they will use for the good of all, is a very different prospect to not knowing whether anyone around you truly understands what is happening.

This, then, may go some way to explaining why things on Caliban began to develop as they did. Another factor is the temperament of those involved, which travelled down two different but somewhat parallel paths.

Those of my brethren who hailed from Caliban had largely come to our ranks directly from the knightly orders of that planet, or at least had an understanding of that culture. Theirs was a world on which brave warriors had ridden out to face down nightmarish beasts armed with weapons the Imperium would have considered primitive, with the intention of either slaying their quarry or dying in the attempt. This was the First Legion's entire history, written in miniature. Having been shown the galaxy, and the myriad of threats it still contained, against which their natures wished to set themselves, it surely rankled the Calibanites to return to their home, where the natural dangers had largely been removed by the sheer obstinance of the Imperium's colonisation.

For me, and other pre-Caliban veterans, things were a little different. I had no connection to Caliban: it was just a world, and neither a pleasant nor appealing one at that. I did not see the savage beauty the Calibanites sometimes did, nor could I appreciate it as a jewel of the Imperium. To me it seemed to be caught halfway between the two states: too dangerous and treacherous to truly be an inspiration to humanity, like such planets as Terra, or Macragge, or even the seat of occult learning that was Prospero, yet no longer somewhere that might appeal to the more poetic soul, like icy Fenris, or windswept Chogoris.

I strongly suspected that I had been slaying the Imperium's enemies since before Luther himself was born. I had no wish to be stuck on his planet under his command, overseeing raw recruits while others tested themselves against the worst the galaxy still had to throw at humanity. Nor did I think it to be a good use of my skills and experience. This was a banishment, an exile from my gene-father, which I appeared to have earned through nothing more than my rank and squad in the Legion's order of battle – and therefore presumably my proximity to those to whom I reported – rather than any action of my own. I could have resented my superiors for this association, but I had no knowledge of any misconduct of theirs, either.

This decision lay with the Lion. He gave us no explanation, and so, though we might abide by his orders, he left fertile ground for our own interpretations of them to take root. This was only compounded when Luther led a task force to aid in the fight at Zaramund, and returned chastened by the Lion for defying him, and stripped of our fleet. The message seemed clear: we were not welcome in the galaxy at large. The Dark Angels had never fought for glory, but even pride in our own actions was denied to us.

What this would have come to had Horus' rebellion not occurred, I cannot say. Perhaps the Lion would have relented in time, finally forced to call upon the resources of the home world he seemed to have forgotten. Perhaps the Emperor would have intervened. Perhaps, even, one of the Lion's brothers might have drawn attention to the oddity of our situation: noble Sanguinius, perhaps, whom it was said could read the hearts of others and might have determined what had truly caused our gene-father to abandon us; or Guilliman. The Lord of the XIII might have sought to increase our Legion's efficiency, and so at least commenced a conversation which the Lion had refused to have even with us, although I cannot imagine that it would have been a good-tempered one.

However, Horus' rebellion *did* occur, although it was some time after the event before we heard of it. Even then, what were we to do, with no fleet? Luther did what he could to prepare us, so far as I could judge from my lowly position within our ranks, but no word came. Even betrayed by their own brothers, even with the galaxy in flames, the Dark Angels apparently still had no need of us.

Rumours grew as time passed, and news trickled in. The Space Wolves had razed Prospero. Baal was under siege. It was not inconceivable that Caliban might come under attack, and some argued the Lion was leaving us in place to defend against that eventuality. However, as time wore on it became less and less obvious from which side that attack might come.

The Lion and the bulk of our Legion had been in the galactic east, we believed, well removed from the fighting. Those who had any sensitivity to the warp – Astartes or human – could tell the rest of us on Caliban that the immaterium was in turmoil, treacherous for both communication and travel. Still, our gene-father was single-minded when his duty required it of him, and ingenious. It was hard to accept that he might be so thoroughly cut-off that he could find no way to influence this war.

And so doubt began to creep in.

The Emperor had created us, and had created the primarchs, and had created the Imperium itself. It was His vision that had sent us out into the stars to begin with, and His vision that we sought to bring about. However, we knew that He had returned to Terra when He proclaimed Horus as Warmaster. The Lion knew only his role as humanity's ultimate defender; was it so hard to imagine that he might see Horus as the new champion of that, with the Emperor apparently distracted by other matters? The Lion had kept his own counsel, even from us, on the meaning for our exile. We would have been fools had we assumed we knew his true intentions with regard to this rebellion, what side he would take. We could not know. We *did* not know.

When the rebellion concluded, and the ships of the Lion's contingent of the First Legion finally found their way into Caliban's skies once more, Luther had us be prepared for anything. We did not wish to meet our battle-brothers with bolter and blade, but we knew it was a possibility. Had we truly been kept here for so long simply because of a slight, real or imagined, suffered by the Lion at some point decades in the past? Had that exile, for whatever reason it had begun, been turned into an unknowing garrison of the Lion's home world to protect it from the threat of Horus and his allies? Or had the Lion turned against Terra in truth, and feared that had he allowed us out into the galaxy we would have gone against him and stood with the forces of the Emperor?

I still do not know who fired the first shot. I saw and heard our defence batteries open up, spitting plasma and las-fire skywards, and although ours is a stoic Legion, hope died in my chest that day. By this point nothing was clear, not even the disposition of our leaders, for there had been quarrels amongst them, and purges ordered of some who were deemed traitors. However, whatever doubts I might hold, I could not imagine that Luther or his lieutenants would open fire on the Lion without provocation.

I had been present when the First Legion killed worlds, and there was nothing about Caliban which would save it from that fate should those above us choose to enact it. Attacking first was to bring a death sentence down, and if there was one thing which our leaders' chafing at the restrictions imposed upon us showed, it was that they had ambitions beyond dying on that world. The only conclusion I could draw was that the Lion had returned to destroy us because he feared we would stand in opposition to his allegiance, whichever way that lay, or would in some way incriminate him to his remaining brothers now he had no excuse to keep us isolated. How he thought we would do that I did not know, but as fire rained down on us, and landing craft fell from the sky bearing our battle-scarred brethren, such considerations became irrelevant.

I had fought for the Emperor. I had fought for humanity. I had fought for the First Legion, and I had fought for my brothers. Now I fought against them, simply in order to survive. We took what shelter we could in the fortress-monastery which had once been the home of the Lion's own Order, protected as it was by powerful force fields, but they were of little use when the Dark Angels' bombardment began to break the planet apart.

And still our brothers came. So determined were they to see us dead that they came on even as Caliban itself died around them.

V

Baelor calmly placed a fresh magazine into his boltgun, heedless of the heavy-slug shotgun fire hammering into the corner of the bulkhead behind which he waited. The auto-cycling mechanism whirred and clicked a shell into place, just as it had done for hundreds of years. Baelor had been the first recipient of this weapon, fresh from the forges. It had never betrayed him, and he had never dishonoured it. Unlike some he could mention.

'What are you waiting for?' Markog demanded from beside him. The green-armoured giant reeked of heavy incense. Baelor did not know if it was his breath, his sweat, or something produced by his armour. Nor did he wish to know. Markog and his Dolorous Guard were effective, there was no doubt of that, but Baelor did not share their view that the changes wrought upon them were gifts. They seemed weak, to have lost their grip on their former nature. And they seemed young, so young.

Everyone in this godsforsaken galaxy seemed young.

'They are not only wasting ammunition, they are also not

alternating their fire efficiently,' he informed Markog. 'More than half will be reloading their weapons...'

He counted down inside his head.

'Now.'

He stepped out. The gun barrels of the ship's defenders tracked him, but he had timed his movements correctly: most of the twenty or so baseline humans in the corridor in front of him were reloading their combat shotguns. They were doing so efficiently and quickly, leaving only a few seconds in which the output of fire was diminished, but a few seconds was a yawning gulf of opportunity for a Space Marine.

He targeted the firers first, dropping half a dozen with shots in the space of half as many seconds, so quickly that an unenhanced observer might have considered it more likely that the humans had simply exploded than all fallen victim to the same weapon wielded by the same warrior. Then he charged the rest.

A solid shotgun round slammed into his left pauldron, but the curved ceramite deflected the shot into the wall. This sort of ammunition would make a mess of most boarders, but it lacked the penetrative power to seriously trouble Mark IV power armour. A direct hit to the faceplate of his helmet might be a problem, but none arrayed against him had sufficient accuracy or reflexes to manage that before he closed with them.

He struck with fist, elbow, and foot, breaking their weak bodies with blows that struck like pneumatic hammers. He did not slow, but ploughed straight through them, destroying those in his way. The untouched remainders at the edges, who had escaped both his bolter and his fists, turned to follow him with the instinctive movements of a flock of prey animals tracking a hunter.

Markog came into the back of them, swinging his long-handled axe, Heartdrinker, with consummate grace. Such was his reach, and the length of his weapon, that he did not need to step either right or left as he followed Baelor's path through the centre of the corridor's narrow confines. The commander of the Dolorous Guard slew the remnants, and the strange, pale metal of his axe-head drank up the blood until it was shining and clean once again.

'Sloppy,' Baelor commented, looking down at the corpses. They were robed in dark green, with gold trim.

'Chapter-serfs,' Markog grunted. His unnaturally long tongue flickered out to mop up the drops of blood that had spattered onto his face, and he shuddered with delight at the taste. 'Only human.'

'Still sloppy,' Baelor said. He activated his vox. 'Knight-captain?'

'You will address him as "my lord Seraphax,"' Markog growled.

'Shut up, Markog,' Baelor said, ignoring the giant's silent snarl. 'Knight-captain?'

'Baelor. Is your level secure?'

Seraphax's voice slid through the vox like an electric serpent. He had always had a good voice, even back as an adept on Caliban, and his ascension to the ranks of the Space Marines had not changed that, it had merely deepened it and enriched it. Seraphax spoke with the same casual mastery with which a blademaster worked his forms: no detail missed, no misstep or error in pacing, everything apparently effortless and unhurried until the observer was mesmerised. He had ruled the world of Bast for a century off the back of his voice, and his sorcerous gifts. The Host of Pentacles had nurtured those, until the Council of Nikaea, but Seraphax had moved far beyond that now.

And where he moved, Baelor moved with him. Loyalty was a strange beast. Baelor had followed Seraphax when he had been a mere company captain, one of many such officers within the ranks of the First Legion, and he followed him now. Baelor was a warrior, but he knew that he lacked vision. He would fight what was placed in front of him, and he would fight it well, but grand strategic understanding was not his strength. The *how*, he could manage. The *why* was something he had always left to others.

'All resistance so far has been eliminated, knight-captain,' he acknowledged. Seraphax had never demanded that Baelor address him by anything other than the title he carried on the day Caliban died, and Baelor had never wished to.

'Glory to the Ten Thousand Eyes!' Markog added.

'Good. Proceed to the reliquary,' Seraphax instructed, but Baelor could practically hear the sorcerer-lord's remaining eye rolling at Markog's fervency.

'Yes, knight-captain,' Baelor acknowledged. He did not look at Markog, but could feel the giant's displeasure. He let it slide off him. Annoying Markog was one of the minor pleasures Baelor took outside of his duty, and pretending that it was incidental rather than calculated only made the whole thing more enjoyable. 'Come, commander.'

That was another little jibe. Markog was the commander of the Dolorous Guard, the remnants of those Space Marines who had once been the Ashen Blades until Chaos had ensnared them. They were Seraphax's personal bodyguard, but instead of being with his lord, Markog had been assigned to assist Baelor. Baelor knew that Markog resented his presence within the Ten Thousand Eyes: resented his close relationship with Seraphax, resented his longevity, and resented the authority he carried not on the basis of any rank he held, but for who he was. Baelor was not Lord Sorcerer, he was not a commander, he was not the Arch-Raptor or the Lord Celebrant or the Unshriven. He was simply Baelor, sometimes known as the Imposter, counted amongst the Fallen by fools, and amongst the deadly by the wise. His word was second only to Seraphax's in the warband, and there was nothing Markog could do about it.

Well, he could kill Baelor, of course – or at least he could try. Baelor had felt the giant's eyes sizing him up more than once, but Markog had always thought better of it. Perhaps he did not trust that he was Baelor's equal, size and Heartdrinker notwithstanding, or perhaps he had not yet conceived a manner of death which would not leave him the obvious culprit, and therefore the target of Seraphax's vengeance. Even the Ashen Blades themselves had not known the origin of their gene-seed, it seemed, but Baelor suspected it was not from a lineage with any subtlety to its name.

However, sometimes subtlety was unnecessary. So it proved when the doors of the grav-lift they were approaching opened to reveal a massive, gold-armoured figure.

It was a Terminator of the Angels of Vigilance, the Chapter whose strike cruiser the Ten Thousand Eyes had ambushed, a storm bolter in its right hand and its left a massive power fist already crackling with energy. It was not as tall as Markog, but it must have matched him for bulk, and its armour was substantially thicker. Of all the foes to encounter, it was perhaps the worst; one of the primary uses of Tactical Dreadnought armour was for close-quarters fighting in confined spaces such as a voidship's corridors.

Markog flew at it with a melodic snarl, Heartdrinker a pale blur as it swept towards the Terminator's helmet. The Terminator's power glove flashed up to swat the giant's blow aside, then the Angel of Vigilance levelled its storm bolter at Markog's chest. Markog seized the weapon and twisted it just enough for the mass-reactive shells to explode in the wall behind him instead of his breastplate. He tried to backhand the Terminator with Heartdrinker, but the Angel of Vigilance grabbed the haft in its power fist, and a strange radiance filled the corridor as the disruptor field warred with the arcane forces residing in the ancient axe. The two behemoths lumbered around in a half-circle, servos whining as each tried to overpower the other, but found themselves equally matched.

Baelor stepped up calmly, dropped to one knee, waited for Markog's attempts to tear Heartdrinker out of the Terminator's reach to pull the Imperial's arm upwards, and fired three times into the vulnerable armpit so revealed.

Even Terminator armour had joints, and joints were weak points. The bolts punched through heavily reinforced plasflex and thundered into the Space Marine's sternum, detonating within. The Angel of Vigilance staggered, yet with superhuman determination and resilience, it still fought. Heartdrinker slipped out of his grip, but the Imperial had enough energy left to drive its power fist into Markog's chest before the giant could bring his axe down. Markog stumbled backwards and fell to the floor with a clatter of ceramite on metal, his breastplate a smoking ruin.

Baelor rose to his feet and fired again. A Terminator's faceplate was the other obvious target of the armour, and unlike the serfs he had so recently killed, Baelor had the reflexes, marksmanship, and ammunition to make his shots count. The Angel of Vigilance's golden helmet shattered, and the head within followed suit. Limbs collapsed like a puppet with the strings cut, and the veteran crumpled into an undignified heap on the deck.

Baelor looked around. Markog was picking himself up again, his chest and armour – if the two were even separate any more – re-forming themselves out of the green vapour the power fist had blasted them into. The giant's eyes glowed, and he gave a shuddering sigh of pleasure as his reconfiguration completed. Then his gaze travelled to the corpse of the Imperial, and his long tongue slithered out between his lips.

'Later,' Baelor told him sternly. '*If* the... the *Lord Sorcerer* says you may. We still need to get to the reliquary.'

Markog snarled, but after a moment he reset his jaw and nodded, somewhat resentfully. Killing the servants of the shell that still called itself the Imperium was one thing. Eating their flesh afterwards was, in Baelor's opinion, quite another.

The reliquary of the strike cruiser *Dread Sentinel* was high-vaulted and dimly lit. Baelor's eyes could pierce the gloom without trouble, but it must have been Stygian indeed for the serfs whose task it once was to tend this place. That would certainly explain the unlit candelabras that lay around, their contents scattered between the corpses of those who would have used them.

'Ah, Baelor,' Seraphax said, turning to greet him. 'Do come in. Commander, you may remain outside at present. Liaise with the rest of our forces, and ensure there are no other pockets of resistance.'

'Of course, Lord Sorcerer,' Markog said, bowing with his hand on his chest. He closed the door, but Baelor caught the glare the giant shot his way. As ever, Markog pinned the blame on Baelor, not Seraphax.

Seraphax.

On Caliban, Seraphax had been a fair-faced youth, with hair the colour of hungry flame and pale cheeks that greeted the sun's rays with a profusion of freckles. Much like his voice, his ascension to Space Marine had not eclipsed this grace, merely altered it. He had never been spoken of in the same terms as someone like Lucius of the Emperor's Children, but Baelor had always considered that amongst warriors generally considered to be bluff-featured and with facial proportions slightly different to the norm, Seraphax occupied a halfway ground between human and transhuman. His face still held some of the beauty of his youth, a history of where he had come from, but altered into something that was never less than striking.

Now, some ten thousand years later by the galaxy's reckoning, although markedly less as Baelor and Seraphax had experienced it, Seraphax's visage had gone beyond 'striking'. Now his hair was hungry flame in truth, along with the left side of his face. No part of his body was consumed by the fire, and he gave no indication that it pained him, but Baelor could see the faint heat haze shimmering above his knight-captain's head. Such was the price of dealing with the warp; the price of what must be done to achieve their goal. Baelor had marked no such changes in himself, not even at the smallest level, and Seraphax had promised to tell him if he noticed any, but the love Baelor bore for his commanding officer was still slightly shadowed by those concerns, these days.

'I know that aspect. What ails you, my friend?' Seraphax asked. The Feverblade, a long knife of ancient and unknown origin, hung at his hip in its scabbard of human skin, and he carried his staff of dark metal, which was topped with an aeldari witch's skull engraved with cuneiform script. Baelor had long ago given up looking at the skull: it hurt his eyes.

'Markog's appetites are growing stronger,' Baelor said. It was not the only thing that bothered him, but it was the easiest to voice. 'He craves the flesh of others more and more, particularly other Astartes.'

'Such are the demands of the Prince of Pain and Pleasure,' Seraphax sighed. 'Markog drinks of Slaanesh's boons, and they do not come without price.'

'These are poor tools with which to bring the galaxy to heel,' Baelor muttered. He reached out and ran his armoured finger down the cover of a battered grimoire standing proudly on a lectern. He had no idea what significance it had held for the

Angels of Vigilance. It was not a weapon, and therefore it was not his concern.

'Markog is powerful,' Seraphax said. 'In what way is he a poor tool?'

'Because he is not *your* tool!' Baelor said, turning to address his knight-captain face to burning face. 'Not fully! He is in thrall to another power. Commander of the Dolorous Guard or not, his loyalty will always be in question when he is sworn to a god.'

Seraphax smiled with the half of his mouth that was still visible. '"God." I remember the days when you would not use that word.'

Baelor sighed. 'So do I. They were simpler times.'

'The times were not simpler,' Seraphax corrected him gently. 'We were. We did not understand our place, or our potential. You and I are on the path to correcting that.'

The sorcerer swung his staff casually, and the plexi-glass front of a cabinet shattered under the impact of the carved aeldari skull. Another skull lay inside, this one the distinctive shape and size of a Space Marine. It was layered with gold leaf. Seraphax muttered something under his breath and the gold began to melt and drip away, leaving the bone beneath unharmed.

'Another psyker skull?' Baelor guessed.

'Well, if our enemies will keep leaving them lying around,' Seraphax said with a chuckle, then sobered. 'This is not a macabre obsession, my friend. With the warp in such turmoil, anything which holds a memory of strong connection to it is invaluable. Abaddon has set the empyrean raging, and only his close allies are protected from its talons. I need to shield and guide us.' He paused, and his remaining eye narrowed as he looked at Baelor. 'What?'

Baelor shook his head, embarrassed at having been caught doubting. 'I will follow you anywhere, you know that, but what makes you think you can succeed where Abaddon has failed? The Ten Thousand Eyes is a mighty force, but it is a flyspeck against what Abaddon commands, and the Despoiler was rightly praised as a general and tactician back when… when things were different.'

'That was then,' Seraphax said simply. 'Abaddon fights blinded by hatred and malice. The Sons of Horus were always too bombastic and full of themselves, and that has only worsened over time. The Dark Angels, in contrast, always had purity of purpose. Then, as now.'

He picked up the skull and regarded it at eye level, then tossed it into the air. Instead of falling to the deck, it began to orbit him in a slow, lazy loop.

'Our tools may be unorthodox, powerful though they are, but we will use them to reshape the galaxy. As our primarch taught us, we will not rest until our quarry is destroyed. So long as you are by my side, my brother, we will succeed.'

Seraphax reached out and took hold of the back of Baelor's neck. Baelor bent forward slightly, and Seraphax touched his lips to Baelor's forehead.

Just like all the other times, the fire did not burn him.

VI

The Space Marine opens fire and bolt-shells roar through the air, but they do not strike their target. This is not because the Space Marine's aim is inaccurate, as such: he expertly placed his shots where he saw the hunter. It is just that in the micro-second between the Space Marine's hands starting to twitch and his transhuman reflexes bringing his weapons up, the hunter has already moved.

The hunter dives to his right, because there are people immediately to his left, and although he could avoid them, he does not wish to draw the Space Marine's shots towards them. They are not as fast, as resilient, or as well armoured as he is, and even being winged by a bolt-shell could be fatal. His hands touch down first as he finishes his leap some twenty feet away, cushioning his impact and distributing his weight. He pivots slightly on his left hand to bring his legs around; they are in contact with the ground for a mere moment before he pushes off again.

The hunter leaves the ground in another stunningly fast bound.

Lion El'Jonson, primarch of the First Legion, collides with the Space Marine and bears him to the ground.

The Space Marine tries to bring his weapons up, but the Lion casually slaps them out of his hands. Thoughts are still sleeting through his forebrain, but enough have found their homes for him to remember who he is, and what has happened to him. Caliban; the Order; his father, and his brothers. Horus, that wretched traitor; Curze, the thrice-damned monster; noble, tragic Sanguinius, and brash, swaggering Russ, and the infuriating Roboute.

Watching his traitorous brothers' home planets burn, at his orders. Watching Terra burn, because he was too late. Returning to Caliban, and watching it burn around him. Facing Luther, and the tidal wave of grief that struck him when he realised what his old friend had become, a tidal wave which strikes him once more and nearly bears him under. And then… and then…

Nothing. Just the forest, and the river.

The Lion pins the Space Marine down before he can reach for the combat knife or the chainsword at his belt. He glances down at the black armour, battered and worn, and still carrying signs that would mean nothing to those outside the Legion, but which to the Lion are as clear as the faces of the people around him.

'Knight of the second Destroyer squad in Third Company, Fifteenth Chapter. Diacon of the Order of the Three Keys, and initiate of the Dreadwing.' More memories rise to the surface, furnishing him with the name that belongs to those ranks. 'Zabriel.'

The Space Marine's expression cannot be seen behind the faceplate of his armour, but Lion El'Jonson feels his struggling stop. It is replaced by a different sort of tension, however, one which the Lion can still sense. Warriors of the Legiones Astartes do not know fear, but something not entirely dissimilar has Zabriel in its grip, if the primarch is any judge.

'Get off him!' someone screams, ten feet behind the Lion and three to his right. 'He is our protector!'

'He is a traitor,' the Lion growls, the words resonating in his throat, and solidifying in his brain as they pass his lips. Yes, a traitor, just like Luther. The Lion remembers the designations of all those he ordered back to Caliban, and Zabriel's squad was amongst them. 'A traitor who has now tried to murder me for the second time.'

'*You* are the traitor!' the Space Marine rages from beneath him. 'You abandoned us, you abandoned Caliban, and you abandoned the Imperium!'

'Lies!' the Lion snarls, but Zabriel's words latch their claws into freshly reopened wounds. The Lion knows he did not intend to abandon the Imperium, but how many times did he question himself whether what he was doing was the correct course of action? Chemos, Nuceria, Barbarus: they all died at the hands of his sons in an attempt to draw the traitors away from Terra, and open a path for Sanguinius and the Blood Angels. Should the Dark Angels have forged on regardless? Should the Lion have turned his Legion into the spear tip so favoured by the Sons of Horus, and gone for his treacherous brother's throat?

Would that have saved his father's life?

'Lies? Then where have you been for ten thousand years?' Zabriel demands.

The Lion opens his mouth to call him a fool, but the words won't come. He wants to demand Zabriel repeat himself, but that would be pointless: the Lion heard him perfectly. The words themselves are not in doubt. It is the meaning behind them that has paralysed Lion El'Jonson into unfamiliar indecision.

He swallows, sits back, and releases Zabriel's arms. 'Take your helmet off.'

'What?'

'Take your helmet off,' the Lion growls, 'or I will remove it for you.'

For a moment, the Lion thinks Zabriel is going to go for his weapons, but then the Dark Angel reaches up and disengages his helmet as instructed. The Lion is already reassessing the state of his traitorous son's wargear. It is battered, yes, but battered and repaired imperfectly, time and time again. These are not the marks of one giant combat, but the result of repeated use, far beyond when Legion protocol would dictate that the parts be replaced.

Zabriel lifts his helmet clear, and his face is revealed. The Lion searches his memory, and finds a near match: Zabriel, Terran, skin a cool mid-brown, hair black, eyes a dark sapphire. A veteran from the earliest days of the Legion, he was already a mature Space Marine by the time the Lion took command.

The face revealed is heavily lined, the dark hair is shot through with grey, and multiple small keloids mark the skin, where Zabriel has been injured and it has scarred. The Lion has never seen a Space Marine this... old. Some of the enhanced, like Lorgar's wretch Kor Phaeron, yes; those warriors were never a Space Marine's equal, being raised up while older, and lacking the advanced gene-smithing that kept the ravages of time at bay so effectively. A true Space Marine, though?

The Lion reaches up slowly with one armoured hand, and rubs gently at the lines he knows mark his own face. He had no idea what he was looking at when he saw his reflection in the river; nothing with which to compare it. Now he remembers how he looked the last time he saw himself, and he wonders.

He shakes his head, clinging to what he knows. 'No. Ten thousand years is an impossibility. A primarch... I cannot be sure how we would age. But a Space Marine would be long dead, I am certain of it.'

'The warp storm scattered us not just through space, but also through time,' Zabriel says. 'I re-emerged perhaps four hundred years ago. Four hundred years of running and hiding from my *little brothers*,' he adds scornfully. 'We were always single-minded once we engaged a foe, but ten thousand years of hatred in an attempt to extinguish guilt? Truly, my lord Lion, you taught your sons well.'

'What mockery is this?' the Lion snarls. 'We returned to Caliban from Terra, only to find the system held against us! You opened fire on us without warning, and your leaders had made pacts with–' He becomes aware again of the people around them, too scared to get close but too fascinated to draw back. Some of them are within earshot, for sure. 'With powers I will not name,' he finishes, lowering his voice. 'I cannot explain how I have come to be here, for my memory was impaired until I laid eyes upon you, and some things are still hidden from me, but one thing is plain – as soon as you saw me, you tried to kill me again! Why should my loyal sons *not* hunt traitors like yourself?'

Zabriel sighs and rests his head back on the ground, his aspect of one who is weary beyond all reason.

'I knew nothing of the powers of which you speak. I had no contact with our leaders, Luther and Astelan and the others, save briefly and in passing. I was not party to any order to open fire upon your fleet. But as for my reaction to seeing you...'

He raises his head, and looks the Lion in the eye. It is not an experience the Lion is used to; even in his old memories there were few that could hold his gaze for any length of time.

'I saw you once only after you ordered us to Caliban. The fleet was raining fire upon us, and our brothers had landed to make war. I caught a glimpse of you, for the first time in years, as you cut your way through some new recruits who had never laid eyes on you, and whose first true battle wearing the armour of the First Legion was against their gene-father and his executioners. They died in moments and you pressed on, presumably in search of Luther. I did not see you again. However, even with what came afterwards, even when the planet splintered and the warp reached out to seize us all, it was the expression on your face that remained with me then, and for all the long years since.

'It was hatred and rage, pure and unfettered. You were intent upon our deaths, and we knew better than any others that once you set your mind to something, you could not be deterred. When I saw you here, having walked out of the forest, I could not mistake your features despite the age that has overtaken you, for your face has haunted my dreams for centuries. Either you were a Chaos-spawned mockery of my primarch, spewed forth from the Great Rift to torment me, or you were the Lion here to finally kill me. I was prepared to tolerate neither without a fight.'

The Lion searches Zabriel's face with his eyes and stretches out with all his senses, but he can sense no falsehood. The Space Marine's twin heartbeat does not betray him, and there is no scent of deception, although to be sure, having been borne to the ground and disarmed by a primarch would trigger a fight-or-flight reflex in anyone, against which background the subtle scents of heightened anxiety would be difficult to make out.

The Lion is bitterly aware that he has not always been the best judge of character. On Diamat, he handed siege machines over to Perturabo in the mistaken belief that his brother was going to use them to crush Horus' nascent rebellion. Instead, those guns spelled doom for the Raven Guard and the Salamanders at Isstvan V. How much grief and bloodshed could have been spared had he been able to trust Guilliman from the moment the Dark Angels arrived through the Ruinstorm at Macragge? Instead, both of them kept their secrets, with disastrous consequences.

And on, and on. Should he have seen what Lorgar's obsessive love of their father concealed? Should he have recognised that Angron's rage would never be satisfied? Should he, most crucially, have perceived the flaws in Horus Lupercal? It was not in his nature – the Lion and the First Legion had always faced outwards, searching for the danger in the darkness beyond humanity's borders, not looking over their shoulders – but it is a failure that gnaws at him nonetheless. But how could Lion El'Jonson be expected to see the worm inside the heart of one of the greatest diplomats and strategists humanity had ever known, when he had not even been able to foresee the thoughts and actions of his own Legion?

He has no answers. None of his brothers are here, even the ones he could trust. He must, as he so often has, do this alone.

'You say I abandoned the Imperium,' he says, his voice low and dangerous. 'Do you swear to me by whatever you hold most dear that you remained loyal? That whatever the allegiances of your commanders, you, Zabriel, loved the Emperor and humanity, and that you only raised your hand to your brothers and to me because you thought you were betrayed in turn?'

Zabriel's eyes still do not leave his. 'I swear it.'

The Lion hesitates, but how can he decry his gene-son for not realising the failures of his commanders, when the Lion himself had never detected his own brothers' treachery until it was too late? Besides which, these people consider Zabriel to be their protector, which at least implies that he has not fallen into the same sort of darkness as the heretics of Horus' rebellion.

'Your story of ten thousand years is hard to accept,' Lion El'Jonson says, 'but I believe these words.' He rises, and reaches down to offer a hand to Zabriel; a gesture as much as it is assistance, for a Space Marine needs no help to get to his feet.

Zabriel does not move. 'And do you also swear?'

Lion El'Jonson frowns. 'Swear what?'

'Do you swear to me by whatever you hold most dear that you remained loyal? That you, the Lion, loved the Emperor and humanity, and that you only raised your hand to your gene-sons because you thought you were betrayed?'

The Lion growls deep in his throat at being questioned so by one of his warriors, but he holds his tongue. It seems he has much to learn, and Zabriel's obvious age immediately suggests that he may know more than any of the humans of Camarth. Besides, the Lion has no reason not to give the honest answer beyond that of stubborn pride, and he has seen how that can tear the galaxy apart.

'I swear it,' he says. Zabriel reaches up to accept his hand, and the Lion pulls him to his feet. He realises a moment later that Zabriel's eyes are moistening with tears.

'So pointless,' the Space Marine mutters to himself. 'If there were any traitors, they were not who I thought. We waged war upon ourselves for no reason.'

'Zabriel,' the Lion says seriously. 'I must know our situation. What of the Imperium? What of my brothers? What of my Legion?'

Zabriel snorts a laugh that is without humour. 'Where to begin? An exact date is... difficult to ascertain, even for someone who has been counting the passage of time for four centuries. The Emperor remains interred on the Golden Throne, or so His subjects believe – I certainly cannot say for sure one way or the other. He is worshipped as a god–'

'He is *what?*'

Zabriel shrugs wearily. 'The Imperial creed. The Ecclesiarchy is just as fanatical as the bastard Word Bearers were in our day, only they have the full power of the Imperium behind them now. To deny the Emperor's divinity is to be sentenced to death. I believe most Space Marines have some clemency on the issue, but I have had little opportunity to engage any in conversation. Every person around you considers Him a god, and I simply keep my own counsel on the matter.'

The Lion closes his eyes. 'I asked myself in the aftermath of the Siege of Terra whether the so-called victory was worth the cost. Now I wonder if we won at all.' He opens them again. 'How did my brothers allow this?'

'They are gone,' Zabriel says with a sigh. 'All the loyalist primarchs were merely a memory by the time I was spat out by the warp. Be assured that I went looking for information, desperately trying to find some link to the life I knew, but I cannot even tell you who was the last to fall, or how it happened. Some say they are dead, some say they disappeared, some believe in the primarchs only as figures of myth and legend. The Imperium is now ruled by the High Lords of Terra.'

The Lion's hands curl into fists without any conscious thought, and he grits his teeth. He remembers the misery he felt when he learned of Ferrus' death, and Corax's, and Sanguinius'. Is it better to be told of all his remaining brothers' deaths in one go, rather than seeing them fall or fade one by one?

He is uncertain, but he doubts it.

'And my Legion?' he manages.

'Rearranged, by order of Lord Guilliman,' Zabriel informs him neutrally. 'All the Legions were dissolved into individual Chapters. The Dark Angels remain, as a force of a thousand or so, with many other Successor Chapters affiliated to them.'

'Guilliman,' Lion El'Jonson hisses, his grief abruptly overtaken by blistering rage. 'Never content with the work of others! He even wanted to improve on the designs of our father! I should have dealt with him when he first raised his hand to me on

Macragge. Why could it not have been *him* who fell, instead of Sanguinius?'

He inhales sharply.

'I must go to Terra. If my father is still on the Golden Throne as you say, then if there is any scrap of life still in Him, any spark of His consciousness left, I will see Him.'

Zabriel shakes his head again. 'Such a thing is not possible. At least,' he adds, narrowing his eyes, 'I would not consider it so. I do not know how you came to be here.'

The Lion thinks back to his awakening by the river. Those forests were definitely not those of Camarth – now he considers it, he realises that they really *were* like the forests of Caliban – but he has no idea how he came to be there, or how *there* turned into *here*.

'That is still something of a mystery to me, as well. But why is travel to Terra not possible? Has humanity lost the use of the warp? Did all the Navigators die?'

'Nothing so prosaic,' Zabriel says. 'Did Halin and Sutik tell you anything of why the people of Camarth are reduced to this?' He gestures with one hand, taking in the camp around them.

'They said the sky opened, and the Bastards came,' the Lion remembers. 'That it twisted everything, even the stars, and that I would see it when the sun went down.'

'Accurate enough,' Zabriel says. 'Dusk is nearly upon us. If you will wait until then, my explanation will be more easily understood.'

The Lion considers. His instinct is to press for more information as soon as possible, but he can practically feel the cracks running through his soul. He lost consciousness fighting the man he had considered a brother, and he awoke to the news that ten thousand years have passed and his true brothers are all dead. He is well aware that this is likely to be just the beginning of the revelations, and any good warrior knows their own limits. Memories are still returning to him as it is; it will do him no good to further pressure his psyche by trying to absorb ten thousand years of history in one go.

Besides, there is another, more sinister possibility: that this entire experience is something concocted by the foul powers that corrupted Horus in order to torment the Lion, showing him the final ruin of his father's vision. If that is the case, then he will bide his time and wait for the flaws in the illusion to show.

'I still require a knife,' he announces to the group at large, turning away from Zabriel. The people shrink back from him in fear and awe, and not a little uncertainty as he strides back towards the corpse of the mutated beast.

'You cannot eat the meat of such a thing, lord,' someone pipes up, then gets nudged in the ribs. 'Well, we can't,' she adds uncertainly.

'I have no intention of eating it,' the Lion declares. He flexes his fingers, as long-ago hunting trips on Caliban come to the fore in his mind.

The simple work of skinning a kill, even with a knife that is too small in his hands, occupies and calms the Lion's mind. The blade is marked with a hand-scratched aquila, and while it is a devotional symbol in these times, he finds that he can think of it simply as a reminder of his father. He pays little attention to the mood of the people around him, although he is aware that some are fearful of him after he bested their 'protector', while others are encouraged that they now have an even more formidable warrior with them. He barely notices when the sun's light, already muted by the leaves and trunks of the trees, disappears completely. It is only when he hears Zabriel approaching that he starts to consider why that is. It is true that his eyes are sensitive, far more so than those of a human, but even so...

The Lion looks up, peering through the gaps in the canopy. He has seen the thick band of the Milky Way from many worlds in his life, but that is not what leers down from the night sky above him now. It is mainly green, but there are other colours in there too, some of which defy description. It looks like someone has taken the biggest axe ever created to the galaxy, and left a long, ravening wound in its wake.

'This is, I presume, what will keep me from Terra?' he asks.

'Yes,' Zabriel replies quietly. 'The Great Rift. So far as we know, it splits the entire galaxy in two, but since the Astronomican is obscured and warp travel is impossible to undertake safely for more than a few light years at a time, actually finding that out is not easy. Similarly, astrotelepathy is extremely limited. Even though we are not in the Rift, the warp is so disturbed that any form of long-range communication is virtually impossible, if not actively dangerous to those involved. Some claim the Rift has actually swallowed the rest of the galaxy, but I do not believe that,' he continues. 'Although I admit I have no evidence with which to support that conviction.'

'The Ruinstorm come again, of a sort,' the Lion mutters. Memories flash up: stars the colour of blood, daemonic fortress walls the width of solar systems, and the bloated, monstrous shape of the *Veritas Ferrum*. He banishes them again. 'So, we are cut off from Terra, and the centre of the Imperium's power. Warp travel is difficult and dangerous, astropathic communication likewise. The fabric of the Imperium has, I suspect, come apart, and reavers have taken advantage?'

'Indeed,' Zabriel confirms. 'Xenos and Chaos alike. "The Bastards" is how the people of Camarth refer to the warband which descended on their planet and ruined it, although they refer to themselves as the Ten Thousand Eyes – mutants, heretics, and some twisted Astartes. I came to this planet in secret, before the Great Rift opened, since it was garrisoned by a Chapter of Space Marines who had no link to the Dark Angels, and therefore my little brothers would find it harder to persecute me here even if they learned of me. The bastion was the first target of the renegades' attack, and it did not survive. The people of the planet who were not killed or enslaved now live like this. I stumbled into this group and have done my best to protect them, since I can neither leave this world, nor summon aid. I do not even know if there is any aid to summon.'

'I have lived like this before,' the Lion says. 'Isolated outposts in a forest, surrounded by malicious, intelligent beasts that would kill us all if they got the chance. You are a Terran, Zabriel, not a Calibanite. Do you know what I did in that situation?'

'You organised the people of your world, and exterminated the beasts,' Zabriel says, nodding. 'The tales were famous.'

The Lion takes a deep breath. 'And I will do so again.'

He was the First; the son who did whatever was asked of him, whatever the cost. He destroyed the nightmares of the galaxy. He annihilated rebellions. He obliterated worlds in his father's name, all in the service of a grand vision that died on the tips of Horus' claws aboard the *Vengeful Spirit*.

'You seek to forge a new Imperium?' Zabriel asks. The Lion growls in response; the memory of Roboute's folly still rankles.

'No. Only my father had the capacity to do that. Now the galaxy burns, my brothers are gone, and I am cut off from Terra.' He pauses, but the Lion has never lacked in decisiveness. 'If all that I know of my father's work has been destroyed, then I shall return to what I knew before. Keeping people safe.'

He wipes the knife clean, and tucks it into his belt. It is a tiny thing, compared to him, but only a fool dismisses a tool solely because of its size.

'My father was a conqueror, and I became a conqueror on

His behalf, but that is not my nature. I kill enemies, and all of humanity's enemies are my enemies. I shall demand no promise from the people of Camarth, and certainly no *worship*' – he spits the word – 'but I will kill their oppressors. They may follow me or not, as they wish.'

'You intend to attack the Ten Thousand Eyes?' Zabriel asks.

'I take it they still have a presence on this world, since the humans are fearful of being noticed.'

'They do.' Zabriel looks away, then grimaces. 'Very well. I can lead you to their closest stronghold, if that is what you wish.'

'Will you fight?' the Lion asks. It is a strange question to ask a Space Marine, but these are strange times. Zabriel is old, and weary, and quite obviously cannot bring himself to fully trust the Lion yet, just as Lion El'Jonson does not fully trust him.

'I was a Destroyer,' Zabriel replies, still looking away at something the Lion cannot see. 'I eradicated humanity's enemies with everything our Legion could bring to bear. I now have nothing more than a pair of bolt pistols and a chainblade, and so I have not brought this filth to battle, since I knew I would be overwhelmed and any protection these people might have from roving bands would be gone. However, if the Lord of the First is going to war...'

He looks back at the Lion once more, and meets his eyes again.

'Then yes, I will fight. My lord.'

VII

The Lord of the First was back. In some ways he was just as I remembered him, and in others he was very different.

You cannot forget the face of a primarch, with the possible exception of that of the Alpha Legion. I had laid eyes on four, besides my own: Mortarion of the Death Guard, Leman Russ of the Space Wolves, Fulgrim of the Emperor's Children, and Horus Lupercal, and each of their features were burned into my memory. Or at least, their features as they were then, in the days of the Great Crusade, before we were exiled back to Caliban. I had no idea how Horus, Mortarion, or Fulgrim had changed when in the grips of Chaos.

The Lion, however, had *aged*. I did not know how. It seemed that he did not, either, as he claimed to have no memory of what had happened to him since the destruction of Caliban. Had the Dark Angels kept him in a form of imperfect stasis, for some reason? Had he merely slept for ten thousand years, and this was simply how a primarch's physiology responded to a hundred centuries? Nonetheless, I still knew him the moment I laid eyes upon him, grey of hair and lined of face though he might be. His armour was different to that which I remembered, but his air, his mannerisms, his aura – however you wanted to put it – were unchanged. He was my gene-sire, and I would have known him had his face been a mass of scar tissue, and had he been clad in beggar's rags.

Lion El'Jonson drew the eye through his glory and his strength, but repelled it through his grim manner. His nature invited adulation, but his character cautioned distance. To speak to him was to become immediately, crushingly aware that your words were being measured and weighed against his standards for what was worthy of his time and attention. He was a being of concentrated and furious purpose and regardless of how or why, he had awakened and returned in the aftermath of the Great Rift opening across the galaxy.

I had never been one to trust in portents or omens, but this felt like something I could not ignore.

I foreswore my Legion long ago, when the rest of it tried to murder me for no reason I could ascertain. I had spent the centuries since my return to the material realm evading the paranoid, spiteful, vengeful descendants of that Legion, in their various different forms. The Lion had no authority over me any longer; even if I believed his assertion that he was the betrayed, that he had only attacked Caliban when his forces had been attacked unprovoked, that was not sufficient to restore my loyalty. I had been alone for too long, too used to making my own decisions and surviving based on my own instincts to readily surrender my will to that of another. He was still my gene-sire, but he had no hand in my creation. Besides, although I was no longer truly human, is it not a human trait to outgrow the authority of a parent?

Therefore, it was not duty, fear, loyalty, or love which compelled me to offer my aid to the Lord of the First when he declared he would make war on the Ten Thousand Eyes. It was something greater.

It was *faith*.

Not a religious faith. I still detested the worship of the Emperor as a god by the misguided humans who populated the Imperium. This was something primal, deeper, and far less proscribed. It was the sensation that the Lion was here, now, at this time, for a purpose. His reappearance exactly when not just the Imperium, but also humanity itself, faced its greatest threat since the Horus Heresy felt like too much of a coincidence. I have heard sorcerers and psykers and charlatans alike speak of the future, of destiny, and of fate, but this was the first time I could say I felt anything like that at work. I did not know where it would lead, but I knew I had a role to play beyond that of a lone, weary warrior guarding a ragtag group of refugees against a threat he could not repel if it descended in force.

We did not move on that first night. The great beasts of the forest were more active in darkness, and although the Lion had little fear of them, the camp would be more vulnerable to them without us there. Besides which, there was an increased chance of drawing attention to ourselves if we were attacked by predators and had to defend ourselves as we approached the traitors. Better to move in the day, when what light the sun managed to throw down through the canopy kept some of the forest's more dangerous denizens in their lairs.

I say 'more dangerous' because I had little doubt that following his arrival, the title of 'most dangerous' went to the Lion.

We left with the first light of dawn. My original chainblade had been lost some three hundred years before in a fight with aeldari renegades, and I had taken my current one from a member of the laughably named Angels of Redemption when I turned their attempted ambush of me against them, thirty years later. However, my two Tigris-pattern bolt pistols had been with me since the Great Crusade, and were still functional despite their age, although my ammunition was low. Resupplying such standard-issue weapons had been easy enough in the days when the Imperium still existed, even for a fugitive such as myself, for there was always someone not averse to selling illegal or restricted munitions to a cloaked and hooded giant. Since the Great Rift had opened I had been reduced to scavenging from armouries not completely looted by the invaders, or taking ammunition from the weapons of those I killed and hoping it was not too tainted.

The Lion had the knife he had been given for skinning his kill, but no other weapon. None of the firearms present in the camp – mainly autopistols and stub guns, with one ancient and highly prized shotgun owned by a woman named Reena – would fit his hand, and he had no wish to deprive anyone there of their scant means of defence. It felt like folly to consider an assault on an enemy whilst so ill-equipped, but I found myself oddly calm at the prospect. I was with a primarch of the Emperor, a being whose like had not walked the galaxy for millennia, and none were better suited for the task that awaited us.

Camarth had been one of the more advanced Imperial worlds on which I had spent time, and the populace did not view their transhuman guardians and overlords with the superstition of more primitive folk who might consider them gods or divine warriors. As such, I knew that the Space Marines stationed here, who had fought bravely against what turned out to be overwhelming numbers, had been the Ruby Crescents. Camarth was an outpost planet, not their home world, but the locals had so honoured them that it might as well have been.

Their bastion, Redmoon Keep, stood in noble isolation atop

lonely Mount Santic, a long-extinct and now somewhat crumbled volcano, the slopes of which were still thickly forested. There was one road leading down from it, which ran off towards the city of Humean Falls, some thirty miles distant. The Lion and I did not venture onto it.

He paused as we crested one of the ridges that led up to the volcano's sides, and looked out across the forest. Even from this elevation, we could see out over the huge, flat expanse of landscape, for Mount Santic was the only natural highland within view. Somewhere to the east wound the mighty Humea River, cutting through the forest until it reached the city.

'That is where your refugees came from?' he asked, pointing at Humean Falls.

'Yes,' I replied. It almost looked like a forest in its own right: a forest of crystalflex, ferrocrete and metal that glinted faintly under the sun. 'Its perimeter was protected by an ion field which incinerated any plant material that touched it. Otherwise it would have been overrun by the forest within a year.'

'As has happened now,' the Lion observed. Many of the city's impressive towers and manufactoria had been devastated by the Chaos assault, but the smothering green I could make out even from this distance hinted that Camarth was in the process of reclaiming it on its own terms. That was nothing brought about by the Ruinous Powers: Camarth had always been hostile to humans. It was only the valuable compounds that could be harvested from the forest which made the struggle to live here worthwhile, and only the fact that those compounds came from the natural synergy of different plants that had prevented the Imperium from trying to farm them in a much more managed manner. In Humean Falls, as with the other tropical cities, the ruling elite had been the families whose techno-magi possessed the fastest, most efficient extraction and purification methods.

'And these shades in the canopy,' the Lion said, pointing out great swathes of discolouration in the green sea below us. 'Are they natural?'

'I have not made a detailed study of the planet's biology,' I admitted, 'but it is my belief that they are not. Deadly though the forest is, some of the locals were familiar with it to an extent, and as we have moved through it they have warned us away from areas they consider to be tainted.'

'Chaos has this planet in its grip, then,' the Lion muttered. 'But it has not closed its fist completely.'

I said nothing. To me, the new variations in Camarth's flora were little different to some of what I had seen in places on Caliban, but I had no intention of provoking the Lion's wrath by voicing this thought. The similarities were not lost on me, however. Strange that the Lion should come, by means he could not explain and after an absence he could not remember, to a world that was not so different to the world on which the Emperor found him.

The Lion began to move again, slipping through the vegetation with the careless expertise of one to whom forests were his natural environment. I followed behind as well as I could, having already learned that his route would be by far the easiest one. I would leave most humans behind in seconds in such terrain, but my progress is graceless, a product of brute force and direct speed. The Lion *flowed* between the trees, leaving barely a trace of his passing. Had he not been matching his pace to my own, I would have already lost him.

'Should we expect patrols?' he asked as he moved.

'I have largely avoided this area,' I replied, 'but I do not believe the filth are that organised. Sometimes they send rampaging parties into the forest to hunt for survivors, or set fires and hack at trees if they find none, but those appear to be at random.

Besides which,' I added, 'the forest has no more love for them than it does for the Imperium. Parts of Camarth's jungles may be truly corrupted, but even the rest will try to strangle or eat anything that passes through it, without care for what powers they are allied to. The traitors know better than to wander without reason.'

'All the better to take them by surprise,' the Lion said. He stepped around an area of ground and continued on; it was not until I was almost on it that I saw the dangling, thread-like constrictor vines, wire-thin but incredibly strong. I had only escaped my first encounter with such a plant through the luck of having one hand free with which I could use my chainsword.

'Do you have a plan of attack?' I asked.

'Eradicate them,' the Lion said, without turning. 'I cannot plan further until we see the terrain.' He paused for a moment, and looked back at me. 'My brother Sanguinius used to talk about fate. He knew the time and manner of his own death. I still find such a thing hard to countenance, but...'

He inhaled, exhaled, and focused on me. It was disquieting, to suddenly be the true centre of his attention.

'Perhaps my brother's destiny was set, whereas others are not,' Lion El'Jonson said. 'I certainly claim no foresight as exhibited by him, or that wretch Curze, for that matter. But I find it hard to believe that you and I survived the death of a *planet*, Zabriel, only to fall here.'

I shrugged, more nonchalantly than I felt. 'I accepted my death the moment I became a Space Marine. I have expended so much effort avoiding it these past centuries only because there seemed no worthy cause for which to give my life.'

The Lion's lined face darkened. 'I have no use for that manner of fatalism. This is no worthy cause, merely a task that must be completed. I expect you to still be living once we are done here, Zabriel of Terra.'

He turned, and resumed his ascent of the ridgeline which would bring us onto the volcano itself. I hurried after him, feeling chastened, yet with an odd kernel of hope nestling at my core. The Lion was practically alone and virtually unarmed, on a world he did not know, with no prospect of aid, and arrayed against a foe of unknown number and lethality, yet he did not view what we were doing as some kind of noble last stand, a mission to inflict as much damage as possible on the enemy and give our deaths some meaning. To him, this was... What? A start? A prelude to a greater work?

My time since emerging from the warp storm had not just been spent in hiding. I had done my best to act according to my nature and purpose where I could, protecting the citizens of this ridiculous new Imperium against threats. Some of those I aided had no idea who or what I was; most of the rest knew better than to enquire too closely. My interventions had by necessity been minor, though. The Lion appeared to have much larger things in mind.

Despite my misgivings about myself, the galaxy in which we found ourselves, and the being that was my gene-sire, I discovered that I was eager to see what he – what we – could achieve.

VIII

They have come through the blasted patches of forest where the fortress' guns cut down the approaching enemies, past the tarnished armour and twisted bones of the dead invaders. The assault was overwhelming and from all sides, judging by the amount of remains, but it was not just numbers that brought Redmoon Keep down, and not the gate that gave way. The Lion points to a dark fissure at the base of the keep's wall, where dull rockcrete strikes up from the rock of the crater.

'Melta bombs?' Zabriel asks. 'They would have needed a lot.'

'I have seen Astartes remains,' the Lion says grimly. 'This was not merely an ill-equipped rabble. However, they have not sealed the entry point again.'

'They have killed anything that can threaten them on this world, and are overconfident,' Zabriel says. 'The ones I have fought in the forest never expect anything other than easy prey.'

'It seems foolish to attempt to scale the walls or breach the gate when the enemy has left us this gift,' the Lion says. He places his helmet on his head, rises from his crouch and moves forward, swift and sure. He is aware of the possibility of a trap, but it is outweighed by his desire to get to grips with the foe. An alert and cunning enemy would have reset the perimeter sensors, cut back the forest to give a wider field of view from the walls, and repaired the smashed and shattered sentry guns, whose dead scopes look out over their surroundings. Everything here matches Zabriel's assessment, and giving your foe too much respect can be as costly as giving them too little.

The Lion reaches the fissure, and plunges in.

It closes in around him, a dark and uneven tunnel through a wall twenty feet thick, but such is his speed that no sooner is he in than he is out again. There are no laser nets, no mines, no foul sorceries lying in wait for him.

Beyond, the only illumination is what splashes in from the outside. He is in a large space; the echoes tell him as much, even before he switches to the low-light setting on his helmet's display. The air entering through his filtration system carries the tang of promethium fuel, engine lubricants, and other such scents. The invaders gained access through a vehicle hangar, then, rather than a Chapter-serf's cell, or a similar bottleneck at which their ingress might have been more easily halted. Unfortunate coincidence, or malign design?

He has taken this in within a second, and then Zabriel is through behind him, both bolt pistols held ready.

'No power,' Zabriel says, scanning the walls. 'The conduits here are dead.'

'Then we go farther in,' the Lion replies, 'and we stay alert for anything which might have sharper senses than our own in this blackness.' His helmet's sensors pick out a doorway in the deep shadows on the far side of the chamber, and he heads for it. The doors themselves are crumpled wreckage, smashed aside during the assault.

The corridor outside the hangar contains the first casualties within the fortress. The Lion's helmet, its picters straining, just picks up the outlines of the dead: largely of human stock, although many show traits that go well beyond humanity's usual variation in form. The Lion switches to infra-red, and sees the faintest glow of microorganisms still giving off trace amounts of heat as they decompose what flesh remains, and he follows this luminescent trail.

There was never such a thing as a standard layout for a fortress constructed by Space Marines, and if there had been then Lion El'Jonson's knowledge of it would be thousands of years out of date, but his sense of direction is unimpeded. He wishes to move towards the centre of the fortress, and so those are the turnings he takes. Zabriel keeps pace behind him. The Lion can hear his gene-son's breathing over the vox-link they calibrated before they left the camp, and is pleased that it sounds level and measured. Zabriel is neither wracked with misgivings, nor overly eager to indulge in violence.

Then they encounter the light.

Power is not out across the fortress, it appears. Light appears through one doorway, casting long shafts into the gloom through which they have been moving. The Lion edges closer, and waits. Although the forces of Chaos are not entirely predictable, it is reasonable to assume that their quarry will still be gathered where there is light and power. What is more, there are no corpses in the light, indicating that the fortress' current inhabitants have cleared them out of the spaces they use, although old bloodstains are still visible on the floor.

'Lord, have you marked the absence of Space Marine bodies so far?' Zabriel subvocalises into his vox, and from there into the

Lion's ear. 'If the defenders had taken no losses for this entire stretch, it is hard to see how they could have been pushed back.'

The Lion grimaces. 'You suggest their bodies have been removed?'

'Stripped for equipment, at least. Quite possibly defaced and… utilised… in some other manner.'

The Lion suppresses a growl. The warriors of this fortress were no gene-sons of his, but the thought of such depravity still lashes at his temper. Therefore, when he hears a shuffle of movement in the lit corridor and a bald-headed shape walks obliviously past the doorway behind which he and Zabriel lurk, he waits only a moment before stepping out after it.

The passer-by is human, dressed in simple robes of dark red marked with symbols upon which the eye does not wish to linger. He is of no more than average height, and his build is unremarkable. The Lion debates for a second between killing him instantly and silently, or interrogating him.

The cultist makes the decision for him when two eyes open on the back of his bald head, immediately followed by a wide mouth at the base of the skull, out of which spills a long, blue tongue, and a shrill scream that somehow goes beyond the simply audible.

The Lion takes a step forward and lashes out with a punch. The cultist's head disintegrates under the force of the blow and his body collapses, but the scream lingers, far longer than any normal echo should. A scurrying in the direction from whence the deceased cultist came rapidly becomes a thundering of boots and other, less wholesome modes of locomotion, and voices are raised in shouts, whoops and gibbers.

'Guard my back,' the Lion tells Zabriel. He would have preferred to get farther before engaging in open combat, but killing from the shadows was always more Corax's style.

They come in a rush, spilling down the corridor and around

the corner of it like the filthy waters of a flash flood. The Lion sees horned heads, purple skin, scales, several tails, cloven hooves instead of feet, and so on; endless and maddening variation, caused by human genetics being pushed far past their breaking point. He gives them one moment to see him in turn, to let their inferior vision and slower mental processes comprehend exactly what it is they are attacking.

His presence registers on the front rank, such as it is, and they begin to slow in terror just before he plunges into them.

The Lion strikes like a thunderbolt, killing with every blow. Bones splinter and skulls split, torsos burst and limbs detach in sprays of blood or ichor. His enemies strike at him with weapons, but on the rare occasion their blows land, they glance off his armour. The dark ceramite in which he is encased turns aside low-calibre autopistol rounds, serrated skinning blades, and spiked bludgeons without difficulty.

Behind him, Zabriel's bolt pistols roar sporadically. The Destroyer is mopping up, executing the few individuals whom the Lion's rage does not cut down and who either seek to launch an attack at the primarch's back or, finding their own retreat blocked by yet more of their companions, try to flee past him instead.

It takes perhaps five seconds of bloodshed for the mass of cultist filth to realise that their numbers are no match for what they are facing. Panic spreads backwards, as those directly in the Lion's path try to get away from him, and the enthusiastic members behind realise that their colleagues in front are not going to have dealt with the threat by the time they get there. The rabble tries to reverse direction, but the Lion's purpose remains unchanged. He will eliminate anything corrupt in front of him, regardless of whether it attacks him or tries to flee.

Some get away. That is inevitable. The sheer weight of numbers is insufficient to overcome the Lion, but it is enough for those at the back of the group to make their escape while he is still dealing with the others. The Lord of the First comes to a halt, his hands and forearms dripping red and his greaves and boots caked in blood, and no longer with an enemy within reach.

And breathing a little hard.

Zabriel activates his chainsword for a moment to finish off those whom the Lion merely mortally wounded. 'I see you have lost none of your deadliness, lord,' he says, as he powers the motor down again.

'If only that were true,' Lion El'Jonson mutters. He overwhelmed the horde, yes, he broke their bodies and was never in danger of succumbing, but unlike during the fight against the predators in the forest, he can now compare it to his previous battles. He finds himself wanting.

They are minor differences, in truth. He is slightly slower, his blows carry a little less force, and his stamina does not seem to be quite what it once was. He is ready to fight again, he could still fight for hours against such opponents, but he can feel the difference.

'There is some malady at work here,' he says. 'I am slower than I should be. Curze would have my flesh off my bones,' he adds in a murmur, as a phantom of his cackling, raven-haired brother flashes through his memory. The Lion has no doubt that the galaxy still contains threats every bit as dangerous as the Night Haunter, even if Konrad Curze has long since succumbed to the fate he saw laid out for himself all those millennia ago.

A new thought occurs to him. 'Zabriel. Are my… *other* brothers also dead?'

'Even more uncertain than the fate of those who stood with your father,' Zabriel replies. 'The Imperium has largely forgotten them, but rumours persist. Some of the circles I have moved in were adamant that the traitor primarchs are still very real. Even if they are, the Imperium would pretend they were not.'

The Lion's lip curls. He can feel the echoes of Malcador reaching down through the centuries, trying to control what everyone thinks and feels, and endlessly fussing around the edges of the Emperor's grand vision. Then again, the Lion's past is not blameless when it comes to secrets. The old man was probably only doing what he thought was right.

'No,' Zabriel continues, 'the greatest external threat to the Imperium is probably Abaddon.'

Lion El'Jonson looks at him curiously. 'Ezekyle Abaddon? First Captain of the Sons of Horus? He still lives?'

'Even allowing for inaccuracies and propaganda, what I have heard suggests that he has gained power to rival that of any primarch,' Zabriel says. 'He recently destroyed Cadia.' He sees the Lion's blank expression, and adds: 'A notable Imperial fortress world, near the Eye of Terror.'

The Lion snorts. 'Well, I will worry about my brother's wayward son should I cross paths with him. In the meantime, we have more immediate concerns. I doubt that those were the only occupants of this place.'

IX

As they press on, the desecration of the bastion becomes more obvious. The Lion had been angered by the bodies of Chaos worshippers left to decompose, but it is clear that this was simply because no one now used those areas, and so the carrion was of no concern. Now the walls are covered with markings: filthy scrawls at first – works of petty vandalism – but increasingly a tight, almost neat script on which the eye nonetheless struggles to focus. The Lion turns into a new corridor and struggles with an unfamiliar wave of dizziness, as his mind refuses to engage with his surroundings sufficiently to be certain of which way is up. The sensation is not helped by the low, moaning hum that has no apparent point of origin, nor has increased or decreased in volume since he first noticed it. It is not loud, but it fills the ears. He reaches up to remove his helm, but Zabriel seizes his arm.

'Best not, lord. We do not know what may be in the air.'

The Lion growls in his throat, but does not shake Zabriel's

hand off. He knows how the warp can infiltrate the mind, and he understands that Zabriel probably has more experience of such matters, given the centuries he has spent in this new, dark millennium. Once upon a time, the Lion would have trusted his physiology to handle any contaminants or poisons, but some threats are not just physical.

'I am getting strong power readings from up ahead,' Zabriel adds. 'If scent and sound cannot reliably lead us to our enemies, energy may serve. We can at least damage whatever our enemies are powering, which may draw them out.'

The Lion flexes his fingers in readiness, and switches his helmet's display to infra-red. Some of his disorientation disappears as the writing fades, but the hum does not decrease.

They encounter no more resistance before they reach a set of heavily engraved blast doors twice the Lion's height. The Lion switches back to normal vision and takes in the decoration: the robed figure, the wings, and the sword clasped between the hands.

'Sanguinius,' he murmurs. But his brother's towering image has been defiled, with the depiction of his noble countenance replaced by skulls – Space Marine skulls – somehow sunk into the metal of the door. Foul sigils have been carved into the metal, as have likenesses of twisted, capering beasts. What once honoured a gene-sire has been transformed into a grotesquery, and most disturbing of all, it seems to be leaking blood. When the Lion flicks back to heat vision for a moment, he sees that the fluid is coming out at the temperature of a human body.

The door controls, however, seem unaffected. The Lion glances over his shoulder.

'Stay behind me until we know what we are dealing with,' he tells Zabriel, then reaches out and activates the door release.

The doors begin to move with what might be the stressed

scream of damaged mechanisms, but which sounds a lot more like a distant voice in pain. Translucent threads stretch and sag in the air between the door's halves as they part, as though their surfaces were starting to merge into one, then finally snap and swing heavily down to rest against the metal with a faint sizzling sound.

The space beyond is gloomy, lit by a sickly yellow-green glow from one side and thick with fumes. The hum is louder here, and a rough voice speaks from out of the murk.

'He comes, the Flawed Knight. Did I not tell you?'

The voice has the tone and timbre of a Space Marine, but the words are not immediately followed by an attack. What is more, it seems as though the Lion's presence, identity, or nature is the cause of some uncertainty.

'You were expecting me?' he demands, striding into the chamber. 'Show yourself.' He cycles through the vision options of his helmet, and his targeting auspexes pick out the other occupants just as another voice speaks.

'What master do you serve?' it demands, as cold and unforgiving as the spaces between the stars.

The chamber is a hall of considerable size, which the Lion presumes would once have been used as a strategium by the Space Marines garrisoned here. It has clearly been badly damaged in the battle for the fortress, for many of the walls are pock-marked with impact craters, or spiderwebbed with cracks. There is no equipment he recognises; no hololiths, or cogitator banks. Instead, thick and glistening cables snake across the floor and connect to a huge, clear-sided vat of fluid against one wall. It is from this that the glow emanates, which also picks out the figures standing in front of it.

There are seven Space Marines, none uncorrupted. Five appear to be a loose squad armed with boltguns, the familiar outline of their power armour interrupted by a horn here, and a bulbous and misshapen limb there. Behind them are two others: a tall shape swathed in a robe, holding a barbed sword; and one whose shoulders seem unnaturally bulky even for an armoured transhuman, until the Lion realises that he is wearing animal skins as a cloak. He can recognise no insignia in the gloom, but their armour is decorated with a repeated pattern of staring, golden eyes.

Most importantly, they do not yet know if he is friend or foe. To them, he is a massive shape in unfamiliar black armour, and even though his breastplate bears the winged sword of his Legion, it seems that this is not an unambiguous symbol in these times.

Lion El'Jonson has never been one to seek the awe of others, nor indeed pay much attention to it, but he knows that his very nature as a primarch often instils such feelings. He tries to draw on that now as he crosses the floor and closes the distance between them, making himself the focus of attention.

'I serve myself,' he declares. 'Whom do *you* call master?' He frowns at a strange sensation, like fingertips of gossamer trailing across his brain.

'His mind is like a blade,' the tall Space Marine says in a low voice. The Lion's lip curls.

'Stay out of my head, witch,' he snarls, without any attempt to hide his aggression or disgust. The muzzles of five bolters that had been held half lowered snap up to cover him in truth, but the Lion does not slow. He is nearly close enough, and they cannot know his capabilities.

'Stop where you are,' says the cold-voiced one in the furs. The Lion ignores him as blithely as he would ignore any order from any Space Marine. Those hungry for power want to be obeyed more than they want anything else: they will repeat themselves and delay giving a command to fire, simply because a dead man cannot obey instructions.

'I said–'

The Lion pounces into the centre of the firing line.

The force of impact bowls two warriors over in a clatter of ceramite. The Lion pivots on his left arm and comes down with his feet under him, then uses the remainder of his momentum to wrench one of his victims off the floor and hurl him through the air into the cloaked sorcerer before the witch can react.

Then the fight starts in earnest.

His opponents are not primarchs, but they are Space Marines, and their reflexes are still far faster than those of mortals. A bolt-shell ricochets off the power pack of the Lion's armour, and another bounces off his left pauldron. He dives back the way he came, seeking to bait them into shooting at him and hitting each other, but the traitors are too well disciplined. Instead, another one jerks and starts to fall as bolt-shells strike him from a different angle.

Zabriel approaches out of the gloom at a charge, both pistols firing. The Lion is still moving, and his fist connects with the faceplate of one of the traitors. Ceramite shatters and the warrior flies backwards, but another lunges forward with one hand extended, his gauntlet's fingers now either shaped into talons, or somehow melded with disfigured flesh beneath. The Lion catches his attacker's wrist and pivots once more, swinging his opponent around and using him as a bludgeon. The Astartes he bore to the ground but whom he did not throw into the sorcerer regains his feet just in time to be flattened once more. Zabriel has advanced past his first victim and charges at the sorcerer with a yell, and force sword clashes with chainsword in a shower of sparks and a snarl of teeth.

'Enough!' the commander thunders, advancing on the Lion at

speed. An energised weapon head crackles into life: a thunder hammer, ready to discharge with armour-splitting force. The Lion watches him come, sees the start of his swing, then lashes out with the edge of his hand.

He strikes the hammer just behind the head. Such is the combined force of his blow and the Chaos lord's attack, the haft snaps and the head flies clean off. The Traitor Astartes staggers into the Lion, unbalanced by the unexpected lack of resistance to his strike, and the Lion tosses him upwards by his furs. The Chaos lord flails, unused to being manhandled in such a manner, and as he starts to descend the Lion grabs his enemy and forces him downwards across one bent knee. The traitor's armour fractures, along with his spine, and the Lion dumps him off to the ground.

Zabriel screams.

The Lion looks up, sees the sorcerer bathing the Dark Angel in a hellish beam of light emanating from the eye slits of his helm, and snatches a fallen boltgun off the floor. He breaks off the trigger guard so his finger fits, and fires the weapon at the sorcerer's back. The bolts strike home; the sorcerer staggers, his concentration breaks, and the spell sputters out. Zabriel recovers himself and swings with his chainsword. It is a weapon designed to chew through flesh and light armour, not solid ceramite plate, but Zabriel angles it perfectly and the blow catches the sorcerer in the neck joint. The traitor jerks and blood spurts as monomolecular teeth tear into his body. Zabriel places one hand on the back edge of his chainblade and forces it deeper, seeking to decapitate his enemy.

The Lion throws the boltgun away – even that brief contact through his armour felt dirty, somehow – and stamps on the traitor whose helmet he shattered with his fist, bursting his skull. That makes three dead, as the sorcerer's head clatters to the floor. The rest are still in the fight, but they are all injured to one degree or another, and the Lion can sense their shock. They were not ready for him.

Then the air shimmers with the distinctive disturbance of a teleport flare, and two hulking shapes shudder into existence.

They were Space Marines, once. Now they are swollen almost beyond recognition, their monstrous physiques having burst out between the plates of their armour and fusing with it. Their exposed flesh crawls with veins that pulse with foul energy, and they are bedecked with twisted guns that extrude from their bodies like growths. Only their heads still seem the same size as they once would have been – they might look comical, tucked away in the mass of flesh and muscle surrounding them, were the rest of their forms not obviously so very deadly.

The Lion reaches instinctively for a sidearm that is no longer there. He only wastes half a second in doing so, but that is enough. His newly arrived enemies have no such problems.

A rocket strikes him in the chest and detonates. The light and noise is indescribable, all-encompassing. He is thrown backwards by the force of the explosion, and lands against a cracked wall with his armour screaming warnings at him, but no sooner has he come to rest than a hail of shells – smaller calibre, but still dangerous – batters into him. The Lord of the First scrambles to one side, trying to get clear of the barrage, but a monstrous shape looms up through the scree of warning glyphs in his helm and swings a fist the size of an ammunition crate.

The blow strikes the Lion with such force that he is knocked not just backwards into the wall behind him, but also through it. Chunks of ferrocrete tumble down, and one strikes his helm as he struggles to rise. Dust is everywhere. The monstrosity that has just struck him bellows in murderous rage and smashes at the wall, seeking to enlarge the hole sufficiently to follow him.

A thunderous explosion a few yards away indicates that its companion intends to simply shoot its way through.

The Lion rolls away to get out of the current line of fire, and tries to take stock. His armour is cracked, and his helm's read-outs suggest that his power pack may go critical if it is smashed through another wall. His instincts are to put distance between himself and his monstrous pursuers, but he has no ranged weapons with which to engage them if he does so. If he remains close, he will have no cover from point-blank shots, and he puts himself within reach of their ferocious strength. He could probably handle one of them, despite the sorcerous malady that still claws at him, but they have already shown their ability to work together. He looks around for something to even the odds, and his heart leaps in sudden hope. This chamber is even more battle-damaged than the one he so recently and violently exited, so much so that the entire back wall has already come down, but he recognises the nature of it as an armoury.

It has been pillaged, of course, but there is always the hope that the raiders missed something. The Lion slips between weapon racks, hunting for anything he can use. An explosion shakes the room as one of the Chaos worshippers' foul guns spits out an incendiary charge and punches a hole a yard in diameter through the Lion's temporary cover. The Lion keeps his head down, and continues searching. A Space Marine would have his own weapons with him at all times, but there was clearly a purpose for this armoury: ammunition, spare weapons, more specialist or esoteric pieces, and items like grenades from which a Space Marine would restock his own supply as needed.

The Lion dislodges a magazine of bolt-shells, and grabs onto it in case he finds something he can load it into. Something else is part covered by a fallen piece of the ceiling, and he snatches it from its resting place. The design is not entirely familiar, but it appears that frag grenades have not changed much in ten thousand years.

One of the Chaos monsters stomps into view, its left foot still sheathed in corrupted ceramite and the other completely bare, the size of a normal Space Marine's chest. The Lion primes the grenade and throws it with effortless accuracy; it lands under the traitor's descending right foot, and detonates.

The traitor howls in a voice that sounds more metallic than organic, and is knocked off balance by the blast. The shots it was about to send towards the Lion skew wide, ripping more holes in the abused weapons racks. The Lion sprints the other way, but the end of the row is suddenly obstructed by the second mutated traitor. Guns erupt from the Chaos Space Marine's forearm, and the Lion throws himself into a slide as they vomit black-tinged flames into the space where his head was a moment before.

He comes up again within the traitor's guard. The thing's massive physique may give it immense strength, but it is no longer fully protected by armour, and the Lion slams a fist into exposed ribs. It is like punching steel. However, the Lion has punched steel before, and it was the metal that came off worse. The monster staggers, and the Lion takes the opportunity to rip its weapon out in a shower of blood, oil, and other more unpleasant liquids.

A new, blood-slicked gun muzzle in the shape of a howling daemon's maw immediately sprouts from the thing's shoulder and levels itself at the Lion's face. He ducks just before a melta blast takes his head off, but that leaves him open to the immense fist that crashes into him instead. The Lion manages to roll with the punch a little, but the force of it still sends him flying again. He comes up and desperately throws the bolt magazine at the creature, and its next blast atomises the entire thing only a couple of feet from its face. The resulting explosion sends the traitor staggering, and the Lion retreats again before it can recover.

Is this what Chaos is? An ever-morphing, ever-changing threat that twists the familiar, and adapts to even the most punishing blows one can strike at it? His determination to bring these abominations down has not decreased, but he needs something which can give him an edge.

He reaches the back of the armoury and, for lack of better options, scrambles through into the chamber beyond. This is smaller, and hung with banners that appear to mark notable battles or great acts of heroism, although they have all been defaced in one manner or another. Even amidst the vandalism, the Lion gets the sense of quiet devotion. This was not a functional space, like the strategium or the armoury, but somewhere the warriors of the Ruby Crescents came for contemplation.

Something streaks past his head, and one of the banners on the far wall is consumed by crawling fire. The traitors are coming, one down each side of the armoury. He can stand and fight them both, or he can try the door to his right and retreat again. It galls him to do such a thing, but he has still not found anything he can use to turn this combat to his advantage.

Zabriel is still back there, though, brought into this fight by his belief in the Lion; a belief that overcame four centuries of hatred and bitterness. He is the only son the Lion knows of at this moment, and the Lion will not leave him to die.

The fire is raging, consuming everything it touches and filling the air with smoke. However, the sensors on the Lion's helmet do not register particulates of ash or atoms of carbon. Instead, the ambient moisture around him increases as grey clouds billow across his vision and obscure the oncoming enemies for a moment. The two sides of the wrecked wall in front of him almost look like tree trunks, with a low canopy of branches above him instead of a ceiling…

The contours of the ruined building material beneath his feet do not change, but now naked rock overlays it in his vision. The pile of rubble in front of him resolves into a boulder, slick and wet, and a glimmer catches his eye. This is not the rough surface of ferrocrete, nor is it the dull finish of structural rebar. The hum in his ears is gone, replaced by a sweeter song.

The Lion reaches out, and his gauntlet closes around the grip of a sword. He seizes it and pulls; it holds fast for a moment, but then slides clear with the faintest whisper of metal on stone.

It is a beautiful powerblade, the perfect size for the Lion. The hilt is a simple cross-guard into which is worked a winged design around a miniature version of the sword itself: the symbol of the Dark Angels, the sigil that the Lion made his own.

His thumb finds the activation stud. The powercell holds charge; the blade's disruption field crackles into existence, causing the barely visible vapour in the air around it to flash into steam.

The Lion smiles, and the forest – illusory, real, or something in between – fades away. His surroundings once more take on the sharp edges of battle-damaged walls, and the air is filled with smoke, through which two hulking shadows are approaching.

The Lion charges.

The corrupted Astartes are taken off guard by his change of tactics, and shots from one track slightly wide of him as he rushes the other: the one whose foot he detonated a grenade under. The monstrosity bellows in anger and tries to retarget its weapons on his rapidly closing form, but the Lion unleashed with purpose is too quick. Now he has teeth: his blade shears through the Chaos worshipper's right elbow and sends its massive fist clattering to the floor, and he finishes his momentum with a shoulder barge that propels it staggering backwards into the wall.

The Lion ducks, his instincts taking over, and a shell from the other traitor blazes over his head from behind and strikes his wounded assailant full in the chest. He lunges up from his crouch and extends the sword, the powered blade driving into the crater left by the shot before even the monster's unholy metabolism can heal it, and skewers the creature to the wall, severing its spine. The Lion spins away, ripping the blade loose and shearing through more internal organs as he does so, and the kill is confirmed by another errant shot from the other heretic that detonates in the first one's skull.

The Lion draws the skinning blade from his belt, and whips it through the air into the other creature's eye. The former Space Marine howls in agony, which ends a moment later as the Lion reaches it, impales it with the powerblade, and wrenches upwards. The blade's energy field and his strength combine to slice right through the traitor's upper body, bisecting its skull, and it drops at his feet.

The Lion breathes hard for a moment, then turns and runs back the way he came, through the armoury and out into the strategium. He arrives just in time to see Zabriel, wrestling with the last upright traitor, angle one of his bolt pistols to put two shots through his enemy's helmet from a foot away. He looks over at the Lion, and his relief is apparent just from the way his shoulders sag.

'What were those things?' he asks.

'They are dead now,' the Lion answers, 'and that is all that matters.' The fur-clad commander, whose back the Lion broke, is still twitching. Zabriel walks over to him and aims his bolt pistol at the fallen heretic's head.

'Wait!' the Lion instructs him. He crosses the floor and glares down at his broken adversary. 'Your sorcerer is dead. What must I do to rid myself of this malady that impedes me?'

'*Impedes* you?' the traitor hisses, his breath coming in staccato gasps. It takes the Lion a moment to realise that he is laughing through pain. 'You slaughtered my best and broke my back as though I were a child. What manner of being are you, that you consider yourself impeded when you can still do such things?'

The Lion reaches up and removes his helm. Perhaps this creature knew his face once, or perhaps not, it doesn't matter. Nor is he concerned about the risk of exposing himself briefly to the air. This is the first time he will declare himself in ten thousand years, and he will not do it from behind a ceramite faceplate.

'I am Lion El'Jonson, primarch of the Dark Angels and son of the Emperor.'

The heretic's eyes go wide, and there is no doubt or denial in them. But then he smiles, exposing teeth that are now merely jagged points.

'There is no malady at work here, *my lord*. You simply got old.'

The Lion stares at him for a moment. Then he turns away, breathing heavily, pursued by the clean bite of the truth.

Zabriel's bolt pistol speaks one final time, and then there is silence.

X

I had been hunted for centuries.

In all that time, I had no true allies. A rogue Space Marine such as myself does not. My Legion was now a many-faceted thing, virtually unrecognisable, and overtly hostile to me. The Lion, fearsome though he was, at least recognised that perhaps some of us exiled on Caliban had not known what was occurring at the Breaking, or who had initiated the conflict. The current-day Dark Angels and their kin had no capacity for such nuance.

Nor could I find allies elsewhere. The regular folk of the Imperium might treat me with respect, wonder, even awe, but a Space Marine draws attention, official attention, and that was something I could not afford. I had spent more time out of my armour than in it, trusting to the protection of partial anonymity more than that of ceramite. I encountered others of my kind twice. One was bitter and self-destructive, and I spent little time with him before taking my leave again. The other had fallen into practices I could not condone. I thought at the time that it was due to a long period of isolation, but perhaps he had already cleaved to such worship while on Caliban.

In all that time, I ran from more fights than I did not, and was rarely the aggressor. At times I even threw my lot in with traitors, claiming a false agenda in the interests of my own survival, although I did my best to ensure that I damaged their cause before I took my leave. Nonetheless, it had been hundreds of years since I advanced into a fight in the service of the Imperium with even one battle-brother beside me, let alone the primarch of my Legion.

I had missed it. A Space Marine's true purpose is war, and there was no doubt in my mind that whatever the Imperium had become, the twisted creatures the Lion and I fought in the bastion of the Ruby Crescents were worthy targets for my blade and bolts. Our victory was bittersweet, however.

There was no mistaking my primarch's disgust at his physical decline. Although he was still by far the greatest warrior I had ever seen, and certainly beyond my own skills, age was an enemy he could not slay. He had never been an open book for observers to read, but I could tell that he was worried. If ten thousand years had wrought these changes on him, he might still be an effective fighter for ten thousand more. However, what if he had been in stasis for much of that time, and this was a more rapid process? His very nature as a primarch was an artificial one: what if, having endured for so long, his body was now failing even faster than that of a mortal?

That was a concern for the future, and one with which I could not help him. Of more immediate concern was what we found in the rest of the fortress.

Much of the Chaos worshippers' leavings we neither understood, nor wished to. However, following the pipes that fed the giant vat of glowing liquid led us to another chamber not far away. When we opened the door, we were greeted by howls and snarls so vicious I thought we were about to be set upon by a horde of mutated beasts. I might almost have preferred if that had come about. Instead, when no attack came, we advanced cautiously within and ignited the lumens.

There were nine figures, bound to the walls with chains I might have considered sufficient for securing a Dreadnought sarcophagus. They howled and thrashed and raged wordlessly, straining to reach us as we walked between them in silent horror. Their eyes were completely black, their faces drawn, their canine teeth grotesquely lengthened, and their armour absent, but their nature was clear enough.

We had found the remnants of the Ruby Crescents.

What foul arts had been used to twist and torment them so, I cannot say. There was no reason left in them, merely mindless savagery. When we realised that there was nothing that could be done, the Lion removed their heads with his powerblade, to grant them a clean end. The first death seemed to drive them into even greater depths of fury, and for a moment I feared we had made a mistake and they were reacting with anger, but when the nearest began desperately licking his fallen comrade's spattered blood from his own shoulder, we realised the gruesome truth. These sons of Sanguinius had been turned by the works of Chaos from noble warriors into mindless beasts, and the Lion was granting them mercy.

Their blood was in turn being drained, and what sorcerous or alchemical process was used to turn it into the glowing liquid we encountered, and to what purpose, we did not find out. We rescued what we could of value from the fortress, then rigged explosives to the remaining powercells and detonated them remotely. The smoke rose to the sky, but only until a rainstorm swept in from the west in the early evening. Anyone watching from a distance would have had a mere handful of hours to notice that the crater of Mount Santic was smoking once more.

The first blow in the Lion's war had been struck.

When we returned to the camp, we came bearing not just news of our triumph, but the arms and supplies we had deemed still fit for use. The people looked upon the Lion with renewed amazement, that he had eradicated this threat in one day, and I felt an echo of my old resentment at that, for had I not been protecting them for far longer? But he was a primarch, and whatever his own opinion of his current capabilities, they were far beyond mine. I could not fight back effectively against the filth that had come to Camarth, but the Lion could.

Whereas he was once the very image of a pagan warrior god, shining and intimidating, now his lined countenance and greying hair gave him an air more akin to one of the patriarchal figures from ancient Terran mythology: certainly not genial, but wise and steadfast. It would be easier for these people to believe that he might care for them, and thus in turn care for him.

Regardless of how he was perceived by the natives, the Lion's focus remained constant. 'I imagine that was not the only traitor stronghold on Camarth,' he said to me in a low voice.

'I greatly doubt it,' I replied. 'The planet had other defences besides the bastion, and they would have to be subdued as well. I do not know what contact there may have been between them, or how soon other heretics might learn of what has occurred here.'

The Lion breathed deeply, his nostrils flaring. 'I do not intend to let them find out in their own time. I was styled as Lord Protector once. The context was misguided, but the sentiment was sound. So long as any part of humanity is threatened, my duty is not done.'

I frowned. '*Any* part of humanity?'

'Indeed.' The Lion looked at me, and the faintest hint of a wintry smile tugged at the edge of his moustaches. 'So we had best get started.'

Part Two

ASCENDANT

XI

'Baelor?'

The hololith on the bridge of the Carnage-class cruiser *Eye of Malevolence* flickered into life, and a wispy image of Seraphax rose out of it. Baelor smiled behind the faceplate of his helmet. At least Seraphax was not simply communicating using his sorcerous abilities. It was not that Baelor disapproved of that as such, especially given the nature of the allies they were surrounded by, but some remnant of his Legion days insisted that psykana powers and their like were best reserved for when they were truly needed.

'What is your command, knight-captain?'

'Camarth has gone quiet.'

Baelor frowned. 'Quiet?'

'It is most peculiar,' Seraphax said, half musing. *'There were mumblings a while back of some local insurgency, a belated fight-back by natives, a mention of a "Flawed Knight". The Imperium's defences had been eliminated, so I thought little of it, as it seems*

did those minds with which I was in contact. Perhaps there was even some infighting. It happens, after all.'

Baelor nodded. Discipline in the massed ranks of the warband varied from stringent to non-existent, depending on the nature of the commander and the troops. 'But this is something more?'

'No one is responding now,' Seraphax said, his one visible eye staring straight into Baelor's. 'No one. *If there are any of ours on the planet, none will open their minds to me.'*

Any sorcerers, was what Seraphax meant by that. Astropaths were all but useless in Imperium Nihilus over any distance. Sorcerous communication using the warp itself was still imperfect, but far superior nonetheless.

Baelor grunted as something struck him. 'Camarth is the location of the Bloodrage project. Could they have got loose?'

'Unlikely,' Seraphax said. *'However, I would hate if our efforts on behalf of our cousins went to waste. We need to find out what has happened. Take the* Eye *and investigate.'*

Baelor placed his fist over his chest, and bowed. 'Of course, knight-captain.' He paused for a moment. 'And if there has somehow been a successful rebellion?'

Seraphax grimaced. *'In that case, save anything that can be saved, and destroy what needs to be destroyed. Hope cannot be allowed to take root. Use your best judgement. I trust you completely, my friend.'*

'It will be done, knight-captain,' Baelor said. Seraphax cut the link, the hololith went dead, and Baelor turned to face the rest of the bridge.

The *Eye of Malevolence* had been dedicated to the gods of Chaos for nearly a millennium. The Ten Thousand Eyes had captured it from a splinter force of the Twelfth Black Crusade, still marauding centuries after the main conflict in which the *Eye* had first turned traitor had ended. Baelor was not certain if the name of the craft had attracted Seraphax to it, given what he had titled his burgeoning warband, or whether his knight-captain had purely tactical concerns. Nonetheless, Baelor had led the boarding party, and Baelor slew the shipmaster, a former legionary of the Sons of Horus in whose face an echo of his primarch's features could still be seen.

The *Eye of Malevolence* was Baelor's to command now, a far greater power at his fingertips than he ever had in the days of the Great Crusade. He turned to Canticallax Dimora of the New Mechanicum, whose body – if it could still be called that – was plugged into the command throne. Baelor had neither the ability nor the inclination to interface with the cruiser's corrupted circuits, but Dimora recognised his authority as stemming from Seraphax's, and the sorcerer's presence was the only thing that still prompted what Baelor might recognise as emotion in the magos. Baelor had still not worked out why Dimora, who essentially *was* now a cruiser in all but name, was quite so terrified of Seraphax, but he cared little from whence her adherence to the chain of command stemmed.

'Prepare the ship for warp travel,' he instructed. 'We are going to Camarth.'

XII

It has been a long time since the Lion needed to take a world without an army of Space Marines at his back, but Camarth is not Caliban. Camarth's jungles, deserts, and high mountain passes are no friend to the unwary, but they do not have the deep-seated malice of Caliban's forests, nor do they contain anything as truly dangerous as the Great Beasts against which the Lion and the Order fought their campaign. Camarth has Chaos worshippers, it is true, but Caliban was not without sorcerous dangers either. The Lion organised the people of Caliban against the Knights of Lupus, and has done the same against those who style themselves Camarth's new rulers, although in a guerrilla war rather than pitched battle. The followers of Chaos destroyed Camarth's chain of command, and much of its infrastructure, but the numbers to repel them still existed. It was just that the spirit and knowledge was lacking.

Until one of the Emperor's sons arrived.

The traitors cowering behind the doors are expecting to hear the thuds of breaching charges being affixed, but the Lion knows better than to give the enemy what they expect, even in a head-on assault. He kicks the thick metal doors in with one blow instead, and is inside Kallia City's space port control room before anyone within has realised what's going on.

The defenders are what he has come to think of as the usual Chaos filth: ragged humans who were happy enough to follow their masters to attack the planet, but have little stomach for a fight now the tables have turned. He ignores the desultory impact of autogun and stubber shots against his armour, and lays about him with his powerblade. He has named it Fealty, for that is what he owes both his father and all the people of the Imperium. Its edge slices through cloth and flesh and bone as the traitors throw themselves at him with desperation but no skill. The fight is over within seconds, but the Lion pivots, his blade extended, and waits. Only when no last opponent lunges out from a hiding place, no hastily rigged explosives detonate, does he sheathe his sword and turn back to the door.

'It is done,' he says, and his followers file in.

They are little more uniform than those he has just killed, but these people have been collected from the planet's refugees and survivors, and their determination to take Camarth back has given them a drive and unity matched by few of the Imperial Army regiments the Lion served alongside during the Great Crusade. Many Camarthans feared him when they first saw him and learned who he was, convinced he was going to execute them for not fighting harder in the first place. The Lion had to persuade them otherwise, had to explain that those battles might not have been winnable, but that he was here to ensure the next ones would be.

Had they died fighting, bravely but pointlessly, he would have had no chance of retaking Camarth. Now, as Pashon and M'kia set up to guard the door, and Jovan, Rezia, and Magos Valdax move severed limbs out of the way to examine the space port's cogitator banks, their goal is nearly achieved.

'Halin, report,' he says into his vox-link.

'The remaining traitor forces were driven back into the industrial district,' Halin replies, his voice stuttering with vox-static. *'First and second armoured units moved in and finished them off. The city is yours, Lord Lion.'*

The Lion smiles briefly. The so-called 'armoured units' are a far cry from the Deimos-pattern Predators, Sicaran battle tanks, and Glaive super-heavies he might have commanded only – to him – a relatively short time ago. These vehicles are primarily Chimeras and similar variants from the planetary garrison which had been neither destroyed nor corrupted by the invaders, along with civilian and industrial vehicles armoured with metal sheeting and armed with jury-rigged weapon sponsons. They are just as ragtag as the Lion's foot troops, but they have helped him take city after city back from the heretics who thought they owned the planet.

'The city is *ours*, Halin,' he says firmly. 'This is a victory for the citizens of Camarth, and one we should all be proud of.' He shuts off his vox, and removes his helm. 'Magos, your assessment?'

Valdax emits a burst of crackling static that is nonetheless interpretable as displeased hissing through teeth, had they still had them. 'I wouldn't want to interface myself with it, that's for sure.'

The Lion's amusement returns. It seems the Adeptus Mechanicus has only grown stranger and more secretive while he has been absent from the Imperium, but Valdax is an outlier in the other direction. They appear to retain much of their human personality traits, despite being at least half machinery. Perhaps that is why Valdax fled from the invasion and lived, rather than dying in defence of their beloved machines.

'Can you make it work?' the Lion prompts. Valdax still needs specific enquiries sometimes, human personality or not.

The magos makes a harsh, two-tone noise that the Lion has come to recognise as a negative, and two mechadendrites waggle in an uncertain manner. 'That depends on your definition of "work", my lord Lion. The machine-spirit still exists, but it is thoroughly tarnished. We have the theoretical capability for long-range auspex and vox, and the calculations necessary to guide voidships to and from the surface, but I can give you no predictions of accuracy or reliability.'

'You are saying that if a ship were to try to land from orbit, the electrogheist might attempt to crash it?' the Lion asks, and Valdax responds with the bright pinging noise they make to signify agreement.

'Indeed. Consider it the equivalent of a blade that may turn in your hand at any time. I will upload the data-scrubbers my comrades and I devised, and attempt to purge the systems of their contagion so we can regain control.'

The Lion sighs. 'I understand.' He activates his vox again. 'Zabriel, have you had any luck?'

'I was just about to contact you, my lord,' Zabriel replies. His tone is heavy. *'It is the same as everywhere else. The astropaths have been butchered, probably as soon as the traitors took control.'*

The Lion grimaces. 'Acknowledged.' He turns back to Valdax. 'Well, magos, if there are any astropaths left alive on this planet, we do not know where they are. Since we cannot call for assistance, we need to find out how feasible it is to take ship. For now, can you at least give us an idea of whether there are any warp-capable craft in orbit?'

It should not be possible for mechanical lenses to eye

something dubiously, but the look Valdax casts the direct interface port on the cogitator bank is downright suspicious. They shake their head after a moment and set to work manually instead, multijointed metal digits skittering across the activation keys while they huff and hiss about how slow the process is.

The Lion walks to the window and looks out over the landing pads. What once would have been a bustling expanse of crew and servitors refuelling craft, travellers embarking and disembarking, and cargos of Camarth's chemical compounds being loaded for distribution across the galaxy, is now lifeless and unmoving. Three huge, sigil-daubed assault boats are arranged haphazardly: the landing craft of the forces that assaulted this place. Skeletons still lie where they fell, although some have been dismembered by scavengers, either animal or human.

'Much of what is in orbit is wreckage, and a reasonable percentage will not remain there for much longer, judging by the degradation patterns,' Valdax says. 'It appears that the traitor fleet destroyed anything sizeable which was not loyal to them, and I would surmise that other ships fled if they could.'

The Lion nods grimly. He had suspected that would be the case. 'Jovan, when we receive confirmation that no pockets of resistance remain, I want you to take a team and assess whatever is still out there.' He jerks his head towards the landing pads. 'It might be that some of the ships in orbit can be repaired, at least enough to get a small crew to the next system. We will not know unless we look, and to do that we will need a shuttle of some sort.'

'Yes, Lord Lion,' Jovan says, bowing. The Lion is as aware as any of them that this is not a likely outcome, but he refuses to let their moment of triumph be tainted by admitting that there is nothing more they can do. He has brought hope back to these people and this planet, and he will not abandon it or them now.

He will continue as though everything is possible, and drag them along with him.

Three days after Kallia City is retaken, the Lion is standing on a landing pad and looking at an Aquila transport with Zabriel, Valdax, Jovan, and ten of the newly formed Lion Guard. He had been inclined to protest the creation of a personal bodyguard for himself, on the basis that of all the people on Camarth he was the least likely to need protection from others, but Zabriel pointed out that this was a gesture of respect and honour from the Camarthans, and refusing would serve no purpose other than to insult them.

'You have run all the necessary checks?' the Lion asks, looking at the landing craft.

'Necessary is difficult to qualify under these circumstances,' Valdax replies, 'given the nature of the foes we have been facing. However, I can detect no scrapcode or infection of the machine-spirit, and the physical structure appears to lack any issues which would impact upon its safety or operation. If there are hidden traps or sabotage, it is beyond my ability to detect them.'

'You have not steered us wrong thus far,' the Lion says. 'If you consider it suitable, I can ask for no more.' He turns to Jovan. 'Do you have a team?'

'People with knowledge of voidships are in short supply,' Jovan replies, looking slightly ashamed. 'The Bastards killed those in orbit, and there were few enough on the ground to begin with, let alone that have survived since the invasion. I've put word out and rounded up those I can, but their knowledge skews between very basic and very specialist, without much in between.'

'It was not so long ago that the thought of getting anyone into orbit to assess salvage potential seemed so far out of reach that we were not even considering it,' the Lion reminds him. 'Let us not sour the taste of this opportunity by regretting what we do not have. Magos, what is the status of the planetary defences, in case our team needs covering fire?'

'We have chased the last few glitches from the system,' Valdax says, with a satisfaction that bleeds through even into their synthetic voice. 'The traitors kept most of the weapons batteries operational, presumably in case they needed them. If anything hostile enters orbit, they will not find Camarth defenceless.'

The magos' words are bold, but the Lion does not need his preternatural senses to detect the unspoken uneasiness in the humans around him. They all know that Camarth is now at only a fraction of its former strength, and that – as well as a small garrison of Space Marines – was still overwhelmed in short order. If the Ten Thousand Eyes return in force, there will be little that can be done to stop them.

Even so, retaking the world is a great achievement. The Lion opens his mouth to give his next order, then pauses. He turns to face north-west instead.

'Lord?' Zabriel asks. 'Is something amiss?'

'I am… not sure,' the Lion admits. He can see nothing, smell nothing, hear nothing unusual or untoward. Nonetheless, there is *something*…

'Should we send a scout team?' Jovan offers, but the Lion shakes his head.

'No. I do not even know if this is a threat. I will go myself.'

As soon as he says those words, he feels more at ease. He knows that it is the correct decision, even if he is not certain why.

'We will come with you, lord,' M'kia says, saluting. The Lion snorts in amusement.

'Was that an offer,' he asks the captain of the Lion Guard, 'or a statement?'

M'kia bites her lip, but does not back down. 'Forgive my presumption, lord, but there seems little point in having a personal guard if you leave them behind to walk into the forest alone.'

The Lion glances at Zabriel, but the former Destroyer is checking the magazines of his bolt pistols – now restocked, thanks to the recovery of Camarth's central armouries – and appears to be deliberately avoiding his primarch's gaze.

'Very well,' he says. 'Zabriel, with us. Jovan, magos, please continue as planned.'

The Goliath truck that serves as the Lion's transport is no Land Raider, despite the winged sword design painted onto it with just as much love and respect as any vehicle from his past. However, it suffices to get the primarch, Zabriel, and the Lion Guard to Kallia City's north-western edge, whereupon the Lion dismounts and stares into the forest.

'What do you sense, lord?' Zabriel asks, climbing down behind him, while M'kia and the others emerge from the transport hold.

'I do not know,' the Lion admits quietly. 'I cannot say that I sense *anything*, as such, but it is as though I am called.'

'A device of the enemy?' Zabriel says warily.

The Lion shakes his head. He can feel something tugging at his spirit, but he has no sensation of it being an intelligence, malign or otherwise: merely a desire to be *there* instead of *here*.

'Stay alert,' he commands, as he sets off into the trees. 'I do not believe we are approaching an enemy, but it cannot hurt to be careful. And I have been wrong before,' he adds softly.

If either Zabriel or the Lion Guard hear his final words, they make no comment, and they follow him beneath the branches. These temperate forests are less choked with vegetation and less hostile to humanity than the jungles farther north, but they are still wild places, for all that they come right up close to the city's boundaries. The Lion has heard of unwary travellers sleeping in the wild waking up to find fast-growing roots have pinned them down and are seeking nutrients from their bodies, and while he is not convinced those tales are completely true, neither is he convinced that they are not.

He advances over soft, moss-covered ground littered with the shrouded shapes of fallen branches and sprinkled with dark purple needles from the tall trees around them. Something calls off to his right: a soft hooting in the distance that is neither threatening nor comforting, merely the sound of the wilderness given voice. The Lion sees where grazers have cropped the undergrowth, where blunt-toothed browsers have stripped the lowest-hanging branches, and marks the spots where the pale, fleshy fruiting bodies of fungi erupt from rough-barked trunks. This is not the work of Chaos; this is merely a forest in its own cycle of life and death.

'Lord?' Zabriel says. It is not technically a question, but the Lion hears the query within.

'A little farther,' he says. He cannot say exactly how far, or in what direction, but he knows that the object of his search is close, even if he does not know what that object is.

They are climbing now, up the sides of the valley in which Kallia City sits, and it is not long before they enter a bank of low cloud. The Lion presses on, but is mindful not to leave his human guards behind. They are fit and healthy, but the incline is as nothing to him, whereas they are already puffing and panting, and sometimes missing their footing.

'Lord,' Zabriel says again, a couple of minutes later. This time it is not a question. The Lion stops and looks around at him.

'Yes, Zabriel?'

The Dark Angel taps the side of his helm. 'My read-outs are malfunctioning, and what they are telling me is making no sense. Where are we?'

The Lion frowns. The sun had disappeared once they'd entered the cloud bank, so he cannot use it to get a sense of direction. He sniffs the air: it is moist, cool, and carries the familiar smells of wet vegetation and decay.

Familiar smells, but not the *same* smells.

He places his own helm on his head, and his frown only deepens as he sees what Zabriel means. His sensors are struggling to lock on to anything, and information such as local time is absent. Even his targeting reticules refuse to focus properly, as though they are no longer able to properly process distance.

He removes his helmet again and breathes in once more, but it only deepens the feeling of unease in his gut. The Lion does not like things he does not understand.

'Zabriel, look around you,' he says. 'Without your helmet on. Tell me what you see.'

The Lion Guard are filing up now, their weapons still at the ready. Zabriel does as the Lion bids, exposing his grizzled head to the wet air. 'The forest, lord.'

The Lion takes a step closer to him. '*Which* forest?'

Zabriel's eyes narrow, and he looks again. The Lion sees in his face the moment he realises the thrust of his primarch's questioning.

'If I did not know better,' Zabriel says slowly, 'I would have said this reminded me of the forests of Caliban, as it was long ago.'

'Not just me, then,' the Lion says. He is not certain whether he is relieved or not. The fact that Zabriel has come to the same conclusion suggests that the Lion's experiences before he arrived on Camarth were genuine, and not the product of illusion, trickery, or a damaged mind seeking familiarity in its surroundings.

It does, however, open up the rather larger question of what is actually occurring.

'Lord Lion, what are you talking about?' M'kia asks. Her face is exhibiting confusion, but no alarm. The Lion realises that despite her role as captain of his personal guard, she has not registered the possibility that something can be wrong when he is there. It is a disconcerting revelation.

'The galaxy is a mysterious place, and not one that I can fully explain,' the Lion says. 'I have not spoken openly of how I came to Camarth, because I did not fully understand it myself. I walked with no memory of myself through a landscape much like this one, until it turned into the jungles where I met Zabriel. Now it seems I am back in that forest, and this time you have come with me. I do not, in truth, know where we are. Nor do I know how to get back to where we were.'

'Surely we just retrace our steps?' says a young man of the Lion Guard, by the name of Kolan. Several of the other guards shush him, as though to imply there is an obvious solution is an affront to the Lion, but the primarch waves their chastisement away despite the nagging feeling that he is not yet where he is supposed to be.

'It is as valid a suggestion as any. Let us try it.'

The party turns and goes back the way they came; or at least, they attempt to. However, they have not gone fifty yards before M'kia comes to a confused halt.

'Shouldn't we be going downhill? It was a bastard climb coming *up*, I know that much.'

Sure enough, the landscape ahead of her seems largely flat. Now the guards' expressions, M'kia's included, are showing worry.

'My lord?' one says, in a voice that quavers slightly. 'What should we do?'

The Lion considers. His rational mind insists that Kolan had the correct idea, but also that continuing to try something that has already been shown not to work is foolishness. Besides which, he can still feel the pull that drew him here, and although mysterious, these misty forests that echo those of long-lost Caliban have not yet harmed him.

As if in response to his thoughts, something howls in the distance. This is not a harmless noise of the wilderness, as he heard back on Camarth. This is a voice with teeth, and the Lion Guard immediately snap their weapons up in response. A mix of autoguns, shotguns, and lasguns scan the trees, but the mist reduces visibility and deadens sound, and even the Lion struggles to tell from exactly which direction the noise came.

'Follow me,' he says, turning. If his rational mind cannot provide him with a way forward, he will trust to his instincts.

He moves quickly, but not so fast that the humans cannot keep up. The Lion leads the way with Fealty drawn, while Zabriel acts as rearguard, both bolt pistols out and ready. The Lion can sense his son's unease at this place, at the oddness of it all, but respects the fact that Zabriel is keeping his thoughts to himself. The Lion Guard are holding themselves together, but if a Space Marine were to be visibly shaken then their nerve would surely go.

The Lion does not know how he picks his route, for the forest is eternally changing yet almost uniform, but he never wavers. Something is ahead of him, like a lodestone drawing him onwards.

The same howl as before comes from behind them, perhaps a little closer than it was before. Then another, definitely a different one, still behind them but off to the other side.

'We are being hunted,' Zabriel says into his ear, subvocalised so the Lion Guard cannot hear, although the Lion can tell that they have come to the same conclusion themselves.

'Great Beasts,' the Lion replies in a low voice.

'I thought you killed them all.'

'I did. But as I understand it, most of Caliban does not exist now either, yet here we are.'

'This must be some manner of warp trickery.'

'If they are Great Beasts, that is something I have the weapons to fight,' the Lion says, squeezing the handle of Fealty. 'But I walked out of this place once before, and we may yet–'

He comes to a halt, staring at something through the trees: a dome of pale stone, barely glimpsed, but unmistakeable. He has seen it before, when he was last in this place.

'Why have we stopped?' M'kia asks, looking around nervously as though the forest is about to disgorge ravenous predators. She might not be far from the truth.

'I do not recall ever seeing anything like *that* on Caliban,' Zabriel says, at a normal volume. A couple of the Lion Guard look at him in confusion, but the Lion ignores his words. A building might provide shelter from the beasts that hunt them, somewhere the Lion Guard could stay protected while he and Zabriel deal with the predators. Great Beasts were fearsome, but they were fearsome to the knights of Caliban who, for all their bravery and martial skill, were not power-armoured Space Marines with genuine bolt weaponry.

However, the words – or equivalent – of the Watcher come back to him. *Do not take that path. You are not yet strong enough.*

The Lion has no way of knowing if he has yet found the strength the Watcher felt he lacked. He has found memories since then, but all they emphasise to him is that the Watchers in the Dark should be heeded. Besides which, if he indeed lacked the strength for something, his companions would surely fare poorly.

His curiosity must wait. The safety of those in his charge comes first.

'Ignore it,' he says, starting forward once more. 'It is of no use to us.'

He does not tell them to hurry, but they do so without instruction as the howls of the beasts come again. The animals making them, if animals they are in this place, are drawing closer. It is still hard to tell exact distance, but the Lion can ascertain that much from the volume.

'We have to find a defensible position,' Zabriel voxes. 'Otherwise the humans will stand no chance. I do not know these creatures, but there are at least two, and I doubt I will be able to hold them both.'

'We are nearly there,' the Lion replies without thinking.

'Nearly where?'

'I know this forest,' the Lion says. 'I knew it in my youth, and I know it now. It may be changed, but it cannot keep its secrets from me.' He pauses for a moment, then cuts right along a stream-bed. 'Everyone keep up!'

The sensation is like a hook in his chest now: not painful, but tugging him insistently along. He could resist it if he wished, but why would he? He knows that he wishes to go where it leads.

He rounds a mighty forest sentinel, a massive tree that rises taller into the mist than he can see, and follows the stream downhill. The mist ahead is starting to clear, providing a better view of the trees. Another roar comes from behind, but although it is still ferocious, it sounds slightly muffled.

And then, between one step and the next, everything changes.

He is still surrounded by trees, but he is no longer in the forests of Caliban. These trunks are thinner and smoother, the trees are shorter, and the sun strikes through their huge, long leaves to hit like a hammer. For a moment the Lion thinks he is back in the jungle, but the air is dry here, and hits the back of the throat like a knife. The ground beneath his feet is soft, but it is not the softness of moss or grass.

It is the softness of sand.

He looks back, and sees the Lion Guard stumbling in confusion, looking around with wide and fearful eyes. Behind them is Zabriel, and although he has replaced his helm, his own uncertainty is visible in the set of his shoulders and the way he turns his head rapidly from side to side, trying to get a measure of their surroundings.

'Hoi! Who're you?'

The voice is shouting in Low Gothic, and it does not belong to any of their number. The Lion turns as a small, four-wheeled vehicle, little more than a buggy, roars up through the trees. It is driven by a man who has clearly spent much of his life under this punishing sun, judging by his heavy brown tan, the glare-shades over his eyes, and the cloth wrapped around his head. His vehicle rolls to a halt as he stares at the Lion in amazement, the aggression gone from his tone.

'What…? Where…?'

'What planet is this?' the Lion asks. He already knows what has happened, although he does not know how.

'Planet? A-Avalus, lord,' the man stammers. 'Please, wh-who are you?'

The Lion stares down at him, but there is nothing to suggest that this is not an Imperial citizen on a world that still adheres to the Imperium's laws.

'I am Lion El'Jonson, primarch of the Dark Angels, and a son of the Emperor.' He sheathes Fealty. 'I must speak with whoever is in authority.'

XIII

Seraphax's understanding of the warp made travel through its domains easier, but still not without risk, especially now it was in turmoil following the creation of the Great Rift. Baelor knew of the charms and wards his knight-captain had woven around the *Eye of Malevolence*, but that did not mean he welcomed his journeys through the empyrean. When all was said and done, only the creatures of the warp – the things he referred to as 'gods' and 'daemons', more for ease of reference than because he was truly comfortable with such labels – could exist there. Any creature of the material universe would die if it came into contact with the pure warp, and so even vessels allied to the powers who ruled that domain had to be shielded from it.

What that meant was that even though half of Baelor's commanding officer's head was now permanently on fire, even though he brushed shoulders with creatures he would have viewed with disgust and hatred in the days of the Great Crusade, even though the ship in which he rode was guided through the immaterium by a daemon bound with chains inscribed with runes of dominion and subjugation in place of a Navigator, he *still* felt the effects of translating in and out of the warp. It was almost always unpleasant, in one manner or another.

This one made his entire skeleton feel red-hot for one agonising second, and turned his saliva to blood. He heaved a shuddering breath prompted by the aftershocks of pain, removed his helmet as the *Eye of Malevolence* juddered back into realspace, and spat a wad of fluid onto the decking. It sizzled gently.

'Are you troubled by the weaknesses of your flesh?' Dimora asked from the command throne.

'You sound like a bloody Iron Hand,' Baelor grunted. He looked over at the Canticallax. 'You still have some flesh. Are you not affected by translation?'

'I would be, if I did not turn off my nervous system's connection to my biological components for the duration of the process,' Dimora replied, sounding smug. The lights of the *Eye*'s bridge pulsed nauseatingly, and the Canticallax buzzed in response. 'We are being hailed.'

'So soon?' Baelor frowned at the instruments in front of him. They flickered into a semblance of life, their static-laced outputs a far cry from the crisp hololiths they would once have produced. However, it was still enough for him to ascertain that they had emerged from the warp significantly closer to Camarth than would be possible through standard navigation techniques. There were *some* benefits to travelling aboard a daemon ship, after all: they were already entering the planet's orbit, rather than making the hours-long journey in from the Mandeville point. 'Raise the shutters.'

The blast shutters which protected the bridge from the churning, madness-inducing sight of the warp began to lift, and revealed the rich greens, blues, browns, and purples of Camarth. Baelor always felt better if he could see whom he was speaking to with his own eyes, even if only on a planetary scale.

'Let's hear it.'

'Compliance,' Dimora buzzed, and the vox-speakers crackled.

'–repeat, this is the space port of Kallia City. You are not broadcasting ident codes. Identify yourselves, or be fired upon.'

Baelor's frown deepened. He had not been back to Camarth since the Ten Thousand Eyes had taken it, but this was not the reception he had expected. It felt too... Imperial.

'Who is this?' he demanded.

'Someone with working surface-to-orbital defence batteries, and very little patience. Identify yourself, shithead.'

That was *not* Imperial protocol, but neither was it something Baelor was prepared to accept. His lip curled.

'Canticallax,' he said. 'Identify us to those planetside.'

The *Eye of Malevolence* screamed.

It began with the bound daemon, goaded by psy-barbs charged with the soul residues of psykers and sorcerers whose skulls Seraphax had collected. Its bellows of rage and pain resonated through the cruiser's superstructure until they reached the vox, whereupon they were broadcast as a torrent of noise and corruption at the planet below. Baelor imagined speakers at the other end blowing out in a shower of sparks, systems malfunctioning, and people recoiling with blood pouring from their ears. He had seen it happen.

When the scream had died away, he activated the vox again.

'Now, identify *your*self.'

Something buzzed an alert, then again, and again: not a regular warning, but the irregular rhythm of something occurring repeatedly, and triggering the system each time.

'Multiple target locks,' Dimora said, just as the vox crackled once more.

'We are Camarth,' the voice came up from the planet's surface. It sounded shaken, but determined. *'We are Camarth, and we hold for the Lion!'*

Baelor stared at the vox, unable to believe his ears. 'What? *What did you say?'*

He was answered only by silence, but it was silence in the form of multiple supra-focused lascannon blasts that stabbed up from planetside batteries to slam into the *Eye of Malevolence*'s shields.

'Taking evasive action,' Dimora declared. Alarms rang out through the warship, and the deck shifted beneath Baelor as the Canticallax fed more power to the drives. The sphere of Camarth began to drop out of sight, but Baelor barely registered it as his mind went back over the sentence he had just heard.

We hold for the Lion.

Camarth was not a recruiting world for the Dark Angels, or for any of their so-called Successor Chapters. If it were, the Ruby Crescents would not have had a presence there, small though it had been. And yes, the names of the primarchs were revered by some worlds within the Imperium, those with sufficient history or learning, but Baelor had not heard anything like this when he and the rest of the Ten Thousand Eyes fleet had swept down on Camarth the first time.

'You seem agitated, Baelor.'

Baelor stared at the tactical hololith, and ignored the Canticallax's words. Or tried to.

'Your pulse rate has spiked, and I can detect heightened levels of adrenaline within your–'

'Keep your sensors to yourself!' Baelor snarled, rounding on Dimora. He realised that one of his hands was resting on the grip of the boltgun mag-clamped to his thigh, and he removed it. He was not actually going to put a bolt-shell through the

Canticallax's primary logic circuits, but the temptation to do so was very high. 'And return fire!'

'Primary targets are protected by void shields–'

'Just do it!'

The *Eye of Malevolence* shuddered ever so slightly as tons of high-explosive death were discharged into the void, to punch down through the atmosphere and strike the planet below. Baelor gripped the edges of the holo-projector until he felt it creak, until every shell detonated in a flurry of static on his read-outs. It was wasteful, no matter what he told Dimora. Seraphax might not have approved.

But then again, Seraphax was not here. Seraphax had not heard what Baelor had heard.

Baelor had spent centuries fighting at the command of his knight-captain. He had seen things he would not have believed possible when he had been a blinkered, naive warrior of the Great Crusade. He did not necessarily like all the things he had seen, either, but he understood the necessity of them. Seraphax had a plan, and it was a bold and brilliant one that could reshape the very galaxy. Any tools, any methods, any cost was worth it.

None of those things had affected Baelor in this way. He had seen violations of the laws of physics, he had heard entities speak that had caused his nose to gush blood, and he had accepted them. They had hardly been pleasant, but the life of a warrior was not supposed to be pleasant. He had been created to fight and kill until he died; there was no scope within that for what he might find agreeable.

This had made him *doubt,* and doubt was a weakness he could not afford.

He took hold of himself, and fought down the wave of rage and uncertainty that those simple words had ignited within him.

'Combat prognosis?'

'We are outgunned,' Dimora replied bluntly. 'We have the advantage of manoeuvrability, but although our targets cannot evade our shots, my calculations indicate a seventy-eight point nine five per cent probability that we will not make a significant impact on any one of them before their batteries abrade our shields and immobilise or destroy us.'

Baelor growled. 'Can you get a reading on the Bloodrage site?'

Dimora clicked and buzzed for a couple of seconds. 'The site appears to have been destroyed. There are no power readings, and the structure is in ruins.'

'Warp take it!' Baelor snarled. The Bloodrage project had been one of Seraphax's side projects: research focused on finding ways to draw out the mindless ferocity which lurked at the heart of the sons of Sanguinius. Camarth was of little consequence in and of itself, other than a loss to remind the Imperium how tenuous its hold on the galaxy was, but the opportunities presented by a small garrison of Ruby Crescents had been too good to ignore. Taking any of them alive had been a great challenge, and Markog would have been dead three times over were it not for the gifts he had been granted.

Baelor glared at the hololith. He could still force a landing, perhaps, but he was the only Space Marine aboard. The ragtag warbands and mutants who roamed the decks in a half-feral existence entirely separate from greater strategic concerns would jump at the chance for ground combat, but the *Eye* was not loaded with a dedicated invasion force. They could storm a single city without a problem, but if the planet's remaining population had truly risen up in rebellion, and somehow had the tactics and tenacity to overcome the forces that had conquered them in the first place, then that was a war of attrition one ship's worth of cultists could not hope to win.

'We withdraw,' Baelor said. 'Lord Seraphax can decide whether we return with a larger force to bring this planet to heel once again. Get us back into the warp.'

'Compliance,' Dimora declared, but Baelor felt he could hear accusation at the edge of her voice. He ignored it, and told himself it was merely his imagination, fired up by the unfamiliar sensation of defeat. In all his centuries of existence, from his first years as a neophyte taken from Gramarye, through the Great Crusade, and now into this new millennium, defeats had been few and far between for Baelor. However, there was one that still lurked in his heart, like a worm that devours a fruit from within.

It had come on Caliban, at the hands of the Lion.

XIV

Avalus was not prepared for the coming of a primarch. But what planet is?

My companions and I were similarly unprepared for how we had got there. I had been convinced I was hallucinating as we travelled through the forests of what could not be Caliban, and yet so strongly resembled the dank, dense woods of the world on which I had spent so many miserable, exiled years. I cannot imagine how it must have been for the Lion Guard, and it speaks volumes for the character of those humans that they did not collapse in fear. Only the presence of the Lion kept us focused; he was our anchor to reality, whatever that reality was, and I found myself remembering once again exactly why the primarchs had been such powerful weapons in war.

It was not just because of their superlative martial skills, or supreme tactical awareness. They were like stars come to earth, both in their brightness and their gravity. A primarch could inspire warriors like no other, and shatter the resistance of an enemy like no other; save for the Emperor, of course. To stand near one was to be in the presence of a force of nature, a being who embodied both an unparalleled ferocity of life, and the promise of instantaneous death.

I sometimes wondered, over the long years, what the primarchs might have become had all of humanity's wars ended before Horus' rebellion. Would Guilliman have been given command of what became the Adeptus Terra? Would Magnus have probed the warp with the Emperor, uncovering even greater secrets? Would Fulgrim have sought perfection in art, while Ferrus Manus worked in partnership with the priests of Mars to devise new and better machines?

Not all of the primarchs fitted into my imaginings. It was hard to picture Angron in a galaxy without war, from what I had heard of him; indeed, I was certain that a galaxy which contained Angron could *not* be without war. Mortarion so strongly resembled the spectre of death which was at one time the symbol of my own Legion that I could not picture him relaxing. Russ, I say without a shadow of a doubt, would have got bored very quickly. And the Night Haunter? What place would that sinister figure, let alone his entire Legion of murderers and sadists, have in a time of peace?

And then there was the Lion.

The Lion was a warrior. Not a brawler, like the Wolf King, or a beast like Angron. He did not fight because there was little else that gave him such pleasure, nor did he fight to release an endless rage that burned inside him. He fought because that was what he was. He fought because the galaxy had never yet run out of threats to humanity, and the Lion's duty was to protect it. He had taken up that duty long before the Emperor found him, and the arrival of our Legion merely gave him the ability to widen his scope. I did not know the Lion's heart, for he was taciturn and withdrawn, but the only thing I could imagine might truly destroy his spirit was for there to no longer be a fight that needed him.

We had arrived, by whatever method it was, in a plantation of fruit trees that grew in the irrigated land around an oasis. The overseer who found us barely comprehended the reality of the Lion's identity, but was overawed enough to get on the vox and immediately communicate the news, and it was not long before troop carriers arrived. I could understand the caution: ten soldiers, a Space Marine, and an armoured giant claiming to be a hero from ancient history emerging from out of nowhere was a security threat, at the very least.

The people of Camarth had been hoping for a saviour, and the Lion fit that bill, so they followed him without question. The forces of Avalus came expecting a battle, and yet no sooner did they lay eyes upon the Lord of the First than they were also staring open-mouthed in awe.

We were taken to the city of Xerxe, the planetary capital, which was a mere twenty miles or so distant. It occupied an entire valley. Flocks of winged reptilians no larger than my hand flapped and screeched around massive hab-blocks that thrust into the sky like artificial cliffs. Between them was the detritus of civilisation: the shanties and shelters, the slums and souks, and lane after lane of squat dwellings which had either been ignored for so long that they had become permanent fixtures, or had actually been there before the hab-blocks were raised.

The Lion Guard were still trying to come to terms with the fact that they were somehow on another planet – a new experience for all of them, I believed. The Lion said nothing other than to address each new tier of military officer for the few seconds it took to convince them that he was, if not who he said, certainly imposing enough to be the problem of someone more important. That left it up to me to find out more about this world, which I had neither visited nor heard of before.

'Have you suffered attacks since the Great Rift?' I asked one of the soldiers, a corporal by the name of Yinda.

'Many, lord,' she said, 'but the fleet and the shields have kept us safe so far, Emperor be praised.' She made the sign of the aquila over her chest. We were on a raised highway now, and she pointed to a splash of char and soot in the distance. 'Only one landing craft ever made it down. It made a mess of one of the poor districts, but it was empty.'

I glanced at the Lion, but he made no indication that he had heard. 'How long ago was this?' I asked Yinda.

'Some six months.'

'It was the strangest thing,' one of the line troopers piped up. He had dark whorls tattooed onto his cheeks, which appeared to be a common affectation here. 'It wasn't even during a battle, but it sure wasn't anything of ours, because a great alert went up about it. We weren't on the detail sent to investigate, but there were no living enemy found, and no bodies in the wreckage.'

'Save for the poor souls whose homes got crushed,' Yinda added. She placed the top of her clenched fist to her lips and pulled it away again, a local custom I later learned indicated a blessing for the spirits of the dead just mentioned, and several of the others in the squad mirrored her action.

'I am glad that this system has held out,' the Lion said from the front of the vehicle's passenger bay. So he had been listening; I was not at all surprised. 'It speaks volumes for the courage and discipline of those who defend it. Camarth, the planet we came here from, was defended no less valiantly, but still fell to the invaders before its people rose up and took it back again.'

Yinda's eyes went wide as she looked at the Lion Guard. 'You took it *back*?'

M'kia, who along with the rest of the Lion Guard had been looking a little dispirited, brightened slightly. In their position, hearing about successful defences against the forces of Chaos when my own world had failed, I would have been wondering if my people had been lacking. The Lion had managed to frame events in a manner that credited the people of Avalus for resisting against an enemy that had beaten Camarth, yet also highlighted the determination of the Camarthans to recover from such a disaster. He might not have been gifted with the same skills of diplomacy as some of his brothers, but I had already noted this change in him during our time on Camarth.

In the years of the Great Crusade, the Lion was the Emperor's tool, as indeed our Legion had been before he joined us. He enacted the will of his father, and there was no space for those who opposed it. Reason and persuasion were the weapons of those who were not backed by the might of the First Legion, and the mandate of the Master of Mankind.

Now, however, things were different. No one could be certain if the Emperor still lived, by any definition of that meaning. The Imperium I had returned to was a long way removed from His original vision, and the coming of the Great Rift splintered even that unrecognisably. Was there anything more to humanity now than scattered islands in a sea of malice and madness, such as they had been during Old Night?

Certainly, the Lion could have railed at these developments. He could have attempted to mould what he found back into the Imperium as his father had intended it to be, even though that was a dream which had never been achieved before it fell apart. Instead, he recognised that Camarth was already too brittle to be forced into anything but the most basic functionality. He neither acknowledged nor raged at claims of his own divinity, even though I could tell he was repulsed by the notion, and he made no comment about the Imperial creed. There was a certain flexibility to him now, a pragmatism that had perhaps not always been there before, and with that came a greater awareness of those he considered it his duty to protect.

But this was not the same thing as weakness. He had certainly aged, and he claimed to be less capable physically, but the Lord of the First was no broken-down old man to be cowed by those of strong will.

The centre of power on Avalus was the Moon Palace. It was ancient, but in a good state of repair, and although I do not count myself as learned in matters of architecture or aesthetics, I felt that it was an example of how humanity could create beauty when it strayed from the prescribed forms of the Imperium. The towering hab-blocks were grim and grey and utilitarian, but the Moon Palace's soaring spires and domes spoke of a joy and wonder that went far beyond functionality. It was there that we were taken with all speed, and it was there that we – or to be exact, the Lion – were greeted at the gate by Marshal Haraj.

Seena ap na Haraj was a lean, stern-faced woman in her middle years, her dark hair thickly streaked with grey, and who bore the same facial tattoos as so many of her fellows. The former planetary governor, we learned on our journey, had stepped down when the initial nightmare of the Great Rift did not fade, and it was determined that martial law was an ongoing necessity. Marshal Haraj was already commander of the system's defence forces, and from then on she found herself in command of the system in truth.

She was flanked by guards, and the Moon Palace's mighty wall guns were declined to cover us, but the marshal stood at ease with nothing between our slowing transport and her. Had I wanted to, I could have shot her dead before anyone or anything was able to react, save possibly the Lion himself.

'This seems foolish of her,' I murmured.

'It is not foolishness that brings her to the gate to meet us, rather than hiding behind yet more guards and checks,' the Lion said back, just as quietly. 'It is hope.'

'Do you need me to remind you that the two are often interlinked, lord?'

'I do not.'

The Lion did not wait for our vehicle to come to a complete stop. Instead he vaulted over its side to land on the ground with a thud of ceramite, his cloak swirling around him. The lasguns of the marshal's honour guard twitched upwards at his sudden movement, but the Lion ignored them. They would have been no threat to him in any case.

'I am Lion El'Jonson,' he declared, his voice powerful but not overpowering. I could tell that he sought to reassure, not intimidate. 'Primarch of the Dark Angels, and son of the Emperor.'

Marshal Haraj stepped forward slowly, as though she were a child approaching a great beast she had been assured was tame, but could barely bring herself to believe it. I could see the wonder in her eyes.

'The return of a primarch would be a miracle,' she said, her voice surprisingly mellifluous for someone whose life had undoubtedly involved frequent shouting of orders. 'We have seen our fair share of miracles in recent times, but they have not been kind ones.'

'I cannot offer miracles,' the Lion said softly. 'Nor can I offer you any proof of my identity other than the evidence of your own eyes, but the warriors with me can account for my deeds on the world of Camarth.'

'Trust is hard to come by in these times,' the marshal said, 'and truth is yet more elusive.' She raised one hand, and a fat, white-bearded man strode out from behind her guards, clad in ornate robes adorned with symbols I had come to recognise. 'Seer Shavar is one of my counsellors and aides, and has helped us ascertain the truth of many a problem. If you have no objection...?'

She left the question hanging, but in truth there was little question about it. For the Lion to refuse scrutiny would suggest he had something to hide, but his displeasure at the notion was easy to read even before he spoke.

'You would have your witch scan my mind?' he asked, and never had he looked more like a disapproving elder.

'My psykana gifts have been sanctioned by Terra itself,' Shavar said. Perhaps he intended to sound reassuring, but it was easy to hear a haughtiness in his words, and the Lion bristled.

'Terra itself? My father banned the use of such powers during the Great Crusade! It was an edict we overturned only in the moment of greatest need, and those were still the disciplined minds of the Legiones Astartes.'

I dismounted from the vehicle and moved to his side. 'My lord, consider the situation. You are practically a being of myth to these people, and this man is being instructed by his commander and governor to determine whether you are whom you claim to be.' I looked at Shavar, and knew the truth of my words. 'His verdict may decide whether they are in the presence of a son of the Emperor who could be their salvation, or an enemy of fearsome power and duplicity standing at their very gates. It is understandable if he is nervous, and his words are not perfect.'

The Lion's cheek twitched, and he snorted. I braced myself for the resurgence of the stone-cold warlord I had known in the Great Crusade, who expected absolute obedience from all and was cloaked in secrets not even all of his sons understood.

Then he nodded. 'Very well. Do what you must, seer, but be aware that I do not share my thoughts with many, and I will not appreciate you lingering longer or prying further than is needed.'

Shavar let out a breath. 'Thank you, lord.' He closed his eyes, and clasped his hands together.

I have never liked warpcraft. Even in the days before the Edict of Nikaea, when the Legions employed their Librarius as they saw fit, it still filled me with a sense of utter wrongness and unease. Nonetheless, I accepted its necessity: we would not have won the Battle of the Black Gate without the Host of Pentacles. I simply hoped for the sake of everyone present that this usage of it would go smoothly, although I surreptitiously readied my bolt pistols in case it did not.

In this instance, I need not have worried. Shavar's eyes moved visibly behind his lids for less than ten seconds before he started twitching, gasped, and fell to his knees panting. He waved away efforts to help him up, instead staring at the Lion with a mixture of awe and terror.

'I have no doubts,' Shavar said hoarsely. 'He is Lion El'Jonson.'

There was a moment of silence after his pronouncement; silence which was broken by a cacophony of unutterable joy. Order collapsed as every human present heard words they had never even dreamed of hearing before this day, let alone hoped for. Many cheered, some laughed, and tears of wonder streaked down most cheeks. A few simply screamed, fists clenched and heads thrown back, as the pent-up stress and misery of their ongoing existence found a release. Nothing had changed for them as such – they were still on the same planet, in the same beleaguered system – yet in some ways, everything had changed. As my cousins of the XIII would have put it, the theoretical was broadly similar, but the available practicals had drastically altered.

Or perhaps they would not. I had not spoken to any Ultramarines since my emergence, and I had no idea whether they still spoke in such terms. Even after so long, I was still capable of giving myself away as someone out of his time.

Marshal Haraj had maintained some semblance of decorum, but she did not wipe at the tears that ran from her eyes down her tattooed cheeks as she sank to one knee. 'Lord Lion,' she declared, loudly enough for us to hear her. 'Avalus is yours.'

'No,' the Lion said. 'It is not.'

That quietened everyone down. No one was quite sure what the Lion could mean by his statement. I saw the doubt in Haraj's eyes: the worry that she had not been fulsome enough, that the Lord of the First required a more emphatic demonstration of their allegiance. However, she was thinking about it in the wrong way.

'Avalus is *yours*,' the Lion said firmly. 'I will not rule. My only intention is to clear the stars of the filth that preys on humanity. Will you grant me command of your forces so that I may do this?'

Marshal Haraj gaped. It was quite something for a military commander to be asked to hand over her authority, but she had been prepared to give up everything. And besides, what mortal would be *asked* for something by a primarch, rather than have it ordered of them? I saw the relief in her eyes as she realised that the fate of this star system no longer rested on her shoulders, and she bowed her head.

'Of course, Lord Lion. They are at your disposal.'

'I thank you,' the Lion said. He paused for a moment before he spoke again, as though considering. 'Marshal, are there any Space Marines present on Avalus, or in the system?'

Haraj shook her head. 'None, my lord, much to my regret.' Her forehead creased. 'But… are the Dark Angels not with you?'

'Only Zabriel, at present,' the Lion said, indicating me. 'My return has been… unorthodox. Regardless, let us begin. I should stress that I have no wish for pomp or ceremony on my behalf. I wish only to address the task in front of us as soon as I may, because I know well that traitors rarely wait to launch their attacks until it is convenient for their enemies. However, it may benefit the people to know of my arrival, so please have the word put out. Even into the warp,' he added, almost as an afterthought. 'You still have astropaths?'

'Yes, lord, we have a choir,' Haraj replied.

'Then let them shout of how the Lion has returned,' the Lord of the First said. 'Let us hope that our allies hear it and take heart, and that Avalus becomes a nexus for a reunification of systems that have been isolated.'

'Our allies may hear,' Seer Shavar ventured hesitantly, 'but our enemies certainly will. The warp is their domain. Your presence is a boon and a blessing, Lord Lion, but to announce it may call new terror down upon us.'

The Lion's expression did not alter. 'Happily, my tactical abilities have been sanctioned by Terra itself.'

There was a lot to be done. Marshal Haraj was an excellent strategist – the system would not have survived so long had she not been – but she was not a post-human warrior created by the Master of Mankind specifically to lead His armies to victory. The Lion had achieved wonders with only a ragtag guerrilla force on Camarth, and now he was dealing with a genuine army, albeit a somewhat battered one. He assessed the tactical situation far faster than any mortal could have managed, then began issuing orders. Defences were to be reconfigured, the fleet's battle groups reorganised, supply lines reinforced, and stores redistributed. He spent a solid hour issuing instructions, never pausing, while runners and vox-operators disseminated them and autoscribes recorded them for subsequent verification. The Lion made sure to comment on the positives of what he was replacing while he did so, but Haraj's eyes were still somewhat glazed by the time the briefing came to a close and the Lion ordered his command staff to get some rest.

His suite had been prepared by this time. It was the largest available in the Moon Palace, not because the Lion had demanded grandeur, but simply because to house such a titanic being in anything smaller would have seemed claustrophobic. Even so, despite the hasty acquisition of the largest items of furniture available, the proportions still looked slightly ridiculous.

'I cannot lie down on that,' the Lion remarked to me after the servants had left. He was looking at a bed that was the size, I had no doubt, of many of the individual units within the massive hab-blocks. 'I would break it.'

'We slept on the ground often enough on Camarth,' I pointed out. 'Is a carpet beneath you now, my lord?'

The Lion's face clouded. 'You mock me, Zabriel? I have done my utmost not to make these people feel inadequate, and when I voice my hesitation about crushing the furniture they have provided for me, you take that as arrogance?'

'No, lord,' I said, 'and I apologise. But what of Camarth? It is free of traitors, but how long can that last? Are we to forget it, and move on?' The Lion Guard had been ordered to bed by the Lion, with his protection – such as was needed – taken over by the Moon Palace's security forces. Camarth was not far distant, it turned out, a mere matter of a few dozen light years. Nonetheless, M'kia and the others were far from home and fearful, both for themselves and for those they had left behind, no matter how hard they fought not to show it.

As for myself, I found that my sense of duty nagged at me. Planets had been afterthoughts in the Great Crusade, no more than a designation stamp and perhaps a memory of some particularly notable battle or dangerous xenos species; we did what we came to do, and moved on. I had promised to protect people on Camarth, though, and I keenly felt my lack of ability to do so.

'No,' the Lion said wearily. 'We will send ships, and try to re-establish links. The people there deserve more than to be left to the mercy of whatever predators might find them. However, the rest of the galaxy deserves the same, and I can do more towards that aim here than I can there.'

'I will go with the ships,' I said, and the Lion looked up at me, his eyes suddenly sharp again.

'You will?'

'You asked the marshal if there were any other Space Marines within the system,' I said. 'I understand that you will need more than just me if you are to achieve your goals, but I have no wish to meet my little brothers of the modern Dark Angels, who will surely seek you out.' I laughed harshly. 'I doubt even you can convince them that I should not be tortured and killed for my perceived sins. I suspect it would be easier for us both if I were to return to Camarth and continue to aid the people there.'

'And if I were to order you not to go?' the Lion said softly.

I said nothing, since I was not sure what my answer was. He was my primarch and my gene-father, but I had resented him, even hated him, for far longer than I had followed him. Part of me wanted to leave before this reunion could be damaged – before he fell back into being the dark and mercurial warlord whose face had haunted my dreams for centuries.

'But then, what authority do I hold over you, Zabriel of Terra?' the Lion asked, apparently speaking to himself as much as to me. 'The galaxy we were created for is long gone, as are the order and structures into which we fitted. You are my son, and I am a son of the Emperor, but so was Perturabo, yet Barabas Dantioch betrayed him and ended up saving my life.'

I did not speak. I had no idea who Barabas Dantioch was, although this was a tale of which I was intrigued to hear more.

'However, you are both right and wrong,' the Lion said, and

now he addressed me in truth. 'You are correct that I will need more Space Marines than just you, but that was not why I asked that question.'

The Lion sat, more than a little tentatively, on the edge of the bed, then waved me to take a massive chair opposite. Neither of us had any need to sit, of course, but it was a gesture which indicated that there was no hostility, so I obliged. I had not been sure how the Lion would react to my statement, but rage had not been out of the question.

'The landing craft,' the Lion began. 'The one that came down mysteriously, and with no occupants.'

'Something did not feel right about that,' I said, thinking back to that conversation. 'If it was not an Avalusian craft, but no hostiles were found within, the obvious conclusion is that they survived the landing but made themselves scarce before local forces arrived. If there has been no conflict then I would assume assassins, saboteurs, or other infiltrators, but there seems to have been no evidence of such things either, even after six months.'

'The forces of Chaos are very capable of playing a long game,' the Lion said, 'but I believe there is a third option, and this is why I need you here.'

He looked at me quizzically, but I had nothing to offer him at this point. Whatever conclusion he had come to, it was not one I had reached.

'I wonder whether the craft contained one of your brothers,' the Lion said.

I blinked. 'My brothers? As in… those the modern galaxy refers to as the Fallen?'

'A melodramatic name,' the Lion said, waving the term aside with one hand. 'But yes. A Space Marine would be capable of surviving such a landing, and Xerxe is easily large enough for him to lose himself in it, despite his nature. Warriors of the

Imperium would report to the governor. Enemies of it would have, as you pointed out, likely made their presence felt. Those in hiding would do neither.'

'It is a possibility, lord,' I conceded slowly, 'but I am not certain it is the most likely option.'

'There is one other factor,' the Lion said. 'I do not know why my original footsteps led me to you, Zabriel, but they did. I still do not understand how that came to pass, nor do I know how to direct myself in that strange non-Caliban, but we must assume that either I could only have come to you, or I could have gone anywhere and something, some instinct or other force, led me *to* you. Just as I re-entered those forests without meaning to, and was subsequently led here.'

I digested my primarch's words. 'You believe you are being led to, or finding, your sons? Specifically, those who were present on Caliban at the Breaking?'

'It is a theory,' the Lion admitted, 'but one that feels right to me. Although I was always a creature of reason, I have learned, sometimes to my cost, that instinct and gut feeling are not without their place.'

'And if you are correct that one of my brothers was in that craft?' I asked. 'What would you have me do?'

'Quite simple, Zabriel,' the Lion said. 'I would have you find him.'

XV

The *Blade of Truth* was the pride of the Ten Thousand Eyes fleet, a mighty battle-barge once of the Ashen Blades, until the warp storm that spelled doom for that Chapter engulfed it. By the time Markog was free of the warp, he no longer had any intention of serving others; his pride, Baelor suspected, had been the chink in his moral armour that allowed Chaos in.

And yet, Markog had willingly bent the knee to Seraphax. That was an inconsistency which Baelor mistrusted, although in truth it was Markog's devotion that rankled. Baelor had seen that kind of deification of a commander at work before, and it rarely led anywhere good. Every leader needed to be challenged and questioned at times, rather than mindlessly obeyed, lest they stray too far down the path of their own ego. Even worse was when a follower suddenly realised that their leader was not the shining beacon of perfection they had assumed, and felt utterly betrayed. That was when love could turn to hatred, with swift and catastrophic results.

All of these thoughts went through Baelor's head anew as he approached the black granite command throne of the *Blade of Truth*, where Seraphax sat with his staff in hand, Markog lurking behind his right shoulder and three more members of the Dolorous Guard arrayed on either side of him. Baelor told himself that it was not just his own insecurities as he returned a failure, and nor was it jealousy of his place in Seraphax's close counsel that troubled him, but he was not sure he believed himself.

'Baelor,' Seraphax greeted him. 'What news from Camarth, friend?'

Baelor saluted with his fist to his chest. 'Camarth is lost, knight-captain. Forces loyal to the Imperium rose up and retook it in our absence.'

The bridge of the *Blade of Truth* was quiet for a moment as the implications of that statement sank in for those assembled.

'And you destroyed them?' hissed Urienz. The Arch-Raptor clicked the talons of his lightning claws together in anticipation.

'The *Eye of Malevolence* lacks the capacity to subdue an entire planet,' Baelor told him coldly.

Discipline broke down among the assembled warriors, who had been withholding judgement and therefore reaction. Howls of rage and bellows of anger rose into the thick, incense-scented air, and Baelor had the sudden impression of having been dropped into a pit of fiends. He flexed his fingers, ready to react if someone tried to gain favour with Seraphax by punishing his failure.

'And you come crawling back to us with this news?' bellowed Varkan the Red. The eyes protruding from the motor of what had been his chainfist glowed in reflected fury, and the weapon's monstrous, tooth-edged tongue began to rev up with a roar which sounded equal parts mechanical and organic.

'My forces would have been lost, and I would have been

unable to report this information,' Baelor said. 'Khorne may not care from whence the blood flows,' he added contemptuously, 'but I retain my tactical awareness.'

It was perhaps foolish of him to goad Varkan. The massive Terminator-armoured Space Marine had been a World Eater once, or so he claimed, although he had already shed anything that marked him as a member of any Chapter or Legion before he joined the Ten Thousand Eyes. He certainly had their temper, though. His eyes widened in shock and rage at being spoken to in such a manner, and he began to drool.

Baelor knew the warning signs. When Varkan lunged for him a moment later, he was ready.

Even encased in Terminator armour, Varkan was fast. The chainfist's blade swept around in a snarling arc that would have decapitated Baelor had it landed, but the Dark Angel had already leaned back just enough for the blurred tip of whirling teeth to slide harmlessly past his helmet's grille, and stepped off to the side. He put two shots into the servos of Varkan's left knee with his bolter, deforming the ceramite; the joint gave a grinding sound as Varkan swung back ponderously towards him, and slowed the Khorne worshipper just long enough for Baelor to squeeze off a shot at his unprotected face.

The aim was true, but the shell never hit.

Golden pain lanced through Baelor's body, holding him in place. Varkan was similarly stilled, but his roar of anger and frustration faded as he noticed what hung in the air between them. It was the bolt-shell fired from Baelor's gun, aimed square at his forehead, the propellant flame burning furiously and futilely as the invisible force held it stationary.

'Baelor,' Seraphax said sternly from the command throne, one hand outstretched. 'I did not give you permission to kill Varkan.'

'I notice that you are not refusing him permission to kill

me,' Baelor managed to get out through a jaw which would not obey him.

'If I thought there was a significant likelihood of him succeeding, I would do so,' Seraphax replied. The bolt-shell's propellant spluttered and died, and it fell to the deck as the sorcerer released his hold on it. A moment later, Baelor could move as well. He did not pull his trigger again, but he kept his boltgun levelled at Varkan, whose pupils were beginning to dilate from pinpoint specks of rage back to something more normal. Even the red-armoured brute realised that he would have been dead had it not been for Seraphax's intervention, and he seemed disinclined to push his luck.

Varkan lowered his weapons and, after a moment more, Baelor did so as well.

'The Imperium is divided,' Seraphax said, as Varkan pushed his way back amongst his fellows. 'Our own nascent empire has been forged out of their isolation. I hear your rage at how a planet has thrown off our rule, but the question that compels me is how have they done this? What allowed the people of Camarth, one of our earliest conquests, to rise up? Did our garrison become lax? Was the planet reinforced or retaken by outside forces? Might those factors come to affect other worlds over which we currently exercise control?'

Seraphax rose from his throne and walked down the steps from it to pass between his assembled warlords and commanders, and stood in front of Baelor. There was no anger in his visible eye, merely calmness. Seraphax was not a man given to prominent displays of temper.

'I asked you to find out what had happened,' he said. 'And I asked you to save what needed to be saved, and destroy what needed to be destroyed. However, I also told you that you had my complete trust. Was I wrong to do that? What can you tell me?'

'The Bloodrage project is gone,' Baelor said. 'The bastion in which it was secreted was destroyed, we were able to ascertain that much from orbit. The defenders have brought a sizeable portion of the pre-existing surface-to-orbit defence batteries under their control, and outgunned the *Eye*. They sounded more like militia than military during the vox exchange, although that was brief.'

He hesitated, but Seraphax was standing in front of him, and would see that more information lurked behind that hesitation. Baelor had wondered how to word this throughout the journey back to the fleet, as the captive daemon navigating the *Eye of Malevolence* through the warp had roared and snarled in the voice of the ship, but now it came to it he could see no better option than stating it bluntly.

'They said they held the planet for the Lion.'

Seraphax frowned. 'For the Lion?'

'Yes.' Baelor took a breath. 'I replayed the exchange to myself after we had withdrawn. They did not say "in the name of the Lion". They said "for the Lion". It is a minor difference, but one which I think raises more questions than answers.'

Seraphax's eye narrowed. 'So a population which mysteriously finds the spirit and ability to overthrow our brethren claims to be defying us for the Lion. As though he would know of this somehow, or approve of it.'

'Standard Imperial-whelp nonsense,' Urienz snarled. 'They try to find courage in long-dead heroes, since they have none of their own!'

'You do not understand,' Baelor said. In deference to not provoking another potentially lethal fight, he kept his tone polite. 'I was there when we took Camarth. The defenders never uttered the Lion's name. I might have understood a reference to Sanguinius or the Angel, since they had Blood Angels successors on the planet. They certainly yelled unceasingly about the Emperor, as though any one of them had stood in His presence when He walked the stars clad in mortal flesh. But the Lion? They have no history, no *reason*, to mention him.'

'Are you sure this is a matter of concern?' rasped Jai'tana the Unshriven. He was a former Ashen Blade as well, a Chaplain who had once been attached to Markog's command and had slain their Master of Sanctity while they were lost in the warp storm. He had found his own path since, and no longer heeded any authority other than that of Seraphax; and, of course, the gods he now worshipped. The faceplate of Jai'tana's helmet had morphed into an eyeless maw that disgorged his prayers between rows of needle teeth, and he was constantly surrounded by a low-level buzz in which, if one listened closely, it was just possible to discern what sounded like faint chanting. Of all the unsavoury allies Seraphax had made, the Unshriven was the one of whom Baelor most questioned the necessity.

'Did I say it was concerning?' Baelor asked.

'You speak, and I hear the whimpering of a child who has heard the name of his father,' Jai'tana declared. 'Why does a long-dead ghost scare you so?'

'I know the name of my gene-father,' Baelor retorted. 'I have seen his face and fought alongside him, ten thousand years ago, and you call *me* a child? You do not even know your own ancestry, *thin-blood!*'

That was not so polite, and Jai'tana's crozius sizzled into life as a howl of rage escaped his altered mouth. Seraphax's lips pursed, and he turned his flaming face towards the Apostle, who quickly quietened himself.

'Brother,' Seraphax said quietly to Baelor, turning back to him. 'Why are you so keen to provoke a fight on my bridge today?'

Baelor bowed his head. 'Because I feel that I have failed you, but I resent that others seek to issue the judgement that should be yours.'

Seraphax smiled. Then he turned away and ascended back to his command throne, onto which he sank with the clank of ceramite on stone.

'My brother Baelor has brought us important information. Our enemies squeal the name of my gene-father as though it means something to them. A primarch of the Emperor, returned after millennia – is this a possibility that should be so easily dismissed out of hand?'

'The Emperor's dogs are all dead,' Varkan growled. 'Only the primarchs who serve the True Powers still live.'

'You know that?' Seraphax said, his voice deadly and quiet. 'You know that for sure?'

Varkan shut his mouth again, which was probably the wisest thing he had done for some years. Seraphax drummed the fingers of his left gauntlet on the throne's arm for a moment, in a series of staccato clicks.

'I will say this for the benefit of those of you who were not, as Baelor and I were, alive at the time when the primarchs walked amongst us. We are but a shadow of them. I would hesitate to label anything impossible where a primarch is concerned, no matter how unlikely it may seem.' He snorted. 'Nor do I pay much heed to a lack of whispers about the Lion's whereabouts thus far. Absence of evidence is not evidence of absence, and the Imperium appears to be just as good at hiding things as it is at genuinely forgetting about them. Besides, the warp storm that scattered my brothers and I at the Breaking of Caliban did not distribute us evenly over space and time. It is entirely possible that the Lion was seized by the same phenomenon, and has only just emerged.'

Baelor saw the other commanders glance at each other uneasily, and experienced a quick flash of pleasure at their discomfort.

'You are saying that you think those wretches on Camarth might be telling the truth?' Urienz asked incredulously, gunning the engines of his jump pack in what felt to Baelor rather like agitation. 'You think Lion El'Jonson might have returned?'

'It is too early to tell,' Seraphax said. 'However, as Baelor points out, there are reasons to consider it a possibility. If so, this potentially changes everything.'

'So why are you smiling?' Varkan the Red demanded roughly.

'Because,' Seraphax said, 'I consider this to be an opportunity. An opportunity we will have to be cautious about seizing, it is true, but an opportunity nonetheless. My path to the Emperor would be difficult even with a mighty hero of the Imperium, but with a *primarch*...' His gaze unfocused slightly, and he appeared to be looking out beyond the *Blade of Truth*'s bridge into the void beyond. 'I only hope he is uncorrupted.'

'He was not on Camarth?' Jai'tana demanded. Baelor laughed hollowly.

'I have no way of knowing. I can assure you that he was not on the vox, however – even after all this time, I would know the voice of the Lord of the First.'

'We should return to Camarth in force,' the Apostle declared, turning to Seraphax. 'We must show the servants of the Corpse-Emperor that defiance brings only pain, and while we are there we can ascertain the truth of these rumours. The immaterium confounds them far more than it does us. If he was there, but is there no longer, there is only a handful of other systems he could have–'

'Lord Sorcerer! Lord Sorcerer!'

That bleating shout did not come from the throat of a Space Marine. Baelor turned in surprise as a grey-furred beastman burst onto the bridge in a clatter of hooves. Four horns sprouted from his head, two spiralling upwards and another two curving down alongside his muzzle. One eye was white with age, but the other was golden and bright, and the horizontal pupil in it was stark black and narrow. He wore tattered robes which had once belonged to an Imperial adept, but it was not his raiment that made his presence noteworthy. This was Krr'satz, overseer of the choir of twisted astropaths Seraphax kept aboard the *Blade of Truth*.

'Peace!' Seraphax shouted, as a couple of the newer warlords brought their weapons up, ready to slay the abhuman who had dared intrude upon their council. 'Krr'satz, you have something for me?'

'The void-whisperers are speaking, lord,' the beastman said, sinking into an awkward kneeling position. 'They say the Imperium is shouting new, shouting loud, from a world called Avalus.'

'And what is it shouting?' Seraphax demanded.

Krr'satz looked up, his one working eye wide with an urgency he felt without comprehending.

'It says, "The Lion is here."'

XVI

I moved through Xerxe's night-time streets with all the caution I could, wondering if I had made a mistake.

Well, I had undoubtedly made many mistakes over my centuries of life. The current question was whether *this* was a mistake.

The Lion's logic made a certain amount of sense, but only a certain amount. Our method of arrival to Avalus, and his own arrival to Camarth, defied explanation. It was tempting to apply logic to it and try to explain how it had worked, but how successful could it be to apply logic to something which was already illogical? On the other hand, warp travel was the definition of something illogical, and humanity still tried to quantify that. The Lion felt certain that he had been drawn to Avalus due to the presence of another of my erstwhile brothers. I had explained to him that even if this were true there was no guarantee that such a warrior would be any more kindly disposed towards him than I had been, and I had attempted to kill him on sight, but he brushed my concerns away.

'I have need of my sons – those who can be trusted, at least,' he had said to me. 'If the war at the Breaking was brought about by malice and deception on the part of some, but honest confusion on the part of others, I owe my sons the chance to prove to me on which side of that divide they fell.'

What this meant in practice was that I was going to be the first one at risk of being shot at. A primarch could not move about a city without attracting a great deal of attention, besides which the Lion was needed to coordinate Avalus' defensive efforts, so finding my theoretical brother was down to me. I was hardly inconspicuous myself, but having shed my ceramite and donned a nondescript, hooded brown robe I could pass for the same gene-bulked servitor or labourer I had used as a disguise on many different worlds before, so long as I remembered to move slowly and more clumsily than was natural. A Space Marine is a warrior, and badly suited for subterfuge, but necessity had forced adaption over the years.

The other advantage I had, and which the Lion had correctly guessed, was that the Fallen were not individuals. Nor, I should stress, were we an organised and coordinated force threaded through the structure of the Imperium; or if we were, I was not a part of it. However, we were still Space Marines, indoctrinated into being part of a larger whole. Any of us who had come into contact with another of our brothers at any point knew that we were not the only one to have been scattered in such a manner, and that kind of shared experience breeds a kinship of a sort, no matter what changes might have been wrought on those concerned.

There are signs that the Fallen use to mark their presence, so that if another passes by we might know that we are not alone, and we will share those signs with others that we meet. They are not Calibanite signs, in the main. Instead, we use symbols linked to the identifiers of the old Hosts by which the First Legion was organised prior to the discovery of the Lion. Sarius, the bitter loner I met first, taught me what to look for, and I passed that knowledge on to Priavel, in the brief time we spent together before I lost my patience for his warp-worship.

Knowing the signs is not enough, since one must also know where to look for them. As such, I made first for the Great Basilica of St Jerome the Pure, the largest cathedral to the Emperor in the city. It was a mighty building indeed, with four domes roofed in pale marble arranged around a larger central one, and its main minaret rose even higher than the spire of the gubernatorial palace. My brothers would never place their mark on a cathedral itself, of course – such an act of perceived heresy would be hard to hide amidst the throngs of the faithful that almost always crowd around such places – but the building opposite the main entrance was a usual starting point.

In Xerxe, I had two choices, one on either side of the street that led onto the square in which the cathedral sat: a liquor house, still open despite the privations of war; and a mortuarium, handily placed for any high-profile funerals that might occur at the cathedral and, at the other end of the scale, any victims of the drink being served across the way. The mortuarium's walls were not free of marks and graffiti, but there was nothing which caught my eye. The liquor house, on the other hand, had a circle carved into it, and within that circle were three crossed lines, one upright and two slanting. Each of those lines had a shorter scratch at right angles across it near one end, to make a very rough approximation of three swords with cross-guards.

It was the sign of the Host of Blades, the most numerous of us and the core of the Legion. Other marks around the edge told me, through their number and placement, where to look next. It appeared that the Lion might have been correct. One of my brothers was here, or had been.

I moved off, skirting around the edge of the crowd of petitioners and penitents who howled their prayers and begged the Emperor for salvation with all the desperation and fury of the most ardent helot cultist. Such displays always made me uncomfortable, but what was even worse was that I could hear the Lion's name being given the same devotional treatment. It was sickening to be reminded how far the Imperium had fallen from its days of rationality.

Two streets across and three northwards, I encountered the next symbol scratched into the metal gatepost of what I took to be a scholam. The surroundings marks guided me onwards, farther into the city, and farther from the palace.

I was into the poorer streets now. The next mark was paint, rather than a scratch, placed unobtrusively amidst the territorial scrawl of the local street gangs on a wall. It was comparatively fresh, too: as I studied it, I noticed that it was a replacement for an older mark which had been partially obscured by the work of others. So, my brother had been here recently, which lent some additional credence to the Lion's notion that he had been in the mysterious crashed lander.

I had travelled on my share of interstellar trading ships before, relying on a mix of currency and intimidation to prevent a private captain from asking too many questions, and sometimes taking my leave before the agreed time in order to avoid potential trouble at the far end of the journey. Sarius had told me of how one captain he had ridden with sent word ahead to slavers she knew, who were eager to take possession of – as they thought – an escaped gene-crafted serf. Then there was the risk of a captain alerting the Imperial authorities in case their passenger carried a bounty; not to mention my modern brothers, who were infuriatingly tenacious when it came to chasing down even the slenderest of leads on us. I could well imagine reaching orbit on a trader ship and stealing a shuttle to make my own way to the planet below, rather than risk the uncertain environment of a space port.

The painted mark guided me deep into the slums, where the streets ran with effluent and the illumination was sparse. This was the territory of the same gang whose marks I had already seen, and I moved with caution. This was not for my own safety – even without my ceramite, I had little doubt in my ability to deal with the sort of footpads and toughs that might lurk here – but simply because any sort of violent confrontation would draw attention, and attention was something I wished to avoid. No recluse appreciates someone dismembering half a dozen criminals, even in self-defence, and then knocking on their door.

The final mark was on a door of cheap plastek, set into the wall of a squat building made out of what I presumed was local stone. This sigil was different: instead of the crossed swords of the Host of Blades, the circle was occupied by a thick horizontal line topped with five vertical ones. It was a crude rendering of the mark of the Host of Crowns, that ancient brotherhood of linebreakers and champions.

I knocked on the door. It might seem an anticlimactic end to my search, but there was no secret code in the rhythm, and nor did I have an ancient password on the tip of my tongue. My basic nature would be immediately obvious to anyone who was familiar with the Legiones Astartes, once I threw back my hood and abandoned the mannerisms I had adopted, and none other than those present at the Breaking of Caliban would have the knowledge required to follow these marks to this location.

Unless, of course, I thought as I stared at a door which remained unanswered, my more modern brothers had prised the secret loose from one of my kin. Then they might set up traps to lure us in, seeking to use our own language against us...

'Move and you die.'

The whisper came from behind me, pitched low enough that someone without a Space Marine's augmented hearing would have no hope of hearing it. It was a Space Marine's voice, I knew that much instantly: there was a pitch and timbre to it that no mortal could have matched.

I have been held at gunpoint more times than most Astartes, I suspect. For the vast majority of my kin, be they ancient or modern, if a gun is pointed at them then either they or the person pointing it are about to die – that is how it works on the battlefield. For those of us who have spent considerable time pretending to be someone or something we are not, however, things are different. I have lost count of the number of times someone with an inflated sense of self-importance, or intimidated by my size, has pointed a gun in my direction with the assumption that doing so will give them control of the encounter. Sometimes I have allowed this fiction, because it has suited me. At other times they have lost the arm holding the gun, or worse.

This was different to those occasions. Priavel and I nearly shot each other when we became aware of our proximity at the same time, and our reflexes to draw and fire were only just overtaken by the realisation of each other's nature, but now one of my kin had the drop on me. I could tell from the direction of the voice where the speaker was: the upstairs window of the dwelling behind me. My weapons were tucked beneath my robe, and I knew that I would die if I reached for them. I did not doubt for a moment that a weapon was being trained on me; even a Space Marine would hesitate before threatening a brother who had not until that moment been aware of his presence, unless he had the ability to make good on the threat.

'Who speaks?' I asked. The fact that I was still alive told me nothing. Another veteran of the Breaking would surely try to ascertain my identity before deciding whether or not to kill me, and my little brothers would seek to haul me to one of their Interrogator-Chaplains to be tortured into confession rather than ending my life outright.

'You are Astartes, then,' the voice said, slightly louder this time. 'Turn around slowly with your hands at your sides, and draw no weapon.'

I did as I was bid, raising my head slightly as I did so, so I could see up from under the cowl of my hood. I could see no figure at the window in the dim light, nor could I see anything of a weapon muzzle as such until I became aware of a darker circle trained on me. The metal surrounding it had been blackened to avoid giving itself away through reflections, but the bore of the barrel itself was just possible to make out. It was a boltgun, and without my armour I would die easily. I silently cursed the Lion. Not for the first time, and I would be very glad indeed if it was not the last, for that at least would mean that I would be alive to do so.

It was time to take what control of the situation I could, which at this point simply meant volunteering information before it was demanded of me.

'I am Zabriel of the First Legion,' I declared. 'I come in brotherhood. Will you at least tell me your name?'

There was a pause.

'Remove your hood,' the voice instructed me. 'Slowly.'

I reached up and did so. I felt oddly vulnerable without it, as though the cloth around my face had been a sort of armour. Although in terms of how much I had kept my face hidden over the years, it had certainly been protection of a sort.

'Emperor's blood,' the voice said, and the guarded hostility was suddenly absent from it. Then I heard a snort of amusement. 'You got *old*.'

That, at least, suggested I was not about to die, but I was growing irritated. Caution was one thing, mockery was another. 'You know me?'

'I *trained* you, old man. Walk through the door ahead of you, but keep your weapons away.'

I crossed the street in two strides, and opened the door. It revealed a dimly lit single room which occupied the entire downstairs of the dwelling, apart from the stairs. I pulled up short as I was about to enter, because it was not empty.

A large figure dressed not so differently to myself stood across the room from me in a duellist's stance, a dormant power sword in his hand. He was another Space Marine without a doubt, but not the one who had been holding me at gunpoint; I could hear that one's steps above as he moved towards the staircase. However, off to my left was yet another warrior, this one in full black ceramite beneath a red surplice, aiming a plasma gun at me. His helmet, the eye-lenses glaring red, was taken from the more modern Mark VII armour.

I swallowed. For some reason, the incineration of plasma was a far less appealing death than mass-reactive bolter rounds, despite the fact that it might well be quicker, and I had not exchanged any words with this individual.

'Come in, and shut the door,' the swordsman told me. He had a cold, clipped voice, one in which the vowel sounds of Caliban still sat prominently.

'Brother,' I said in greeting, doing as he bid.

'We shall see.'

Footsteps on the stairs heralded the arrival of the third warrior, the one with whom I had been exchanging words. The room was crowded enough with the three of us in it; his arrival made it positively claustrophobic. I saw his face, and a shock of recognition ran through me.

'Aphkar?'

'I said I trained you, did I not?' Knight-Sergeant Aphkar replied with a grin. He had been one of my instructors when I was first raised into the ranks of the First Legion; a Gyptian with long, smooth black hair. That hair was still just as black and lustrous as when I had last seen him, bellowing orders during the defence of Caliban.

'You have not aged,' I said in wonder.

'It has been a mere thirty years for me,' he replied. 'You must be twice my age now, in real terms.' His glance slid sideways, and he sighed. 'Lohoc, will you put the gun away? You will bring half the street down if you fire it in here.'

'I will not,' Lohoc replied. His voice was hoarse and breathy, even taking into account the slight distortion from the vox-grille of his helmet. 'We do not know his intentions.' His plasma gun was a Ryza Thunderbolt, a design considered ancient by modern standards, but which still looked comparatively new. I suspected it was one of our Legion's original weapons, made when the Imperium's understanding of plasma was superior to its current level of technology.

Aphkar sighed. 'Zabriel, meet Lohoc, also known as the Red Whisper. This is Kai.'

The Calibanite inclined his head to me in a slight nod. The Red Whisper did not move.

'This is Zabriel, whom I trained,' Aphkar continued. He smiled. 'It is good to lay eyes upon you again, even if you are somewhat changed from when I last saw you.'

'Four hundred years in this galaxy will do that,' I muttered, and I saw him wince.

'Alone?'

'Near enough. I met a couple of others, but in each case one or other of us quickly decided we preferred our own company.' I fought down the envy I could feel rising up inside me at the notion of having like-minded brothers at my side while attempting to deal with the insanity my life had turned into. I could not afford resentment to creep into my voice.

'The streets are already abuzz with rumours,' Kai said. 'They claim that Lion El'Jonson is here, in Xerxe.'

'They are correct,' I said simply. 'He has returned.'

Each of them tensed. I had expected denial, but it seemed they trusted one of their brothers to know his own primarch when he saw him.

'And you are with him?' Lohoc asked. I was very aware that his finger was still on the trigger of his weapon.

'I am,' I told them.

'Even though he and the rest of his traitors tried to destroy us all?' Aphkar said, his voice roughening.

I shrugged. 'I tried to kill him when I first saw him. I failed. He did not kill me in turn. Instead, we spoke about that day. The Lion swears that he remained loyal to the Emperor, and I believe him. He also swears that Caliban fired on his fleet first, and I believe that he believes that. If there was treachery, I fear it came from our commanders – Luther, Astelan, and their cohorts.'

'I told you there was something off about Luther,' Kai murmured. Aphkar shushed him with a wave of his hand.

'Was he taken by the warp storm with the rest of us?' he asked.

'He does not know,' I said. 'He has no memory of what happened between the destruction of Caliban and just before he met me.' I decided not to mention the strange, pseudo-Calibanite forests at this juncture; there would be time enough for that later, assuming Lohoc did not decide to incinerate me. 'But my guess would be not. He is *old*, Aphkar – he looks older than me now. If I were to speculate, I would say he has been kept somewhere else, and aged as naturally as a primarch can.'

'Kept where? Kept by whom?' Kai demanded. I could only spread my hands.

'As I said, brother, that is merely my speculation.'

'Why did he send you to find us?' Aphkar demanded. My old mentor clearly had no trust for our gene-father.

'He needs our help. He wishes to protect as much of humanity as possible, and he needs Space Marines to do that.' I hesitated, then continued. 'And to be frank, I think he is lonely. He awoke, like we did, into a galaxy vastly different from what he knew before, where all his father's designs have fallen into ruin. He faces it with the same stoicism he always had, but I think he craves familiarity, and I am only one. I have convinced him that at least some of us on Caliban knew nothing of any hostility between us until his forces attacked, and now he wishes to find those of his sons who still live. I think he wishes for reconciliation.'

'Reconciliation?' Aphkar growled. 'He slaughtered our brothers, warriors who had been with the Legion since its inception and neophytes alike, and we are expected to believe that it was a *misunderstanding?*'

The Red Whisper lowered his weapon. 'I will go with you, brother.'

My surprise was mirrored on the faces of Kai and Aphkar. Lohoc did not seem to feel that any further explanation was necessary; he merely shouldered his plasma gun and turned to a chest behind him in which were, I assumed, whatever personal effects and ammunition he had accumulated.

'Lohoc?' Aphkar said, that one word containing all the question needed.

'I never believed that the Lion betrayed us,' Lohoc said. 'I assumed the fault lay with us somehow. Caliban was a strange world, which twisted much. Who is to say it had not twisted us?' He opened the chest and pulled out a bandolier from which hung two plasma flasks. 'Since I returned to the galaxy I have hunted the mightiest beasts preying on humanity, and I have dedicated each kill to the Lion. If he means to turn a hunt into a war, I will go to him.'

Aphkar scowled. 'And what are you ordered to do if I refuse to go with you, Zabriel?'

I faced him openly. 'The Lion sent me with a request, not an order. He *asks* for your help in protecting humanity. If you refuse him, but do not oppose him, he told me he will not pursue you. Besides,' I added, 'we had no idea there would be more than one of my brothers here. If Lohoc alone joins us, that is all we had hoped for.'

Kai grunted. 'This is not an opportunity I can ignore. To see my primarch again with my own eyes, after all this time?' He sheathed his sword. 'I will come with you, Zabriel, although I may not stay.'

I looked at Aphkar. His nostrils flared, but after a moment, he nodded.

'Fine, we will see what he has to say for himself.' He glanced at Kai, then back at me. 'Zabriel, I do not wish to ask you to demean yourself, but–'

'But this would go quicker if I assisted with your armour.' I gave my former instructor a knowing smile, and stepped forward willingly. 'Brother-sergeant, I have been alone for four hundred years, more or less, with no serfs to help me with my battleplate. I have had to choose when to don it and when to remove it, always thinking about if and when I will be able to reverse that decision, and the dangers of revealing my identity to anyone whose assistance I enrolled. Of course I will help you.'

XVII

The Lion is woken from sleep by the chime of the vox. He sits up on the floor and reaches for his sword first, then for the communication equipment on its pedestal next to the unused bed. This seemed like the perfect opportunity for sleep: he had issued instructions which were in the process of being carried out, and there was no immediate threat. Now he looks at the sky outside the window, still shrouded by night, and wonders if the fact someone is rousing him at this hour means he misjudged.

'Yes?'

'Your... attendant has returned, my lord.'

The Lion snorts in amusement. 'If you refer to Zabriel, he is not my attendant, he is my son. Is he alone?'

'No, my lord. There are three others with him.'

'Three?' Lion El'Jonson gets to his feet. 'Three Space Marines? Armoured in black?'

'Even so, lord. Shall I conduct them to the Twilight Garden?'

'Do so.' The Lion breaks the connection, and reaches for the robe laid out on the bed: a gift from Marshal Haraj, created by her personal tailors within two hours of his arrival. The fabric is a beautiful soft cream, and the winged sword of his Legion is emblazoned on the chest in black. He pulls it on, ignoring his armour. He has no need to remind these sons of his that he is a warrior; indeed, their last image of him might well be him clad in the Leonine Panoply and coming for their brothers with his blade bared.

The Lion is not incapable of considering the thoughts and feelings of others, but it takes him conscious effort. His reunion with Zabriel was unforeseen and sudden, when he did not know himself, and he has thought about how to approach others of his Legion ever since. However, this does not mean he can discern the approach that will work.

'Father, why did you create us so? So… incomplete?' he mutters, acutely aware once again of his own shortcomings. 'I am a weapon, only of use within the structure you had already forged. Now that structure has crumbled, and I have scant authority save that granted to me by its remnants. I can lead by example, but little else.'

The Lion sighs. He has no time to dwell on such things now; he sent Zabriel to retrieve one son, and the former Destroyer has returned with three. Keeping them waiting will do nothing to endear him to them.

He leaves his chambers and takes the quickest route through the palace: he has already assessed the defensive capabilities of the building, and memorised its layout while he was doing so. Most of the guards stationed where corridors meet jerk to alert and salute as he passes. One or two bow their heads and murmur as if in prayer, which the Lion chooses to ignore.

The Twilight Garden is a large balcony, three storeys above ground level, aligned towards the setting sun. The Lion enters it through double doors made of squares of frosted glass set into ancient wood. He breathes deeply, inhaling the scents of the night air and the garden's plants, but along with those comes the faintest hint of ceramite, and the slight tang of ozone from the waste heat vents of power armour. The telltale smells of Space Marines.

'Zabriel?' the Lion says, coming to a halt. The immediate comparison that springs to his mind is that his sons are skittish wild animals whom he does not wish to spook. The likeness is not a flattering one, and he tries to forget it.

Zabriel emerges from behind a shrub bearing flowers the size of a woman's fist; they are closed now, but slight remnants of their perfume still lurk in the air. 'Lord, I found three of my brothers. They have all agreed to see you.'

The Lion takes a deep breath. 'I am glad.'

Three new shapes come into view. The first is tall, and walks with a duellist's balance, an impression only heightened by the power sword sheathed at his waist. His power armour is Mark IV, like Zabriel's, although not as battle-damaged. Behind him comes a warrior carrying a plasma gun, wearing a variant of power armour with which the Lion is not as familiar, although much of it is hidden beneath a hooded red surplice. Finally, if a Space Marine could be said to skulk, the one with the bolter at the rear is doing so. He wears an ancient suit of Mark III 'Iron' armour, although despite its age it looks in better condition than the newer versions.

'I failed my father,' the Lion says, the words coming unbidden to his lips. 'I fear I also failed my brothers. I do not wish to fail my sons.'

'Your sentiment is somewhat late,' the rearmost warrior says caustically. The Lion looks over the marks on his armour, placing him.

'Knight-Sergeant Aphkar. It is good to see you again.'

'I cannot say the same,' Aphkar replies. His finger is not far from his boltgun's trigger. The Lion suddenly wonders how wise this meeting was. He is unarmoured, and even a primarch has reason to fear a point-blank blast from a plasma gun.

'I presume Zabriel explained that I placed no onus on you to come here?' the Lion asks. 'I was deceived by Horus for years, while he pretended to be loyal to the Emperor. I was deceived by my brothers, and I was deceived by the powers they served. When I returned to Caliban, it seems that many of us were deceived again. I witnessed Luther wield foul sorcery of the kind I had only seen used by the traitors, but I now believe that many of my sons who were on that planet with him had been deceived as well, and knew nothing of his fall. I am trying to see past deception to the truth, and leave recrimination aside.'

'It is very convenient that you should come to this conclusion now you have returned to an Imperium in ruins, and seek to rebuild it once more,' Aphkar says sarcastically. He removes his helmet, and his dark, distrustful eyes lock on to the Lion's own. 'Where was the benefit of the doubt when you had most of a Legion at your back?'

'I learned to survive on Caliban by acting with certainty, and that was the mindset I took with me into the galaxy,' the Lion says. 'It evidently was not foolproof. Perhaps, burned as I was by betrayal and grief, I reacted too swiftly, and with too much choler. However, Caliban fired on its own brothers, without warning. If you truly believe the fault was mine alone, why are you here?'

'Can this truly be our primarch?' the swordsman interjects, waving the hand that does not rest on the pommel of his blade. 'His height is right, Zabriel, but his visage is much changed, and he is less vengeful than I expected.'

The Lion's temper flares at being spoken of in so casual a

manner, but he keeps a firm grip on it. 'Knight-Commander Kai. I see your humours are unchanged.'

'Thank you,' Kai says, sketching a slight bow.

'That was not necessarily a compliment.'

'That depends on how accurate one's opinion of me is.' Kai draws his powerblade. 'I see you came armed, my lord Lion. I wonder whether your skills have decayed as much as your face has aged.'

'Do not be a fool, Kai!' Zabriel snaps, but Kai simply laughs.

'If he wishes us to follow him, then I wish to test him in the only way that matters. After all, I was always best with a blade in the Legion, save for our lord himself.'

'Corswain might have disagreed,' the red-robed Space Marine rasps.

'Corswain might have given me some trouble, but only on his better days,' Kai replies airily. 'And besides, he is not here.' He activates his blade.

There is no further warning, no salute with his weapon or statement of intent. He simply attacks.

The Lion steps back from the first thrust and draws Fealty on pure instinct, the power field crackling into life just in time to deflect Kai's second swing. The former knight-commander is pressing forwards aggressively and with speed, switching between single- and double-handed grips from moment to moment, his every movement an attack. However boastful Kai's claims about his pre-eminence within the Legion may be, they are not entirely without merit: he is undoubtedly an expert swordsman. The Lion has waded through a host of foes with nothing more than his armoured hands, and slain members of the Traitor Legions and their younger kin on Camarth with Fealty without pause, but none of those foes possessed Kai's ability.

The Lion circles to his right, but Kai's footwork is excellent, and his attacks do not relent. The Lion slaps the point of his opponent's blade aside just before it grazes his chest; Kai has come close to landing a blow three times now, despite his reach disadvantage.

And this is because he is leaving himself open.

The Lion jerks his blade back from the instinctive thrust that would take Kai in the side, and the unnatural movement spoils his balance for a moment. Kai seizes on the opportunity and presses hard, feinting for a strike at the Lion's face and then changing it to a chopping blow which nearly leaves the primarch's right arm truncated below the elbow, and Fealty lying in the grass.

'Do you want me to kill you?' the Lion demands.

'I am attacking you!' Kai shouts. 'Why would you not?'

The Lion makes a grab for Kai with his free hand, and nearly loses it.

'Will you fight me?' Kai roars, swinging for the Lion's head. 'Where is the Emperor's foremost warrior?'

The Lion leans backwards to avoid the blow, knocks aside the next thrust that comes for his belly, and lashes out with a kick.

His bare foot connects flush on Kai's chestplate, and knocks the former knight-commander backwards through the air for some ten feet. Kai lands in the grass with a thud, but he is back on his feet within a moment, his sword still in his hand. Now, however, the Lion is moving into the attack.

He does not aim for Kai's body or head, for he suspects that his son will still not be guarding himself. Instead, his next strike is for Kai's weapon. The powerblade is knocked to one side. Kai manages to hold onto his sword, but the next blow knocks it from his hand completely, and the Lion brings Fealty's point up to rest a finger's breadth from Kai's gorget.

'Do not test me again,' the Lion growls. Kai kneels and removes his helm, but the face so revealed is smiling.

'Forgive me, lord. Words of reconciliation are easy to utter, but little reveals the spirit like swordplay. You could have killed me, but did not. If your intentions are to safeguard this world, and others, then I pledge my blade to you once again.'

'What if I *had* killed you?' the Lion demands.

'Then my companions would have known that your words were empty,' Kai says.

The Lion snorts. He remembers Knight-Commander Kai as a braggart, about whom it was whispered more than once that he might better belong in the Emperor's Children, but also as a warrior who would never ask anything of others that he was not willing to attempt himself.

'And if you had killed me?' he asks.

'Then he would have died,' says the red-robed Space Marine, from where he, Aphkar, and Zabriel had been watching the combat. He too goes to one knee when the Lion looks at him, and bows his head. 'I am Lohoc, my lord, and I am sworn to your service now as I was then. There is no excuse for our actions, long ago though they now were, and I wish only for the opportunity to redeem myself.'

The Lion frowns. 'I thank you, but I cannot place you, Lohoc. Will you remove your helm?'

'Forgive me, my lord, but I will not.'

The Lion glances at Kai, who shrugs. 'Aphkar and I found the Red Whisper two years ago, and we have never once seen his face. He eats alone.'

'In the building in which I found you?' Zabriel asks incredulously. 'There was barely room for the three of you in there as it was.'

'My brothers have been most accommodating about my... preferences,' Lohoc rasps, his head still bowed.

The Lion deactivates Fealty and sheathes it. 'Kai, Aphkar. You have known him for two years? And in that time he has given you no cause to doubt him?'

'It is hard enough to move around without attracting attention,' Aphkar says. 'Lohoc's preferences made that even more difficult, to the point that Kai and I needed to take almost all responsibility for sourcing supplies, interacting with others, and so on. He has undoubtedly made our lives harder, but doubt him? No. He has saved our lives before now.'

'He shot down that great xenos beast that was about to gut you on Llarraf Beta,' Kai agreed. 'Burned its head clean off.'

'It was going to gut *us*, Kai.'

'I was ready to parry its talons with my blade,' Kai said with a sniff, 'and then disembowel it in turn. It is just that as fast as I am, a plasma bolt is faster.'

'And how were you intending to recall your blade to your hand from where the beast had knocked it, ten paces away from you?' the Red Whisper asks, still with his head bowed.

Kai smiles. Even Aphkar does not look as sullen as he did. The Lion realises that this is a dynamic the three of them have forged over their time together: Kai making exaggerated boasts that even he does not believe, specifically so that Aphkar can puncture his pomposity, while Lohoc interjects here and there. It is a far cry from their days in the Legion, but they no longer have a Legion. For a soldier trained into decades or centuries of service within a command structure, even a structure as multifaceted and fluid as that of the Dark Angels, losing it was like losing a part of themselves. They had to remake that part in order to survive.

The First Legion as it was will never exist again. Adaption is critical.

'I will not rule,' the Lion says. 'I have no wish to. I will command those who are willing to be commanded, and I will lead those who will follow. I know Kai, and he has said his piece. Lohoc has also given me his answer, and with your recommendations, I will accept him. What of you, Aphkar?'

Aphkar's jaw works for a moment, but he finally mag-clamps his bolter to his thigh, and straightens. 'You will give the same opportunity to any of our other brothers whom we might encounter?'

'If they are corrupted, I will not stay my hand,' the Lion says firmly. 'But I will not make the same mistake I did on Caliban, and assume corruption without proof.'

'Then you will be out of step with the Imperium,' Zabriel remarks.

'We are *all* out of step with the Imperium,' the Lion says. 'Determining the exact nature of those differences, and the reconciliation of them, is for a time when humanity is not threatened by extinction.' He raises an eyebrow. 'Aphkar?'

Aphkar still hesitates, but when he does move, he moves swiftly. He drops to one knee quicker than either of his brothers, as though finally succumbing to a heavy weight; or, perhaps, as though long-held tension has finally been released.

'If you are not who we thought you were, then we were fools,' he says, his voice choked. 'Fools who fired on their own battle-brothers for no reason.'

'Say not for no reason,' the Lion says. He tries to keep his tone neutral, for condescension could be as counterproductive as anger. 'Say that you were deceived, as was I, and that you now have the opportunity to atone for whatever mistakes you feel you made – beside me, instead of from the shadows.'

Aphkar nods. 'I will not spurn this opportunity.'

The Lion takes a deep breath of the night air, savouring the smell of the plants. They are a welcome reminder of the forests of his home, without any of the threat.

'Come with me, my sons. We have a campaign to plan.'

XVIII

Reality shimmered and wavered, and the fleet slipped out of the darkness between the stars and into the Avalus System like a shoal of ocean predators.

It was not a uniform force. The Furious-class grand cruiser *Lord of Dominion* was the centrepiece, a blood-soaked, crenellated beast of dark majesty around which the rest of the ships were arrayed, like outsized planets circling a star on an orrery of ancient Terra: three Hades-class heavy cruisers, the *Terrorlight*, the *Fane of Ancients*, and the *Downfall*; two Styx class, the *Blood Oath* and the *Crowbane*; two Devastation-class cruisers, the *Overwhelming* and the *Shroud*; no fewer than four of the fast, heavily armed Slaughter-class cruisers, the *Ash'katon*, the *Doleful*, and twin vessels the *Merciless* and the *Fearless*, built in the shipyards of Selethan and which turned traitor on the same day; the *Stormbreak* and the *Defiling Gaze*, both Hellbringer class; a single Gothic class, the *Longblade*; the former Angels of Vigilance strike cruiser *Dread Sentinel*, already consecrated to new gods; and innumerable smaller light cruisers and escorts.

And, at the rear, the Carnage-class cruiser *Eye of Malevolence.*

The holo-projector on the bridge of the *Eye of Malevolence* buzzed. Baelor tapped the activation rune and it sputtered into life, motes of light combining into the figure of Varkan the Red. The Champion of Khorne was addressing the entire fleet with a ferocious glower, and wiped a strand of drool from his lower lip with his ceramite gauntlet.

'Avalus has been clinging on,' he growled, his voice thick with bloodlust. *'We let it survive because there were other, more tempting targets, but that has changed. Avalus thinks it can shout defiance into the warp without consequence. We are here to show them how wrong they are. Burn hard for the main planet, and destroy anything in your way! One exception only – if the Imperial fools are correct, and the Lion is somehow with them, then Lord Seraphax wants him alive. If he is on a ship then it is to be boarded, not destroyed. If he is in a complex on the planet then you are to land, not bombard. Otherwise...'*

He smiled, showing his metal teeth, blackened and corroded by the acidic qualities of his spittle, but still sharp.

'Let the blood flow.'

The glowing figure of Varkan jabbed at something out of view of the vid-imager capturing his likeness and broadcasting it, and the display flickered, but remained active. When the Khornate warlord next looked up, his eyes were for Baelor alone.

'Baelor.'

'Varkan,' Baelor acknowledged. He could see plasma drives flaring into life ahead of him, as the fleet answered its blood-thirsty master's call to battle. 'That was quite an impressive speech. You managed full sentences.'

Varkan bared his teeth again, this time with no semblance of a smile. *'Seraphax still tolerates you, Imposter, but your time runs short. Why else was I able to give you the role of rearguard without the Lord Sorcerer overruling me? He knows you are weak and unreliable, and not even his brotherly affection for you will keep you intact for much longer.'*

'I seem to recall that it was not my skull that was going to be split, had Seraphax not intervened on the *Blade of Truth*,' Baelor said, and Varkan's cheek twitched at the memory. 'Besides, I am sure that your headlong rush will give the *Eye* ample opportunity to engage the enemy when they encircle us.'

'Then let us hope your ship remembers how to fight,' Varkan snarled, and ended his broadcast.

Baelor sighed, and turned to Canticallax Dimora. 'Engage the plasma drives, and keep pace with the fleet. I want sensors at full. Varkan still retains some tactical awareness and low cunning when it comes to a frontal assault, but he will not pay any mind to enemy elements who evade the battle group's thrust, and he will rage at any who break formation to engage them. We may need to be busier than I would like.'

'You appear unconcerned about his assessment of your character,' Dimora observed. The deck beneath Baelor thrummed as she fed power to the main drives, and they began to move towards the faint, distant orb that was the world of Avalus. 'It is my observation that members of the Astartes such as yourself ordinarily place great and disproportionate worth on concepts such as honour. To be assigned to the rearguard, although statistically and tactically a position of comparative importance with regard to the welfare of a group, is often seen as a mark of shame.'

Baelor snorted. 'Varkan's opinion of me is inconsequential. We are assigned to the rearguard because that is where Seraphax wants me, and he knew that if he gave Varkan the command then that is where he would place me. The success or otherwise of the coming battle is not what is important. The only thing that matters, and my purpose in this company, is verifying whether the Lion is truly here. If he is not, then Avalus will fall, and Varkan will glut himself on its blood.'

'And if he is?'

Baelor took in the spread of the fleet on his auspexes, the sheer might of it. Avalus had been isolated for a long time, holding out against raids and acquitting itself well with its limited and dwindling resources, but the size of Varkan's battle group would surely be enough to overwhelm what remained.

Unless...

'If he *is* here,' Baelor said, feeling his gut twist as he gave voice to the possibility, 'then things are about to get very interesting.'

XIX

There is no subtlety about the Chaos fleet, but something does not have to be subtle to be dangerous. It is a mailed fist punching towards Avalus with speed and ferocity, a haymaker that will cause devastation if it lands flush. And planets, as the Lion knows very well, are poor at dodging.

'Sixteen capital ships,' breathes Admiral Torral Derrigan, staring at the blizzard of icons which fills the tactical hololith on the bridge of the *Lunar Knight*, the Armageddon-class battle cruiser that anchors the Avalus fleet. 'Perhaps two hundred vessels in total–'

'One hundred and eighty-four,' the Lion corrects him. He was borne to the fleet's flagship by shuttle as soon as the first sensor returns came in.

'We are outnumbered two to one overall, and three to one at capital level,' the admiral says heavily. 'Lord Lion, I cannot see a path to victory in this engagement.'

'Would you surrender?' the Lion asks, and the admiral glares at him until he remembers himself.

'Never, my lord. Quite apart from the shame, better a clean death in battle than to be taken prisoner by these monsters.'

'Would you flee, then?'

Derrigan swallows. 'In times past, perhaps, my lord. Tactical doctrine cautions a senior officer against committing their forces to a battle that cannot be won, if those forces may regroup with other elements and return to exact vengeance. But in these times, the warp is more treacherous than ever for us, while our enemies' – he gestures at the hololith – 'are able to emerge from it in battle order. Were we to flee, we might lose half our strength or more, to no purpose. At least in realspace we only have one enemy to fight.'

'So we fight,' the Lion says, with satisfaction. 'We fight to defend the planet and the system, and those who live within it. And if our only recourse is to fight, then the likelihood of victory is irrelevant, is it not?'

Admiral Derrigan frowns, but then his face clears into an expression of slightly baffled agreement. 'I... suppose so, my lord.'

'Vox-officer,' the Lion says, looking up from the hololith. The man so addressed, a distinguished veteran to have such a role on the fleet's flagship, looks petrified at being addressed by the black-armoured giant out of legend, but manages a salute.

'Y-yes, my lord?'

'Broadcast to all the ships in our fleet,' the Lion orders. 'For full dissemination. I want everyone aboard to hear, not just the bridge crews.'

The vox-officer's nerves do not impede his execution of his duties; he adjusts the settings of his console appropriately, and sits back. 'So marked, my lord. The vox is yours.'

The Lion takes a breath.

'Defenders of Avalus. I am Lion El'Jonson, primarch of the

Dark Angels and son of the Emperor. We face an enemy force intent on destruction – not only of this fleet, and this planet, but whatever remains of the Imperium, and humanity as a whole. I will not deny that the odds appear to be against us in this fight, but as I saw when the people of Camarth rose up and overthrew the invaders who thought they had conquered that world, appearances can be deceiving. The forces arrayed against us are vicious, and they are merciless, but they are often without discipline or structure. They do not fight for each other. Not as we must.

'As individuals, any one of us would fail. If we remember that we are part of something greater, if we refuse to give in to fear and despair, and if we perform our duties swiftly and efficiently, then we can frustrate and infuriate our foes, and force them into mistakes – mistakes for which we will make them pay in blood. I cannot promise you that our struggle will lead to victory, only that our victory will not be achieved without struggle.'

The Lion looks up and out of the main viewing gallery of the *Lunar Knight*, towards where he knows the Chaos fleet to be. It is still only a star-speckled darkness even to his eyes, with nothing to betray the force bearing down on them.

'But I did not return after ten thousand years to fail in the task I have set myself. I want each and every one of you, from captain to bondsperson, to know that I will give my life in defence of your world, if that is what it takes. However, I do not believe that my father guided me to you simply in order to die. So crew your stations, ready the weapons, and prepare to strike down these traitors and heretics for Avalus, for the Imperium, and for the Emperor Himself!'

There is a moment of silence across the bridge. Then:

'THE LION!'

'THE LION!'

'THE LION!'

The vox erupts with shouts – first from dozens of throats on bridges, but then the volume increases as they are joined by other relay stations throughout the ships of the fleet, when anyone within range of a vox-unit sets it to broadcast. Within a matter of seconds, thousands of voices are bellowing their defiance and allegiance into the void, and the vox-speakers begin to crackle and overload.

The Lion gestures, and the vox-officer cuts it off. The quiet which takes its place on the bridge of the *Lunar Knight* feel empty by comparison, but it is an expectant emptiness, one charged with weight and determination, and in which the crew resume their duties with renewed purpose.

'Do you really believe the Emperor guided you here?' Zabriel asks the Lion quietly.

'Something did,' the Lion replies, just as softly, 'and something which I do not believe has malicious intent. I do not think my father a god, as these people do, but I cannot dispute His power. Did He not maintain the Astronomican for ten thousand years, a beacon for all humanity's travellers, even if it cannot now be seen by us? His mastery of warpcraft is unparalleled by any mortal being. If anyone was capable of reaching out and guiding me here, then it is Him.'

'And such a statement can boost the morale of our fleet,' Zabriel adds. The Lion sighs.

'In such circumstances, I must use all the tools at my disposal. Matters of theology can wait.' The Lion has so far refused to meet with Avalus' representatives of the Ecclesiarchy, much to their dismay.

'You are going to have to deal with the priests at some point,' Zabriel says, as though reading his thoughts. All such figures in authority on Camarth had been killed, either in the initial attack or hunted down and executed by the Ten Thousand Eyes as an object lesson, and after hearing Zabriel's tales, the Lion privately considered this a mercy. 'The Imperial creed is too powerful to ignore for long.'

'One battle at a time, my son,' the Lion says, returning his attention to the tactical hololiths and starting to mentally draw up his plan. 'One battle at a time.'

XX

The Chaos fleet did not slow, alter course, or display any sign of strategy other than a brutal directness. They were approaching Avalus from the nightside, which, by accident or design, allowed them to head straight for Xerxe. The capital was protected by two Gaugamela-class star forts locked in geostationary orbit above it, but they were in no way sufficient to fight off a force of that magnitude. Crude though the assault was, it gave us two bleak options: to hold position and meet their force head-on; or to evade their superior strength, but thereby let them have a free run at the capital city.

I had taken part in such planetary assaults before, as of course had the Lion. We both knew the devastation that would ensue if the traitors were allowed to make it that far. They might not be a Space Marine Legion, with the discipline and equipment we had at the height of the Great Crusade, but the foul powers they worshipped could make them just as destructive, and even more indiscriminate. Our options were an illusion; there was only one choice the Lion could make.

The fleet drew up into a battle order of three spheres, each one centred around two of our capital ships, with the planet and the star forts at our backs. The *Lunar Knight* was central, along with the Dominator class *Adamantine Will*; the starboard wing was taken by the two Lunar classes *Lady Varin* and *Peregrine*, and the port wing anchored by the Dictator class *Righteous Wrath* and the Gothic class *Traitor's Bane*. We were spread out across a wider front than the close-knit Chaos fleet, with our wings advanced, in order to do as much damage as we could from both sides, but had sacrificed height for width. The traitors, in contrast, were a loosely spherical block, smaller escorts surrounding the capital ships in an ugly fist which could easily punch through our middle.

'Captain Seryan,' the Lion said into the vox. 'Make your presence known.'

Void combat can take place over huge distances. Ships fire torpedoes to disrupt their enemies' movements as much as they seek to land significant strikes with them. Weapons batteries fire over hundreds of miles, and even the supra-focused energy blasts of lances can be unleashed when an enemy ship is a mere speck that must be targeted by auspex. However, some armaments stretched the ranges still farther.

The nova cannon on the *Adamantine Will* pulsed into action, and the distant spark of an explosion flowered instantaneously in the midst of the enemy fleet. Nova cannons fired their enormous projectiles at almost the speed of light, and far outranged any other conventional weapon. It would be minutes before the traitors could return fire.

'Our enemy has already shown his eagerness to close with us,' the Lion remarked. 'I do not think he will appreciate his current inability to fight back.'

'The enemy fleet is starting to disperse, my lord,' I said, for the

Lion had charged me with command of the auspex station in the place of its normal mortal crewer, searching for any advantage he could get in the fight. The icons denoting our enemies were gradually breaking apart, as each captain decided that the explosive power of a nova cannon was a good reason to put some distance between themselves and their comrades.

'*Adamantine Will*, continue firing!' the Lion ordered. 'Priority targets. I want as much damage to their largest vessels as possible before we start exchanging in earnest. All other ships, let us corral them – concentrate torpedo fire on these vectors.' He highlighted sections of the hololith to be broadcast to the other captains, although I heard a muffled curse from him as the display refused to obey him momentarily. The Lion had accepted that the technology on a planet recently retaken from the rule of Chaos would be patchy and unresponsive, but he had expressed dismay when he found similar issues prevalent on warships, and I could tell he missed the clinical efficiency of the *Invincible Reason*, back in the days of the Great Crusade.

The *Lunar Knight* shuddered as gigantic warheads streaked away into the inky blackness. Our torpedoes were not aimed at the central mass of enemy ships, but their surroundings, giving the traitors a choice of their own: to stay clumped up and risk the nova cannon, or to veer off into the path of death. For their part, the Chaos ships were largely unequipped with such munitions, focusing instead on a higher concentration of weapons batteries and lances. Of course, we could not cover all areas with our barrages, but even that meant our enemies' next movements were more predictable. We could squeeze them into certain lanes of fire that would concentrate them for our other weapons, and leave ourselves less vulnerable to theirs.

'Fire from the Furious class, reading as *Lord of Dominion*,' I reported, as alerts flashed up.

'We are surely still too distant!' Admiral Derrigan said, although I could hear the uncertainty in his voice. However, this was not the fear of a weak-willed man, but the understandable alarm of a warrior who well knew that the forces of the Ruinous Powers could produce horrendous surprises.

'They appear to be firing at their own ships,' I said, our sensors picking up the telltale flares and debris showers. It was tempting to find such infighting reassuring, but much like the admiral, I distrusted everything about the enemy.

'Our adversary attempts to restore what he considers to be the correct order of battle through the only means he knows,' the Lion said with some satisfaction. 'To whit, brute force.'

'He wants his own ships to fly straight down the throat of our nova cannon?' Derrigan asked incredulously.

'Some factions of our enemy view any attempt to minimise casualties as the most heinous cowardice, worthy of immediate execution,' the Lion said. 'It appears that faction is in command here, which will undoubtedly provide its own challenges, but also its own opportunities.'

The *Adamantine Will* fired again, and although the shot did not strike the *Lord of Dominion*, a pair of its escorts flared and died in the resulting massive explosion. The next shot impacted on a vessel I identified as the *Fane of Ancients*; the mighty cruiser was not disabled, but it slowed, and began to list downwards and to starboard.

'Another volley, high and low,' the Lion commanded, highlighting more sections of the hololith. The fleet had limited supplies of all ammunition, including torpedoes, but conserving it would be pointless if there was nothing left to fire it. Every captain of the Avalus fleet believed that the Lion was best equipped to ensure the system's survival, and so they did as they were bid.

'Enemy are launching fighters,' I said, then frowned at the display. 'Or possibly not.'

'Give me visual,' the Lion ordered, and the hololith flickered as the tactical display was replaced by grainy images captured by the *Lunar Knight*'s picters at extreme range. I peered closely at it, although I was no expert in void warfare. There were swarms of dots pouring out of the shadowy smudges in starship hulls that signified launch bays, which looked normal enough. However...

'There,' I said, pointing at a cluster of shapes that looked to be dropping from a ship's keel, although of course such concepts as 'up' and 'down' were arbitrary until we were in the gravity well of a planet. 'Where are they coming from?'

'Can we magnify further?' the Lion asked. A sensor ensign managed to coax a slightly higher resolution from the ancient machinery, and the pict-feed enlarged again, just sufficient to get an idea of the outline of the things I had seen. There was a suggestion of fanged maws on protruding necks, sharp talons, and jagged wings that glinted brassily in the dim light reflected off distant stars and from nearby running lights.

'Beast's blood,' the Lion breathed, falling back on an invective of ancient Caliban. 'What manner of monstrosities are they?'

'Daemon engines, riding through the void on the ships' underbellies,' I answered him. 'I believe the Imperium designates them as Heldrakes.'

'Is there nothing in this millennium which is not worse than in the one I left?' the Lion muttered. I could tell that the sight of the creature-machines had shaken him with their casual reminder of the warp's corruptive power. 'Do they die, at least?'

'I saw one shot down once,' I said, my memory throwing up a two-centuries-old image of something black and brass screaming out of the sky in a cloud of flame, smoke, and screeching pain. 'That was on a planet coming under attack, rather than ship-to-ship combat, but the Hydra battery accounted for the thing well enough.'

The foremost ships of the Chaos fleet were coming into range of their forward-mounted guns, mainly lance weaponry. Now the advantage shifted to them, for other than our torpedoes we had little that could match them at this distance.

The *Adamantine Will* fired again, and a cruiser identified on the hololith as the *Blood Oath* flared and died – a lucky shot, perhaps, or the result of poor maintenance of shields or the superstructure in general, characteristic of heretic forces. The *Lunar Knight* added its prow lances to the fray, coupled with our escorts and lighter cruisers which had surged forward to meet the enemy's outriders and so closed the range, but this was where the defenders of Avalus were going to be outmatched. Our void shields began to shimmer with unhealthy rainbow colours as some of the incoming rain of fire splashed onto us.

'All ahead full,' the Lion ordered over the vox, and the idling plasma drives of the defensive fleet roared into life.

It was simple, in one respect: if the enemy outranges you, close distance to engage. The Chaos fleet had done the same when we were peppering them with shots from the *Adamantine Will*'s nova cannon and our torpedo salvos. We would minimise the time for which we were at a disadvantage by closing in. But unlike the traitors, who were flying according to little ascertainable strategy, the Lion was coordinating our defence. A navigation plan appeared on the bridge of every capital ship and escort aside from the *Adamantine Will*, plunging into the gaps in what passed for our enemy's formation.

It was aggressive and direct, and unpredictable. Faced with a larger force intent on closing with us, most of our capital ships should have presented their flanks to the enemy and prepared broadsides. We would have suffered more hits, thanks to our side-on profile, but when the enemy closed we would, if we had sufficient craft left, have been able to match them gun for gun; at least until they drew abeam, at which point their flank weapons would have come into play.

Instead, the Lion had us advance. I must admit that I switched my glances between the auspex and the viewing ports frequently, expecting at any moment to see the flare of our void shields failing, followed immediately by the rapidly expanding shape of a warhead or the instantaneous brightness of a lance beam which would spell my death, but it appeared that our tactic had caught the enemy off guard. Having previously been faced with a passive defence that kept its distance, they were unprepared for this new response, and their guns were overshooting us.

'All crew, brace!' Admiral Derrigan bellowed, as the *Lunar Knight*'s powerful engines began to carry us abeam of the first Chaos vessels. 'Batteries and lances fire at will, dorsal lance concentrate fire to starboard!'

The high and low torpedo volleys the Lion had ordered had flattened the shape of the Chaos fleet, forcing their ships to bunch up to avoid the munitions' flight paths. Now we thrust ourselves into their midst, and while we had targets on both sides, most enemy ships would only be able to use their weapons on one flank lest they hit an ally, which was now confounding their firing solutions. In fact, some would be unable to draw a bead on our ships at all. In terms of minimising what was never going to have been less than an extremely punishing exchange for us, it was the best we could hope for.

'*Righteous Wrath* reports Starhawk bombers are away!' the vox-officer called. Those tiny attack craft punched above their weight when delivering their payloads to capital ships, and would menace any enemy cruiser unable to defend itself properly. Now, however, we were coming into the angle to fire upon our enemies, which meant, of course, that they could fire upon us in turn.

The *Lunar Knight* shuddered and slowed as it opened fire. The Lion had instructed us to move directly between two Slaughter-class vessels, the *Merciless* and the *Fearless*, which if anything out-gunned us, and the darkness of the void lit up as their brutal armaments began to test our shields. In turn, I saw explosions from our weapons along their flanks, and the pulsing brightness of our lances attempting to pierce their shields and cut deep into their hulls.

Warning klaxons blared as the ship's systems registered the punishment it was taking, an electronic hooting ruthlessly silenced by Admiral Derrigan as he continued barking orders and receiving a stream of updates from the bridge crew: power levels, shield levels, remaining armaments…

'Shields failing!' someone shouted.

'Dive!' the Lion bellowed.

A battle cruiser the size of the *Lunar Knight* is not built for quick manoeuvring, but the crew was spurred to new efforts by the presence of the Lion, and our prow began to tilt downwards. The Slaughters were slow to react, and as we began to sink beneath the plane of our previous exchange, some of their fire flew above our dorsal spine and hit each other. The *Merciless*, to our starboard, had taken the brunt of our fire thanks to the contribution of our dorsal lance, and these shots from its sister ship knocked out its last void shields.

'Roll to port, maintain starboard fire!' the Lion ordered. The vessel began to obey him, and our starboard weapons raked the belly of the *Merciless*, but in doing so we took our port weapons beyond the angle of elevation at which they could hit the *Fearless*, which was now starting to roll in turn in order to pursue us with its batteries before we passed to aft and the exchange was over. I held my breath, waiting to see if the Lion's gambit had worked.

A trio of Dauntless-class light cruisers swept in to take advantage of the now unshielded *Merciless*, and cut it to pieces with their disproportionately powerful forward lance armaments, although the *Merciless* took one of them with it. However, that was not the true gamble. That came up when, just as its guns began to clip us once more, the *Fearless* was torn apart in an eruption of sheared metal and oxygen fire.

'There he is,' the Lion said, a predator's smile on his face.

Beyond the wreckage of the Slaughter-class cruiser was the hulking shape of the *Lord of Dominion*, its port weapons blazing. Its captain, caught up in bloodlust and infuriated by the fact that his own ships on either side were preventing him from engaging any of ours thanks to the Lion's carefully planned attack routes, had taken matters into his own hands and simply eliminated what his violence-obsessed brain viewed to be a problem.

'My lord, how could you know the traitor would turn on his own forces?' Admiral Derrigan demanded.

'You never met Angron, did you?' the Lion murmured absentmindedly. I expected Derrigan to blanch, or make the sign of the aquila and call on the Emperor for deliverance, but he simply looked blank. Even four centuries after returning to the galaxy, I still sometimes forgot how little the Imperium's citizens knew of their own history, let alone those forces that sought to destroy them.

However, now we had a new problem. The sheer weight of fire from the *Lord of Dominion* was punching through the remains of the *Fearless*, and beginning to rake us. We had barely survived our exchanges with the two Slaughter-class vessels; the Furious-class grand cruiser would annihilate us in a straight fight.

'Engines to full!' the Lion ordered, and the *Lunar Knight* responded, accelerating away from the engagement. However, it was not quick enough.

'Shields down!' came the shout, just as a new and more insistent alarm began wailing. A moment later I felt thunder roll through the *Knight*'s superstructure, and our forward momentum juddered.

'Engines hit!'

'Hull breaches in sections Delta and Epsilon, decks three and four...'

The Lion said nothing, but simply watched the sputtering hololith. After another moment, the icon of the *Lunar Knight* passed out of the cone of the *Lord of Dominion*'s projected firing arcs. We had escaped that fate, for the moment at least, and were passing through the rear of the Chaos fleet.

'Carnage class dead ahead!' I reported, frowning at it even as I did so. This ship was showing no intention of engaging, despite being under power; it was almost as though it was simply observing the battle.

'Torpedoes!' Admiral Derrigan responded. 'Clear the way!'

The rest of our task force was emerging along with us, or at least what remained of it. We had lost the *Peregrine* and the *Righteous Wrath*, leaving no refuge for the latter's squadrons of fighters and bombers, currently duelling with traitor craft of similar size, design, and function. The *Traitor's Bane* was limping, too, although the read-outs suggested that its lances had done murderous work close-in. We had lost perhaps half of our light cruisers and escorts, but we had punched above our weight: nearly half of the Chaos fleet was on fire too, or cut apart, or floating without power or weaponry.

'Come about,' the Lion ordered. 'And target that Carnage class as we do so.'

The Chaos fleet had taken a mauling, but it had, in theory at least, achieved its objective: it was past us now, and it could commence planetfall if it so wished. Even with the Lion's leadership, we would never have been able to stop it through force of arms. The *Adamantine Will,* still gamely firing away at point-blank range with its nova cannon and destroying a pair of Idolator-class raiders even as it was savaged from both sides by larger warships, was the only ship left between the traitors and the planet. The twin star forts opened up with their lance batteries as the first heretic vessels came into range, but even the greatly reduced Chaos fleet would be able to bring them down.

However, the Chaos fleet did not press on; or at least, not all of it did. The two Hellbringers were advancing into range to duel with the star forts, but most of their companions did not support them. Instead, led by the *Lord of Dominion*, they began to turn.

The Lion nodded. 'He cannot ignore our bloodying of his nose. Only our total destruction will satisfy him now. He will seek to kill every ship, and in doing so will allow the star forts to engage his landers piecemeal.'

Sure enough, the Hellbringers had the vessels and landing craft to rain havoc on the planet once established in orbit, but they seemed to have only just realised that they were going to be taking the Gaugamelas on more or less alone. That was a fight they could not win, and I saw the Chaos fleet's best methods of effecting a quick landing start to come apart under relentless fire from the star forts.

'Prepare remaining torpedoes,' the Lion ordered all ships. 'Form up on the *Lunar Knight*, and–'

A glyph flashed up an alert on the auspex, and I drew my bolt pistols even as I shouted my warning.

'Teleport flare from the *Lord of Dominion*!'

We were at extreme range for effective teleporting, at least as I understood it, which admittedly was not well. However, that did not necessarily mean anything. The forces of Chaos were often adept at using the warp in ways the Imperium could not predict; and besides, given the bloodthirsty nature we had already seen demonstrated by their commander, it was not out of the question that they might try such a tactic even if there was a low chance of success.

'Emergence flare location?' the Lion snapped, drawing Fealty from its scabbard and activating it with one hand, and locking his helm into place with the other, but the air in the main crew well of the *Lunar Knight*'s bridge was already shimmering with telltale distortion.

I aimed my pistols and activated my vox to speak two words. 'Bridge! Now!'

Then the shimmering resolved into dark shapes, and between one breath and the next the distortion cleared entirely to be replaced by six huge warriors in armour of blood red and brass.

Terminators.

XXI

'Seraphax can burn! If the Lion's here, I want his head!' roars the apparent leader of the new arrivals. He is a monster, bloated by the foul powers of Chaos in his Terminator armour so that he near rivals a primarch in size, and is surrounded by other warriors nearly as massive, each one armed with a brutal collection of close-combat weapons. The Lion sees chainaxes there, and lightning claws, and power fists. The leader clutches a power sword in his right hand, while his left is enveloped in a huge powered glove from which the toothed tongue of a chainfist protrudes, already powering up to speed with a bone-jarring whine that is nearly a weapon in its own right.

'Then come and take it, if you can!' the Lion shouts, striding to the rail and looking down at them. His challenge is not mere theatricality; the bridge crew are scattering away from the Terminators, and with good reason, since they could no more fight them than they could a supernova. The Lion can see the minuscule twitches in the warriors' limbs as their instincts press them to pursue and butcher the fleeing humans. He has to keep their attention on him.

He raises his sidearm, and opens fire.

Marshal Haraj presented it to the Lion as a gift: the Arma Luminis, a plasma weapon of ancient and unknown origin, which local myth has that the Emperor left on Avalus at some unspecified point in the past. There is no other evidence that the Master of Mankind ever visited the planet, but the Avalusians are so convinced of this divine legacy that the weapon has been stored in a stasis chamber in the governor's palace for as long as any records of it exist. One thing that is undeniably true is that it does not appear to be sized for a mortal, for it fits the Lion's hand like a pistol.

The other undeniably true thing about it is that it still works.

The Arma Luminis spits a bolt of energy as bright as the sun straight at the Chaos lord. However, instead of vaporising ceramite and punching into the flesh and bone beneath, the shot is enveloped and consumed by a crackling darkness that disappears as quickly as it materialises. The sigil emblazoned on the Chaos lord's chest, a crude and blocky thing that weeps what looks like blood, flares with an ugly light that is echoed by other runes which flash into existence across his armour. The Lion's skin prickles, and thoughts of his blade biting into flesh rise unbidden in his mind.

'BLOOD FOR THE BLOOD GOD!' howls the Chaos lord, and he and his bodyguard rush for the stairs that will carry them up to the command deck where the Lion stands.

'Admiral! Clear the bridge!' the Lion snarls, but Derrigan is already moving and ushering other crew members ahead of him. There is bravery, and then there is foolishness, and the admiral is no fool.

'Zabriel, hold the door!' the Lion orders as he moves towards the stairs and holsters the Arma Luminis. Zabriel says something in response, but the Lion does not hear the words. He is filled with revulsion and fury at the sight of the interlopers, and with a mighty leap he launches himself clean across the guard rails, over the crew well beneath, and into the foremost Terminator before it is halfway up the stairs.

Strong though a Space Marine is, and enhanced in both power and mass by the bulk of Terminator armour though these warriors are, the sheer weight and speed and fury of a primarch is too much. The impact sends them sprawling back downwards, and the Lion with them. He recovers his feet with a roar of rage and seizes Fealty in a double-handed grip, then drives it into the neck joint of the nearest Terminator, who is still on his back. The energised blade, propelled by a primarch's muscles, slides through the weak armour like a serpent through wet grass and bites into the Terminator's throat, and on into the spinal column. The heretic first stiffens, then goes limp, and his blood flash-burns into ash as it tries to ooze out around the wound that Fealty has inflicted.

A power fist thunders into the Lion's side with a crackling discharge of energy that splinters ceramite. The Lion is sent stumbling by the blow, leaving Fealty wedged in the neck of the fallen heretic, and the sudden stab of agony informs him that his armour is not the only thing to be damaged; some of his ribs are surely cracked, if not outright broken. The sharp clarity of his pain washes away the rage which grips him, and he turns to face the traitors with grim understanding. The foul deity they worship hungers for blood, and the aura they project managed to taint even his perceptions for a moment.

The Terminators thunder forwards with weapons raised, their battle cries turned into bloodcurdling hymns of slaughter by the distortion of their vox-grilles. The Lion's instinct is to spring to meet them and then plough through them, breaking them apart with nothing but his hands, but he restrains the impulse. He might have been able to do that in times past, even against foes like these, but this is a different age, and he is already wounded. He was never careless, but now more than ever he cannot afford to trust to his strength and vitality alone. His victory, and indeed perhaps his survival, will come down to one thing.

Focus.

Roboute Guilliman was able to focus on dozens of things at once and give them attention in excess of what most mortal minds could achieve dealing with just one such subject. It was what made him such a good logistician, and while the Lion might not have a great many compliments ready for his brother, the Lord of Ultramar's organisational skills could not be denied: many of the Ultramarines' successes came down to simply never encountering a situation for which they were not prepared. Guilliman himself had only ever been an adequate combatant in person, however; at least so far as their brotherhood went. The Lion has sometimes wondered if that was because Roboute was never able to properly give his full attention to *anything*.

In contrast, the Lion has always viewed that extraneous details are what subordinates are for. A single focus, a task from which his mind will not deviate until it is resolved to his satisfaction: this is second nature to him. He is aware that this has made him seem cold and detached to others, at times, but that too is an extraneous detail.

Whatever else the Emperor made His sons, He made them resilient. The Lion banishes the pain in his side with an effort of will, and flows into battle.

He already knows that the Terminators can wound him if they land a blow, but they are slow and cumbersome, and their momentum can be used against them. The Lion kicks out at the first one, armed with twin chainaxes; not at the face or the chest, but at the right knee. The impact jars the Chaos worshipper's leg backwards just as he is about to plant on it, and even the auto-balancers built into the weighty suit are unable to properly compensate. The Terminator stumbles over onto his front, the Lion sidesteps to his left to avoid the mass of clattering ceramite, and the second, wielding a chainaxe of his own as well as the power fist which has splintered the Lion's armour, falls over the first.

The third combatant is the Chaos lord himself. He pulls up short of his fallen warriors and lunges for the Lion with his chainfist, emitting a bloodthirsty growl as he does so. He favours his left hand, clearly his dominant one: the better blow would have been a thrust with his power sword, since the Lion is moving towards that side of him. Instead, the chainfist strike is chasing the Lion, and the Lord of the First is already reacting to it.

The Chaos lord's swing appears to be caught in a grav-field, given how slowly it is moving to the Lion's vision. He catches the inside of the traitor's left arm at the elbow with his right hand and slams his left into the Chaos lord's chest, then uses this leverage and his enemy's unbalanced attack to hoist him off his feet and spin him around, dumping him into a command terminal that crumples as the heretic hits it. He will be unharmed within his armour, and only out of the fight for a matter of seconds while he recovers his feet, but seconds are crucial.

Another Terminator attacks, this one with a diagonal downward slash of his chainaxe. The Lion catches the weapon by the haft, just above where the Terminator's hand grips it, and wrenches it out of the warrior's grasp in the same motion. He uses it to knock aside a lightning claw thrust from the last attacker, backhands the butt of the haft into the original wielder's faceplate, cracking an eye-lens, then steps aside as the lightning-claw-armed traitor lunges again with both weapons extended. The energised talons bite deep into the body of the Chaos worshipper from whom the Lion wrested the chainaxe, who bellows in pain.

Chainaxes are brutally effective against flesh and light armour, but almost useless at piercing Tactical Dreadnought armour. Instead, the Lion hurls his stolen weapon end over end at the Chaos lord, who is still extricating himself from the command terminal, and the impact on the traitor's pauldron tips his balance just enough to send him slumping down again with a roar of rage and frustration. The heretic who has just been impaled by his fellow's lightning claws reacts as those in the grip of the Blood God's frenzy are prone to: he lashes out with his power fist at the source of his pain, knocking the other traitor back with a thunderclap as the weapon's disruption field pulverises some of the ancient ceramite it strikes. The lightning claws are wrenched out of his body, and blood spills from the eight wounds left in their wake.

The Lion reaches behind him and his fingers close on the grip of Fealty, still embedded in the neck of the Terminator he killed. He wrests it out, and moves back into the attack. *This* is a weapon which can make a mockery of even Tactical Dreadnought plate.

He kicks the bleeding Terminator in the back, sending him staggering forward into the one with the lightning claws. Lost in pain and bloodlust, the injured traitor no longer seems to care whom his original target was, and he lashes out at the warrior in front of him, who, for his part, has no compunction in finishing his fellow off if it means his own survival. The Lion leaves them to it, and moves to meet the Chaos lord and his other two warriors, all of whom have finally extricated themselves from their respective predicaments.

The Lion half expects his enemies to show some caution now,

to encircle him and for one or two of them to feint at him to draw him out and leave him exposed to a strike from a third direction, but he immediately realises that such subtleties are not the way of Khorne. The Blood God has no patience to wait for blood to be spilled, and so all three warriors charge the Lion at once. In doing so, they almost succeed, for even the Lion takes a moment to adjust to such relentless berserk savagery. Only his focus saves him.

He ignores the chainaxes for now: their teeth can scrabble and shatter against his armour, almost as ineffective as they would be against Terminator plate. He concentrates on the power fist, the power sword, and the chainfist, because these are the weapons that can most readily hurt him. Of those three, the power fist has the least reach, and so it is the Chaos lord who is the centre of the Lion's attention. However, even a warrior steeped in the power of the Taker of Skulls can only swing one of those weapons at a time, and so the Lion backs away parrying, catching chainaxe blows on pauldrons or the sturdy, solid plates of his vambraces instead of in vulnerable joints, his defences a whirling shroud of empowered silver metal while he looks for his opportunity.

It comes when the warrior to his right, infuriated by his inability to draw blood with his twin chainaxes, loses any semblance of composure and hurls himself bodily at the Lion with both of his weapons raised. The Lion ducks for a moment, allowing the traitor to collide with him, then straightens and raises his right shoulder as he does so. The Terminator is thrown head over heels into his opposite number, knocking them both to the floor again.

The Chaos lord thrusts with his powerblade, a blow aimed straight for the Lion's chest. The Lion cannot avoid it, but he turns and leans into it with his left pauldron, on which the image of a hooded spectre stands proud. The heretic's power-blade drives deep into the thick ceramite, and sticks fast for a moment.

And a moment is long enough for the Lion to bring Fealty up and around in a two-handed grip, and shear through his enemy's sword hand at the wrist.

The Chaos lord, caught up in his rage, barely pauses to register the loss of his hand and weapon. He bellows in fury and swings wildly with his chainfist, a scything blow from which the Lion steps back. The traitor lashes out again on the backswing, but although a chainfist is a powerful weapon, it is not a subtle one. They were designed for cutting through bulkheads and jammed doors when clearing bunker complexes and space hulks, and they confer little ability to alter the direction of the blade. The Lion waits for the backswing to pass him, then pivots like a fencer and extends Fealty straight through his enemy's faceplate.

The enemy commander staggers backwards, and falls. The Lion wrenches Fealty out as he does so, then turns and draws the Arma Luminis to put a blazing-hot shot into the heads of the other two Terminators. Each one dies with their brains flash-boiling within what remains of their skull.

The Lion uses Fealty to knock loose the power sword still embedded in his pauldron, then turns. The Terminator armed with lightning claws has finished butchering his former comrade, but he has suffered for it. One arm hangs limply, and his faceplate has been smashed away to reveal the damaged visage beneath. Spurs of bone jut from the Chaos worshipper's cheeks and chin, to the point where his helmet would surely not have fitted for much longer in any case, and his skin is an unhealthy maggot-pallor traced with thick, dark veins that pulse in time with his laboured breathing. He staggers forwards, drooling corrosive spittle over torn lips, reaching out with the arm over which he still has control as though his shuffling gait will be enough to impale the Lion on his bloodied talons.

The Arma Luminis cannot be fired again yet lest it overheat, so the Lion brings Fealty up into a guard position, for he will not make the mistake of underestimating this enemy. However, before either one of them advances into range of the other, there is a distinctive double roar of bolter fire and the traitor's head explodes. He slumps sideways, and the Lion looks up at the command deck to see Zabriel standing there with both his bolt pistols aimed at the heretic's corpse.

'Forgive me, lord, I did not wish to interrupt,' Zabriel says. 'But now I actually had a target I might stand a chance of damaging–'

'I take no issue with expediency,' the Lion assures him, and lowers his blade. 'I am not the Wolf King, to growl and defend my kill.' A strange wave of regret washes over him at the thought that he will never see that obnoxious savage's face again, but there is no time to examine his thoughts. 'What of the rest of the battle?'

'The fleets have not yet begun to engage again,' Zabriel assures him. 'You killed the intruders remarkably quickly, my lord.'

The former Destroyer is correct: less than a minute has passed since the Terminators teleported onto the bridge according to the chrono in the Lion's helm read-out, although he was lost in his battle-focus and could not have said how much time had elapsed. Ceramite footfalls announce the arrival of Kai, his own power sword drawn. He comes to a halt next to Zabriel and looks down at the slaughter with a disappointment that is communicated even through the impassive faceplate of his helmet.

'Oh. I thought you meant there was actually a problem, Zabriel, not a mild workout for the Lord of the First.'

'We have a damaged bridge that is now polluted by corrupted corpses, and a void battle yet to win,' the Lion snaps, his tone made slightly more acerbic by the returning pain in his side, which is now reminding him that he just fought six Terminators with broken ribs. A couple of crew members are creeping back out of alcoves where they secreted themselves while the combat took place, but most fled the bridge completely. The Lion points at the nearest. 'Get on the vox and order everyone to return to their stations immediately, or we will have repelled boarders only to be blown apart while we sit inert.'

Zabriel taps keys at the auspex, and administers a ritual blow with the gentle ring of ceramite on metal. The tactical hololith sputters back into life above them, and the Lion assesses how the battle has altered.

'What is that cruiser doing?' he demands, pointing to a single hostile-flagged icon on their flank.

'Nothing, lord,' Zabriel reports, turning a dial. 'Sensor scan says they have drive power, and I have nothing to suggest that their weapons are inoperative, but they are not engaging.'

'I do not like an enemy who holds his fire,' Kai remarks.

'Under the current situation, I prefer him to one who does not, and we have plenty of those inbound,' the Lion says. The tactical situation does not look promising, at least in terms of Avalus maintaining a navy. The Chaos fleet has been mauled, but so have the Imperials, and for all that the Avalusians have punched above their weight so far, the best outcome the Lion can see is for mutual annihilation.

He does not regret this outcome. He is certain, without undue arrogance, that no other commander present could have achieved anything close to even this level of success. The ability to defend Avalus against future attacks is inconsequential if this one is not defeated first. Perhaps more ships will come to Avalus before the traitors send another fleet. If they do not, there is nothing he can do about it. He ascends the stairs back to the command deck, and moves to the hololith.

'Vox! General broadcast to all, including the enemy!'

'Ready, my lord!' shouts back the crewer who has taken over the vox-station at his order.

'This is Lion El'Jonson,' the Lion growls. 'My ship was boarded by teleportation slightly over one minute ago. The attackers, including your lord, are now all dead. You may expect the same fate if you remain.' He signals to the crewer to cut the transmission.

'Most of our ships are reporting low ammunition stocks, Lord Lion!' the crewer informs him a few seconds later. 'However, they have taken heart from your message, and are expressing their eagerness to take the fight to the enemy again!'

'The majority of the enemy are pursuing us away from the planet, though,' Kai says. 'Should we retreat, and draw them out further?'

'We would have to present our sterns to them, leaving us with little ability to engage,' the Lion says with a sigh, 'and to try to turn now would almost certainly leave us still in the middle of manoeuvres when their guns came into range. No, we will have to see this through to–'

'New contacts!' Zabriel shouts. 'New contacts coming in fast, from above the orbital plane!'

'Heading?' the Lion snaps, as the new icons blink into existence. Behind him, the bridge doors open and begin to admit the crew who had fled from the Terminators, the men and women rushing back to their respective stations.

'How did we not see them until now?' Kai asks. He has removed his helmet, and is peering up at the contacts with a mix of trepidation and distrust.

'The fog of war applies in void battles as well,' Admiral Derrigan says, joining them at the hololith. 'Once engaged in combat and surrounded by explosions, gas vents, debris, fighters, and so forth, even the best auspexes can fail to register things. I suspect these ships were running dark, using only minimal thrust and power in order to remain hidden. The question is, why?'

'Their heading has them on course to join the Chaos fleet,' Zabriel calls from the auspex station. 'Starting to get ship ident codes–'

Names flash up on the hololith, attaching themselves to the new arrivals, along with designations. They are a mixed bag indeed, the Lion sees; he is still unfamiliar with modern ship classes, but he can tell that this ragtag fleet is made up of a few smaller military vessels and some that were clearly once civilian, but which now appear to be upgraded with weapons of a sort.

'The *Umbra*, the *Perfecti Vagari*, the *Starward Coil*, the *Saint Lott's Light*...' Derrigan mutters, reading off the display.

'They have a ship named after a saint?' the Lion queries. 'Surely that is a good sign?' He finds the canonisation of mortals in his father's name just as unappealing as the Emperor's deification, but at least it displays an allegiance to the same broad goals.

'If only that were true,' Derrigan says grimly. He points at the foremost icon. 'That is the *Honour's Edge*, a Nova-class frigate. It's a ship-killer, and this is her pirate fleet. They have been harassing shipping across half a dozen systems for the last few decades, and defied all attempts to capture or destroy them even before the Great Rift opened. They have no love for the Imperium.'

'A Nova class?' Zabriel asks. 'That is a... Space Marine vessel, is it not?' The Lion hears the hesitation in his voice where he was about to say 'modern Space Marine vessel'. None of them have seen any point in explaining to the Avalusians the exact age of the Dark Angels who are accompanying their primarch, or exactly how they came to be here.

'It is,' Derrigan agrees. 'Hence my concern. I can only assume that its captain and crew are allies to the foul monstrosities currently attacking us.' His eyes wander towards the guard rail at the edge of the command deck, but he does not move towards it to look down into the main crew well: it appears that his curiosity does not outweigh his fear over what he might see.

The Lion nods. Irregular though the new flotilla might be, they have numbers and firepower enough to be a significant factor in this engagement where both sides are already battered. Even a stalemate of extinction may now be unachievable. In which case, the question becomes one of prioritising the damage they can still deal.

'Signal all ships,' he orders. 'Prepare to concentrate fire on the *Lord of Dominion*. Capital ships of that size can carry a battle, so we shall at the very least leave them with one fewer.'

'My lord!' Zabriel says. 'The enemy fleet is pitching and rolling. They appear to be seeking firing solutions on those approaching from above.'

The Lion frowns at the hololith again. 'Admiral, I understand your logic with regard to these ships' character, but surely you must agree that their approach vector gives the appearance not of a rendezvous, but of an attack run?'

Admiral Derrigan bites his lip. 'I cannot bring myself to hope, my lord Lion, but–'

His hesitation ends as the hololith sparkles with simulated weapons fire.

'Target?' the Lion snaps. The pirates appear to be on the wrong heading to attack the Avalusians at present, but he is not prepared to take anything on trust.

'The *Lord of Dominion*!' Zabriel shouts joyfully. 'They are giving it everything they have!'

'All ships are to advance at full speed and engage!' the Lion orders. 'Hurry! Our unlooked-for allies will not last long against that fleet alone, but together we can eliminate this threat entirely!'

'We're being hailed!' the vox-officer shouts. 'Signal origin is *Honour's Edge*!'

'Patch it through,' the Lion orders. A small part of the tactical hololith, closest to the generator, fizzles with static for a moment as the signal is established. The Lion tenses, waiting. Will this be more traitors, corrupted by the power of Chaos and simply taking the opportunity to strike at an internecine rival? Or could they be genuine allies, pirates who will nonetheless stand and fight alongside those upon whom they have preyed when presented with a greater and far fouler enemy?

He is not prepared for the visage which appears. It is grizzled, and scarred, and one eye socket is obscured by a solid metal patch since it appears no bionic replacement has been available, but the nature of it is unmistakeable.

It is a member of the Legiones Astartes, and what can be seen of his scuffed and battered battleplate is the night-black of the First Legion.

The legionary's remaining eye widens. *'My... my lord Lion? I knew that the astropaths of Avalus had not lied when I heard your voice on the vox, but–'*

'I am somewhat altered, it is true,' the Lion says. He fights down the emotion that swells up inside him at the sight of another of his sons; he cannot be taken off guard by sentimentality now. 'As are you. The admiral alongside me informs me that your vessel is a pirate. State your name and purpose, legionary.'

'Knight-Captain Borz, Twelfth Company, my lord,' the one-eyed legionary declares instantly. *'I will make no excuses for our predation upon this so-called Imperium, although they are far from the only faction from whom we have made our living. However, now you are returned, our vessels and the warriors under our command are yours.'*

The Lion frowns. 'There are others with you?'

'Indeed so, my lord. Knight-Sergeant Perziel, and Knights Rufarel, Cadaran and Breunan. Each has a ship – the rest are allocated to mortal commanders we trust.'

'And do you stand against the forces of Chaos, knight-captain?'

'My lord, we have harried them wherever we have found them,' Borz declares forcefully. *'We came here merely to ascertain the truth of your return, but when we saw this filth had arrived and were attacking the planet, and we heard your voice–'*

'Then let us finish them,' the Lion cuts him off. The *Lunar Knight* is opening fire, as are the rest of its fleet. The traitors, now attacked on two fronts and lacking any true leadership, are foundering; they are still many, and will not die easily, but die they shall. 'Kai! Get down to the vox and disseminate my instructions to Knight-Captain Borz using the Legion's battle code.'

'As you command, my lord,' Kai replies, and vaults down into the crew well. 'No, young man,' the Lion hears him add, 'I am perfectly capable of operating this device myself, thank you...'

The Lion regards the hololith once more, then reaches out and begins to highlight attack routes, insertion points, which of the enemy should be isolated from which, and in what order. A mortal commander would still struggle to achieve anything from this combat beyond a glorious and probably spectacular death, but the Lion is not mortal.

He is a son of the Emperor.

XXII

On the *Eye of Malevolence,* Baelor turned to Dimora. 'Return us to Lord Seraphax.'

'You are not going to order me to engage?' the Canticallax asked. There was no judgement in her mechanical tone, but Baelor heard it anyway.

'The fleet is doomed, and our participation will not change that,' he snapped.

'And what of your orders? Are you satisfied that the primarch genuinely lives?'

Baelor took one last look at the death claiming those with whom he had made common cause. He would not mourn the loss of Varkan the Red, but those ships, and the troops they contained, were hard-won assets. They were not irreplaceable, but neither were the Ten Thousand Eyes' resources inexhaustible.

'I will report what I have witnessed to Seraphax. He can make his own decision based on the evidence.'

It is hard for a member of the New Mechanicum to sound

tentative. Dimora managed it nonetheless, and her words appeared to be uttered despite her better judgement rather than because of it.

'The level of tactical ability demonstrated by the Imperial commander suggests a ninety-eight point two per cent likelihood that they are not a baseline human, and only a sixteen point five seven per cent probability that they are transhuman Astartes–'

'Enough!' Baelor thundered. 'Get us into the warp and back to the rest of the fleet, before that commander decides we are more of a threat than we have given him reason to believe!'

'Compliance.'

The *Eye of Malevolence* turned and began to burn towards the Mandeville point. They did not need to reach it in order to translate – having a daemon bound into the ship gave advantages beyond those of simply navigating the warp once in it – but they would need to drop the void shields first, and Dimora had no intention of taking any form of damage just as they entered the immaterium.

Baelor stared out at the stars, but without seeing them. Instead, his mind was filled with a deep voice, worn and roughened by age, but still alarmingly close to the one he knew centuries ago.

The Lion was lost in the Breaking. Baelor, who had no faith in gods of any kind, and little faith in anything else, had held fast to that belief ever since he landed in this damned future. It was only now that what he previously viewed as simple fact was questioned that he was finding out just how stubbornly he believed in it. The Lion could not be back. He could *not*. There were other Fallen out there, and they knew how the Lion had sounded; how he had looked, for that matter. It must be a ruse, a desperate ploy by those fools still loyal to the Imperium to rally some last few pockets of resistance by use of a symbol which might pass examination even from those in this age with some knowledge of history. Their mummery would undoubtedly be unconvincing in person to anyone who had ever actually laid eyes on a primarch.

And yet, as the stars were replaced by the swirling vistas of the warp, which were to colours what a chainsword was to a flint knife, Baelor could not get that damned voice out of his head.

Part Three

ATONEMENT

XXIII

Lion El'Jonson has a singular focus, allowing him to concentrate absolutely on something to the exclusion of all distractions. It is an ability he has possessed for as long as he can remember; it was the only thing that kept him alive during his youth in the forests of Caliban before Luther found him, when he was hunting its mega-predators and being hunted by them in turn. Keeping something in his thoughts is not a problem.

Not thinking about *anything* is a great deal harder.

The Lion sits cross-legged in the chambers set aside for his use on the Endeavour-class light cruiser *Glory of Terra,* and attempts to clear his mind. The *Lunar Knight* and the rest of the fleet are licking their wounds in the Avalus System, undertaking what repairs they can and salvaging anything worthwhile from the wreckage of the battle, but the Lion is not content to sit idly. He has taken this ship to travel with most of the pirate fleet of Borz One-Eye, as he is known to his crews, in a series of short warp jumps to where the knight-captain swears there are more of the Fallen. Each jump is a matter of a few light years at a time, followed by an extended period of waiting as the scattered flotilla reassembles itself: this is how Borz has been travelling ever since the Great Rift cut him and his Navigators off from the Astronomican, and he claims that his ships have become experts in knowing exactly how far they can risk jumping each time. The Lion has little to offer this process other than bad memories of trying to reach Terra through the Ruinstorm, so he is trying to meditate.

The problem is that his mind is desperately searching for something, anything, on which to fixate. Clearing it simply provides space for a new thought to enter unbidden: the sound the ship makes as it flexes in the warp, and whether that might be the precursor to a hull breach; the likelihood of the Techmarine to whom Borz claims to be leading him being able to repair his armour; how long it would take to reach Terra while making jumps of this duration and frequency, even without the presence of the Great Rift; exactly what condition his father is in now; and so on and so on, an apparently endless procession of problems, dilemmas, and calculations that extends off into the distance of his own brain, each one waiting its turn.

The Lion sighs. What he would not give for the serenity his brother Sanguinius was able to achieve, troubled by visions of his own future and death though he was. Then again, few things are as serene as death, and the Lion is not yet ready to join the Angel in that.

He exhales, and tries again. Meditation was something many of the knightly orders of Caliban valued highly, as a way of achieving clarity and focus. Clarity and focus were ever-present for the Lion, so his need for the techniques were limited. Now, however, he seeks an understanding for which concentration appears to be of little use, if not actively hindering. Perhaps clearing his mind will allow insight to visit him, if only he can keep the other thoughts clamouring for his attention quiet for long enough...

He breathes in, and he breathes out. He focuses on the rhythm of his breathing, in the hope that will help his mind find the necessary balance between emptiness and activity. He envisages the forests of Caliban as he remembers them: the mighty trees, the thick foliage, the click and whirr of insects and the distant cries of forest beasts, the rustle of wind in the canopy of leaves overhead, the occasional shaft of sunlight striking down into the dimly lit understorey like a lance strike from an orbiting ship–

His train of thought derails as other memories flash up: fighting through his sons, those who were traitors and those whom he damned by association, as his fleet bombards Caliban from overhead. He never intended to destroy the planet that was and will always be his home, but his fleet had practice by that point. Chemos, Barbarus, and Nuceria, most recently, not to mention all the nameless worlds they blasted clear of hostile xenoforms when the Great Crusade was still ongoing. Still, even a ferocious orbital bombardment should not have done such damage to a world unless true planet-killing munitions were used. Perhaps the level of destruction was the result of some unforeseen interaction with the foul sorceries with which Luther was involved...

The Lion grunts in irritation, banishes that line of thought from his mind, and tries again.

He is not sure how much time has passed, which is an achievement in itself given how readily his mind will latch onto tracking its passage in the absence of other stimuli. However, quiet though he has tried to keep his thoughts, his senses inform him that the nature of his surroundings has changed.

He opens his eyes, and finds that instead of sitting on the floor of his chamber in the *Glory of Terra*, he is seated on grass in the forests of Caliban: not the true forests that he remembers, but the mist-shrouded echo of them in which he first came back to awareness. He was meditating in an attempt to gain some understanding of this phenomenon, how it came to be, and whether he could control it. He was not anticipating a reoccurrence of it, but he supposes that he should have. The galaxy is a strange place now, stranger even than it used to be.

Off to his right, the river is singing its silver song to him again. He becomes aware of a presence behind him, and he rises to his feet and turns. A wall looms over him, several times his height. It is the castle he saw before, he is certain of it; it is built of the same blue-grey stone, and it is next to the river. He looks to his left, but the water is empty of the fishing king in his small boat. Nor is there any sign of a Watcher in the Dark.

There is a gate in the castle wall, a thing of weathered wood studded with dark iron, and it is slightly ajar. The Lion approaches it cautiously, then reaches out with one hand and pushes it. It is heavy, but easily moveable for a primarch.

The Lion walks through the arched stone portico with the confidence of someone who ended up ruling the real Caliban, but with the alertness of someone who knows that the threats of the real Caliban were myriad, and did not come just from the wild beasts of the forests. There seems little reason to assume that this echo of it, whatever it is, will be any different.

The entrance is a dim tunnel in which the black shapes of murder holes lurk above, ready to rain death down on attackers. Halfway along it, the Lion sees the spiked iron slats of a portcullis in the ceiling. It is a second line of defence should the gate fail, but it does not drop at his approach. He passes through, and into the courtyard beyond.

The castle is not any of the fortresses he came to know on Caliban, but it is familiar in its layout nonetheless. To his right, away from the river, is a small orchard of a dozen or so fruit trees, close-packed together, and quarters that would accommodate most of the inhabitants, although the castle has a decidedly empty feel to it. In front of him are the stores, and then to the left of them, the kitchens. Farther to his left is the castle's great hall, although it hardly seems great to a warrior who has commanded a Gloriana-class battleship several miles in length. That tower will contain the well, and that tower will be the chambers of the castle's ruler, and that tower...

The Lion realises that he can see flickering light, as of a fire, in the windows of the great hall. So, perhaps there is someone in the castle after all. He moves towards the hall, and realises that he has taken the decision to move silently, but does not halt to announce himself even though he is by any definition an intruder here. There is something oppressive about this place; he feels that to break the silence with speech would be unwise, although he cannot say why. Perhaps this is just his memories of Caliban, where making undue noise was a good way to draw the attention of predators. Perhaps it is some other instinct.

The Lion is not armed or armoured, for his plate was damaged in the fight against the boarding party and he had no weapons either in hand or belted to him when he began his meditation, given that he was not anticipating being transported to this place. He wonders whether his body is currently still sitting on the floor of his chambers aboard the *Glory of Terra* and it is merely his mind which is here, but he does not think so: these forests took him and his companions from Camarth to Avalus, after all, so they are certainly capable of being a conduit for physical objects. He feels the lack of his wargear, despite his own natural deadliness. Only a fool enters an unknown situation unarmed, yet here he is, drawn to the light of a fire like a winged insect fluttering to its doom.

He continues to approach the hall, despite the analogy his mind has thrown up. He does not know exactly how he got here, and nor does he know how to leave. He does not feel the same tug in his chest as he did when someone or something guided him to Avalus, but there has to be a reason he found himself next to this castle, and his alternative is to turn his back on a recognised landmark and wander the forests at random.

At least here he might get some answers.

The hall's doors are open. The Lion enters cautiously, ready to respond to a challenge or to violence, but neither comes. Instead he finds himself in a long chamber with a pitched ceiling perhaps twice his height at its lowest and three times at its highest, braced by beams of dark wood. The fire is in an alcove halfway along the far wall, and so natural does it seem that it takes the Lion a moment to notice that the flames which writhe and coil there so merrily are burning nothing. The slab on which logs would rest is empty, and there is no sign of outlets for flammable gas or any other form of more exotic fuel. It is oddly unsettling; the familiarity of this place makes it easy to nearly forget that it does not fully conform to natural laws as he understands them.

He looks away from the fire, and down the length of the hall. Candelabras spaced evenly along the walls provide additional lesser light, and between them these different sources illuminate woven tapestries and banners that hang vertically between the windows. They too are familiar, although the detail is hard to make out, and the Lion cannot place them. Nonetheless, their nature is clear enough: they are records of battles, great triumphs of arms achieved by the castle's ruler, or their commanders.

And at the far end of the hall, seated on a high-backed chair behind a wooden table, is the wounded king.

He does not move nor speak, but the Lion can feel the intensity of that gaze. He sets off down the hall towards the monarch, expecting at any moment to be ordered to halt, or to state his business, or to give his name, or any number of other demands or enquiries that the master of a castle such as this might utter to an unknown intruder. However, the king says nothing. He merely watches the Lion approach, his dark eyes unblinking beneath his lank grey hair and the golden circlet on his brow.

The Lion pauses when he is a few paces away from the table. The lustre of the wood is hidden beneath a patina of dust, but three objects sit on it, arranged as though with ritual significance. A golden candelabra, more ornate than those decorating the walls, is in front of the king and on his right. On his left is a spear or lance, also golden, the blade of which is wet with blood. Directly in front of the king is a broad golden chalice with figures moulded around the bowl.

The Lion sniffs. The lance is not the only blood in the chamber: the king is still bleeding. There is a dark stain on the clothes covering his lower stomach, and the Lion's ears detect the faint sound of a drop falling from the edge of the throne and landing in a puddle on the floor below.

The king continues to stare, showing none of the intimidation the Lion might expect from a wounded mortal alone in his own hall and confronted with a towering post-human warrior. His eyes bore into the Lion, and indeed through him, as though he is seeing things far beyond the walls that surround them. Nonetheless, the Lion is certain that the king knows he stands there; it is just that he does not warrant the king's full attention.

There is an expectant expression on the king's face. The Lion recalls what the Watcher said to him after their first interaction.

You did not ask the correct question.

The Lion has little patience for such games, but he cannot

avoid the feeling that the king's reticence is not due to personal choice. This is a riddle of some sort; there is something actively preventing the king from communicating unless the correct words are spoken first. It would hardly be the strangest thing the Lion has seen in his life.

'Who are you?' he asks. The king's eyes focus on him momentarily, as though fully seeing him for the first time, but then they drift away. There is no other movement or sound, no slump or sigh, but the Lion can sense the king's frustration.

He tries again. 'How may you be healed?'

The king's eyes flicker back to him, and for a moment the Lion hopes that he might have hit the mark, but no reply is forthcoming. Instead, the king's gaze manages to communicate a warning, although the reason for that warning is not immediately obvious. The Lion frowns in annoyance, and opens his mouth to try again.

'Where–'

The shadows of the king's chair, cast by the light of the fire and the candelabras on the walls, begin to shift of their own accord. They lengthen and deepen, and reach out across the floor towards the Lion. He recognises them then: these are the same dark shapes that swirled in the water beneath the king's boat when he was fishing on the river, and into which the king's blood has been dripping.

The same things the Watcher warned would destroy him.

The king's gaze sharpens still further, into something that conveys both rage and disappointment. The Lion takes a step back, uncertain of how to fight a foe which on the face of it appears to be nothing but shadow, but he does not get the opportunity to try. The king's eyes flash, and the Lion's vision goes white.

When it clears, he is standing in his chambers on the *Glory of*

Terra, and his vox is chiming to alert him that they have arrived at their destination.

XXIV

It was a strange feeling to be moving openly after four centuries of hiding.

This was not to say that I had no qualms about it. My modern brothers and their affiliated Chapters were fanatics whose clutches I had only narrowly escaped on three occasions, and whose presence or arrival had sent me fleeing dozens more times over the decades. Even though I now possessed a vid-imager on which was a holographic recording of Lion El'Jonson naming me, and instructing anyone who saw it to offer me all aid in the name of the Emperor and the Lord of the First, I had little doubt that the Dark Angels of this time would view such a thing only as an even greater heresy than whatever they thought I had already committed. None of them would have seen or heard the Lion before the Breaking, and so they would have little reason to believe that the message was genuine.

Nonetheless, it was a strangely welcome sensation to once more be walking the bridge of an Imperial starship, and to be treated with respect by the crew. They did not know the exact nature of my history, but I was a Dark Angel of the Emperor and a companion of a primarch, and that was enough for them. I had command of the *Pax Fortitudinis*, a Cobra-class destroyer. As one of the smallest warp-capable ships in the Avalus fleet at just over a mile long, it would normally be deployed in a squadron as part of an order of battle rather than sent out alone, but my mission was not intended to be a combat one.

We had come to Gamma II, the second moon of Trevenum Gamma, a massive gas giant in the Trevenum System. Borz said he had heard of at least one Fallen who had taken up residence here, although he had not come to verify the stories since the system was reckoned to have little pickings for his pirates. I could tell there was something he left unsaid, too: that he did not investigate the business of other Fallen unless they wanted him to. His companions had found him by chance or by design, but I got the feeling that Borz had not searched for his Fallen brothers, in case he did not like what he found.

I understood this. I had gone for centuries believing that the Lion had betrayed us, but there had been times after I met Priavel, and left his company again, when doubt had clawed at me. It was easy to assume that Priavel had fallen into foul practices as a result of some character flaw or desperation at being alone and hunted in an unfamiliar galaxy, but what if I had been the outlier amongst my brothers? What if I had been rendered oblivious to the widespread corruption of those around me back on Caliban by my resentment of the Lion, and my own exile? The more of my brothers whom I encountered, in this future where we were hated fugitives and so all masks could be dropped, the more likely I was to encounter uncomfortable conclusions. Space Marines know no fear, but that does not mean we are able to face our own preconceptions and prejudices without bias, and nor does it mean that we relish having our mistakes exposed. There is too much baseline human left in our natures for that.

The Trevenum System was a mess, and an example of the chaos inflicted on the galaxy by the arrival of the Great Rift. Trevenum Theta, a frozen world on the edge of the system primarily mined for exotic ices, was endlessly broadcasting a chorus of screams. The vox signal was quickly routed away from the main console for the wellbeing of the vox-officers, and was monitored by Magos Toran, one of the ship's tech-priests. The magos informed me after four hours that ze had detected no exact repetitions, and so had to conclude that it was not on a loop but was a constant and continuous transmission, possibly live.

The high-atmosphere luxury palaces of Trevenum Epsilon, the system's second gas giant and previously a location of some status, had reportedly been hit so many times by aeldari raiders that the few inhabitants not carried off as slaves had taken their chances with the warp storms. Trevenum Alpha, a rocky planet close to the star, just went silent in the immediate aftermath of the Great Rift's appearance. According to the system's public navigation records, ships which approached it now disappeared from auspexes without apparent cause and ceased all transmissions as soon as they entered the orbit of its singular moon.

Amidst this pain and misery the moons of Trevenum Gamma still nominally belonged to the Imperium, although in name only, since they had had no real contact with its wider structures since the Great Rift. The inhabitants had, so far as we could determine, kept their heads down and avoided looking too closely at what was occurring elsewhere in their solar system, just in case it came for them too.

The *Pax Fortitudinis* was challenged by the planet's defence fleet, which exuded all the enthusiastic aggression of a fighting force finally faced with something it felt it could definitely destroy if it needed to. However, their belligerence evaporated when I identified myself as Zabriel of the Dark Angels, and emissary of Lion El'Jonson, the returned primarch.

'This is a wonder!' exclaimed Captain Raulen, the commander of their fleet. He was a rail-thin man, and the dark hollows of his cheeks as interpreted by the somewhat fuzzy hololith display gave his face a rather skull-like appearance. *'We will inform the lords immediately. Lord Launciel was adamant that he be informed as soon as any Space Marines arrived in the system, particularly other Dark Angels.'*

I had several hundred years of practice at keeping my expression blank, at least well enough to fool mortals, but I cannot deny that shock ran through me at the man's words. I was expecting to conduct a search similar to the one that led me to Kai, Aphkar, and Lohoc; hunting for secret signs through streets or, as it would be in the great hive cities of Gamma II, across the different levels. The notion that the object of my search would be known to the inhabitants had not crossed my mind.

Of course, the alternative was that this was not one of the Fallen at all, but a modern Dark Angel who had perhaps been stranded here. If he ordered my capture, the *Pax Fortitudinis* would find itself drastically outgunned, and swift though the Cobra class was, it was undoubtedly not swift enough to outrun munitions targeting its engines.

'One of my battle-brothers is on Gamma II?' I asked, stalling. 'I was not aware of this.'

'Two, my lord!' Captain Raulen said eagerly. *'The lords Launciel and Galad graciously took charge of Gamma's defences.'*

Two Space Marines, and Dark Angels no less, who had assumed positions of authority much as the Lion had done back on Avalus. That was certainly one explanation why Gamma and its moons had managed to see off xenos raids, and cult activity appeared not to have flourished out of control. Still, I was now more apprehensive of my mission than I had been: I did not recognise either name, and so I still did not know whether these Space Marines were truly old brothers of mine, or warriors who would wish me captured and interrogated.

Even if they *were* old brothers of mine, what did it mean that they had announced themselves openly? Did they assume that no modern Dark Angels would make it here through the warp storms, and so they were safe from persecution? Or did their assumption of command hide a more sinister purpose? A cult would have far more freedom in its operations if its activities were sanctioned by the highest local power, after all.

'Please inform them that I will be landing imminently, and wish to speak with them at once,' I said.

Captain Raulen's expression twitched slightly; I suspected he lost money at cards, if he played. *'My lord, I can communicate your wishes, but we must wait for–'*

'I need to wait for nothing, captain,' I said firmly. 'As I explained to you initially, I am the representative of Lion El'Jonson, primarch of the Dark Angels, who has returned to us after ten thousand years. He is the Emperor's son, and the gene-father of my two brothers and I. Whatever authority they have in this system is eclipsed by his.'

I signalled the vox-officer, who cut the transmission. Captain Montarat of the *Pax Fortitudinis*, who was so advanced in her career that she was now nothing more than an ancient body interred within a pod of amniotic fluid and connected directly to the ship's functions via mind-impulse, clicked her vessel's vox-speakers to attract my attention. Her mind-voice, as emitted by the speakers, was surprisingly light and lilting.

'Was such a peremptory missive wise, Lord Zabriel?' she asked. *'I am one ship against many, and trust is in short supply.'*

'My Legion has always been one for which trust is in short

supply,' I told her quietly. 'In this, we take after our gene-father. I do not wish to be kept waiting while my two battle-brothers second-guess our intentions, and I want them to be in absolutely no doubt not just that I have invoked the name of the Lion, but that I believe in it, too. If I hesitate, I show doubt that they will accept his authority, and therefore suggest I myself may not believe in his identity. If I proceed as though there is no question of them refusing me, I make it more likely that they will at least see me in order to understand why I act in such a fashion when we are immensely outgunned.'

The vox-speakers made a sound which I interpreted as the captain laughing. *'That is either admirably cunning or admirably direct, my lord, and I cannot decide which. In either case, the course is set. We are on approach to Gamma II, assuming I do not get blown apart between now and our arrival in low orbit. I have instructed Blue Hangar to prepare a shuttle for you. Do you require an escort?'*

'No need,' I replied, turning away. 'These are Space Marines, after all. If I cannot persuade them to join us, nothing a mortal can say would succeed.'

The Aquila transport touched down in the primary landing bay of Crown Hive some fifteen hours later. We had not come under any fire, although the clipped nature of the transmissions guiding the *Pax Fortitudinis* in past the weapons platforms, and then detailing the course changes my shuttle should make, suggested that my manner had ruffled some feathers. There had been no communication from either of my battle-brothers, though, which I took as a sign that they wished to judge me themselves and in person.

The ramp began to lower, and I took stock of myself for the final time. My bolt pistols were holstered and my chainsword clamped to one hip, while my helmet was on the other, leaving my features visible and vulnerable. I was not approaching these warriors as a supplicant, but neither did I wish to appear as though I were a second away from opening fire. Our Legion nearly destroyed itself once through distrust and misunderstanding, and I had no intention of reliving that, albeit on a far smaller scale.

Now I just had to see what sort of brother awaited me.

It was only a moment before my question was answered. The ramp lowered enough for the massive, hulking shoulders of Cataphractii Tactical Dreadnought armour to come into view, and exquisitely decorated armour at that. It was surmounted by a pair of wings above the helmet, and our Legion's iconography was everywhere: feathered wings, swords, skulls, and other more esoteric devices identifying the warrior's ranks and specialist knowledge. This was a suit of the very best armour the First Legion had ever manufactured, and the wearer was a giant. His beard was shot with grey, and his right hand was clamped around the hilt of a massive blade as tall as many a mortal human, which rested point down on the deck. That entire arm was bone-coloured, in contrast to the black of the rest of the armour, marking him as someone who had taken a wound meant for another and thereby saved their life.

This was a Cenobite of the Inner Circle, one of the most knowledgeable and skilled warriors in all of the Legion as it had been. Old instincts rose up even after centuries removed from any sort of command structure, and I had to fight myself not to salute him as a superior immediately. The warrior standing next to him was a far more normal sight, clad in Mark III armour, although the great ablative shield and power sword he carried were less common: the marks of a breacher squad veteran, by my guess, although it was always possible that he had simply picked them up as the only weapons available.

One of my questions was answered, because there was no

doubt that they were from the 31st millennium. The simple nature of their wargear was enough to convince me of that, even without the fact that theirs was the same black as mine rather than the deep forest green of our modern brothers. The next issue was how they would receive me, and whether their rule here hid something unsavoury.

'Well met, brothers,' I said, starting down the ramp before it had finished touching the ground. It was a continuation of the tactics I had begun with my message to Captain Raulen: to proceed as though there were no possibility things would not go as I expected them to, and let others deal with that how they would. 'I am Zabriel of the Third Company, Fifteenth Chapter.'

'Knight-Sergeant Launciel of First Squad, Twenty-Fourth Chapter,' the breacher replied in a sonorous bass, gracing me with a smile. He wore a neatly trimmed beard of tight black curls in which white was liberally sprinkled, and his brown skin was as deep and rich as his voice.

'I am Galad,' the Cenobite said simply. I looked at him, expecting more, but he met my gaze impassively.

'Galad believes that our former ranks are unnecessary,' Launciel explained, looking up at his companion with amusement but sparing me a twinkling glance.

'They no longer have relevance,' Galad replied, turning to Launciel, and I got the feeling that this was a discussion they had had several times before which was being voiced mainly for my benefit. 'We neither command nor are commanded by anyone, and the Legion as we knew it no longer exists.'

'I was led to believe that you *do* command people,' I put in, eager not to let the conversation get away from me. 'I was informed that you command the defences here. Although,' I added, 'I might expect such commanders to have an honour guard, regardless of whether or not it was needed.'

'We did not know your intentions,' Launciel told me. 'And you were a Destroyer, after all – better not to risk the mortals against the tools you might have available.' He laughed at my frown. 'We never met in person, but we both hunted the rangda through the warrens of their accursed war-moon at Advex-Mors. I remember your name and designation from the duty listings.'

'Launciel has an uncommonly good memory,' Galad put in.

'I ran out of phosphex about four hundred years ago,' I said dryly. 'But enough pleasantries, brothers. The Lion has returned to us.'

'So your message said,' Galad acknowledged. 'Do you have any proof of this claim?'

For answer, I reached into a belt pouch, pulled out the vid-imager, and pressed the activation rune.

The hololith skittered into fitful life, motes of light forming themselves into our gene-father. The Lion wore a heavy robe with the cowl thrown back to reveal his lined face, framed by his shaggy hair. He looked like an ancient warrior-king, rich with the wisdom of years but still ferocious in battle.

'I am Lion El'Jonson, primarch of the Dark Angels and son of the Emperor. If you see this message, then know that the bearer, Zabriel, is my emissary.'

The image panned out a little to reveal me standing at the Lion's side, armoured but unhelmed. Even with the added bulk of my ceramite, the difference in our stature was immediately noticeable. That was the idea, after all: not only to prove that I was the message's intended bearer, but also to make it clear to the viewer the true nature of the being speaking to them.

'I have been absent from the Imperium for a hundred centuries, and I have returned to find it in disarray. I do not come to you with any intent to rule, and I have no wish to set myself up as Emperor, or as Regent, or any other title. My duty is simply to protect humanity

against the perils that lurk in the dark. The Lion's Protectorate is centred on the world of Avalus. Any who wish to join us merely need to send word there, and we will come to you if we can.

'I am aware that my sons are abroad in the galaxy, both openly and in secret. I have no wish to reopen old wounds. I call upon all *Space Marines of Dark Angels lineage to join me, because both I and the galaxy need you now more than ever. If your hearts are true then a place will be found for you to help in this endeavour.'*

The Lion's face grew stern.

'Be aware that although I do not seek to rule any part of the Imperium, I am still the Lord of the First. Anything my sons wish to do in my name, any matters of judgement or censure, should be abandoned until I am able to give a pronouncement on them. Do not think to know my mind on a matter until you have consulted me, my sons. There has been too much misunderstanding already.'

The message ended, and the hololith sputtered into darkness once more.

I could tell immediately that Launciel and Galad had no doubt as to its veracity; their expressions were evidence enough of that. Whether it would have convinced my suspicious modern brothers was another matter entirely, but the Lion and I had agreed that at the very least, if they encountered it then they were likely to send as much of their fleet as they could spare to find him. The Lion was confident that he could then convince them not to obliterate whatever ship or city he was in at the time without at least seeing him in person.

I hoped he was correct. I might have found grim amusement in the prospect in the past, until the Lion swore to me that he had already been fired on unexpectedly by his sons once before, rather than being the initial aggressor. The notion of him now travelling with members of that force and coming under attack from those who had always considered themselves loyal to the

Imperium would be a grim joke indeed, but the galaxy had never been a forgiving place.

'It *is* him,' Launciel breathed, a look of wonder upon his face.

'It is,' Galad agreed. A frown creased his brow. 'Although I wonder at the truthfulness of his words. He is a warlord, just as the Emperor was – perhaps even more so, since the primarchs were created for that purpose. Why would he *not* wish to rule, given the state of the Imperium?'

'The Lion was many things, brother, but a liar was not one of them,' Launciel argued. 'He kept secrets, yes, but that is not the same as uttering falsehoods. If he says that he does not intend to become a new Emperor, I believe him.'

'And the other part? About his sons?' Galad eyed me appraisingly. 'That was hardly plainly worded.'

'The Lion chose his words carefully,' I said. 'He did not know to whom I would be showing the message, and he felt that to openly mention the schism within our Legion might cause a loss of morale amongst those who do not know of it, not to mention antagonising our modern brothers, who have spent ten thousand years attempting to keep that secret and persecute all those involved.'

'And he understands the nature of those who call themselves Dark Angels in this day and age?' Galad asked. 'He knows of their fervour and vindictiveness? He knows that they will even abandon their own allies to pursue a mere rumour of us?'

I grimaced. 'I have explained to him as best I can. Whether he can truly fathom it remains to be seen, but that is what lies at the heart of his message – that the Lion, not his sons, will judge us, and that he will do so based on our actions now, not what happened at the Breaking.' I looked from one of them to the other. 'Will you come with me?'

Galad looked uncertain. 'We promised these people that we would protect them...'

'And how better to protect them than by going to the Lion and seeking his help?' Launciel asked him. 'Gamma and its moons cannot survive remaining isolated forever, Galad. We always knew that either some facet of the Imperium would make contact, and we would have to reckon with that, or that we would be overwhelmed by raiders. A joint venture of worlds, a protectorate which does not seek to supplant the Imperium but merely to preserve what remains of it – that is more than I could have hoped for before Zabriel's first message reached us. Tell me truly, my brother. Do you doubt that the Lion could protect this system, even take back those elements of it which are lost, better than we ever could?'

'I do not doubt it at all,' Galad said. 'But what of *us*, Launciel? The Lion was ever mercurial in his temper.'

'Do not pretend you are concerned for your own welfare,' Launciel said with a laugh. 'I know you better than that! Galad is far too noble,' he added to me, his eyes twinkling. 'He would protect me from all harm if he could.'

'You would do the same,' Galad said stolidly. 'That shield of yours has taken as much damage defending me as it has defending you.'

'Well, you make such a large target, and a slow-moving one at that!' Launciel said, then sobered. 'But truly, brother, I can see no reason why we should not go with Zabriel. Even if the Lion still seeks revenge on us as individuals for our perceived misdeeds, that is no reason to deny the people of Trevenum the protection a primarch can offer. We only ever wished to serve humanity, and this is the best way we can do that, rather than remaining as lords of our tiny kingdom and waiting for doom to find us.'

Galad sighed, and placed one hand fondly on Launciel's pauldron. 'If that is your wish, then I will go with you.' He looked at me. 'What of our other brother? Did you wish to seek him out as well?'

I frowned. 'Other brother? I had been told of rumours that one Dark Angel was here, not two, and Captain Raulen spoke only of the two of you, not more.'

'Bevedan,' Launciel said, by way of explanation. 'I found him when I was searching for Galad, decades ago, but he was always a melancholy one. He has completely forsaken battle, and when we arrived here he decided to go and live as a hermit in the Umbran Mountains. We have visited him on a few occasions and he seems happy enough, but entirely uninterested in larger events.'

'The Lion wished me to take his message to as many of his sons as I could find,' I said. 'I would be remiss not to do this.'

'We will arrange you a transport to go and find him while we prepare the mortals here for our departure, and explain our reasoning,' Galad said. 'But Zabriel, you should not go there expecting success. Bevedan is stubborn, and will not be swayed.'

'I am not going to attempt to sway him,' I replied. 'I go with the same offer and message I made you, no more, and no less. The decision to accept or refuse will be his own.'

XXV

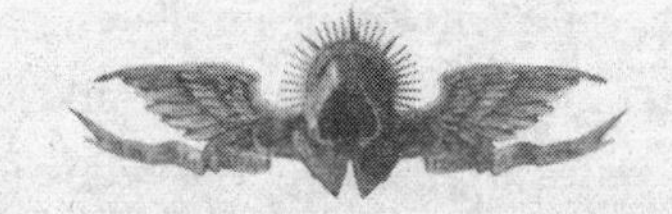

Echo Station is a dark speck in interstellar space lurking at the edge of the Cordova Nebula, and consists of five extended arms around a globular core. The Lion can see no obvious reason why such an installation has been placed here, far from any planets for it to guard, but that is not the only source of his uncertainty.

'This construction does not look like it was made by humans,' he states. 'Although it is of no other design that I recognise, either.'

'And we destroyed enough different xenos civilisations in the Great Crusade that it is surprising we do not know it,' Borz agrees over the vox from the *Honour's Edge*. *'But it is true, my lord, Echo Station does not seem quite human. Still, the scale and layout is similar enough for humanity to use it.'*

The Lion grimaces. 'And this does not trouble you?'

'We are all damned in the eyes of the Imperium anyway,' Borz replies honestly. *'I could have turned myself over to the tender mercies of my modern brothers, but I chose to stay alive. Out here, that*

means using what you have available.' He pauses for a moment, then speaks again. *'Without Echo Station, my ships would not be operational today, and then you would have had a far harder fight against that Chaos filth at Avalus, my lord.'*

Kai tuts beside him, and the Lion sighs. He does not like it, but he has to accept the logic of Borz's argument. The Emperor wanted the galaxy scoured clean of xenos civilisations because He knew that any of them could and would be a threat to humanity's domination, and their artefacts might pose just as great a threat as the beings themselves. However, the Emperor, as any Navigator could tell you, is not here.

And besides, it is fair to say that the Dark Angels were not unfamiliar with xenos technology. The holds of the *Invincible Reason* contained some of the most dangerous relics from the times of Old Night, to be used by the Dreadwing in cases of extreme necessity, and the Lion knows well enough that not all of the weapons his father gifted him were entirely of human origin. There was a difference, though: those artefacts had been approved for use by the Master of Mankind.

But what was the Lion to do? The Emperor's vision of the galaxy never came about, having foundered on the reefs of Horus' treachery. All that remains is for the Lion to step out from his father's shadow and make the decisions he thinks are best, here and now, and with that logic, and with him similarly absent, it is unsurprising if his own sons have taken the same step.

'What I would not give for another loyal brother of mine,' he mutters. 'This is a heavy burden to bear alone.'

'Even Russ?' Kai asks.

The Lion thinks about it for a moment. 'Even Russ.' The Wolf King had a savage simplicity about him which would be almost welcome now, although doubtlessly infuriating. The Emperor sent the Space Wolves when He wanted to make an example of an enemy that would linger in the memories of all, and He sent the First when He wanted no record of the enemy to remain. Russ might not be right, about anything, but he would be certain that he *was* right, and that could at least throw the available options into stark relief.

The vox crackles, but it is not Borz. They are being hailed by the station itself, and the deep voice that emerges does not sound happy, an impression only heightened by the chiming of alerts as the *Glory of Terra*'s systems register various weapons systems locking on to it.

'Borz, you sump-swilling wretch,' the vox rumbles, *'if you have brought the hells-damned Imperium down on us–'*

'Is that you, Guain?' Borz cuts in. *'You are not still sore about last time, surely?'*

'That was a full shipment of supplies–'

'Enough,' the Lion says into what is rapidly turning into an argument. 'Borz, you did not tell me that your piratical exploits had extended to the very place you were guiding me!'

There is a momentary pause from the vox.

'Who is speaking?' says Echo Station.

'This is Lion El'Jonson.' He searches his memory. 'You would be Knight-Sergeant Guain, if I recall correctly. You lost an arm in the second Karkasarn engagement.'

'Lion El'Jonson is dead, and a traitor to boot.' It takes a lot for a Space Marine to sound shaken, but Guain's voice is unsteady. *'And I was raised to knight-captain by Lord Luther during the exile on Caliban.'*

'I am no more dead than you are, Knight-Captain Guain,' the Lion says firmly, 'and I would argue, no more of a traitor either.'

'You know I would not have come back without good reason, Guain,' Borz interjects. *'What he says is true, impossible though it seems. At least get your brothers together and meet him.'*

The vox is silent for several long seconds. The Lion waits patiently. Words can always be added to a situation, but they can never be removed once uttered.

'Very well. One shuttle only. And Borz, you and your pirates had better stay well back.'

The angles are wrong.

That is the Lion's first impression of the hangar bay once he has exited the shuttle. There is something very inhuman about the design, although it is a far subtler dissonance than the night-marish interiors of khrave ships, or the structures of the rangda. If anything, that makes it more disturbing. Something which is truly alien can be rejected out of hand, whereas something which is *nearly* but *not quite* the same as what the eye expects draws attention to itself again and again.

There are seven of his sons waiting for him. Whether out of habit or deliberate choice they are drawn up in something close to parade form, helmets in place, but the minor discrepancies tug at his eye in the same manner the surroundings do. A mis-sing company marking here, a scavenged armour plate there, or a weapon that was never part of even the First Legion's exten-sive and varied armoury. Five of them wear First Legion black, but the one on the far right is in the white of an Apothecary, and the many-limbed figure at the rear is in the rust red and servo-harness of a Techmarine.

The Lion is not wearing his armour – it is damaged, after all – but he has Fealty on his belt. Kai and Lohoc flank him, the swordsman to his left and the Red Whisper to his right, while behind them come the Lion Guard. M'kia refused to let him go on this mission without them, after hearing of the combat on the bridge of the *Lunar Knight*. The Lion would have pre-ferred to send them back to Camarth on one of the ships that his fledgling protectorate has sent there to re-establish contact, but he knew that such a statement would only induce pleading from the Camarthans, and he has no wish to see them reduced to that. He took them from their world without meaning to; the least he can do is let them keep their dignity.

Still, no one has their hands on a weapon, including the Lion Guard. Even Lohoc has his plasma gun slung away. Borz got them here just as he promised, but his economy with the truth about his relationship to his estranged brothers on Echo Station means that the Lion is walking into a more hostile situation than he previously anticipated.

'It is good to see all of you,' the Lion says. The statement is more true than he expected. He found Zabriel alone and guarding refugees on a tainted world, Kai, Lohoc, and Aphkar hiding in the slums of a city, and Borz and his crew predating on whatever ships they could find out in the void. The notion of some of his sons making a home of sorts for themselves is an oddly pleasing one, even if the home is an alien place, and it is a far cry from the life of war for which they were created. The Lion can see baseline humans peering around the edges of the doorways that open into the hangar, looking on with wonder. Serfs and servants? Or equals, in this strange place?

'Are you here to kill us?' asks the leftmost Dark Angel as the Lion looks at them. He holds a meltagun, and does not sound either angry at the notion of dying, or eager about the prospect of a fight.

'Again,' adds another, second from the right. The Lion has already marked him as Knight-Captain Guain by his bionic right arm, but the voice would have given him away in any case.

'I am not here to kill anyone,' he says, and he speaks of what he has learned: of the treachery of Luther, and Astelan, and others allied to them, but of how he has since found sons who he believes had no part in or knowledge of the attack. He speaks of Camarth, and Avalus, and he speaks of his purpose.

'If you wish me to, I will leave you in peace,' he finishes, 'and I will attempt to make those sons of mine who wear the mantle of Dark Angels in this time do the same. The only exception is if you prey upon humanity. And continue to do so,' he adds, thinking of Borz.

The warrior at the rear steps forward with the clanking of metal foot upon metal hull, and when he removes his helmet the Lion sees that half of his head is metal too. The Techmarine of whom Borz spoke is ancient, and the remaining flesh of his face is pallid and sagging.

'It has been seven hundred and thirty-seven years since the Breaking of Caliban for me,' the Techmarine says, with a wheeze in his voice which speaks of at least partially artificial airway or lungs. 'I am Ectorael, son of Caliban and adept of Mars, and I can tell you that the galaxy is a worse place than ever, Lord Lion. The Imperium is wretched, short-sighted, superstitious, and hateful, and it clings to tenets it does not understand in pursuit of goals it cannot remember and will never realise. Why should we fight to protect what is left of it?'

'The Imperium is by all accounts gravely flawed, but many of the people within it bear no responsibility for that,' the Lion replies firmly. 'They are beset on all sides by ravening xenos we failed to exterminate, and by foul powers to which our brother Legions, and indeed some of your own battle-brothers, enslaved themselves. Should we leave these mortals to reap the consequences of their forebears' decisions, and the failures of the Legiones Astartes and the primarchs?' He extends a hand towards the humans lurking by the doors, and they recoil despite him being a hundred yards away from them. 'You have humans with you here, and I presume they receive your protection as you protect this station. Why not extend your boundaries?'

'Because they are scared,' Kai says, stepping forwards. The Lion turns to him, a harsh rebuke on his lips, but it is too late. The tense stillness of the standoff has been shattered, and the Dark Angels of Echo Station are raising their weapons.

Kai, however, appears unconcerned.

'I know the feeling,' he announces, spreading his arms. 'I felt it too. Back in the days of the Great Crusade, I was part of something huge. I had my brothers around me, and I knew my purpose. Even when we were exiled on Caliban, I felt that connection – more so, even, because I knew that there was so much good that I could be doing if I were simply allowed to get out there and *do* it.' He drops his hands to his sides. 'And then the Breaking happened, and the storm threw me through space and time, and I ended up alone and without purpose. Even when I found a pair of companions, we had no plan other than to keep our heads down and survive. How could we three make a difference to the galaxy?'

He points at the Lion.

'But now we can, brothers. Our gene-father says he has no wish to rule, and I believe him, but you must realise that everywhere he goes, humanity will cling to him like a drowning person to a flotation device. They will hang off his words, and take his statements as law. Even if it is only a handful of star systems, that is still trillions of lives that the Lion will be protecting. You have the choice of joining him, finding a new purpose standing next to other warriors, and having no enemies other than those who seek to destroy humanity – or refusing him, remaining here, and waiting for a passing xenos fleet to grant you a meaningless death, or to finally be captured and tortured by the Unforgiven.'

There is a few moments of silence.

'I would not have been sad if you had never come back out of that warp storm, Kai,' says the Dark Angel holding the meltagun, with considerably more feeling than was in his voice before.

'Nor I you, Kuziel,' Kai replies with a sniff. 'But I am speaking the truth, and I suspect you know it.'

'And what of your other companion, my lord Lion?' Ectorael asks. His mechanical eye clicks and whirrs as it focuses on Lohoc. 'Does he have similar eloquence?'

'I do not,' Lohoc rasps. 'I do as the Lion wishes me to, and that is an end to it.'

'Brother, that sounds like an old injury,' says another of Echo Station's Dark Angels, the one in the white plate of an Apothecary. 'Does it require attention?'

'It does not.'

'But–'

'Lohoc does not remove his battleplate within the sight of others,' the Lion interrupts him. 'But we thank you for your concern.'

'Does he not?' Ectorael says, and the half of his face still capable of movement settles into a considering expression. 'And this does not strike you as strange, my lord?'

'I suspect that many of my sons have developed quirks since the Breaking,' the Lion says levelly. 'I will not condemn without proof. Lohoc has pledged himself to me, and given me no reason to doubt his word. I will extend the same trust to any of you.'

There is a slight shift of stances amongst the Echo Station garrison, and the Lion can tell that his words have struck something. His Legion always prided themselves on being the very best, the first, the template which the rest of the Legiones Astartes had to follow. He wonders what insecurities have developed during their respective long times of relative solitude, when they could not influence the galaxy. Kai is correct, he suspects: there is fear here, but not fear of death, or pain, those things that a Space Marine will face unflinchingly.

It is a fear that they have lost the only thing that told them who they were, and that any attempt to reclaim it will see those fears confirmed.

'My sons,' he says, as gently as he can. 'You and I spent centuries doing what we were told. Now I simply wish to do what is *right*, and I need your help to do it, for as long as you are willing to give me that help.'

'Who are you fighting?' asks a new voice. An Assault Marine, the Lion notices, with an ancient jump pack still attached to his back.

'Currently, our most prominent enemy appears to be a Chaos force going by the name of the Ten Thousand Eyes.'

The Assault Marine steps forward. 'Knight Lamor, my lord Lion. If you are hunting Seraphax's filth, I am with you.'

The Lion frowns. 'Seraphax. I fought a boarding party who shouted that name. That is their overall commander?'

'Knight-Captain Seraphax, as he was,' Ectorael growls. 'One of Luther's favourites, back on Caliban. I have not met him since the Breaking, but I have seen his handiwork, and that of his followers. He *is* a traitor, that one, to everything the Emperor taught us. You will have my aid.'

The Lion smiles, and it only broadens when Guain steps forward as well.

'Not alone, brother.'

'He is not alone,' Lamor says, turning to address Guain. 'Did you not hear me pledge myself before he even spoke?'

'He will be alone the moment you fly off at the enemy, you hot-headed–' Guain begins. However, the Lion's comm-bead chimes with an urgent message alert.

'This had better be important, captain,' he says quietly.

'Forgive me, my lord, but it is. Mellier the astropath has just received a distress call.'

The Lion bares his teeth.

'From where?'

XXVI

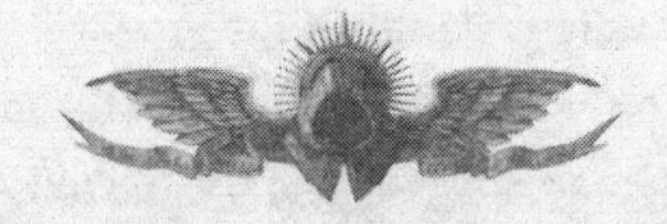

The Umbran Mountains were starkly beautiful, and I arrived there at their second dawn, which was, by their nature, also noon. The range stood just where Gamma II, which was tidally locked to its parent planet, emerged from Trevenum Gamma's shadow and into the full power of the overhead sun. I had seen many strange sights during my centuries travelling the galaxy, but the Trevenum star slowly rising above the enormous dark sphere of Gamma, its upper atmosphere backlit and glowing by the star's rays, to illuminate the rugged, rocky landscape of the second moon was certainly one of the more memorable, at least amongst the events which had not directly threatened my life.

Some of the Blood Angels had made art, back in the days of the Great Crusade. I wondered whether this spectacle might be the sort of thing that would have inspired them. I also wondered whether any of their descendants still did the same, and if not, what that said. Had my modern brothers and cousins lost touch with their human origins, despite still being taken from human stock, and was that a failing? Or had we, the originals, clung to an identity we were never meant to hold onto, rather than accepting our role as inhuman weapons?

The transport I had been assigned was an RE-45, a civilian shuttle craft, which touched down in a rocky valley. I could tell that the crew were none too impressed at their assignment or their destination – Space Marines unsettled them, and the hydraulic landing gear was making whining noises of complaint about the uneven ground – but they did their jobs quietly and efficiently. I set off up the slopes and left them to their craft, and I think they were grateful for my absence, despite needing to wait around in the middle of nowhere for my return.

Mountain ranges are areas where the altered nature of Space Marine physiology is particularly noticeable. We are not particularly nimble, as a rule, and although our power armour boosts our strength and actions, it also greatly increases our weight. Rocks dislodge far more readily, and scree slopes are virtually impassable. On the other hand, we are more or less tireless, and sheer blunt strength sometimes provides the tools to conquer climbs that even an experienced mortal mountaineer would baulk at.

What I mean to say is that I trudged upwards towards the location I had been given for Bevedan's retreat without any particular ability or grace, but at a steady, slogging speed which made me feel somewhat like a member of the Death Guard. I had already discarded the brief aesthetic appreciation I had for the scenery, and was now firmly back into regarding it as terrain: something to analyse and use to my advantage, noting the best routes and potential hazards, and always being aware of the points from which a sniper could gain a good vantage point on me. I was not expecting enemies here, as such, but no Space Marine ever disregards the possibility.

Bevedan apparently lived in a cave on a high slope that faced west, catching the long afternoon. There was a rough path up, although I was unsure whether it was made by humans or animals. I startled a pair of cloudhoppers, as the locals apparently called them: furred and bipedal beasts about a foot and a half high, which chittered angrily at me through sharp teeth before leaping off the cliffside and catching the robust mountain wind beneath outstretched flaps of skin to glide away to safety. There were signs of larger denizens, too: the sandy dirt bore the multitudinous pockmarks of something with many chitinous legs that splayed at least a yard apart, and I saw the deep, heavy print of what I presumed was some kind of mammalian predator, judging by the pads and the faint tips of claws. In my years on Caliban I had grown more accustomed than I would have liked with its accursed forests and the various biological dangers that lurked within them, and I had some familiarity with hunting and tracking.

However, it was more mundane tracks which next caught my eye, some half an hour later: the distinctive imprints of ceramite boots like my own, going in the same direction. A Space Marine had come this way, and not too long before, judging by how distinct the prints still were even as the wind eroded the edges of them. I was glad for this evidence that my ascent was not in vain, because although I did not doubt Launciel and Galad's honesty it seemed that this Bevedan was somewhat eccentric to say the least, and I had no guarantee that he was still where they had last known him to be.

Gamma II's orbit of its parent planet, and therefore its day, was somewhere in the forty-hour region, so the sun was only halfway to the horizon by the time I emerged from a thicket of the gnarled, stunted trees which appeared to be the only form of sizeable vegetation up here, and came into sight of the cave that was my destination. A few terraced ledges of thin soil in which some form of crops had been planted suggested that Bevedan had turned to agriculture to support himself up here, far from anyone with whom he could trade.

But given that very isolation, with whom could I hear him talking?

My helmet's audio receptors picked up the faintest edges of something which I could identify as a Space Marine's voice, although I could not yet make out any words. I made my way closer, trying to hear what was being said in order to gain some idea of what I would be walking into. Launciel and Galad had told me that Bevedan had forsaken combat, but that did not mean that he might not react violently to the arrival of an armoured stranger. Once more, I found myself wondering how to approach a situation and deciding that, against the habits of my Legion and the instincts that had kept me safe for centuries, being direct and open might serve me best. The loud and obvious newcomer might or might not be welcome, but he is unlikely to be mistaken for an assassin.

'Bevedan!' I shouted, still far enough away that I could not make out the individual words being spoken. 'A brother wishes to speak with you!'

When the echoes of my own voice died away – I realised in the aftermath that I had perhaps been incautious, but the tales I had heard of loud noises in mountains sparking a rockfall or snowslide were not borne out on this occasion – I could hear that the speech from within the cave had also stopped. A black-armoured figure stepped out a few moments later, its bolter held in both hands but with the muzzle pointed down and to the side.

'Brother Bevedan?' I asked, but I realised at once that it could not be. Launciel and Galad had not mentioned whether

Bevedan still habitually wore his armour plate, but they had been very clear about one thing: namely, that he lacked his left hand, and had no bionic or prosthesis to replace it. This warrior, however, held his boltgun in two hands.

This was a stranger.

I did not draw my bolt pistols, since to do so was to invite being shot. If I decided I needed to kill this warrior then I would draw and work from there, rather than risk sparking an unnecessary confrontation. Besides which, the Lion had asked me to take his message to any and all of his sons, and the iconography on the black armour told me that this was one of my brothers.

Another shape emerged from the cave, one-handed and clad only in simple cloth. This, then, was Bevedan. He was blond-haired and pale-skinned, with eyes of entirely colourless grey, and a sober aspect that bordered on the morose. He pursed his lips when he saw me, an expression of rueful consideration. I got the impression that my presence was not immediately welcome, and I wondered what I had interrupted.

'And who might you be?' Bevedan called to me. He beckoned with the stump of his forearm; his other hand held no weapon. 'Come closer, since you have come this far.'

'I am Zabriel,' I replied, walking towards them. I attempted to give the impression that my attention was fixed on Bevedan, but I was in fact monitoring my other brother for any indication of hostility, as I had no doubt he was doing to me. 'I come with a message from the Lion.'

Bevedan glanced at the armoured brother beside him. 'From the Lion?'

'Indeed,' I replied. 'It is for all of us, so that includes you, brother,' I continued, openly addressing the mysterious warrior for the first time. 'I did not know another would be here. What is your name?'

He reached up and removed his helmet, revealing features I recognised. 'Zabriel. It has been a long time.'

I frowned, and did the same. 'Baelor? I heard the Dark Angels got you.'

'They were on my tail in the Nephilim Sector,' Baelor said, nodding. 'But they did not have the stomach for the pursuit.'

We had not known each other well on Caliban, but Baelor and I had been at least passing acquaintances. I had sparred with him in the practice cages on occasion, and our respective squads had shared a purging mission once – one I now looked back on with some distaste, as I no longer had any certainty that the traitorous lords we had been sent to eliminate had been anywhere near as dangerous or disloyal as Astelan's orders had made them out to be. Baelor had aged nearly as much as I, from what I could judge, but appeared otherwise unchanged from the solid, dependable warrior I had known him to be.

'The Lion's return is a grand claim,' Bevedan said.

'It is,' I agreed. 'And I have proof of it.' I produced the vid-imager, and played the same message that I had delivered to Launciel and Galad.

My two brothers reacted very differently, although perhaps not obviously so to those unfamiliar with our kind. Bevedan's lips were pinched and his nostrils flared as some strong emotion gripped him, but reading the nature of that emotion was beyond me, other than it was certainly not unbridled joy. Baelor, on the other hand...

His face was completely blank, as unreadable as a fortress wall designed by the Imperial Fists. It set my hackles rising, because what son of the Lion could see and hear that message and not feel *something*? Whether it was incredulity, relief, or rage, I could have understood him falling to his knees and crying out to the hololith for forgiveness, spitting at it in disgust, abusing me as a worm-ridden liar peddling falsehoods, or anything in between.

No, Baelor felt something, but he wished to hide it, and that instantly garnered him my mistrust.

'It sounds like him, as I remember his voice,' Bevedan conceded, his speech somewhat halting. 'And we survived – might he not have, too? What I find harder to believe is that he let you live, given our treachery. And now he sends this obtusely worded message to suggest that he bears no grudge?' He shook his head. 'If this is indeed the Lion, I struggle to believe that he is doing anything other than attempting to gather as many of us together as possible to execute us all at once.'

'Execute us with what?' I demanded. 'His mortal followers? He has perhaps a dozen of us rallied to his banner – more, if he has had any success since I have last seen him, and he is *old* now, Bevedan. I saw him kill five Terminators of the Ten Thousand Eyes, it is true, but it cannot be long before we would be able to overwhelm him if he tried to turn on us–'

I broke off, because Bevedan had looked at Baelor, and was not looking away.

'Is something amiss?' I asked cautiously.

'You did not say that you had tried to kill the Lion, Baelor,' Bevedan said, and there was a dangerous undertone beneath the calmness of his voice. 'You might have mentioned that, when you came here to recruit me.'

I considered his words, and drew the obvious conclusion.

'Baelor,' I said, 'whom do you serve?'

'I serve whom I have always served,' Baelor replied, and I could feel the tension coming off him. 'Knight-Captain Seraphax, who was my commanding officer throughout the Great Crusade, and during the exile on Caliban.'

'And warlord of the Ten Thousand Eyes,' Bevedan added. He

raised his hand. 'Brothers, I came here to escape conflict, and keep my mind calm. Please do not raise your weapons. My days with the Host of Pentacles are long past, but I would wager that I can still draw on the breath of the warp before either of you could pull a trigger, and what is more, *I will do so*.'

I froze. Launciel and Galad had not mentioned that Bevedan had once been of the Librarius. Perhaps they had never known. That might explain his desire for solitude, at any rate: my limited understanding of psykers was that some of them could find the presence of other minds thoroughly unpleasant, even with training.

'You are with the Ten Thousand Eyes?' I asked Baelor. It was hard for me to countenance. Luther or Astelan as traitors, perhaps; they had been high command figures, far removed from me, and I had not known either well. There were sinister rumours about other brothers too, but few and far between – any word of our presence was a lead for our modern kin to chase – and never a name I recognised. We had been a large Legion split into different fleets that only rarely came together in the name of a larger war, so there were countless other Dark Angels from my time whose names I had never heard and faces I had never seen.

Baelor, though; he was someone I had known, and it was hard to reconcile that with an allegiance to the gods of Chaos. What was more, I had faced servants of the Ruinous Powers before, and Baelor bore little resemblance to them. He had removed most of the identification marks from his armour, else I might have recognised him before, but his battleplate bore none of the foul glyphs I had come to associate with Chaos, let alone the twisting and malformation. Even his face looked much the same as I remembered it, allowing for the ageing that had found us all.

'I am with Seraphax,' Baelor said. His tone was bored, as though he were simply repeating a truth, but I could sense the tension within him. He was not certain whether I would risk Bevedan's intervention and attack him anyway. 'And let me assure you, brothers, Seraphax has no wish to kill the Lion, if indeed he has returned. The boarding party who attempted it were disobeying his direct order.'

Something slotted into place for me. 'You commanded that cruiser. The one that did not engage. Throne of Terra, Baelor, you are allies with filth like those berserkers? And you hold to it, even though you have heard the Lion's words, and seen his image?'

'I have seen and heard something you claim to be the Lion,' Baelor said. 'I can understand why you do so. With the galaxy as it is, why would humanity not flock to a mythical figure arisen out of the past? It would allow you to exert some measure of control once more.'

'And attract a lot of attention, and with attention will come our little brothers,' I pointed out. 'Do you honestly think that I – that we – would do this unless we knew we were right? I have avoided the Dark Angels' knives for four hundred years. If I wished to hand myself over to them now then there would be easier ways to do it than raise up a false primarch!'

'You assume that our "little brothers" are even still alive,' Baelor said with a snort. 'They are a thousand callow youths adrift in a galaxy which they have suddenly found is even less hospitable than they thought. There is nothing to say that they have not been swallowed up by it.'

I thought about it for a moment, but shook my head. 'Whatever differences divide us from our modern kin, they inherited our stubbornness. They might be wounded or reduced in number, but they would not have fought the galaxy's darkness for ten thousand years only to succumb to it now. They will not deign to die unless they know that all of us have been killed first, at the very least.'

'I am far from the worst thing abroad in the galaxy, but they were not stubborn enough to capture me,' Baelor sneered. 'They might bear our name, but we fought horrors which they can only imagine.'

I gestured to the sky above, and the galaxy in general. 'I suspect they are catching up. But I think there is little point in wasting words with you, Baelor. I have seen what the Ten Thousand Eyes do, and I cannot imagine that you would turn your face from them, although I wish that you would, and ask the Lion for his mercy.'

'His *mercy?*' Baelor snapped. 'What right does he have to grant me anything, after he betrayed us?'

'He did no such thing,' Bevedan said.

We both looked at him. His expression was even more morose than it had been.

'Neither of you were senior enough to know, I suppose,' he said. 'The Lion was never to be allowed to land on Caliban. Some of the commanders feared he had turned from the Emperor, and had returned to claim all the resources he had us accumulate while he was gone, only to use his largely undamaged Legion to overwhelm his remaining brothers and take control of what was left of the Imperium. A few, I think, feared what he would make of them when he returned. I never broke the Edict of Nikaea on Caliban, but I know others who did, and there were always rumours that some had sought refuge in rituals and practices of which the significance was not understood at the time. Some, I have no doubt, had decided that Horus had a point. But mainly, we were angry. Angry that we had been cast aside and abandoned, and angry that even amidst a galactic war, we had not been trusted enough to help.'

I stared at him in shock. 'Then... Caliban *did* fire first? We fired on our own primarch?'

'A primarch who watched the entire Imperium fall rather than let us fight!' Bevedan said sharply. 'Horus used every asset at his disposal to bring the Emperor low, but the Lion left thirty thousand Astartes sitting on a backwater rock!' He looked me directly in the eye. 'So yes, we fired upon the *Invincible Reason*, because we knew that we had been created for one thing – warfare – and yet in the greatest war humanity had ever known, we were ignored. Our gene-father was either a traitor or an incompetent, or he viewed us to be at least one of those two things. How could there be reconciliation after that?'

I was staggered. I had felt resentment during the exile, of course, but how did resentment lead to attempting to obliterate your own battle-brothers? What was more, I could see that Baelor was going through exactly the same thought process as I; or indeed, a worse one. I had at least come to terms with the notion that the Lion believed he had not attacked us first, and that there might have been treachery in my own higher ranks. I could accept my primarch's belief as genuine, even if I did not know the truth. Yet Baelor had clearly believed for all this time that he was wronged, but here was one of our old battle-brothers telling us that yes, the attack on the Lion's fleet was not only deliberate but *premeditated*.

If misplaced resentment could lead to such treachery against your brothers ten thousand years ago, it could certainly lead to treachery against humanity here and now. I looked back to Baelor, hoping this might be what it took to rebalance his humours.

'Do you see now, brother? The Lion left us in exile, it is true, and perhaps he did not fully trust us, but he did not initiate the battle which saw Caliban destroyed and us scattered. *We* did that, and yet he is willing to put such things aside. Humanity still has hope, certainly while a being such as the Lion exists. Why not leave your path and join him?'

For a moment, I thought my appeal might work. Baelor's cheek twitched, and he looked uncertain. However, then his doubt was replaced with stiffness.

'Humanity has hope, but I am afraid that it will not come from anything you do, Zabriel. Even if your "Lion" were the real thing–'

'Do not give me that,' I interrupted him. 'Do not deny him! You *know* he is real, I can hear it in your voice!'

'Even if he were real, he and you are clinging to outmoded thinking!' Baelor shouted. 'Have you not seen the galaxy, Zabriel? Humanity can huddle around the few fires it has left and wait for the embers to flicker and die, or it can take a radical new course!'

'Worship of the Chaos gods, you mean?' I asked, not bothering to hide my disdain. 'I have seen what happens to their followers, and death is the better outcome.'

Baelor shook his head. 'You think too small. Seraphax would be able to explain it better, but he is not here, and I was never his equal with words.' He looked at Bevedan. 'Will you come? I know you will make a powerful ally, but more importantly, I suspect that you could find purpose in Seraphax's designs. Let him speak with you, brother.'

Bevedan shook his head. 'If Seraphax desires my presence so much then he should have come himself. I settled here for a reason, and I will not leave it for vague promises of undefined hope. It was good to see you, brother, but I will not be going with you.'

Baelor's lip twitched, but he turned to me. 'I know better than to think you will listen to me, Zabriel, but you judge too quickly. Seraphax does what he needs to in order to achieve his goals, just like our Legion always has. Do not assume that those who fight for him are his allies as you understand the term.'

Emperor help me, I wanted to believe him. Baelor himself

could have been any one of my brothers: older, somewhat battered, and with the inevitable weariness that afflicts even a Space Marine once they have been alone and hunted for a century or two. There was nothing about him to suggest that he was tainted by the powers of the warp, and yet I had seen the forces of which he was a part. To think that anyone could fight alongside such perversions of nature and not become corrupted was foolishness at least, and more likely wilful ignorance.

'I will not fight for Seraphax, as an ally or otherwise,' I said. 'And I fear that the next time our paths cross, brother, we will no longer be sparring.'

'That will be interesting,' Baelor said carefully, 'but it will be a shame. In that case, I will take my leave of you both.'

He replaced his helmet and trudged past me, without any further acknowledgement. I expected some form of trick or attack, but he simply carried on walking back down the track up which both he and I had come before, until he reached the knot of twisted trees and disappeared from sight.

'I had expected something more dramatic from a servant of Chaos,' I commented to Bevedan, as much to break the silence as anything else. 'Not that he would just... walk off. Where is he going, in any case?'

'He has a ship in orbit,' Bevedan said. 'I presume he has a shuttle somewhere.' I looked at him, but he waved away my concern. 'Be at ease, brother. Baelor knows better than to aggravate Launciel and Galad by having his ship fire on yours. They will have allowed his presence on the understanding that he starts no fights.'

'They knew he was here?' I exclaimed. 'They allowed him to land?' My suspicions about the pair of them, which had receded after meeting them, came flooding back.

'He is our brother, is he not?' Bevedan asked. 'We might

have our disagreements, but when it comes down to it, we still struggle to kill each other. Launciel and Galad would not tolerate a Chaos fleet arriving in orbit, but a single vessel captained by another of the Fallen? So long as he makes no trouble, they do not order their defences to engage him. By the same token, they know that whatever other powers might cast their attention towards Trevenum Gamma and its moons, the Ten Thousand Eyes would be amongst the last to come as enemies.'

I wanted to argue, but I could not. I had killed servants of the Dark Powers before, but I did not raise my hand to Priavel despite his practices: I simply left him and travelled alone once more. Unpleasant though he had been, there was still a bond between us. At that point there had been no one else I knew of in the galaxy who understood who I was and what I was experiencing, and the same held true for him. Indeed, there was no one else we knew of in the galaxy who could even be *allowed* to know, lest our lives be endangered.

I do not know if Bevedan's threat of psychic action would have stayed my hand if Baelor had not been one of my brothers. If Bevedan himself had not been one of my brothers, I do not know if I would not have tried to kill him first for interfering. Yet I was always more willing to listen to my brothers, to reason with them, to try to find some way in which we need not come into conflict, or at least not yet.

Perhaps this is a flaw in us. Or perhaps the flaw is that we so rarely seek any other option.

I turned to Bevedan. 'I presume your answer to me will be the same – that if the Lion wanted you, he should have come himself. Especially since you tried to kill him once before.'

Bevedan's expression shifted, and I worried that although I had spoken the plain truth, I had provoked him into attacking me. However, he merely sighed.

'Baelor did not come just to try to recruit me for the Ten Thousand Eyes, you know. He came to warn me of the rumours abroad in the galaxy that the Lion had returned. He wished me to be on my guard against those who might seek to use them to manipulate me.'

I nodded as understanding came. 'So when you heard that the Ten Thousand Eyes had already fought the Lion...'

'I suspected that Baelor was not telling the whole truth. Which in fairness, I had already guessed.' He gave me a smile, although it was as lacking in real humour as the rest of his face. 'We are Dark Angels, after all. The Alpha Legion liked to think that they were masters of deception by all assuming the same name, but we guarded secrets that would have stripped their minds bare. An open and honest Dark Angel is as rare a thing as a civilised Space Wolf.'

I snorted a laugh. 'A fair assessment.'

'When the Lion returned to Caliban, I was angry,' Bevedan said. 'I do not know if I felt that it was right to do as we did, but I was surrounded by others who seemed to think so, and I certainly did not feel strongly enough about it to raise my voice against them. I followed orders, I suppose, which as a soldier, was all I was supposed to do.'

'Things feel different now,' I ventured cautiously. 'Rather than having him placed above us by the Emperor, this time the Lion is *asking* for our help.'

Bevedan was silent for a while.

'You made the same offer to Launciel and Galad?'

'I did.'

'What did they say?'

'They are coming with me,' I told him. 'They want the protection the Lion offers for Trevenum.'

'And Launciel said yes, so Galad is going with him,' Bevedan said.

I nodded.

'I... regret what I was a part of,' Bevedan said, after a few more seconds. 'It might have been difficult in those days to work out what was truly right, but I should have known that what we did was wrong. Even if the Lion had turned, had all of those with him? And we called down such ruin on our own, including those who had no concept of what we had done, or why, and who might not have stood with us had they known it. I cannot make that right, but if some of my old brothers are standing with the Lion now then perhaps I can help protect them from whatever dangers they are going to face.'

I blinked in surprise, feeling the unexpected warmth of hope rise in my chest. 'You will come with me?'

'I should see your Lion for myself,' Bevedan said, nodding. 'I suspect he is genuine, but I must make up my own mind. Once I know that, I can decide what to do next. If things are as you say, I can still walk away if I choose to. And if not, then perhaps I will bring our gene-father's falsehoods into the open. You have transport?'

'A shuttle in the valley,' I replied, gesturing downwards and to the west. 'We can likely reach it before nightfall.'

'I will need your help armouring myself first,' Bevedan said ruefully, raising his stump of a left forearm. 'Assuming it still goes together.'

'We will get you back into it,' I said with a smile. 'Come, let us–'

My vox chimed with a priority notification from the *Pax Fortitudinis*. I frowned, and activated it.

'My apologies, Lord Zabriel, I know you ordered that you were not to be contacted unless it is a matter of extreme urgency, but I believe this qualifies,' Captain Montarat said into my ear. *'The astropaths have picked up a distress call.'*

Distress calls were commonplace in Imperium Nihilus; so much so that other astropathic communication struggled to make itself heard above the psychic din of a galaxy in torment, or so I was given to understand. For the captain to assume that this was something which would be of great importance to me...

I grimaced. 'A distress call from where?'

XXVII

Camarth burns.

Most of the largest continent is on fire. Vegetation is aflame, the remaining fuel dumps have gone up, and even natural gas is blazing as it spews up through fissures opened in the land by bombardment. The Ten Thousand Eyes took Camarth with a certain level of efficiency the first time, wiping out the main military strongpoints and executing the leadership. It was a conquest; almost a compliance operation, from the days of the Great Crusade.

This, the Lion knows better. This is much more akin to the extermination operations the First Legion engaged in, although not as comprehensive. Seraphax – and he has no doubt that it was Seraphax – had no interest in completely obliterating the planet's life. He left enough of it untouched that the survivors of his wrath can huddle together, and weep, and wonder why their saviour Lion El'Jonson abandoned them. The feeling of failure, and the rage it provokes, are like twin spectres that lurk at the Lion's shoulders.

He tries not to think about whether Caliban looked like this, before the end.

Camarth still has no astropaths; it was the Lion's relief ships that he sent from Avalus which broadcast the distress call that brought him here. The Ten Thousand Eyes are long gone, of course, leaving nothing behind them but a damaged, burning world.

Or almost nothing.

'Sensor focus, here,' the Lion orders, highlighting an area on the tactical hololith. His voice is clipped and focused, but no one around him is in any doubt about the tight fury contained within it. The bridge crew of the *Glory of Terra* move with the quick, slightly nervous efficiency of people who are not scared of that anger being directed at them, as such, but definitely do not want to cause any delay in it being directed at those responsible.

'My lord Lion!' the vox-officer calls. 'Incoming transmission from Lord Zabriel on the *Pax Fortitudinis*, making its way in-system.'

The Lion taps a control rune, and a new display flashes up. Zabriel is there, and with him are three other faces that could only belong to the Legiones Astartes. The Lion blinks in surprise.

'Zabriel. I see your trip was even more fruitful than we hoped.'

'This is Launciel and Galad, who have assumed command of the defences of the moon Gamma II in the Trevenum System,' Zabriel says, gesturing to a giant in Cataphractii plate and the Tactical Marine beside him. *'And this is Bevedan.'*

'My lord Lion,' Launciel says, in a deep voice as smooth as butter. *'I had not expected to see this day.'* Galad smiles, as though the sight of the Lion has brought him a certain amount of peace. However Bevedan, the left arm of whose armour ends not with a hand but in an ugly plug of ceramite that was surely not fashioned by any Techmarine, has a shadowed expression. There is an internal conflict there, the Lion can tell that much immediately.

'I am glad to see all of you,' he says. 'However, a more detailed reintroduction will have to wait. Zabriel, you have seen what has befallen Camarth?'

'I have,' Zabriel acknowledges, grim-faced. Space Marines are not sentimental beings, but the Lion can imagine Zabriel's grief and rage at seeing the world on which he fought so hard to defend people being consumed by flames.

'Then I would like you to direct your attention here,' the Lion says, transmitting the coordinates of the area he just identified for a sensor focus. It appears to be an island of untouched land amidst the flames, although the choking clouds of smoke billowing across make it difficult for the instruments to get proper readings. 'That is Redmoon Keep, is it not?'

'It is not easy to determine with so much of the surrounding land on fire,' Zabriel says, *'and I only saw it from ground level, never from orbit. But yes, my lord, I think it is.'*

'I do not believe in coincidence, even when dealing with the followers of Chaos,' the Lion says. 'I consider it very unlikely that this location, a former Space Marine fortress and the place where I first attacked the Ten Thousand Eyes, has been left by accident. I suspect there is something there for me to find.' He absent-mindedly rubs the hilt of Fealty, feeling the indentations of the wings against his fingertips. He does not like to think of what further atrocities could have been visited on the place where his brother's sons once lived.

'They have set half the planet on fire,' Zabriel says, his voice tight. *'What more message do you think they could have for you?'*

'I do not know,' the Lion admits. 'But this is a demonstration of power, as much as it is anything else. It is intended to intimidate – or at the very least tell us that our enemies are not intimidated by *us*. No, I feel that Redmoon Keep will hold something more personal to me, some communication from a son to his father.'

'You intend to make planetfall?' Zabriel asks, and the Lion nods.

'I do.'

'Then we will come with you,' Zabriel says firmly. It is neither a request nor an offer, but the Lion is not minded to refuse him in any case.

'I will welcome your company, and that of any of your brothers who wish to join us. I am well aware that I am not invulnerable, and the environment will be too hostile for baseline mortal troops.' He breaks the communication, and turns to exit the bridge. 'Make a shuttle ready!'

Two members of the Lion Guard fall in beside him as soon as he walks through the blast doors into the main area of the ship. They are both tight-lipped and grim-faced, but the Lion can sense no judgement from them for the fate that has overcome their world, no resentment or malice for taking them from it, or being too late to protect it. If that is true, then they are kinder to him than he is to himself. Still, perhaps the mortals have the right of it. There is only one party at fault here, and it is the one which chose to rain destruction down on this world from orbit in order to take petty revenge on an enemy who was not even there at the time.

'Ectorael,' he says into his vox. 'Have you been able to complete the repairs to my armour?'

'Yes, my lord,' the ancient Techmarine replies. He approached the suit with a quiet awe bordering on reverence when he first saw it, and wasted no time in expressing to the Lion exactly how fine a piece of craftsmanship it was. All the same, ceramite was ceramite, and Ectorael set about repairing the damage dealt to it by the Terminators of the Ten Thousand Eyes. His workspace had been granted at the sufferance of the tech-priests of the *Glory of Terra*, and lacked the dedicated tools of a Legion armoury, but the Lion could tell that Ectorael was relishing even this freedom.

He sees it amongst his other sons, too. Zabriel watched his own back for so long that he had almost become twitchy, but that is fading, although there is a certain keen alertness above and beyond that of a Space Marine which the Lion doubts will ever go away completely. Aphkar and Lohoc are so used to keeping a low profile that they instinctively stay in corners and shadows and lack the usual forthrightness of Space Marines, even with mortals, but that is starting to change. Even Kai's brashness now feels less like a performance to overcompensate for a similar timidity and more like a natural part of his own personality, although the Lion is not certain he counts that a positive change as such.

Borz clearly achieved and kept his position through ruthlessness, and while that is hardly a poor character trait for a Space Marine, the Lion thinks he can sense a certain relief from the one-eyed warrior now. Borz is a natural leader, perhaps, but not a natural general. He feels more at ease within a command structure where he has orders to follow; he is slowly coming back to that mindset, and bringing his flotilla with him.

The Lion is hardly in the process of forging a new Legion out of these few warriors, but he is hopeful that they are beginning to remember what it feels like to belong to a brotherhood. He has no idea how far he can go in terms of protecting the galaxy, or what other forces will eventually flock to his banner. Ideally, word will spread – slow though that will be, given the limits on both warp travel and astropathic communication – and he will be joined by the modern Space Marine Chapters. Perhaps then he can do more than help a few isolated star systems. However, in the meantime, he has to rely on these few sons of his.

He recognises that there is a certain irony in that, given that not so long ago – at least by his experience of time – he considered them all traitors. Nonetheless, they are his sons. He does not believe that all grudges have been buried, but he understands that decades or centuries had largely ground down the jagged edges of spite to leave only weariness. They are all adrift in a time not their own and looking for purpose in lives which had once been laid out for them, and there is something shared in that.

Besides, the Lion does not trust unreservedly. He never has. This is a second chance for them all, himself included, but while the Lion is not necessarily expecting betrayal, he will be watching for it.

And should he find it, he will have no mercy.

The Corona-class lander is an old vessel, a model that the Lion is almost surprised still flies, but then he has become accustomed to the fact that the Imperium has not progressed since his day. Indeed, in many matters it has positively *re*gressed, although he keeps such thoughts to himself. However, this shuttle was present in the bays of the *Glory of Terra*, and it was functional, and it suited his needs.

'The air is thick with ash,' Ectorael mutters. 'If too much builds up in the engine intakes…' The Techmarine has one hand splayed against the wall, as though he is monitoring the shuttle's spirit like it were the breathing of a wounded animal. Perhaps he is.

'Do not worry, old friend,' Lamor says with a chuckle. 'If we start to fall from the sky, I am sure I can carry you to safety.' He slaps the harness of his jump pack for emphasis.

'He will be heavy, with all that extra weight,' says Breunan, one of Borz's warriors, looking at Ectorael's servo-arms. He too is a former Assault Marine, with a jump pack of his own. 'You will need help.'

Lamor bristles, and nods towards Borz. 'Will you not be helping your own, *pirate?*'

'Not likely,' Borz calls, from the other side of the hold. 'He knows who the more valuable is out of the two of us!'

A ripple of laughter passes through the Corona, mainly from those who had not been part of Echo Station, but Borz's self-deprecating humour seems to thaw the tension, even if only slightly. The Lion did wonder about the wisdom of putting all of his sons together like this, after so long apart and when at least two of the factions within them had been in opposition at times, but he decided to trust them. They do not have to follow him, after all; if they do, he expects them to bury old arguments.

'Status?' he says into his vox.

'Altitude four thousand feet and descending,' the servitor pilot replies from the cockpit. *'No enemy fire detected.'* The Lion can see their escort of half a dozen Lightning fighters flanking them, but none of them have taken hits either. Whatever is waiting for them at Redmoon Keep, it appears that it is not merely a lure to then shoot them out of the sky.

'Three thousand feet and descending.'

The Corona is starting to shake now, buffeted by the massive thermal updraughts from the enormous fires below. Visibility is decreasing as the smoke thickens, and what can be seen begins to waver in a heat haze. The Lion waits, expecting each new jarring tilt or pitch to herald the impact of a weapon, but the descent continues uninterrupted.

'One thousand feet.'

'Be ready,' the Lion tells his sons. He places his helm on his head, and checks the read-outs. His armour is as good as new, according to the displays of structural integrity and power feed, and he is grateful once more for Ectorael's work. He intends to be more than just a figurehead to whatever remains of humanity, but he is well aware that humans will cling onto images, and it is difficult to look like an inspiring protector without armour that fits.

'Five hundred feet. Landing sequence initiated.'

The Lion's audio receptors pick up a faint grinding noise as the Corona's landing gear extends. The Lightnings pull away and start to circle. If anyone wishes to rid the galaxy of Lion El'Jonson and those of his sons who have pledged themselves to him once more, now is the time for them to make their move.

The Corona settles onto its landing skids. They are down.

The Lion does not need to issue any orders. Kai has already activated the door release, and the lander's access ramp drops to reveal a scene that might have come straight from the hells of Old Earth.

The Lion remembers these forests, lush and verdant and packed with life. They were dangerous places, filled with plants that would strangle or poison and animals that hunted with rending claws or lethal venom sacs, but there was a certain savage beauty to them nonetheless.

Now they burn, greedy flames consuming the trunks and leaves, and leaving nothing but black char and floating ash so thick it looks like swarms of insects carried upwards on the breeze. From this vantage point, where the Lion and his sons have landed on the road that leads up the slope of Mount Santic, they are surrounded by a ring of fire. However, a wide area of land has been cleared around the mountain's base to prevent the flames from spreading to it: a firebreak, presumably cut in by those who committed this monumental act of arson.

'To the fortress,' the Lion orders, 'and stay alert. I suspect our enemy intends me to remain alive at least for long enough to encounter whatever he has left for me, but there is no guarantee that he will not consider you expendable. He has set half a planet on fire just to wound me – I doubt he will think twice about killing his brothers to achieve the same result.'

They are a mismatched group of twenty-one, many of whom

have not seen each other for centuries before this day – if indeed they ever knew each other at all – but they still settle into a formation without needing to exchange words. Breunan and Lamor take point, making short hops ahead on their jump packs. The Lion comes behind them, flanked by Zabriel on one side, both bolt pistols drawn and tracking, and Lohoc the Red Whisper on the other, his plasma gun charged and ready, while Kai walks directly behind them. Borz One-Eye and his other three pirates, Perziel and Rufarel with their bolters and Cadaran with a flamer, are on the left flank, while Guain, along with Kuziel's meltagun and the bolters of Elian and Meriant – also formerly of Echo Station – take the right. In the middle walk the three specialists: Ectorael the Techmarine, Asbiel the Apothecary, and Bevedan, formerly of the Librarius, who is yet to meet the Lion's eye. Bringing up the rear are Launciel and Galad, along with Aphkar, and the final member of the Echo Station Space Marines, Danidel, who bears an ancient Sol Militaris-pattern heavy bolter on his right shoulder.

They are a formidable force indeed, but the Lion is still wary. He knows only too well how the forces of Chaos can twist reality so that strength becomes weakness, and bravery becomes foolishness.

A turn in the road brings them within sight of the ruins of Redmoon Keep. There is little left of it that one could call a building, since the Lion and Zabriel destroyed it with the detonation of its power cores. There are a few semi-intact walls poking up here and there like damaged teeth in diseased gums, but the fortress is mostly rubble.

Most of the gates still stand, however, and in front of them is a lone figure.

'Lord?' Breunan asks. Both he and Lamor are, perhaps unconsciously, cycling up the outputs on their jetpacks, ready to launch themselves into the air.

The Lion focuses on the figure, and his helm obliges by magnifying the image. The nature of it is immediately clear.

'Heretic,' Zabriel says from alongside him, having come to the same conclusion.

'Advance cautiously,' the Lion orders. 'He is obviously here for a reason, and if that reason is to speak with me, I will do so. Anything our enemy says can be useful, even if it is lies.'

'That is no Dark Angel,' Lohoc rasps. 'Nor ever was.'

'I hope you are correct,' the Lion says. The half-machine monsters the primarch fought here were grotesquely swollen and distorted, but although this Space Marine is a giant like them, his proportions are normal, and one hand rests on a tall-handled axe with a pale blade. However, the uneasiness that gnaws at the Lion's belly eases as they approach closer. The traitor's armour is green, but this is not the dark forest green the Lion hears that his modern sons now wear; this is an iridescent shade that shifts and glitters in the uneven light from the surrounding flames, and whatever the local star manages to get through the billowing, smoky atmosphere. There is no familiar iconography or markings, even corrupted or altered. Whoever this warrior is, he was never a Dark Angel, and the Lion breathes a little more easily for that. He has no doubt that the day will come when he sees one of his sons so corrupted, but he is glad it is not this day.

'Name yourself!' the Lion shouts. He is glad to see that his escort are covering their surroundings, rather than focusing on the mysterious figure. The Lion can see no other sign of life, either within the ruined fortress or amongst the trees which line the road, but he does not trust that this is the case.

'I am Markog, commander of the Dolorous Guard,' the heretic says. His voice is surprisingly melodious, with the faintest thrill of strange harmonics that the ear only just registers, and then wonders if it has done so. 'I am bodyguard to Seraphax, Lord Sorcerer of the Ten Thousand Eyes.'

'Is he here?' the Lion demands.

'No.'

'Then you are in the wrong place, bodyguard, and you are wasting my time,' the Lion declares. He raises the Arma Luminis, although it would be a long shot to hit Markog at this range. 'If you have a message for me, then speak it, but be warned that I have little patience for games.'

'Lord Seraphax wishes to become reacquainted with you, his gene-sire,' Markog pronounces, as the Lion continues to advance. 'I have been ordered to tell you where you can find him, should you wish to discuss...' He pauses, and gestures around him. 'The current situation of Camarth, or indeed anything else. You have interfered in my lord's designs, and he would like to explain them to you in more detail, to prevent further misunderstandings.'

'This one is markedly too polite for a Chaos worshipper who has burned a planet,' Kaï comments from behind the Lion.

'How observant,' Aphkar replies, sarcasm dripping from his voice. 'I suddenly get the feeling we should not trust him.'

They are closer now, close enough that the Lion is confident the plasma weaponry he holds can burn Markog's head from his shoulders. 'Do as you have been bid, and have done,' he orders the traitor. 'You might enjoy the sound of your voice, but I do not.'

'I have a condition,' Markog says. He reaches up and removes his helmet – the mouth grille of which seems to be grinning obscenely, even though it is only metal – to reveal his face. A growl rises involuntarily in the Lion's chest at what is revealed.

Markog still looks human, or at least transhuman, but there is nothing about the features revealed that sits quite rightly.

His eyes are too large, with pupils so swollen that they leave only the faintest rim of colour at the edge of the iris. His cheekbones are so sharp they look like they could cut flesh, his chin is too long, his mouth and nostrils too wide. When he smiles he reveals pointed teeth of gleaming white, with an overlong tongue lurking behind them that stirs impatiently. His skin has a pearlescent sheen, not dissimilar to the iridescence of his armour. Everything about his face suggests that it is changing to maximise the sensory stimulus to his brain, intensifying what he witnesses and experiences. He sighs and rolls his eyes as the Lion's growl reaches his ears, as though he were an epicure delighting in sampling a new delicacy from a distant world, but when he focuses again there is a literal hunger in his gaze.

'Ah, the distaste of your Legion has a tang all of its own, fermented and rotted by all your years in the darkness,' Markog says. 'Baelor is more like the rest of you than he knows.'

'You weary me,' the Lion tells him, 'and I have no patience for any condition you may set. Give me your message, or I will strike you down and hunt your master myself.'

'But that is my condition!' Markog replies eagerly. 'You must strike me, and then take my blow in return. Only then will I reveal my master's location to you, Flawed Knight.' He licks his lips with his long tongue in anticipation, opening narrow wounds on the organ as he drags it across his sharp teeth.

The Lion frowns. 'What did you call me?'

'The warp knows you as the Flawed Knight, or so my master informs me,' Markog says, a touch of impatience entering his tone. 'Come, Emperor's son! I yearn to feel the kiss of your blade!'

The Lion aches to strike him down, but the thought of giving this heretic what he claims to want is anathema to him. Nonetheless, nor is he prepared to let Markog live another second.

'Zabriel,' the Lion says, and gestures.

No further instruction is needed. The former Destroyer steps forward and brings his blade around in an arc that catches the grinning Markog just under his jawbone. Whatever has happened to the traitor's skin to make it glisten in the light, it appears to have done nothing to harden it: the chainsword rips through into the meat of his neck, then judders through that and out the other side. Markog's head comes away in a shower of flecks of torn meat and drops to the ground; Zabriel steps back, waiting for the giant Space Marine's body to catch up with events and fall.

It does not.

Instead, when it begins to move downwards, it does so in a graceful kneeling motion, bracing itself on the hand still holding the haft of the large, pale-bladed axe. Markog's free hand reaches out and plucks his own severed head off the floor, then holds it out at Zabriel's eye level. Eyes still wide and moving, and mouth still smiling, Markog's lips and tongue form words without sound. Then the traitor takes a step backwards, and simply disappears.

The sudden departure of a potential threat is almost more unnerving than the arrival of one. Weapons which had been held ready snap up to cover the suddenly empty spot where Markog had been standing, and power weapons are activated with a hum, and the *pop* of immediately ionised air.

The Lion fires the Arma Luminis. The superpowered energy bolt vaporises part of the gate without striking anything else first. Markog has gone.

'Cutting the head off doesn't work,' Kai says, apparently to himself. 'Something to remember.'

'Maybe not,' Zabriel says, turning to face the Lion. 'But at least we know where they are. Or where they say they are.'

'Where?' the Lion asks. 'I heard no words.'

'Nor I,' Lohoc agrees.

'Hmm.' Zabriel's face is hidden by his helm, but he sounds even more uneasy at that revelation than he did after he had beheaded a warrior without killing him. 'He said that Seraphax is on the world of Sable.

'And Markog said that he would be waiting for me there, to give me the blow that is my due.'

XXVIII

Practice does not come naturally to a primarch, simply because everything else *does*.

Lion El'Jonson has sometimes wondered what it would be like to be human, actually baseline human. He presumes that there is more to it than being a frail sack of watery meat for whom the galaxy seems to offer little more than uncounted numbers of ways in which to die. The greatest of humans might manage, with considerable effort, to come close to a primarch's competence in some matters; at least, one in which the primarch in question has no particular interest. Most humans will never achieve even this. They are lesser beings, by any definition that makes rational sense.

The Lion does not see any problem with this view. Humanity evolved naturally, and evolution requires only that genes are passed on successfully. Some of humanity's biology is redundant. In some individuals biology fails catastrophically, but evolution does not care; if the genes are passed on then it was good enough, and if they are not then it was a dead end. Humanity as a whole is trial and error on a massive scale, whereas the Lion was one of a handful of genetically crafted beings, designed from the ground up. Whatever else the Emperor may or may not have been, He was still an incredibly gifted geneticist, scientist, and military commander. It is unsurprising that His hand-created sons are so far beyond baseline humanity that they might, in more superstitious times, have been taken as gods. It does not reflect any underlying value, simply differing levels of ability.

However, when everything comes so naturally – if 'naturally' is the correct word, given such an artificial genesis – the notion of having to practise something is almost utterly alien. Practice is for mortals. Even Space Marines have to drill and train to learn their combat skills, and ensure they do not degrade. The only purpose practice has ever served for Lion El'Jonson has been to enhance his abilities from 'very good' to 'superlative'.

To find something that he has not mastered before he has even tried it is infuriating.

'Clear your mind, and try again,' Zabriel advises. He is seated cross-legged opposite the Lion, dressed in a hooded robe.

'Clearing my mind is a near impossibility,' the Lion growls. He opens one eye and glowers at his son, who looks outwardly serene. 'You truly find this easy?'

'I did not at first,' Zabriel admits. 'It took some time to master.'

'Why did you persist?'

Zabriel's cheek twitches. 'I was alone in the galaxy, hunted and without allies, and without purpose. Fear might not have found me, but desperation has its own claws. There were times that my continued existence seemed… pointless. Meditation helped me shed those feelings, or at least examine them dispassionately.'

'I see.' The Lion purses his lips. 'I am glad, Zabriel, that you did not succumb to them.'

'As am I, my lord, or I would not have seen your return.' Zabriel shakes his head slightly. 'But this discussion is not helping us address the matter at hand. You are certain that you wish to continue?'

'I am,' the Lion replies. 'I may not fully understand this gift that I have been granted, but it is a foolish commander who does not use the assets he has available when his forces are otherwise outmatched.'

He closes his eyes and begins again, noting and discarding the sounds and sensations around him, then focusing on the rhythm of his own breathing. Zabriel matches his breaths to those of his primarch, to minimise distractions. The Lion visualises the forest once more: not the forests of Caliban exactly as he remembers them, but the strange world into which he has previously slipped, which is like Caliban, yet with echoes of every other forest he has ever seen. Nor does he shut Zabriel out of his awareness, but holds his son's presence close.

He has until they reach Sable.

The *Pax Fortitudinis* slips out of the warp with not much more than a notable judder, and brief flares of unnatural colours at the edges of its passengers' vision. It is an uncommonly easy transition, especially in these times, and the Lion wishes that he did not suspect it might have something to do with the sorcerer who awaits them easing their passage for his own ends.

Seraphax. Knight-Captain Seraphax, as he was. The Lion remembers him, although not in any great detail. He was a good commander, and a good warrior. Now he has apparently become a sorcerer and a warlord, in this cursed far future. Seraphax's choices were his own to make, and the Lion knows he should not self-flagellate over the decisions made by another, but he cannot help but wonder how much misery has been unleashed on the galaxy by his lost sons, and how much of that might have been avoided.

'Report,' he orders, pushing the other thoughts from his mind, at least for now.

The ship's crew obeys, feeding back information and analysis with a clipped precision that belies the tension the Lion can smell on the air. It was his decision to come in one small ship, this Cobra-class destroyer, rather than bring what passes for his war fleet. His reasoning is simple: even though the surviving ships of Avalus have been bolstered by those of the other nearby systems with which contact has been made, it is far from an armada to match the reported strength of the Ten Thousand Eyes. The Lion has no intention of leading them all into a trap in which Seraphax could snuff out their naval strength in one engagement.

The invitation was to the Lion, and so the Lion has answered. He has to trust that Seraphax has a purpose, one which goes beyond a simple military engagement. Whether his arrival in such a small ship is greeted with amusement, scorn, pity, or any number of other emotions is inconsequential to him. All he intends to do is spring this trap and turn it upon its maker.

If he is wrong, however, he intends to limit the number of those who will die with him.

The Lion pieces together the information he receives as the *Pax Fortitudinis* makes its way inwards from the system's Mandeville point. The star is a red giant, bloated and swollen as it approaches the end of its cosmic life cycle, although it will burn for millions of years yet before it gutters out and fades into a white dwarf. Sable would have once been a dark, icy outer world, far from its parent's light, but now it is bright and warm.

And overrun.

'There are *voices* on the vox,' the officer reports, pulling her headset off and setting it down with a shudder. 'Unnatural ones. Forgive me, my lord, but–'

The Lion waves her apology away before it has fully formed. 'I know the foulness our enemies can spew, and I would not have it corrupting your mind. Bevedan?'

'My lord Lion,' Bevedan replies, stepping forward, and the vox-officer stands aside and surrenders her console to him. The Lion asked Bevedan to be ready to undertake this role, since he has experience of mental discipline thanks to wielding his psykana powers, and the one-handed Space Marine acceded without complaint. Zabriel told the Lion of what Bevedan said on Trevenum Gamma II, and Bevedan presumably knows this, but the Lion has not broached the subject: he is content to judge his son on his actions, not his history, and if Bevedan wishes to make a confession to him then he will do so in his own time.

'Long-range scans suggest significant defensive capability,' the auspex officer reports, not without a hint of nervousness in his voice. It is understandable; he knows that should it come to a fight then the *Pax Fortitudinis* is as good as dead, and the farther they get from the Mandeville point, the less likely they are to be able to escape.

The tactical hololith flickers into life. At this range the sensors are unable to make out the full detail of what may be waiting for them, but the blobs in orbit around Sable suggest a significant number of warships. However, one return is different.

'What is this?' the Lion asks, highlighting it. He has to wait for an answer as the auspex slowly processes the available information into a conclusive response. All that while, the *Pax Fortitudinis* moves farther and farther inwards from the Mandeville point; a shell of metal barely a mile long, heading for the stronghold of a Chaos warband.

Finally, the auspex officer has an answer. 'Read-outs suggest a low-density octagonal structure, detecting high levels of… calcium?'

'Bones,' Zabriel says flatly. He points to the information. 'Throne of Terra, that thing's bigger than this ship!'

'The bones of the planet's population,' Kai says. The Lion looks at him, and he shrugs. 'That is my guess, at any rate. These heretics do like their grand, horrific statements.'

The Lion bares his teeth. His own Legion made use of grim iconography, but such a foul ossuary is an offence to all dignity, and it sickens him to think that one of his sons might have been responsible for it. However, he has learned that little that this enemy does is without purpose, no matter how twisted or incoherent it may seem.

'It is in geostationary orbit?' he asks.

'Yes, my lord.'

He taps control glyphs, and the answers he seeks flash up. 'And situated over the governor's palace. It seems likely that location is of some import to Seraphax, and therefore will probably be our destination. But let us find out. Bevedan, are we ready to transmit?'

'Yes, my lord,' Bevedan reports. The Lion waits until the rune goes green, then speaks.

'This is Lion El'Jonson. Seraphax, my son. You invited me here, and I have come.' It burns the Lion to be so civil to a monster who has turned a planet's population into an orbiting ornament, but he has ever kept his true thoughts hidden, and his voice remains level. He has no illusions that Seraphax's intentions are genuine, any more than his own are, but they will each play this game of pretend until one of them feels he is in position to strike. 'Your messenger boy said you wished to explain your designs to me. I am here, and I am listening.'

He ends the transmission, and the *Pax Fortitudinis* waits once more. Then Bevedan signals that he is getting a response, and the signal comes through.

'My gene-sire, how remarkable it is to hear your voice once more,' Seraphax says. He has a richly melodious tone, and it triggers some more of the Lion's memories: a brief exchange about a world brought into compliance; Seraphax laughing as he sparred with one of his company in the duelling cages; a concise report of losses taken in a boarding action against an ork vessel. Minor things and unremarkable moments, snapshots from a life that could have belonged to a thousand other Dark Angels.

'I must admit I am surprised that you came to me with only one vessel,' Seraphax continues. *'I am taking this as a gesture of trust, and I am willing to extend the same. Your ship will not be fired upon or boarded so long as you make no hostile moves. I have included the coordinates for where your shuttles can make landing, if you wish to conduct this conversation in a more immediate fashion.'*

'Bastard almost sounds convincing,' Kai observes, as the message ends. 'But then he always did have a glib tongue on him.'

'The governor's palace,' Zabriel says, pointing at the coordinates that have flashed up. 'You were right, my lord. Assuming he intends to let us make planetfall at all, rather than destroying us in transit, that would appear to be his seat of power.'

The Lion smiles tightly. 'It is good to have one's suspicions confirmed.' He extinguishes the hololith and turns to the cocoon which houses Captain Montarat. 'Captain, please instruct the shuttle to be ready to launch as we discussed.'

'Of course, my lord Lion.'

The Lion takes a step towards the bridge doors, then pauses. 'And captain? Once our deception is discovered, please launch a torpedo volley at that construction of bone before you make yourself scarce.'

'My lord,' Montarat says, her electronic voice taking on a tone of grim satisfaction, *'it will be my pleasure.'*

XXIX

Baelor stalked the halls of the ridiculously named Palace of Glory on Sable, dissatisfaction and unease growing within him in equal measure. He barely responded to the various salutes, obeisances and other acknowledgements of his rank made by the warriors of the Ten Thousand Eyes whom he passed. In part, this was born of his own displeasure: Seraphax had decided to surround himself with a battalion of the Broken Horn, a warband of beastmen led by the odious King Mehgrud, a massive abhuman even bigger than most Space Marines. Despite Baelor's words to Zabriel about not judging Seraphax by those that followed him, he found beastmen a distasteful reminder of how easily humanity's genetic code could be mutated. The grunting brutes were everywhere, bleating worship of their gods and stinking of their foul musk.

He turned a corner and came out into an atrium, which had at one point been decorated by the governors to show the planet's proud history. Now the tapestries and paintings had been torn down to build the blazing fire that sat in the middle of the floor, blackening the tiles on which it stood, and the hololithic art projectors had been smashed and cast aside. The walls were covered with the beastmen's scrawls instead, angular splashes of blood and filth which spoke of primitive bestiality, yet also somehow hinted at an innate understanding of the workings of the Ruinous Powers. The space had become a herd pit, a place for the warband to sleep and eat, and indulge in whatever passed for the finer points of their society.

A lot of them were indeed sleeping, huddled up together in a mass of horned heads, mismatched fur, and cloven hooves. Others were seeing to their weapons. Even now, Baelor found it strange to see their animalistic features creased in concentration as humanlike hands loaded ammunition into an autogun, or dismantled and cleaned out a firing mechanism. However, a large group were in a loose circle around two individuals, and judging by the roars and hoots and hollers, a fight was taking place. Baelor heard the impact of knuckles on flesh, and then the crowd parted as one of the combatants staggered out, bleeding from several small wounds.

The beastman, apparently knocked woozy by the most recent punch thrown by his opponent – a white-furred individual, still within the circle, and breathing heavily as though trying to muster the energy to pursue his foe – stumbled into Baelor. Baelor would have simply shoved him away in disgust and left them to their amusement had the beastman in question, its mind inflamed by violence and humiliation, not turned and lashed out at whatever it had just collided with.

Baelor caught the creature's wrist without effort, then reached out with his other hand and clamped it around the beastman's throat. Its eyes widened in alarm and fear, and he considered throttling it, but found that the prospect gave him no enjoyment.

He made a fist, and the bones of the mutant's neck gave way beneath his ceramite-encased fingers with a soft *snap*.

Baelor opened his hand again and let the beastman fall to the floor. The shouting and yammering had stopped as soon as his presence had been noticed, and it did not start again. The crowd slunk backwards away from him, heads lowered cautiously and eyes fixed on him to both watch for an attack or be ready to obey his orders.

He considered saying something, but what would he say? He had no need or desire to apologise for his temper, but nor did he wish to issue a warning or chastisement. They were beasts, and were acting according to their nature. That nature had annoyed him, and so the culprit had died. That was the way of things in the Ten Thousand Eyes.

Baelor flexed his fingers once, growled in the back of his throat, and stalked off.

The governors of Sable had not been ones for subtlety or modesty. The centre of the court was a throne room in truth, with the governor's seat in question raised high on a dais from where they had overlooked the lesser beings over whom they ruled. The floor around the room's edge was a wide terrace on which the courtiers and officials had gathered, clustered together in groups of rank or function as dictated by the differently coloured tiles. In the middle was a hexagonal pit where, as Baelor understood it, petitioners and criminals had stood to receive their respective judgements. Baelor found it bleakly amusing that the governor's bones were now mingled with those of his subjects in the *ostella*, as Seraphax called it, that orbited above them, given that the throne room was as eloquent an example as any of how humans could come to see themselves as utterly and unquestionably superior to those to whom they were essentially the same, when viewed from the perspective of a centuries-old transhuman warrior.

Now, of course, things looked different, but these were not the haphazard, vandalistic alterations made by the Broken Horn. Seraphax had prepared for his ritual with characteristic thoroughness, from the ritual pyres positioned at the corners of the sigil of the Eightfold Path in the pit, to the glyphs daubed in triple-distilled blood on selected floor tiles, to the giant mirror of polished silver, shaped from a piece of one of the daemon engine towers of Tzeentch, that hung over the throne. Baelor remembered the battle in which that particular trophy had been claimed: some of the Ten Thousand Eyes had been fearful of angering the Changer of Ways by despoiling one of the god's instruments in such a manner, but Seraphax had argued that Tzeentch would be appeased since the metal in question was destined for one of the grandest schemes the galaxy had ever seen. As it turned out, it was going to be even grander than Seraphax had envisaged at the time, thanks to the re-emergence of the Lord of the First.

'Ah, Baelor,' Seraphax greeted him, looking around. He appeared much the same as always, apart from the chains of dark iron which now criss-crossed his chest. Markog lurked behind the sorcerer like a giant green shadow, and his expression was notably less pleased. Baelor ignored him; Markog's head was firmly reattached to his body now, after his encounter with the Lion's Fallen, but his recovery was less impressive when – as Baelor did – you knew his secret.

Seraphax sniffed. 'You have the scent of death on you, my friend.'

'More so than usual?' Baelor asked. He had kept a kill counter active on his helmet's display back when he was a green initiate of the First Legion, and even been proud of himself as the tally rose and rose. He abandoned that practice when the numbers became meaningless, well before he even first laid eyes on the

Lion, let alone the long years doing his knight-captain's bidding since they had escaped the warp storm. He was not sure how Seraphax could sense any individual death when set against the mountain of lives he had taken over the centuries.

'A fresh one,' Seraphax said. He sniffed again. 'And catalysed by… irritation? It is not often that you kill for such a reason, brother. What vexes you?'

To deny Seraphax's assertion was to do a disservice to his commander's power of perception, and to hide behind a non-answer was to refuse to give insight which had been requested. Baelor sighed.

'The Lion vexes me. This entire situation vexes me.'

Markog's eyes lit up, and his hand tightened on the haft of Heartdrinker at the notion that someone might be insulting his lord and therefore required punishment, especially since that someone was Baelor. However, Seraphax merely nodded.

'It is a difficult thing, to be sure. We seek to bring down the being whose genetic code made us what we are today, and through him strike at the heart of what we once served. It is easy to be overwhelmed, or fall into doubt.'

'It is not that,' Baelor said, shaking his head. 'Or at least, not that directly. He has come with one ship, and a Cobra-class destroyer at that? Where is his fleet? Surely you cannot think that he intends to take you at your word?'

'It matters little,' Seraphax said, smiling reassuringly. 'Perhaps he does indeed wish to offer me a chance at redemption, as he sees it, and will approach us peacefully. Perhaps he has ascertained that I need him alive, and seeks to use that to get close to me before betraying me. It is inconsequential. His escort will be killed and his transport destroyed as soon as he sets down.' Seraphax placed one hand on the chains hanging over his breastplate. 'And even a primarch can be bound, with the correct tools.'

Baelor grimaced. 'I still do not like it, knight-captain. This is the Lion. *The Lion!* You know as well as I that he is uncompromising, grim, and merciless, perhaps the greatest of the Emperor's generals. If he had come at the head of a war fleet then I would be happier. This feels like he is walking too meekly into your trap, and I do not trust it. The Broken Horn are numerous, but they are not Astartes. If we had the Arch-Raptor and his warriors, or Jai'tana's Possessed, then–'

'The Unshriven commands the ships,' Seraphax cut him off, 'and Urienz has his own instructions to follow elsewhere. The Broken Horn are more than a match for any mortal allies the Lion might bring, and we have the Dolorous Guard.'

Baelor glanced at Markog. 'All the same...'

'Well, the bones are cast now,' Seraphax said with a shrug, while behind his back Markog's eyes flashed at Baelor's doubt of his warriors' capabilities. 'No great venture can be undertaken without risk, and by setting ourselves against a primarch we are certainly engaging in risk. It is possible that we all may die today, as our gene-sire stuns us with some unforeseen tactic, or a surprise dredged up from the Dark Age of Technology.' He smiled again, the visible half of his mouth quirking upwards. 'So be it. I have worked too long and too hard to abandon my dream when the key to it is within my reach.' He walked over to Baelor, and reached up to cup his cheek. The ceramite of his gauntlet was cool against Baelor's flesh.

'We have the ability to reshape the galaxy,' Seraphax said softly, 'and we are so close. The Lion has one grand purpose left, whether he chooses to see it or not, and if we can help him achieve it then everything we have done, *everything*, will be worthwhile. But I cannot do this without you, Baelor. I need your certainty.'

Baelor laughed despite himself. 'Look at you. You wield power I cannot comprehend, and you strike bargains with beings I cannot name. I am little different to how I was back on Caliban. You have surpassed me by so much that I scarcely know where to begin in counting the differences.'

'Nonsense!' Seraphax said, dropping his hand. 'I may have changed, but that is why I need you. You keep me grounded, Baelor, else I would have lost myself to the gods long ago and become nothing more than their puppet! Instead I am still myself, with my own thoughts.' He shook his head, the flames flickering, then leant forward and planted a kiss on Baelor's forehead. 'You are the only one on whom I can totally rely.'

For a moment, Baelor saw the look of fury on Markog's face before it was replaced by the giant's more usual expression of sensuous hunger. For a wonder, the commander of the Dolorous Guard's anger did not seem to have been directed at Baelor, but rather at Seraphax himself. Something stirred uneasily in Baelor's gut, and he took a step back from his captain, ready to reach for his bolter if Markog lashed out.

In the distance, something exploded.

Baelor whirled towards the noise and vibrations, snapping his bolter up and opening a vox-channel at the same time. 'What was that?'

Nothing answered him apart from muffled noises which even his superlative hearing could not parse into much that made sense, and he cursed silently at the Broken Horn. Beastmen might be stronger, faster, more resilient and more ferocious than most mortal troops, but at least your average cultist or militia deserter knew how to speak into a warp-damned vox-unit...

However, there was a sound that he could identify.

'Bolters,' he reported tensely. 'We have bolter fire, somewhere in the palace.' He altered the vox settings to broadcast to the ships above them. 'Unshriven, has there been any shuttle launched from the Cobra?'

There was nothing but the hiss of static for a few seconds, until Jai'tana's voice replied, as unpleasant to the ear as ever. *'No, the destroyer is still some distance from orbit.'*

'Any teleport flare?'

'You are aware that the palace is covered by a teleport jammer–'

'Of course I am aware!' Baelor shouted. 'I oversaw its deployment! But we have hostiles firing boltguns within the palace perimeter, so has there been a bastard teleport flare?'

'No, there has not,' the Apostle replied, and even he sounded discomforted. *'Wait... The Cobra has opened fire. A full volley of torpedoes. It has broken off its approach, and is fleeing.'*

'What is the torpedoes' target?' Seraphax interjected.

'Initial triangulation suggests the ostella, Lord Sorcerer.'

'Shoot the ordnance down,' Seraphax ordered. 'And get some ships in their path, just in case you fail to do so. The Cobra is a secondary consideration – the ostella is to be protected even if you have to take the strike yourself, am I understood?'

'Of course, Lord Seraphax.'

'Now,' Seraphax snarled, summoning his skull-tipped staff to his hand through the warp with a flex of his fingers. 'We have intruders. I do not know how they got here, but it is of little consequence. Let us go and see exactly whom my gene-sire has brought with him to die.'

The green-armoured forms of the Dolorous Guard began to converge, forming up around them as they left the throne room, but Baelor's misgivings were not eased by their presence.

Somehow, the Lion had outflanked them. And Baelor knew only too well that when the Lion outflanked his enemy, that enemy was usually doomed.

XXX

I cannot truly say which was more disconcerting: the first time I travelled through the forest with the Lion, when we stumbled into it by accident on Camarth and emerged in the fruit grove on Avalus, or the attack on Sable, when my brothers and I assembled in the cargo hold of the *Pax Fortitudinis*, closed our eyes at his bidding, and opened them again to find ourselves surrounded by mist and trees.

The others had been told what to expect, and the stoicism of our bloodline counts for a lot, but I still caught the twitching of helms as warriors looked about them in shock, and heard the startled whispers hissing through the vox-net. I think as much as anything else, what unnerved them was the change in our gene-sire. Travelling from place to place by means largely unknown to us was hardly a new concept for Space Marines who had voyaged through the warp on many occasions. However, the Lion had never possessed the sorcerous gifts of Magnus, or even the prophetic vision of noble Sanguinius, or that twisted monster Curze. It was hard to imagine a being more grounded in the material universe than Lion El'Jonson, and no sooner had my brothers come to terms with the fact that the Lord of the First had returned, and was considerably altered by age, than they had to confront the strange abilities he now possessed, and which even he did not fully understand.

However, in one aspect at least the Lion had not changed: if he could see a tactical advantage, he would take it. Seraphax might expect any number of tricks from his primarch, but this was very unlikely to be one of them.

We hoped.

Our journey through that mysterious forest was shorter than my previous one, for which I was grateful. The surroundings themselves were not too disturbing, other than the unnatural manner in which we had arrived there, but I remembered the howling from my first trip, and had no desire to meet whatever made it. The flesh-and-blood enemies that awaited us on Sable were one thing, even taking into account the foul sorcery and inhuman allies upon which they might be able to call. However, Caliban's forests had been deadly enough in the material universe; I did not fancy our chances against whatever might lurk in this echo of it, which had to be warp-adjacent in at least some manner.

Even with our greater numbers, it seemed our presence was too brief to come to the attention of anything that might be stalking beneath the branches of mirror-Caliban. We followed the Lion through the damp, muffled world of mist and tree trunks, until we came to a place where the trees were spaced a little more uniformly, and their branches started farther from the ground, leaving tall expanses of bare bark all around us.

'We are here,' the Lion said. He drew his weapons, and activated the power field around Fealty. 'The Emperor may not still live, in any sense of the word. The Imperium as we knew it may be dead. The cause we served long ago may no longer exist. If so, now is the time that we find our own purpose. If anything in this galaxy can be said to matter, perhaps it is how we choose to act when the old constraints laid on us are gone, and we are free to choose our own path. You have all chosen to stand with me to do whatever is possible to help whomever we can, and for that you have my deepest gratitude. We will be what we were always meant to be – humanity's weapon against the darkness. Are you ready, my sons?'

We chorused our assent. In truth, I think any one of us was more ready to face whatever we were about to walk into than we had been the forest. Battle, pain, and death: these were things for which we were prepared centuries ago by our reckoning, and millennia ago so far as the galaxy was concerned.

The Lion stepped forward, and we moved with him, our weapons at the ready. Between one step and the next I noticed that the trees around us suddenly looked less like trees, and when my foot came down for the step after that my boot did not land with a soft thud in the earth and leaf litter of the forest floor, but with the hard clink of ceramite on stone. The tree trunks had turned into columns – tall, bare, and evenly spaced – and we were in an atrium.

And we were surrounded.

They came at us in a bawling rush, and if our sudden arrival had caught them unawares, there was little hesitation on their part to show it. I put a bolt-shell through the skull of one before I had even registered how misshapen that skull was, and it was only as a second creature rushed me with a weapon that was less an axe and more a massive, long-handled cleaver, that my brain was able to put a name to it. *Beastman.*

A semi-stable form of abhuman, considered barely better than true mutants on most Imperial worlds. I had met several beastmen in my travels through the galaxy, of varying character. A few were indentured slaves, miserable with their lot, with their status as sinful degenerates having been drilled into their heads since their birth. The rest were renegades and outlaws, tired of the abuse heaped upon them and fighting back by taking what they could. I found more common ground with those than I might have expected, although one named Raan tried to kill me when he realised I was a Space Marine. He quickly learned his error, although given I killed him in turn I cannot say that he remembered it for very long.

The way the Imperium treated such creatures created fertile soil in which discontent and anger could take root, and now we reaped the fruits of it. I heard brayed prayers to the foul gods of Chaos to give the horde strength enough to bring down the hated tools of the Emperor, as they saw us, and whether or not those deities answered the entreaties made to them, the beastmen certainly lacked neither strength nor savagery as they came for us. I lashed out with my chainsword and severed one arm of the creature attacking me with its enormous cleaver, but although it screamed in pain it neither fell to the ground or backed off, instead switching to a clumsy single-handed grip and striking at me nonetheless. I was so surprised by its resilience that I failed to either evade or parry the blow, and the notched edge of the weapon struck me on the breastplate.

The creature's strength was considerable, and that combined with the weapon's weight was enough to knock me to the ground. My armour saved me from bisection with merely a new, bright line in the black paint to show for it, and I fired from my sitting position to blow a hole right through my attacker's chest and spine. Not even its robust physiology could stand up to that, and it collapsed with a truncated scream. I shot the next one down as well, then hurriedly regained my feet before any of my brothers could trip over me.

'Ugly brutes, are they not?' Kai said jovially, flourishing his power sword. It looked like a showman's move, designed merely to impress with wrist technique, but when he returned to his guard position, the beastman that had drawn back its arm to smite him with the spiked mace it carried was falling to the ground, its head now some distance away and its neck already cauterised by the blade's power field. Kai stepped forward and swept his weapon through the air in a simple, double-handed figure of eight, after which two more of our attackers were quite literally falling apart.

'Typical officer,' Meriant commented from my other side. His bolter barked, and the chest of another beastman exploded. 'We could all do that if we had his weapon.'

I was inclined to agree. My chainsword would tear through flesh, bone, and light armour well enough, though it was an ugly process. But then, powerblades were far more expensive and difficult to build and maintain, which was why a knight-commander like Kai would have had one. The simple and robust construction of a chainsword was more suitable for the line trooper I had been.

Or, it seemed, for an abhuman. A new foe threw itself at me, its lolling tongue hanging out of slavering jaws, and swung its own roaring, promethium-powered blade of monomolecular-edged teeth at my face. I batted the blow aside with my forearm – ceramite could deflect such weapons with little more than a scratch – and stabbed, driving my weapon into the creature's chest. Blood gouted as the chainsword plunged inwards, accompanied by the drill-like whine of its teeth slicing through ribs. The stench of friction-heated bone reached my nostrils even through my helmet's filters, and the beastman spasmed in agony.

I felt my blade judder as it shredded my enemy's heart, and I wrenched it out and away with such force that I turned the beastman into a bloody missile which collided with another of its kin lining up an autogun shot.

Even against such devastation as we were wreaking upon them, I think the beastmen might have stood their ground, for they were driven by both hatred and fierce determination – the very qualities that made them such effective troops in the Imperium's armies for those few commanders willing to use them. We were towering foes, and mighty ones, but they knew that we could be hurt and killed, and even if they died while attempting such a goal, their death might buy a critical opening for the one behind them to exploit. However, we were not just twenty Space Marines, nor even just twenty veterans of the Great Crusade. We were led by a primarch, *our* primarch, and he was always death incarnate.

The creatures that attacked us were thrown back and slain, but they never got near the Lion; at least, not through their own volition. There was no exchange of blows there, no combat between foes, unevenly matched though they might be. The Lion simply killed anything that got in his way, flowing through the atrium as easily and swiftly as the wind. Beastmen were carved apart or run through before they even registered that the huge, terrifying leader of their attackers was coming for them next. Against such an enemy, even their resolve crumbled.

By the chrono in my helmet, it took sixteen seconds of visceral combat before the beastmen panicked and began to flee from the Lion and the trail of corpses he was leaving. The effect on the rest was almost instantaneous, like a herd of prey animals taking to flight when one scents a predator, and the creatures that were piling forwards in an attempt to reach and kill us one second were turning tail in the next. I put a bolt between the shoulder blades of one, more to encourage its fellows on their way than anything else.

'There are more coming,' the Lion announced over the vox, his helm turning this way and that as his preternaturally sharp senses gave him information which even we did not have. 'We must not get pinned down by weight of numbers – we must find Seraphax.'

'Allow me to help you with that, *Father*,' said a voice from the far end of the atrium, and someone stepped out of a shimmer in the air.

It had to be Seraphax, the sorcerer. I had no memory of him from either the Great Crusade or our exile on Caliban, but although some parts of his armour had obviously been replaced over the years, it was still painted and marked in the manner of the First Legion. He wore a surplice over it, much as Lohoc and some of my other brothers did, but instead of simple cream with our icon of a winged sword, Seraphax's was marked with fantastically complex runes and glyphs that hurt my eyes to look at. His actual armour plate was not greatly deformed or disfigured – certainly not in the manner I had seen with other worshippers of Chaos, whose ceramite had often flowed into spikes, horns, or leering mouths – but his *face*...

Half of his head was on fire, burning with bright yellow flames that appeared to neither cause him pain nor consume his body, or at least that was what I surmised, since they were so ferocious that I could not make out what lay beneath them. No wonder Baelor had been so unconcerned by the nature of the sorcerer's followers, if this was the warrior to whom he gave his allegiance.

Seraphax clearly saw no more need for words after he announced his arrival. He raised a staff tipped with a skull which looked like it had once belonged to an aeldari, and a coruscating bolt of sorcerous energy erupted from it and streaked towards the Lion.

And dissipated a foot from the grilled visor of the primarch's helmet.

The Lion raised the Arma Luminis and fired back in his own fashion, but the superheated plasma simply splashed off whatever arcane protection Seraphax had conjured for himself. Seraphax tried his own attack again, but it once more faded away just before it struck home. The visible half of the sorcerer's face was shocked; shock which shifted to alarm as the Lion leaped forward, intent on ending him with Fealty since his plasma weapon was apparently incapable of doing so. Seraphax turned and fled through a door, with the Lion in hot pursuit. We followed, but neither our reflexes nor our speed were the equal of our gene-sire, and so by the time he had exited the atrium none of us were directly on his heels.

The iridescently green-armoured warriors emerged from similar shimmers in the air as the one that had disgorged their master, arrayed around us in a loose semicircle, and between us and the door through which the Lion had just gone. These were no abhumans; they were Astartes, like us, although the similarity ended there. While Seraphax's armour in and of itself gave little hint as to the foul powers he now served, the allegiance of these warriors was immediately obvious. Some bore horned helms, the protuberances appearing to be bony eruptions from their own skulls that had pierced the ceramite from within, rather than an external decoration. I saw that one clutched his boltgun with a normal right hand on the stock, but supported the barrel with fleshy tendrils emerging from his vambrace. Another had a scaled tail that ended in a spiked mace of bone, while a third roared at us with a fanged mouth that had replaced the Imperial eagle on his chest.

I did not need to see the massive shape of Markog to know that this was the Dolorous Guard; altered though their forms were, the colour and nature of their armour was similar enough to his that the resemblance was obvious. Both they and we had half a second to take in the enemy arrayed against us, and then the shooting started.

This was an exponentially more intense, more brutal affair than the fight in which we had just been engaged. Bolt-shells were never designed to pierce ceramite, because back when the weaponry was first conceived there was no notion that humanity's enemies would ever be wearing such armour. In the millennia since, the Imperium had been hamstrung by its own refusal to embrace progress, and renegades such as we now faced – or indeed, such as ourselves – were largely limited by what weapons they could scavenge from their former masters. Much like my chainsword, bolt weaponry was more than sufficient for most purposes to which it was ever going to be put, but lacked the specialism to be similarly effective against the armour of the one wielding it.

Two bolt-shells struck my chest in the same instant as I fired my own weapon. I was knocked backwards, but the ceramite held, although the sigil of my Legion took more damage. I put a bolt-shell into one enemy's knee, staggering him; three more shots ricocheted off my right pauldron and one took a second deflection off the side of my helmet, staggering me sideways. There was no cover to take, here: this was a point-blank engagement at one end of the atrium, decided by volume of fire and sheer luck. I emptied my bolt pistol's clip almost blindly, hoping to strike a weak point such as a faceplate, but unable to aim properly due to the shots I was taking myself.

Some of my brothers did not have such problems. Out of the corner of my eye I saw the incandescent smear of the Red Whisper's plasma gun discharging, and striking a target's well-armoured central mass was of no concern for a weapon of that power. One of our enemies screamed and died as the ravening energy tore through him, and another was vaporised by Kuziel's meltagun. I saw one of the Dolorous Guard go down, I thought from one of my bolt-shells, but then something struck me in the side with the force of a mag-train.

Our enemies had heavier weapons too, and read-outs in my helmet flashed red and flickered as I was knocked to the floor. Something big – a heavy bolter, or perhaps an autocannon – had hit me and splintered my ceramite like my weight had done to the tiles on which I had just landed. Power vanished for a moment, leaving my limbs unnaturally heavy and my vision dark, then sputtered back as a loose connection made contact once more. I hoped someone was going to deal with that weapon; if it struck me in the same place again, I was unlikely to survive.

As it turned out, I had other things to worry about.

'Zabriel!' roared a voice, but that was not one of my brothers coming to my aid. I stumbled to my feet to see the massive form of Markog bearing down on me, his enormous, pale-bladed axe clutched in both hands.

'I owe you a strike!' the commander of the Dolorous Guard bellowed, almost jovially. Borz flew at him from his left, his power fist drawn back to lay the traitor out, but Markog was too quick: the haft of his axe lashed out and caught Borz on his helmet's faceplate, spinning him to the ground, and by the time my brother had regained his feet one of Markog's warriors had fallen on him from behind with a power knife, and Borz was fully occupied with trying to save his own life.

I dropped my empty bolt pistol and drew my spare, hoping to at least injure him before he closed with me, but the giant's size belied his speed, and the butt of that damned axe knocked the weapon from my hand before I could fire. I swung my chainsword, but Markog was wearing his helmet this time, and in truth I do not know what I hoped to achieve, given that the last time I decapitated him he simply picked his head back up again. The teeth threw up sparks as they grated against his armour, but in a moment he had brought the haft of his axe down on my arm with such force that I felt both ceramite and the bone within snap, and the chainsword dropped from my grasp. His next blow was a punch that hammered into the cracked armour over my ribs, and even my enhanced pain threshold was momentarily overloaded. I stumbled backwards and fell, and he raised his axe high.

'I owe you a strike,' he growled, strange harmonies emanating from behind his helmet's faceplate, and swung. The pale-bladed axe descended like death, too fast for me to roll clumsily aside from.

The edge stopped a mere finger's breadth from my helmet seal, but this was not an act of mercy or mockery on my enemy's behalf. Instead, his weapon was thrown up and back again by the blade of the Terranic greatsword which had intercepted the swing just below the axe's head.

'I owe him a strike!' Markog roared at my saviour. 'This is a matter of honour!'

'You think we conquered the galaxy with *honour*? You children are all the same,' Galad snorted, and attacked.

The Cenobite's Cataphractii armour made him a match for Markog in size, and apparently in strength as well: their weapons clashed together, but the commander of the Dolorous Guard was unable to throw Galad away from him, despite his straining. Instead each warrior took a backward step, then swung again. Markog was blisteringly quick, and his axe spun through the air faster than should have been possible, but Galad was his equal, calmly parrying and deflecting as though he knew what strikes were coming even before Markog did. Destroyers fought and bled in the crucible of brutal, close-in killing, with no quarter asked or given, so I was no stranger to the cut and thrust of combat. Seeing Galad at work, however, took me back to when I was a raw recruit, watching my instructors handle their weapons with what seemed at the time to be godlike speed and skill.

But I had no time to gape. I lunged for my dropped pistol, raised it, and opened fire. The bolts detonated on Markog's leg, arm, and pauldron, and although his armour repaired the damage within moments of it occurring, the impacts knocked him off balance and caused his next strike to miss its mark completely and bite deep into the floor.

'Cowards!' Markog roared, just deflecting Galad's next blow. 'Fight me–'

He cut off as Launciel appeared on his right, and drove his power sword through Markog's armour and right through his ribcage. The giant stiffened in what could well have been agony and which might, given what I suspected of his allegiances, possibly be ecstasy, but Galad was in no mood to leave him to the experience uninterrupted. The Terranic greatsword lashed out again, and Markog's left arm was cut clean from his body, his pauldron severed in two by the disrupting power field and razor-sharp edge of the ancient weapon.

Launciel withdrew his own sword and stepped back from Markog's clumsy, unbalanced counterstrike. The giant was roaring wordlessly now, his pain and rage too overwhelming for anything else. I rose to my feet and fired another bolt, shattering his helmet just as Galad swung again and took his right arm off as well.

That changed things. The haft of the axe was still clutched in his hand, but Markog's unnatural resilience vanished now that hand was no longer attached to his body. He staggered, and blood began to drip thickly from his shoulders. It started to clot almost immediately, since he was still a Space Marine with our enhanced biology and healing abilities, but it appeared that it was the weapon itself which had granted him the ability to survive decapitation rather than any innate ability of his own.

'No!' he bellowed thickly, and took a step towards Galad.

Galad was clearly taking no chances: he crouched and swung his blade horizontally, and severed both legs with one blow. Markog clattered to the floor with a howl. Galad rose back to his full height, reversed his grip on his sword, and plunged it into Markog's chest.

The blade was wide enough to strike both hearts simultaneously, and I had no doubt that Galad had directed it with the requisite skill for it to do just that. Markog spasmed as much as he could without any attached limbs, but Galad did not linger over his kill. He wrenched his sword out with one hand and raised the other, firing his plasma-caster. I followed the direction of his shot, my bolt pistol raised and ready, but I found myself with a dearth of targets.

The Dolorous Guard had been overcome. Ferocious though Seraphax's bodyguard were, they had proved no match for the First Legion, even such remnants of it as us. Our victory had not come without cost: my own broken arm was but one of several immediately noticeable injuries amongst my brothers, and Asbiel the Apothecary was tending to the fallen Lamor, who had clearly attacked with the fury common to assault squads and had suffered the consequences, which were equally common. However, the enemy's elite warriors were dead, and there appeared to be no malign magics threatening to reanimate them.

I walked to Markog, and stamped on his helmet. It shattered and fell away to reveal his face, twisted in pain and hatred. He reached up towards me with his unnaturally long tongue, then cackled at me.

'I will taste your flesh yet, twice-cursed traitor, and you will–'

I emptied the rest of that pistol's clip into his head without waiting for him to finish, until I had blown a hole in the floor beneath and the legs of my armour were speckled with fine particles of his skin, bone, and brain. Perhaps I should have been more careful about allowing his obviously tainted flesh to touch my armour in such a manner, but I had been a Destroyer – I *was* a Destroyer – and our enemy's annihilation always took priority over our own safety.

'Are they all accounted for?' Guain asked, the blade of his power axe smoking as the blood coating it was vaporised. 'None disappeared in the same manner as they arrived?'

My brothers confirmed in the negative, but a chill had taken hold of my hearts as I scanned our surroundings. Our force was here, in various states of health and injury, and the green-armoured bodies of our foes, but there was one notable absence.

'Baelor,' I said, ejecting the magazine of my bolt pistol and fumbling another into place with the hand of my broken arm. 'Our last brother, and Seraphax's lieutenant. He is not amongst their dead.'

'Which means he has somewhere more important to be than here, trying to stop us,' Bevedan agreed. I wondered if he regretted not striking Baelor down atop his mountain – I certainly did – but I held my tongue. There was little to be gained by confronting him about it; nor indeed Galad and Launciel, who had let Baelor leave their system freely, but who had undoubtedly just saved my life.

'The Lion,' Guain said.

'The Lion,' I agreed, and my brothers and I moved as one towards where our gene-sire had disappeared in pursuit of the Lord Sorcerer of the Ten Thousand Eyes.

XXXI

The Lion pursues Seraphax like a hunter with his quarry in his sights.

He has no qualms about this. Some of his sons have remained as true as they can to their purpose, in this future where they are hunted fugitives. Others became wayward, but have now returned to him. The Lion does not judge them; he saw well enough in his own brothers how being too long removed from guidance could lead to poor decisions and selfishness. Even now, he cannot help but wonder how many of the primarchs might have taken different courses had they been found sooner. What if Curze had met their father before taking the first step towards establishing his empire of terror? What if Angron had been found before the Butcher's Nails had been inflicted upon him?

Seraphax, however, is not lost. He has chosen his path, and it leads to a damnation of the soul from which there is no return. The Lion is as certain of that as he is of anything, for all that he is a practical being grounded in the material universe. Whatever is left of the warrior that was Lion El'Jonson's gene-son is now twisted almost beyond recognition, either a slave to the powers of Chaos or willingly doing their work.

Seraphax is a threat to humanity, and the Lion has always exterminated such threats.

He trails the fleeing sorcerer through the palace, cutting down the occasional beastman or other cultist that gets in his way. He is faster than Seraphax, but Seraphax knows the building better, and the Lion is not so eager to end this that he intends to run headlong into a trap. Seraphax's sorcery has left the Lion untouched, but he was still a warrior of the First Legion, and the Lion knows better than to underestimate one of the Legiones Astartes. So it is that when he reaches the end of what was once a particularly grand corridor, now defiled with spatters of bodily fluids and hideous glyphs, and encounters a massive set of double doors so richly carved and decorated that even the invaders' vandalisms have not completely marred their beauty, he does not charge through them unheedingly. Instead he enters cautiously, the Arma Luminis poised to fire and Fealty held ready in his other hand.

It is, or was, the throne room. On the other side is the dais where the governor's throne still stands untouched; Seraphax clearly had his own designs for it, although the Lion does not know whether the large silver mirror above it is the sorcerer's addition, and the sorcerer himself is nowhere to be seen. In the middle of the floor is a pit, surrounded by a wide terrace of tiled floor, but the daubed additions to those tiles bear far too great a resemblance to the sigils that decorate Seraphax's surplice for it to be coincidental. The Lion is wary of any form of trap, but a sorcerous one would concern him the most. He has seen what warp sorcery can do, and while Seraphax's energy bolts might not be able to hurt him, he has no wish to get embroiled in a prepared ritual.

On the other hand, what the Lion has also learned about warp sorcery is that it is, in its own way, as ordered as any physical structure. There is always an anchor point, something upon which the rest of the construct depends, and if that is destroyed or removed then everything else fails, sometimes catastrophically. He scans the room quickly, trying not to look too closely or think too logically, but instead see the patterns and upon what they are centred. It is not the easiest thing, for someone so attuned to detail, but a second's consideration gives him an answer: the mirror.

The Lion raises the Arma Luminis, and in that moment Seraphax rises into view out of the central pit, borne aloft on nothing but sorcerous power, and unleashes a new bolt of energy at the Lion's chest.

This one does not dissipate before it strikes him.

The Lion is no stranger to pain, but this is a new and unpleasant variety of it. It feels as though someone has routed electrical current directly into his nervous system, not just flooding his muscles, his tendons, and his very bones with agony, but preventing them from responding to his will. He can overcome even this given a few moments, but Seraphax does not allow him that luxury. The sorcerer touches down on the edge of the terrace and the heavy chains wrapped around his shoulders and over his chest spring into life, flashing through the air with the speed of striking serpents. The Lion tries to twist aside from them and cut them from the air with Fealty, but his body will not obey him quickly enough. The chains wrap around him, pinning his arms to his sides and binding his legs.

'I feared you would recognise that my earlier strikes were not thrown in earnest,' Seraphax says with a smile, 'but then I suppose you were never that familiar with pulling your punches, were you, Father? That was what made you great, and it will make you great again. Come.'

He gestures, and the chains rise into the air, taking the Lion with them. He struggles, but he can neither move them nor break them, simple though they seem to be.

'They are not normal iron, those chains,' Seraphax says. 'I will grant you that if a tech-priest analysed them then they would find nothing unusual other than the extraordinary purity of the iron used, but science does not tell you everything. You should be able to snap an iron chain without effort, but it is the process of their creation which gives them their strength, not the materials used.' He pauses, and purses his lips. 'I suppose the same is true of the primarchs. Flesh and bone, blood and genes, and yet the Emperor created something truly remarkable.'

He gestures again, and the chains begin to lower the Lion down into the pit. The floor is marked out in a sickeningly familiar eight-pointed star, at each corner of which burns a brazier. The Lion senses a presence behind him, and as he is forced down to his knees he is able to turn his head far enough to see a black-armoured shape. For a moment he thinks that help is at hand, but then he realises that this warrior is none of the sons who came here with him. This, then, must be Baelor, Seraphax's ally.

'Do you know how much iron the body of an average human contains?' Seraphax asks from above, then answers his own question. 'Not a lot. I am sure you saw the ostella, in orbit above us – the bones of the population, put to good use. However, I did not waste their blood, either.' He gestures to the chains. 'Not much from each subject, it is true, but when you have enough subjects...'

'If you seek to horrify me with tales of your deeds then you forget to whom you are talking,' the Lion growls. 'You know full well that our Legion murdered entire planets, entire *species*, in the interests of humanity.'

'And what I am doing is for the same purpose,' Seraphax says, walking around the pit's edge to stand beneath the mirror. 'I had hoped to find some great hero of the Imperium for this, but I never dreamed that I would be able to seize a primarch, and my own at that! Baelor, prepare him.'

Baelor moves forward, and reaches out for the Lion's helm. Despite his best efforts, the Lion is unable to prevent Baelor's fingers from finding the clasps and removing it. Baelor himself is wearing his own helmet, and so the Lion cannot see his face, but the Dark Angel pauses for a moment after the Lion's features are exposed to the air, as though taking in how much his gene-sire has changed.

'You have been gone for so long,' Seraphax says, shaking his head. 'The galaxy is riven, the Imperium is a shell. There is no hope for anything other than Abaddon's endless wars. The flame of humanity will sputter out and die, and the stars will be reclaimed by the sort of xenos bastards we should have eradicated ten thousand years ago. I can do nothing to stop this. *You* can do nothing to stop this, primarch though you are. Only one being exists who can.

'The Emperor.'

The Lion stares at him, mistrust and hatred warring with hope. 'He still lives? The Emperor still lives? You know this?'

Seraphax's smile is like lightning, there and gone again almost before it is seen. 'The warp tells me many things, and some are not to be trusted, but yes, Father. The Emperor still clings to existence on the Golden Throne. Were that not the case, there would be such a disturbance in the immaterium that the bluntest of humans would feel it, even on this side of the Great Rift. No, He survives, and I will be sending you to see Him.'

The Lion blinks in shock. Has he misjudged the situation somehow? Is Seraphax truly as forsaken as he seems? Or is he merely delusional? Yet his words do not feel like disconnected rantings.

'One of the Imperium's many mistakes was in imprisoning the Master of Mankind on the Golden Throne,' Seraphax announces. He raises a finger. 'Baelor, the Feverblade.'

A long knife appears in Baelor's hand. The edge glints in the shifting light of the brazier flames, and the blade itself has an unpleasant sheen to it. Baelor slashes with it, and opens a cut on the Lion's cheek. The Lion feels the sting of the wound, and then his flesh knitting back together as his father's genecrafting does its work, but Baelor's blade is now wet. The Fallen flicks the knife, and drops of blood fall onto the design of the eight-pointed star on which the Lion kneels.

'The Emperor must be allowed to die,' Seraphax says, raising his staff. The drops of blood begin to smoke, and the smoke weaves outwards, along the lines marked into the floor. 'Death is only the beginning for one such as Him. Only then can He ascend fully into the warp as the true god He is. Once there, no longer enfeebled by the anchor of His broken mortal body, He will destroy the Ruinous Powers and the wailing deities of the xenos races, and oversee humanity's second Great Crusade.'

The Lion stares at him. It sounds ridiculous, fanciful, foolish. And yet, the forces worshipped by the followers of Chaos are undoubtedly powerful, foul though they are. To label them as gods offends the Lion's sensibilities, but there is no other convenient word that will encompass them. In that case, while the Lion does not and will never consider his father a god, might the term not similarly be used for an immensely potent psychic who lived for millennia before revealing Himself to humanity, and has now persisted for ten thousand more years after taking what should have been a mortal wound? For a psyker capable of sending a psychic signal out through the warp so powerful that most of the galaxy was able to use it to navigate? Who created such remarkable beings as the Lion himself, bringing about life in a process which must have involved more than just the skilled manipulation of organic matter?

'I hoped Abaddon would kill the Emperor,' Seraphax continues, 'but I do not believe that even the gods themselves know what he is up to. Regardless, he has not yet taken Terra, because he wishes to batter down its gates. I, on the other hand, intend to walk through them unchallenged.'

The smoke from the Lion's blood reaches the braziers, and the flames shoot upwards. The Lion swallows, fighting a sudden dryness in his throat.

'It is fascinating, how the soul and the body intertwine,' Seraphax says. 'Yet they can be separated. A sufficiently powerful soul, bound with the correct processes, can become a fearsome weapon – a tame daemon, of a sort. The soul of a primarch is one of the mightiest spirits to roam our galaxy, so just imagine what I could do with that at my command!'

The Lion coughs as something wrenches inside his chest with a sensation of overwhelming *wrongness*. His breaths feel thin, as though there are holes in his lungs.

'I will have to leave some behind, though,' Seraphax says. Sweat beads his forehead now, and the xenos skull that tops his staff is glowing with an eldritch light. 'Enough to fool everyone, but not enough to stop me from exercising my control over your mortal shell. After all, who stands a chance of gaining an audience with the Emperor Himself, other than one of His long-lost sons? I had hoped that a mighty general or a Chapter Master would suffice, but a primarch? Even the Custodian Guard would hesitate to stop you!'

The Lion is trying to fight Seraphax's sorcery, but he barely knows what he is fighting, or how to do so. It feels as though someone is trying to pull his skeleton out through his skin, and all he can do is concentrate as hard as he can on remaining whole, and himself.

'Why resist?' Seraphax shouts angrily. 'Is this what you want your life to be? Meaningless protection of meaningless worlds while the darkness closes in? I am damned already, but I am giving you the chance to do one final great deed! Rather than slaying a single foe, or even an entire species of them, you will be killing the very thing that keeps humanity shackled and downtrodden!'

The silver mirror seems to be growing larger and brighter, whilst somehow not changing, and the Lion cannot look away from it. He can *feel* the artefact somehow; the surface is incredibly smooth, yet contains infinite complexity. It is stretching him out, pulling him across its surface and letting him sink into it, twisting and locking him away from his own body.

The Lion wavers in that one second, because now the surface of the mirror is showing him the true scale of the galaxy he starts to wonder how much difference even he can make. He is a great general and a deadly warrior, it is true, but he does not know how to heal the rift that has opened across a hundred thousand light years of space. He cannot defeat it with an army, and he cannot pierce its heart with a blade, so what use is he? He woke up after betrayal and injury to find that things were even worse than when he had left them, and he has no solution. It would be so easy to let go, to abandon control, and let himself be used. He was only ever his father's instrument, in any case; is this so different?

Then the mirror pulls his consciousness up further until it brushes against the ostella, and the Lion recoils. It is the mirror's counterpart, a grotesque construction of endless angles that are scented with death. It is not just the killing that repulses him;

it is the foul energies he can feel wreathed throughout it. The touch of them brings him back to himself somewhat. He is the Lion, he is a son of the Emperor, and he will live or die as himself, and as a father to his own sons, who have placed their trust in him when many of them had little cause to do so. He blinks, the silvery sheen of the mirror fades a little, and he is back on his knees staring defiantly up at Seraphax.

'I hoped you would see the necessity, and surrender willingly,' the sorcerer snarls. 'But I can splinter your soul and drag it out of you, with or without your consent!' He slams the butt of his staff down on the tiles, the braziers flare once more, and the Lion convulses as another spasm of pain wracks him. He bites down and glares, daring his gene-son to do his worst, because if this is a battle of wills then the Lion knows he can triumph.

As it turns out, he may not have to.

Seraphax looks up, startled, then brings his staff across in front of himself in a warding gesture. A moment later there is a thunder of gunfire, and the air in front of the sorcerer shimmers as it absorbs a rain of bolt-shells and plasma blasts.

The Lion hears Baelor snarl, and the Fallen sheathes the Feverblade, unclamps his bolter, and runs for one of the access points into the pit. He disappears just as Seraphax unleashes a bolt of his own arcane energy, and a scream rings out as one of the Lion's sons is caught by it. However, the Lion's attention is grabbed by something else.

The chains around him have loosened slightly.

XXXII

'Shoot the mirror!' the Lion bellows over the *crump-roar* of bolters and the scorching sizzle of plasma. His brief out-of-body experience confirmed to him that it is key to the sorcerer's plans, and regardless of whether or not the sorcerer would have been successful in his attempt to split the Lion's soul and wrench most of it away, completely removing his ability to do so has to be the priority.

His sons do not question his instructions. Seraphax howls in rage and lashes out with his staff as though to knock their shots out of the air, but it seems that his ability to shrug off weapons fire is reduced when he attempts to extend the range of it beyond his immediate vicinity. The silvered metal begins to buckle as bolter shells strike home, the impacts sounding like dissonant bells, and the perfect reflection the mirror casts becomes distorted. However, the Lion sees something in the dents and craters that now mar the mirror's surface: shadows with eyes, and claws, and teeth. Then a plasma blast strikes the mirror dead centre, and molten droplets of silver begin to fall.

Directly onto Seraphax.

The sorcerer screams as a white-hot lump lands on his head, but the fire that covers half of his skull simply sweeps across to engulf it. Now there is nothing to be seen of his features except flames, and the other drops of silver are swirling around his armour as though they have a mind of their own. Within moments his surplice has burned away, his black armour is edged with glinting light, and silver claws erupt from the ends of his fingers, punching through the ceramite and then melding with it. New whorls and decorations of incomprehensible complexity spread across his battleplate like creeping frost over a window. The Lion tears his gaze away, even though his eyes and mind yearn to explore and understand the patterns because some intuition tells him that within them lurk the secrets of the universe, just waiting to be discovered.

'You fools,' Seraphax snarls. His voice is no longer remotely human; it sounds like a metal-stringed harp being sawn in half. A claw-tipped hand sweeps up to casually swat aside a bolt-shell fired at the flaming ruin of his face. *'You have doomed me, yourselves, and the entire galaxy!'* the sorcerer adds, as wings of blue silver erupt from his back and spread wide.

Faces appear in the mirrored surface of the wings: the faces of those of the Lion's sons who came with him to Sable. Their features reflect the screams that erupt from above him, accompanied by the clatter of ceramite as warriors fall to their knees, or land supine on the tiles. Space Marines can weather a great deal of physical pain and suffering, but there are some things against which their enhanced constitutions give them little assistance, and the predations of the warp are one of them. Powerful muscles and hardened bones are no defence when the psyche is being torn from its housing.

Baelor appears behind Seraphax, having found his way up

to the dais level. He is holding his bolter ready, but pauses and does not fire when he sees what is occurring. Although his helm hides his face, something about his stance implies shock.

The Lion strains once more against the chains which hold him, but while there is some give to them now, he still cannot break free. He hears a yell, and a one-handed, black-armoured body topples from above to land in the pit not far from the Lion.

'Bevedan!' the Lion barks. The former Librarian fumbles at his helmet with his remaining hand, and claws it loose. The face he turns on the Lion is wracked with pain.

'Forgive me, lord,' Bevedan murmurs, now unmoving. 'He is too strong, and I have not used my powers in decades.'

'Bevedan, I am secured by chains upon which there is some mystic binding,' the Lion says, quickly and quietly. 'Seraphax's concentration is weakening, but I cannot loosen them sufficiently. I need your gifts.'

'I am not yet so overcome as I make out,' Bevedan says through gritted teeth. 'Be ready. He is pulling my spirit from me, but this connects me to him. I can turn this into a weapon, but for a few moments only before I am gone.'

There are many things the Lion would like to say to his son, but there is seldom time for warriors to bid each other farewell as they would wish, so he merely nods. Then Bevedan sets his jaw, and his eyes blaze with light as he stops fighting Seraphax's spell and forces all his power at the sorcerer at once.

'No!' Seraphax shouts, as the glow in his wings flares chaotically. The sorcerer staggers, lashing out wildly as Bevedan's consciousness burns into him, but he regains control of himself almost immediately.

However, it was enough.

The Lion rises to his feet, and this time when he strains the iron shatters as it always should have done. His leap takes him up out of the pit in one bound, directly for Seraphax. The sorcerer swings his staff, but his reflexes are no match for the Lion's speed. The Lion slashes with Fealty and slices the staff in two, then crashes into Seraphax and bears him to the ground.

'Release them!' the Lion bellows, reversing his grip on his sword and placing the point of it over Seraphax's hearts.

Seraphax laughs. *'The time was that you would have already slain me, and called the death of twenty Dark Angels an acceptable cost.'*

'That was ten thousand years ago,' the Lion growls, trying not to look at the agonised expressions staring imploringly at him from out of Seraphax's wings. 'I will see no more of my sons die this day.'

He does not know what killing Seraphax now would do. All Lion El'Jonson knows is that he owes more to the warriors behind him than leaving them to an uncertain fate while he eradicates one more enemy. These so-called Fallen are giving him a second chance, just as much as he is them. He brought them here with appeals for them to do something good, and he cannot let that be nothing more than dying so that he might live.

'Your terms are acceptable,' Seraphax says, and a blaze of silver force erupts from his wings. It strikes the Lion and knocks him sprawling, numbing his fingers so that his weapons slip from his grasp and skitter away across the floor. He scrambles back to his feet, but finds himself anchored to the ground. Sigils painted onto the tiles flare into life, and lock him in place.

'You thought I would not have prepared the ground on which I was going to face you?' Seraphax snarls as he rises. *'You disappoint me, my lord Lion!'* He spreads his wings wide once more, and the faces of the Fallen disappear. In their place the Lion sees his own, repeated again and again, old, and wracked with pain, and he feels the tug on his soul once more, now tinged with hungry claws.

'You talk to *me* about disappointment?' he roars, still fighting against the hex which holds him in place. 'You are a mockery of all we ever stood for! Take my soul then, if you can!' He must keep Seraphax's attention on him; if he does so, perhaps others may recover enough to resume the battle. Now the lives of his loyal sons do not hang in the balance the Lion will have no hesitation in ending Seraphax's, and all he needs is one more distraction.

Seraphax takes a step closer. *'That was the plan originally, but my foolish brothers had to interfere!'* He snorts with laughter. *'Brothers! I am sure you can sympathise with my frustration on that front. However, I am simply doing what must be done, no matter the cost, the same as we always did!'* He takes another step. *'I will have your soul, my lord, but they shall join you in servitude. Together, there is nothing we cannot do! Baelor–'*

Seraphax stops, and stiffens, and something sharp parts the ceramite of his breastplate from within. The Lion tenses, ready for something even worse to be ripping its way out of the sorcerer's body, but the wrenching at his soul dies away, and he recognises the foreign object as something even more unexpected.

The tip of the Feverblade.

The long knife remains where it is for a moment, while Seraphax shudders around it, then flesh, bone, and ceramite yields before it as the sorcerer tears a massive wound in his own body to whirl around and plunge his silver claws into the Dark Angel behind him with a scream of rage. Seraphax's attacker cries out in pain, and the Lion sees the knife flash dully again, severing the sorcerer's wings. Seraphax collapses, and convulses, and the edges of his wounds begin to creep outwards, everything dissolving and boiling away into foul-smelling vapour.

Baelor falls to his knees, bleeding copiously from multiple claw marks in his torso which show no sign of clotting. He throws down the Feverblade and removes his helmet. The face so revealed is a world apart from the fire-ravaged features of the sorcerer, for there is no mark of mutation or disfigurement that the Lion can see, other than the small marks and scars any warrior will have accumulated over time. However, the wound of grief is deeper than any other mark.

The glyphs on the floor stutter and fade, and the Lion can move again. He approaches Baelor cautiously, for Seraphax's blade is clearly a potent weapon and it is still within Baelor's reach, but the warrior makes no move to take it up again. Instead, as the fires die away across Seraphax's head and leave only bare skin behind, he leans down to kiss the sorcerer's brow before the flesh begins to disintegrate entirely.

'My son,' the Lion says. Baelor looks up at him with haunted eyes, but an expression of grim acceptance on his face.

'My lord.'

The Lion lowers his head in a gesture of acknowledgement. 'Thank you.'

Baelor swallows. 'I followed him for so long. He was my captain. My brother. My friend. And… everything he did had a purpose. I believed he knew what was right. We were traitors, lost in time – all the battles we waged, all the hateful followers he gathered, were simply the only way he had a chance to get close to a mighty hero of the Imperium. Even when he told me the details of his plan, he said we would be freeing the Emperor, not killing Him. I thought he must be right, because he knew so much more of the warp than I do. Nothing in this galaxy makes sense any more, anyway.'

The Lion nods slowly. 'What made you change your mind?' he asks, as gently as he can.

'He was no longer Seraphax,' Baelor says quietly, looking down again. 'Not really. My brother held onto himself for so long, but when I heard him speak and saw how he had been altered, I knew he was gone. And you... you protected my brothers from him. That is not the Lion who attacked Caliban.'

'They are with me because they choose to be,' the Lion says. 'The day may come when I have to ask them to give their lives for a cause, but it will never be simply because it is convenient to me for them to do so. The galaxy might call them Fallen, but I call these sons of mine the Risen.'

He extends his hand. 'Rise, Baelor.'

Baelor looks up sharply. 'Lord, I am a traitor and heretic. I believed it was the only way to do what was right, but–'

'My Legion is my responsibility,' the Lion interrupts him. 'I did not see what festered in the hearts of my sons, or my former brothers of the Order. Had I done so, all this might have been avoided. You turned from that course, of your own will.'

Baelor blinks once. Then he sets his jaw, nods, and rises to his feet.

'But too late.'

The Lion nods sadly. 'But too late.' He reaches out and clasps Baelor's forearm. 'I wish I could trust that you might be able to advise us on how best to destroy your allies, but the wiles of Chaos run deep. However, know that in coming to the aid of my sons and me today, you have earned my gratitude and forgiveness.'

Baelor smiles, but pain catches at the edge of it. 'I do not believe I will survive the wounds that Seraphax dealt me, in any case. I would ask for a cleaner death, first.'

The Lion picks up Fealty, but hesitates despite knowing that Baelor cannot be trusted and must die, and despite the fact that Baelor himself has asked for it. The Lion said that he would see no more of his sons die this day, and he is loath to prove himself a liar so quickly.

Zabriel limps up beside him. The former Destroyer is obviously battered, and looks to have a broken arm, judging by his splintered vambrace. 'Baelor.'

'Zabriel,' Baelor responds, meeting his brother's gaze with some effort. 'I–'

'You killed Seraphax,' Zabriel says before Baelor can say anything further. 'Actions speak louder than words. Thank you.' He looks up at the Lion. 'Lord, I can undertake this duty, if it is your wish.'

The Lion shakes his head. 'No. Fealty is too heavy for you, with only one arm, and Baelor deserves the clean death he wishes. And as I said,' he continues, 'my Legion is my responsibility.'

Absolute focus. The Lion brings his blade up and strikes in one smooth motion, and the powered edge of it severs Baelor's head from his body in an instant. Bright red blood fountains from the stump of the Fallen's neck as the body collapses.

The Lion allows himself a second of sorrow, as he looks at what remains of his two sons who fell into darkness and treachery. Then he raises his voice.

'Cadaran! Does your flamer still have fuel?'

'Aye, lord,' Cadaran says, although he is unsteady on his feet, weak and wrung out after fighting Seraphax's attempts to wrench his spirit from his body.

'Burn as much of this as you can,' the Lion orders. 'Then we must depart before reinforcements arrive.' He does not relish the effort of summoning the forests again, but it is the only way out for him and his sons. 'This victory is significant, but there is much we have left to do.'

XXXIII

Without Seraphax, the Ten Thousand Eyes have splintered as each warlord seeks to fill the vacuum left by his death. The Lion should be satisfied, since his slowly increasing alliance of human worlds has been hunting down and eliminating the different elements one by one. Still, he cannot help but wonder if the naked power struggle upon which he is capitalising is simply a mirror of what happened to the Imperium after the Emperor was interred on the Golden Throne.

What's done is done. The Lion can do nothing about the past, but the present is another matter. The Lion's Protectorate is expanding, gradually taking in more and more systems. Only the ones who want to join, the Lion keeps reiterating; his forces are stretched thin defending their own territory against raiders, without trying to subjugate populations who will resist. However, most have welcomed the arrival of other humans after their isolation, and none who have met with the Lion in person have refused him, no matter how deliberately unwarlike his bearing has been. In contrast, he has been hailed as a hero, a rescuer.

A god.

He has stepped back from that, always, but it is inescapable. The Emperor is seen as a divine being, and so, in the reckoning of today's galaxy, His sons must by definition be at least semi-divine. It matters not that the Emperor always said He was merely a man, or that the primarchs were creations of science rather than the combination of DNA through crude biological means. The Lion has been left with the option of endlessly repeating the same arguments when he knows that those to whom he is speaking will simply assume that he is being modest, or letting them believe what they wish to believe. In his lower moods he has considered ordering punitive measures against the most vocal proponents of his deification, but then he remembers Guilliman's account of Monarchia. If people are so eager to find a god nearby, rather than the distant figure of the Emperor on Terra, then better Lion El'Jonson than the alternatives.

Now, however, he faces a different challenge. He has left orders that he is not to be disturbed, and has returned to the mist-filled forests that bear so much resemblance to his home world.

He has not gone looking for the castle which houses the wounded king. He does not feel like he belongs there, nor that he is welcome; at least, unless and until he finds the correct question, if the Watcher in the Dark's words are to be believed. However, there is something else that he has seen more than once amongst the mighty trees, and it is that for which he now searches.

It does not take him long. Indeed, it previously appeared to him even when he was not looking for it. The forest's geography seems to respond to his needs and desires, at least to an extent, but this particular landmark has been a constant. He does not even know what it is, but its recurrence has convinced him that he should find out.

The start of the path is the same as before: a route of short grass hemmed in on either side by bushes and tree trunks. In the distance, he can see the roof of pale, curved stone. And standing next to the path is the Watcher in the Dark.

'You told me before that I was not strong enough for this,' the Lion says.

+You were not.+

'And now?'

+That remains to be seen.+

The Lion nods. It will do.

He is not sure what he was expecting, but the path itself offers him no obstacles. It is an easy route, almost enjoyable by the standards of these woods. It is not long before the Lion brings his destination into view, and he is able to look upon it properly for the first time.

The marble dome stands atop a square stone building, but this is not like the king's castle. That was a structure which fitted its surroundings, for it was not so different in nature to the fortifications raised on Caliban to protect its people against the threats that world held. This is almost alien in comparison. The exact fit of the stone, the cornices carved into a repeated, flowing shape, the mighty columns flanking the black arch of the doorway: this is the architecture of the Imperium, not Caliban. It does not belong here.

The Lion approaches cautiously. He does not know how such a structure could come to be here; but then again, he is still not entirely certain where 'here' is. He theorises that it is some manner of space adjacent to the warp, a halfway house through which the distance and time of realspace could be bypassed to some extent, but that is merely guesswork. Regardless, the building must have been constructed to contain something, and the Lion intends to find out what that is.

There is no door, but the interior is so dark that not even the Lion's eyes can make out what is within, at first. It is not until he is quite close that he sees the faint hint of a glow, and that is only for a moment.

Mainly because someone has stepped in front of it.

Despite himself, the Lion's jaw drops when the figure steps out into the gentle, mist-shrouded light. Blond hair, so much like the Lion's own, but tangled and part-braided, and not faded with age; ornate armour, so much like the Lion's own, but the grey of death in winter rather than the black of night. The ferocity that lurks within the Lion's heart is mirrored here, but worn on the surface in the flashing blue eyes, and the elongated canine teeth that are exposed as the upper lip lifts in a snarl.

Relief, anger, joy, and alarm all swell within the Lion's heart.

'Russ?'

'Hello, traitor,' growls Leman Russ, and launches himself forward with his hands reaching for the Lion's throat.

The Lion wastes no more time with words. He has fought Leman Russ before, and he knows that such things only end when the Wolf King is either incapacitated or chooses to stop of his own accord. He sidesteps Russ' lunge, then swings a fist. He knocked Russ unconscious once, on Dulan, but his brother was laughing then. Russ is not laughing now. He swats the blow aside and slams a punch of his own into the Lion's chest, his face twisted in rage.

The foolish see the savagery of the Space Wolves and dismiss it as nothing more than that, but Lion El'Jonson knows better. There is a calculated rage within his brother that longs to spring forward and lay waste, but Russ usually keeps it under tight control, and only lets loose when sanctioned. He is no mindless berserker; every action has a purpose, which is the destruction of his enemy as efficiently as possible.

The Lion meets him toe to toe, furious concentration against concentrated fury. Punches are thrown and dodged or ducked, or land with the crash of ceramite on ceramite. Hands grapple, seeking purchase. The Lion shakes off Russ' grip on his forearm and pivots, using his own hip as leverage to hurl the Wolf King off his feet and into one of the columns.

'Traitor?' Lion El'Jonson demands, as Russ picks himself back up. He knows better than to think he can talk his brother down, but the accusation stings. 'You know that is not true!'

'Then why does it bother you so?' Russ says with an ugly laugh, but it is not Russ' voice, and the shape now rising to its feet stands taller than Russ ever did. A mighty figure encased in a massive suit of Terminator plate is now where the Wolf King stood a moment before, the fingers of one hand long and deadly.

'You are dead,' the Lion tells Horus. 'Russ' fate I did not know for sure, but *you* are dead. This is some warp-trickery.' His heart sinks, because even a furious, vengeful Russ carried the prospect of a future in which they might have been able to resolve such differences.

'An ancient Terran sage said that a man never truly dies while his name is still spoken,' Horus declares, gesturing with his talon. He moves and sounds just as the Lion remembers, with effortless grace and a force of personality that is practically a weapon in and of itself. 'And so I will live for as long as humanity survives, because I am the mirror against which all of my brothers are now compared. You know that. You have done it every day since you first learned of my actions. You can never again truly be yourself, because you will only ever be focused on not being me.'

The Lion clenches his fists. 'You may not be Horus, but wearing his face does not reduce my desire to see you destroyed.'

He makes the first move this time, heedless of the fact that Horus was powerful enough to mortally wound the Emperor. That was a different Horus, one swollen with foul boons from the Chaos gods. This is the Lion's memory of Horus, and mighty though the much-loved Lupercal was, the Lion remembers what Guilliman told him once, back on Macragge: that Horus had resented the Lion, for he knew that they were equals.

Even within his massive armour, the Serpent's Scales, Horus is still deceptively fast. He wards off the Lion's blows, laughing as though they are friends engaging in sport, then lashes out with a backhand that staggers the Lion into the column against which he threw Russ. Horus snarls and lunges with the elongated fingers of his talon, seeking to impale Lion El'Jonson against the stone.

The Lion ducks, and as Horus' blades punch deep into the masonry, he slams his fist into the Warmaster's face.

Now it is Horus' turn to stagger, raising his other hand to shield his face as he does so. When he lowers it again, his features have changed. His skin is paler, and cables snake out of his skull and into his armour.

'Well anticipated,' Perturabo says in a voice like a leaden hammer. 'A shame you lacked that foresight on Diamat.'

'You might at least have found a brother for whom I ever cared,' the Lion retorts. He boosts off the column behind him into a flying punch, but Perturabo catches him in mid-air and slams him into the ground, then balls both his fists together and brings them down at the Lion's face. The Lion rolls aside and lashes out with his legs, sweeping Perturabo's feet from underneath him, but when his brother lands on his back his armour is white, and it is the Khan who vaults straight back up to his feet.

'Had you been quicker, you might have reacted to Horus' treachery in time,' Jaghatai Khan says. He feints a strike with his right hand, then lashes out with the straight fingers of his left and tears open the skin on the Lion's forehead. He follows up with a kick thrust straight into the Lion's midsection; the Lion catches it, then hurls the Khan to one side.

'And if you had been smarter, you would have seen it coming,' intones Magnus the Red. The crimson-haired giant is as tall on one knee as the Lion is standing, and his hand closes around the Lion's skull in an agonising grip. The Lion manages to prise the fingers apart, but Magnus' other hand punches him full in the face and sends him flying backwards.

'Now I know you are a fraud,' the Lion spits. 'Magnus never hit that hard.' He ducks under the giant's grasp and hauls himself up behind him on one of the horns adorning the Crimson King's armour, then lands a blow to the top of his adversary's head. A hand reaches up to grab him, and throws him to the ground once more.

'Perhaps you are merely getting old,' Mortarion rasps, stamping down on the Lion's chest so hard that he is momentarily winded even inside his armour. 'Worn-down and *broken!*'

The Lion evades the Death Lord's second blow, but as he is scrambling back to his feet Mortarion throws a punch which clips him around the head and sends him staggering. He is only wobbled for a moment, and recovers his equilibrium to grab a handful of dirt and throw it into Mortarion's eyes. The lord of the Death Guard shakes his head, blinded, and reaches out with one hand to ward off whatever attack is coming. The Lion grabs that arm, and uses it to haul himself up and plant a kick straight into the Pale King's face.

The Lion drops back to the ground, but it is no longer the drab colours of Mortarion's armour in front of him. Rogal Dorn raises fists clad in the same burnished gold as that which armoured their father.

'The Emperor never trusted you,' Dorn grates, lashing out with two quick punches. The Lion should have been able to dodge them both, but he is starting to feel the effects of being repeatedly battered by his brothers, or at least by the being which is mimicking them, and the second lands flush.

'That is why He sent you far away into the galaxy's darkest corners, while keeping me close,' Dorn continues, reaching out to grab and strangle. The Lion seizes one of his arms and pivots, throwing Dorn over his shoulder and dumping the Praetorian of Terra onto his back.

'You think He trusted you with His secrets?' Alpharius laughs from the ground. 'I know secrets you could never guess at, *First*.'

Arms seize the Lion from behind, wrapping around his neck and hauling him around in a half-circle, but he reaches up to prise them loose and drops down to one knee to throw his attacker off again. Alpharius rolls up to his feet, no longer smiling. The version of him that had been lying on the ground is nowhere to be seen.

'You never did have the stomach for a fair fight,' the Lion growls, and when the Lord of Serpents throws a punch he twists Alpharius' arm around and drives him face first into the column which bears the scars of Horus' talons. The impact pleases the Lion so much that he does it again, and then tries to do it a third time.

This time, however, the arm that braces itself against the pillar is stronger than his.

'A *fair fight?*' Angron roars, throwing the Lion off. He piles forward in a furious rush of blows that have all of Russ' savagery, but none of the control. The Lion is struck in the chest, in the ribs, in the chest again, a glancing blow off his shoulder, and then in the face. Something hits him from behind, but he realises it is the wall of the building against which he has stumbled. He does not try to dodge the strike that he knows is coming, not against Angron, but throws himself low instead, clipping the onrushing Red Angel's knee and sending him head first into the wall with a crash. The Lion gets back up and tries to throw a punch of his own, but it is caught in a hand of metal.

'Where was your vengeance?' Ferrus Manus bellows, as his other fist slams into the Lion's stomach.

'Where was your guile?' growls Corax, snapping the Lion's head back with a kick.

'You never were good enough,' Fulgrim sneers, jabbing him in the throat.

'Yet now you accept the worship due to a god,' Lorgar says, tutting. The Lion lashes out for him, but a blue-armoured foot trips him and he lands on his face.

'You dared preach to me about my faults, but when the chance came to return to Terra, you decided to burn some planets instead,' Roboute Guilliman says from above him.

Red-armoured fingers lift the Lion's chin.

'Had you not done so, would I have lived?' Sanguinius asks sadly. The Angel walks out of view, and an incredible strength hoists the Lion upwards.

'Would I have died?' Vulkan hisses in his ear, and then the Lion is tossed through the air towards the building's door. He strikes the lintel on the way through, and crashes down into shadow. Head whirling, the Lion struggles up again, straining with all his senses. The light from outside is faint, but even so it does not penetrate into the building's interior like it should. He cannot see.

And he knows what is coming.

First there is a presence behind him on his right, as soft as thought. He whirls towards it, but it is gone. Then there is another to his left, as light as memory. That disappears as well. And then the darkness in front of him splits to reveal a pale face in which sit two dark orbs of eyes, eyes that see the future, eyes that have no pity.

'At least I knew which of my Legion deserved to die,' whispers Konrad Curze, the Night Haunter.

'They all did,' the Lion growls.

Curze smiles. 'And I knew that.'

He fades backwards again, disappearing from sight. The Lion is well aware of his brother's hunting tactics and turns for the door, expecting to see the Night Haunter swooping at him. Instead, Curze's talons puncture his armour to pierce his ribs from behind.

'They called me a fiend because I terrorised worlds, but you just killed them!' Curze hisses into the Lion's ear, through the agony. 'My reputation made planets capitulate when they heard of my approach, but you dropped from the sky unannounced and burned the very soil to ash!' He shifts his fingers, sparking a new wave of pain through the Lion's body. 'Why is it, *brother*, that you are a hero and I am a villain simply because I left some wretches alive to talk about me?'

The Lion manages to get his hands on Curze's and wrenches the claws out, then staggers away. When he turns, the Night Haunter is nowhere to be seen.

'I am not a hero,' the Lion says through gritted teeth. 'I did what was required of me by the Master of Mankind, the man I believed knew best. I was a necessary part of His plan to unify and save humanity.'

'So noble...' Curze whispers from the darkness.

'You are a villain,' the Lion continues, flexing his fingers, 'because you *enjoyed* what you did, and you did it even when you had been ordered *not* to!'

'Perhaps Father did His work too well,' Curze hisses, and lunges into view with his talons aimed at the Lion's eyes. The Lion rolls aside from the strike, and comes up against the far wall.

'You can only blame the Emperor because you refuse to take responsibility for your own actions,' the Lion says, watching for Curze's inevitable next attack. 'You liked to say that you could see the future, but you let yourself be a slave to it instead of forging your own path.' He stands up, cautiously. 'Father has not failed yet. Not while I am still alive to protect this galaxy.'

'You know nothing of which you speak,' Curze snarls, too close for comfort yet not close enough to place.

'Perhaps,' the Lion says. 'But you are long dead, and I am through bandying words with ghosts.'

The light he saw from outside flares up again from the wall behind him. He turns, and sees it emanating from a kite shield which hangs there. It is richly decorated, and embossed with an icon of an eagle crowned with laurels.

The Lion reaches for it, and as his fingers touch it–

fire

fury

he stands on a battlefield with the shield on his arm under a dark sky but he can see all the stars and he knows their names and he can feel everything around him all the humans hurting and bleeding and dying all the xenos those abominations and all the tiny creatures burrowing through the soil and the trees and the grass and the wind he can feel it all it is all connected a web of power and this is not overwhelming this is just how he lives instant to instant to instant

The Lion staggers. The shield is on his arm. He knows the touch of that mind; he has felt it before.

'Father?'

'He is dead, you fool,' Konrad Curze hisses, and the shadows split again to give birth to his rangy figure, stabbing for the Lion with his talons.

The Lion brings up the Emperor's Shield, and Curze's claws clash futilely against it. Curze – or the thing wearing his face, the thing the Lion's father set to guard this place to keep away the unworthy – shrieks and recoils, but not far enough. The Lion can feel the energy running through the shield, and feels within it the echo of the Emperor's Aegis that covered the Imperial Palace on Terra, which is anathema to the warp. He lashes out, slamming the shield into the Night Haunter and bearing him down to trap him beneath it.

The warp-thing collapses, boiling away from the inside as its essence is destroyed. The Lion watches it shriek and shrivel into non-existence, then stands. Konrad Curze is indeed dead, long dead, and watching his likeness die the death the Lord of the First could never inflict upon him gives Lion El'Jonson no satisfaction. The past is done; it can be buried and left behind.

In the grim darkness of this far future, there is only war.

EPILOGUE

The Lion has been waiting for word that the Imperium still survives in some form. He has sent expeditionary ships out, and has astropaths screaming their silent messages into the void, but with every new system his forces find the message is the same: they have been isolated, they have been cut off, they have no knowledge of the wider galaxy.

The Lion still desperately hopes that the Imperium survives, and that he has simply ended up in a part where the isolation and warp storms are particularly bad. Indeed, according to the rumours that run through the worlds he now protects, that is exactly *why* he is there: a champion to protect them in their time of greatest need. He does not comment on such speculation, because he still cannot truly say what drew him to Camarth in the first place, nor why he regained awareness at that time.

However, another part of him worries. These people were desperate, they wanted a saviour and were only too happy to cast him in that role, but what happens if the Lion encounters a bastion of Imperial space, besieged but still resistant, in contact with other areas and holding firm to their old systems? Will they accept who he is? Or will whoever rules there, driven by genuine doubts or simple fears of losing their own authority – or both – denounce him as an imposter, and call for war against him? Against his protectorate? The Lion has not created an empire nor attempted to supplant the Imperium, but he fears how it might appear to suspicious outsiders.

When word of the Imperium does come, it comes in a manner he had not expected.

'Translation!' the auspex officer of the *Lunar Knight* shouts, as the Lion studies the damage reports of the fleet he led against the ork pirates that had been lurking in the asteroid fields near the world of Denerair. 'Multiple warp wakes!'

'Xenos?' the Lion asks, dismissing the read-outs and bringing the tactical hololith online, as the bridge readies itself for a combat footing once more.

'Negative,' the auspex officer says after a moment. 'Bringing visual up for you now, my lord.'

The Lion frowns at the grainy image that appears. The shapes are difficult to make out, but it is a small fleet: several light cruisers clustered around a central capital ship. This, however, is not any of the Imperial battleships he has seen so far since his reawakening. This is something new, yet also familiar.

'That is a battle-barge,' the Lion says. He raises his voice. 'Do we have an ident?'

'It's reading as *Baal's Fury*, my lord!' the auspex officer reports.

'Blood Angels,' the Lion breathes. The sons of his most beloved brother. A joyous sight... and yet potentially disastrous, if they do not accept his tale.

'They are hailing us, my lord,' the vox-officer says. 'They say their commander wishes to speak with you. They are asking for you by name.'

The bridge goes quiet. Everyone knows how significant this moment could be.

'We will receive them,' the Lion says immediately. 'All ships are to power down weapon systems. I do not want anyone in that force to think that we are not glad to see them.'

He turns, and leaves the bridge. Now he just has to hope that his brother's sons give him no reason to regret his orders.

The Lion stands on the deck of the hangar, with Zabriel to his left. The rest of his sons are commanding other forces and other fleets, lending their skill and experience to the protectorate, and with orders not to stray too far. All of the so-called Fallen are keen to prove their worth, but the Lion has impressed the need for caution upon them. Their only chance of survival is to stay in close contact, and be ready to aid each other if needed; the days of Dark Angels crusading fleets venturing into the unknown are long gone.

But here are the Blood Angels in a trio of Thunderhawk gunships, sweeping in through the ion field that prevents the hangar's atmosphere from leaking out into the void of space. They touch down as one, as neatly as if this were a parade ground back in the days of the Great Crusade – a flashback to a time before the twin knives of treachery and betrayal were buried into the Imperium's heart.

The Thunderhawks' forward ramps lower, and warriors armoured in blood red descend them in unison. The Lion feels a pang of sorrow at seeing Sanguinius' sons. It is one thing to know that his loyal brothers are gone, but quite another to see this reminder of one of them. Quite unexpectedly, the Lion feels a rush of guilt. *Why should I have been the one to survive? Out of all of us, why should it have been me?*

However, another part of him is weighing and assessing what he is seeing. Sixty Space Marines is a potent force; even more so if they are armed, supplied, and organised by squads in a manner his sons cannot currently be. What he could do, if these sixty warriors were under his command! But of course, they are not. They are here to do him honour, plucked away from what must undoubtedly have been other vital engagements simply because of his status.

And if their current commander decides that he is a fraud, then the Lion is under no illusion that these warriors are here to kill him.

Then a new group of ten Space Marines emerge from the central gunship, and between them comes a warrior in incredibly ornate golden plate, with a jump pack rising from his back, and his face masked.

The Lion's eyes fall upon that mask, and rage fills him.

'Who are you?' he demands, striding forward. The assembled Blood Angels, who had their weapons held neutrally in parade form, bring them up to ready positions as one, although they do not yet aim them. The Lion does not care. 'Who are you,' he repeats, louder and more angry, 'to wear my brother's face?'

They are Sanguinius' features, cast in gold, and drawn in an expression of rage and grief that reaches out and tears at the Lion's heart all over again.

'Stand down, brothers,' the masked warrior orders, and the Blood Angels lower their weapons once more. Then the gold-armoured commander reaches up and removes his helm, revealing the face beneath.

The Lion can see the distant echo of the Angel there, but greatly distilled by time. The warrior's long hair which spills loose is jet black, but threaded with silver, and his pale skin is drawn tight over high cheekbones, with faint blue veins visible beneath it. For all the power and command this Space Marine radiates, the Lion can tell that he is ancient.

'I am Dante, commander of the Blood Angels,' the golden-armoured warrior says. 'I greet you, Lion El'Jonson, lord of the Dark Angels and son of the Emperor.'

The Blood Angels drop to one knee, just as smoothly as their Thunderhawks landed. The Lion frowns, abruptly feeling as though he has been wrong-footed.

'You are satisfied with my identity?'

'If you will forgive me, lord, you are... older than I expected,' Dante says, still on one knee. 'But to have so readily and unprompted recognised the face of our gene-father says much. Besides, I have served the Emperor for over a thousand years, and I have yet to meet a being with the same bearing as a primarch, save for another primarch.'

The Lion blinks. *Over a thousand years?* Dante was ancient indeed! And–

'Wait,' he says, his mouth dry. '*Another* primarch? Get up, all of you,' he adds, 'just tell me – one of my brothers yet lives?'

'My apologies, my lord Lion,' Dante says, rising back to his feet along with his warriors. 'I assumed word had arrived ahead of us. Lord Guilliman of Ultramar was revived and healed from the stasis in which he had been locked for millennia, and has launched the Indomitus Crusade to take back the Imperium from its enemies. He fought his way through the Great Rift and came to the rescue of my Chapter and our blood-brothers, and brought reinforcements with him in the shape of the Primaris Marines, a new breed of warrior developed over ten thousand years.'

The Lion's thoughts are whirling. The Imperium still exists. He is not being denounced as an imposter, and plunged into an ugly civil war against his brother's sons. There are other bastions of humanity out there in the galaxy, with which he can link up and fight back the darkness. However, one thought rises to the surface above all others.

Roboute.

I am not alone.

ABOUT THE AUTHOR

Mike Brooks is a science fiction and fantasy author who lives in Nottingham, UK. His work for Black Library includes the Horus Heresy Primarchs novel *Alpharius: Head of the Hydra,* the Warhammer 40,000 novels *Rites of Passage, Warboss* and *Brutal Kunnin,* the Necromunda novel *Road to Redemption* and the novellas *Wanted: Dead* and *Da Gobbo's Revenge.* When not writing, he plays guitar and sings in a punk band, and DJs wherever anyone will tolerate him.

YOUR NEXT READ

AVENGING SON
by Guy Haley

As the Indomitus Crusade spreads out across the galaxy, one battlefleet must face a dread Slaughter Host of Chaos. Their success or failure may define the very future of the crusade – and the Imperium.

For these stories and more, go to **blacklibrary.com**, **games-workshop.com**, Games Workshop and Warhammer stores, all good book stores or visit one of the thousands of independent retailers worldwide, which can be found at **games-workshop.com/storefinder**

An extract from
Avenging Son
by Guy Haley

'I was there at the Siege of Terra,' Vitrian Messinius would say in his later years.

'I was there...' he would add to himself, his words never meant for ears but his own. 'I was there the day the Imperium died.'

But that was yet to come.

'To the walls! To the walls! The enemy is coming!' Captain Messinius, as he was then, led his Space Marines across the Penitent's Square high up on the Lion's Gate. 'Another attack! Repel them! Send them back to the warp!'

Thousands of red-skinned monsters born of fear and sin scaled the outer ramparts, fury and murder incarnate. The mortals they faced quailed. It took the heart of a Space Marine to stand against them without fear, and the Angels of Death were in short supply.

'Another attack, move, move! To the walls!'

They came in the days after the Avenging Son returned, emerging from nothing, eight legions strong, bringing the bulk of their numbers to bear against the chief entrance to the Imperial Palace. A decapitation strike like no other, and it came perilously close to success.

Messinius' Space Marines ran to the parapet edging the Penitent's Square. On many worlds, the square would have been a plaza fit to adorn the centre of any great city. Not on Terra. On the immensity of the Lion's Gate, it was nothing, one of hundreds of similarly huge spaces. The word 'gate' did not suit the scale of the cityscape. The Lion's Gate's bulk marched up into the sky, step by titanic step, until it rose far higher than the mountains it had supplanted. The gate had been built by the Emperor Himself, they said. Myths detailed the improbable supernatural feats required to raise it. They were lies, all of them, and belittled the true effort needed to build such an edifice. Though the Lion's Gate was made to His design and by His command, the soaring monument had been constructed by mortals, with mortal hands and mortal tools. Messinius wished that had been remembered. For men to build this was far more impressive than any godly act of creation. If men could remember that, he believed, then perhaps they would remember their own strength.

The uncanny may not have built the gate, but it threatened to bring it down. Messinius looked over the rampart lip, down to the lower levels thousands of feet below and the spread of the Anterior Barbican.

Upon the stepped fortifications of the Lion's Gate was armour of every colour and the blood of every loyal primarch. Dozens of regiments stood alongside them. Aircraft filled the sky. Guns boomed from every quarter. In the churning redness on the great roads, processional ways so huge they were akin to prairies cast in rockcrete, were flashes of gold where the Emperor's Custodian Guard battled. The might of the Imperium was gathered there, in the palace where He dwelt.

There seemed moments on that day when it might not be enough.

The outer ramparts were carpeted in red bodies that writhed and heaved, obscuring the great statues adorning the defences and covering over the guns, an invasive cancer consuming reality. The enemy were legion. There were too many foes to defeat by plan and ruse. Only guns, and will, would see the day won, but the defenders were so pitifully few.

Messinius called a wordless halt, clenched fist raised, seeking the best place to deploy his mixed company, veterans all of the Terran Crusade. Gunships and fighters sped overhead, unleashing deadly light and streams of bombs into the packed daemonic masses. There were innumerable cannons crammed onto the gate, and they all fired, rippling the structure with false earthquakes. Soon the many ships and orbital defences of Terra would add their guns, targeting the very world they were meant to guard, but the attack had come so suddenly; as yet they had had no time to react.

The noise was horrendous. Messinius' audio dampers were at maximum and still the roar of ordnance stung his ears. Those humans that survived today would be rendered deaf. But he would have welcomed more guns, and louder still, for all the defensive fury of the assailed palace could not drown out the hideous noise of the daemons – their sighing hisses, a billion serpents strong, and chittering, screaming wails. It was not only heard but sensed within the soul, the realms of spirit and of matter were so intertwined. Messinius' being would be forever stained by it.

Tactical information scrolled down his helmplate, near environs only. He had little strategic overview of the situation. The vox-channels were choked with a hellish screaming that made communication impossible. The noosphere was disrupted by etheric backwash spilling from the immaterial rifts the daemons poured through. Messinius was used to operating on his own. Small-scale, surgical actions were the way of the Adeptus Astartes, but in a battle of this scale, a lack of central coordination would lead inevitably to defeat. This was not like the first Siege, where his kind had fought in Legions.

He called up a company-wide vox-cast and spoke to his warriors. They were not his Chapter-kin, but they would listen. The primarch himself had commanded that they do so.

'Reinforce the mortals,' he said. 'Their morale is wavering. Position yourselves every fifty yards. Cover the whole of the south-facing front. Let them see you.' He directed his warriors by chopping at the air with his left hand. His right, bearing an inactive power fist, hung heavily at his side. 'Assault Squad Antiocles, back forty yards, single firing line. Prepare to engage enemy breakthroughs only on my mark. Devastators, split to demi-squads and take up high ground, sergeant and sub-squad prime's discretion as to positioning and target. Remember our objective, heavy infliction of casualties. We kill as many as we can, we retreat, then hold at the Penitent's Arch until further notice. Command squad, with me.'

Command squad was too grand a title for the mismatched crew Messinius had gathered around himself. His own officers were light years away, if they still lived.

'Doveskamor, Tidominus,' he said to the two Aurora Marines with him. 'Take the left.'

'Yes, captain,' they voxed, and jogged away, their green armour glinting orange in the hell-light of the invasion.

The rest of his scratch squad was comprised of a communications specialist from the Death Spectres, an Omega Marine with a penchant for plasma weaponry, and a Raptor holding an ancient standard he'd taken from a dusty display.

'Why did you take that, Brother Kryvesh?' Messinius asked, as they moved forward.

'The palace is full of such relics,' said the Raptor. 'It seems only right to put them to use. No one else wanted it.'

Messinius stared at him.

'What? If the gate falls, we'll have more to worry about than my minor indiscretion. It'll be good for morale.'

The squads were splitting to join the standard humans. Such was the noise many of the men on the wall had not noticed their arrival, and a ripple of surprise went along the line as they appeared at their sides. Messinius was glad to see they seemed more firm when they turned their eyes back outwards.

'Anzigus,' he said to the Death Spectre. 'Hold back, facilitate communication within the company. Maximum signal gain. This interference will only get worse. See if you can get us patched in to wider theatre command. I'll take a hardline if you can find one.'

'Yes, captain,' said Anzigus. He bowed a helm that was bulbous with additional equipment. He already had the access flap of the bulky vox-unit on his arm open. He withdrew, the aerials on his power plant extending. He headed towards a systems nexus on the far wall of the plaza, where soaring buttresses pushed back against the immense weight bearing down upon them.

Messinius watched him go. He knew next to nothing about Anzigus. He spoke little, and when he did, his voice was funereal. His Chapter was mysterious, but the same lack of familiarity held true for many of these warriors, thrown together by miraculous events. Over their years lost wandering in the warp, Messinius had come to see some as friends as well as comrades, others he hardly knew, and none he knew so well as his own Chapter brothers. But they would stand together. They were Space Marines. They had fought by the returned primarch's side, and in that they shared a bond. They would not stint in their duty now.

Messinius chose a spot on the wall, directing his other veterans to left and right. Kryvesh he sent to the mortal officer's side. He looked down again, out past the enemy and over the outer palace. Spires stretched away in every direction. Smoke rose from all over the landscape. Some of it was new, the work of the daemon horde, but Terra had been burning for weeks. The Astronomican had failed. The galaxy was split in two. Behind them in the sky turned the great palace gyre, its deep eye marking out the throne room of the Emperor Himself.

'Sir!' A member of the Palatine Guard shouted over the din. He pointed downwards, to the left. Messinius followed his wavering finger. Three hundred feet below, daemons were climbing. They came upwards in a triangle tipped by a brute with a double rack of horns. It clambered hand over hand, far faster than should be possible, flying upwards, as if it touched the side of the towering gate only as a concession to reality. A Space Marine with claw locks could not have climbed that fast.

'Soldiers of the Imperium! The enemy is upon us!'

He looked to the mortals. Their faces were blanched with fear. Their weapons shook. Their bravery was commendable nonetheless. Not one of them attempted to run, though a wave of terror preceded the unnatural things clambering up towards them.

'We shall not turn away from our duty, no matter how fearful the foe, or how dire our fates may be,' he said. 'Behind us is the Sanctum of the Emperor Himself. As He has watched over you, now it is your turn to stand in guardianship over Him.'